The Hustler Next Door

Also by K.A. Tucker

The *Hustler* Next Door

K.A. TUCKER

ISBN 978-1-990105-32-6 (paperback)

ISBN 978-1-990105-13-5 (ebook)

Edited by Jennifer Sommersby

Cover design by Hang Le

Published by K.A. Tucker Books Ltd.

Manufactured in the United States of America

To the readers who have waited two years for Justine's escapades. I hope you're ready for her.

Chapter One

"HALF OF BOSTON MUST BE HERE." My calf muscles strain as I stretch on my tiptoes, striving to see over the bulky winter jackets and capped heads. It's pointless. There are too many people and, as usual, my diminutive stature works against me.

Mom waves off my protests. "It'll move fast. It always does."

She's right, of course. Rain, snow, or sunny summer skies, mornings at Sam's Pastry are always hectic as Bostonians flock to the iconic downtown bakery for their cannoli fix. Even now, only days after everyone has renewed their gym memberships and made New Year's resolutions about pious lives of salads and spin classes, bodies are stuffed into this storefront like the rows of cream-filled pastries in the display cases ahead. Five separate lines wait impatiently for service while a crowd loiters outside in the frigid January air.

Mom and I have always been Saturday regulars. Even after I moved out, I'd insist on coming here every visit home, just so I could taunt my brother Joe with unflattering pictures of myself shoveling pistachio—his favorite—into my gaping mouth. But it's been ages since I've faced this crowd, and I'm not in the mood for it. "We picked the slow line."

"Stop fussing."

"I'm *boiling*." I tug at the collar of my knit sweater for effect.

"And you'll be cold once we step outside." Mom toys with a strand of my lengthy hair. I'd dyed it black for years but recently made the switch to a rich chestnut brown. "I'm so happy you're here."

I meet my mother's gaze, see her sincere smile, and I swallow the other complaints waiting to spill out. "So am I." There's something about walking into Sam's and inhaling the sugary-sweet icing sugar and pastries … it transports me back to childhood every time, if only for a moment.

She hesitates. "Especially since you missed Christmas."

Oh my God. "*Please* don't start now." I'm already irritated; a guilt trip will put me over the edge. "You know why I didn't come home." Why I did the unthinkable and skipped the holidays with my family for the first time in my thirty years of life. It's not that I didn't want to see them. It *killed* me not to see them. But holidays with my family include our longtime friends, the Wrights, and there was no way I was spending Christmas watching a certain six-foot-three Wright—the one I was supposed to marry—and his new woman suck back eggnog while canoodling in matching reindeer sweaters. "If you'd wanted me there badly enough, you should have banned them from visiting."

"That would have put a strain on the relationship. And punishing *everyone* for his mistake—"

"I don't want to talk about this anymore."

"These things always happen for a reason. One day you'll look back and—"

"Cheating is cheating. Do *not* make excuses for Bastard Bill." I stab the air with my finger in warning.

"I'm not! The truth is, I don't think I'll ever look at him the same way again. But, for Molly and Craig's sake, would you please stop calling their son that, or *I'm* liable to do it in front of them accidentally."

"Would that be so bad?" I know Mom's in a difficult position. The Wrights have lived next door to us for almost three decades.

Our families have a long, entwined history. When my father injured his back and couldn't work construction any longer, Craig put his reputation on the line to get him a job at his company, even though my father didn't have the first clue about insurance or office work. Mom and Molly must have burned a trillion calories together over the years on their daily walks while venting about their husbands and children. They travel to Mexico every winter together. I can't expect my parents to cast away those friendships because of what Bill did.

I can't even blame my brother. When Bill and I first hooked up years ago, Joe was *pissed*. He wouldn't talk to either of us for days, and when he came around, he swore he'd never take sides between his sister and his best friend if we broke up, no matter what.

I was shocked when Joe showed solidarity, punching Bill across the jaw and ignoring his calls for a few weeks. But I knew that wouldn't last. They've been best friends since the day they met. They went to college together and have never lived more than a twenty-minute subway ride apart. They start every day swapping sports stats over the phone while sitting on their respective toilets.

"Look, we're *all* disappointed with the situation—"

"The *situation*?" She says it like Bill got a flat tire and was late to work one day. "You mean when he got caught sticking his dick in his coworker?" Close enough, given the explicit texts I discovered on his phone.

"*Justine*." Mom's cheeks flush as she scans around us to see if anyone heard her daughter's crass remarks.

"Whatever," I huff. "It's my own damn fault. I should *never* have taken him back in the first place." We dated while I was in college until Bill broke it off to "figure things out." I was crushed. I'd been in love with him since I was twelve. Imagine my surprise when he showed up at a family barbecue with *Debra*. One wedding, a daughter, and a divorce later, he came crawling back to me. I should've seen myself for what I've always been to him,

3

though—a fill-in until something better comes along. No wonder he was so hesitant to live together.

And now he has *Isabelle,* who Joe begrudgingly informed me has asked Bill to move into her midtown condo with her.

He probably didn't blink when he said yes.

"Do they still have the Oreo cannoli?" I ask, abruptly changing the subject to keep my emotions in check before I turn into a lip-quivering mess.

"I don't see why they wouldn't." Mom lifts her chin, trying to spy over the sea of shoulders. It's no use; she's even shorter than I am.

"They better, or Uncle Jay is gonna ride my ass hard."

"Honestly, I don't know where you earned that mouth of yours."

"From your father."

Mom grunts but doesn't deny it. She can't. Gramps was a sweet old man, but he could have headlined a Quentin Tarantino movie for all his cussing.

"Speaking of your uncle, he's not happy with the man he hired to replace you."

"I warned him that guy didn't know his head from his asshole, but he didn't listen." Through a narrow crack in the crowd, I spy the tray of limoncello cannoli dwindling. They're not the most popular, but they're my favorite, and they never make enough.

"Your uncle is as stubborn and hardheaded as your father." She pauses. "But he'd let you come back in a heartbeat."

"I know." That's why Jay's driving to Boston this weekend: to promise me the sun, the moon, and the North Star until I agree to work for him again. "I already told him no. I just … I *can't.*" I needed a big change.

"You know what he said to your father the other day?" Mom drops her voice conspiratorially, though no one's listening. "When he kicks the bucket, he'll leave the company to you."

"Come on." I snort. "Jay isn't kicking any buckets anytime soon." My dad's baby brother is a fit fifty-two-year-old who has no interest in retiring. "And running a skilled trades agency isn't the life I want." Even though I had become a master at matching candidates with the right employers. I'd even started recruiting clients. Of the new companies we partnered with in the past year, I brought in eighty percent of them.

Mom worries her lip as if weighing her next words. "But selling refrigerators in a tiny town in Pennsylvania *is*?"

There it is: the judgment I've been waiting for. When I told her I'd started at Murphy's Appliances in Polson Falls a few weeks before Christmas, she asked the usual questions but didn't share her opinion. I knew it would come. "I don't just sell fridges. Ovens too. And washing machines. The occasional microwave."

"Justine—"

"Like I said, it's temporary. The hours are good, there's no stress, and it's a four-minute drive from home."

"I don't see why you had to uproot your *entire* life."

"There was nothing to uproot. Besides, Scarlet's in Pennsylvania." There should be no need to elaborate. My best friend and I lived together for a decade before she bought a house in her hometown. When I caught Bill cheating, she's the one I ran to. I sure as hell wasn't running back to Boston, where *everything* reminds me of him. "*Look,* I am in what they call a transition stage of my life. Nothing is permanent. The world is my oyster." I hold out my hands for dramatic flair. "Now, can we talk about something *other* than my poor life choices?"

Mom purses her lips. I know what she's itching to point out: that I'm borrowing a room in my friend's dilapidated house in a sleepy town, I have a dead-end job in a store that's barely surviving, and my custom T-shirt that reads "I hope your penis falls off"—I had it printed in three colors—isn't about to woo future dating prospects.

"Tell me about Sara," I prompt. "I still can't believe Joe brought her home for Christmas." They only met in November, but literally, every text from my brother is Sara *this* and Sara *that.* It's nauseating.

"Oh, Justine ..." Just hearing her name has my mother smiling. "She is lovely."

"She has great taste, I'll give her that." Joe's gift to me this year was an adorable pair of Sorel suede booties that I know he didn't pick out.

For the next ten minutes, I'm content to shuffle a few steps at a time and listen to my mom drone on about the many ways Sara Walton is perfect—how smart and kind she is, how elegant and yet down-to-earth, how tall and pretty, how proud her parents must be that she's taken up nursing when, according to Joe, her family comes from "old money"—the kind that earned them a penthouse in Manhattan and summers in Newport, Rhode Island.

"I've never seen Joseph *so* smitten." Mom's eyes light up. "She's the one. I'd bet money on it."

"Wow. *Must* be serious." A gambler Joan MacDermott is not. She still rolls loose pennies to take to the bank. "Do you think it'll last, though? A woman like that with Joe?"

"Why wouldn't it? Your brother's no slouch. He just got that big promotion at work. He's one of the youngest executives his agency has ever seen!" she declares proudly.

"He also eats Froot Loops for dinner and spends half his paycheck on baseball cards."

"That's an exaggeration."

"He's thirty-four and sleeps on an air mattress."

"Not anymore. He just bought a proper bed."

"Either way, the MacDermotts of Boston don't run in the same circle as the Waltons of the Upper East Side."

She seems to consider that for a moment. "Maybe not, but your brother's circle must have crossed with Sara's at some point, otherwise they never would have met."

"Fair point." I still haven't heard the details of their meet-cute. "I guess I should say hello to my potential future sister-in-law soon, then, huh?"

We're next in line for the counter. Mom is deciding out loud which six of the nineteen flavors we should order while I glower at the worker who collects the last three limoncellos and tucks them into a large box. Who would take *three*? That's excessive.

I stretch up on my tiptoes as the clerk veers back toward the customer, curious who the culprit is.

My stomach drops.

Bill is at the far end of the counter, his long, skinny index finger pointing out other flavors for the worker to fetch.

I haven't seen him since I discovered the string of racy messages last October. The day I moved my belongings out, I threatened bodily harm if he showed up.

He stayed away.

How dare he come *here*, to *my* cannoli spot, and buy up *my* favorite flavor?

The brunette standing beside him leans in, her plump lips moving as she reads out flavors, and a sinking realization hits me. I've seen that face before, attached to a naked body on my boyfriend's phone.

Rage simmers as I grit my teeth against the urge to scream. Not only did he come here, to *my* cannoli spot, but he brought *Isabelle*. They're probably visiting his parents. They'll be right next door.

"Justine?"

"Huh?" My head whips back so fast, I kink my neck and a burst of heat explodes.

Mom has moved ahead to the counter where a server with latex gloves and a tight smile awaits, box in hand. "They're out of the lemon. Can you believe that? No one ever wants the lemon. What about the peanut butter or the mint, or ..." Her voice trails. "What's wrong?"

I feel like I'm going to vomit. "He's here," I hiss.

She frowns. "*Who's* here?"

"*Bastard Bill*. And he's with *her*."

Her focus shifts over my shoulder, and she inhales sharply. "Oh dear ... this is awkward."

"Ya think?"

"Has he noticed you yet?"

"Not that I know." But the longer we stand here, the more likely a run-in will become.

Sympathy twists her features as she studies the panic splayed across my face. "Tell me what you want to do."

"Shove the biggest cannoli they have down his throat until he chokes to death?"

The worker in the hairnet raises an eyebrow.

In truth, all I want to do is run, and my mom figures that out.

"Let's pick our flavors and get out of here, okay? How about two of the—"

"Kitty!" A shrill child's voice carries over the buzz in the bakery.

Fuck me. Bill's daughter is here, too, and she's seen my mother, who answers to that nickname as readily as her own. Bill and Joe coined it years ago on account of Mom's laugh sounding identical to that of the mother in *That '70s Show*.

Can this day get any worse?

"Pretend you didn't hear her," I say.

Mom cuts me a glare before smiling wide and waving. "Hi, Rae!"

I groan inwardly. Of course, that's the right move—Rae had no part in her father's treachery. With a deep inhale, I peer over my shoulder. The six-year-old is perched on Bill's arm, held high enough to glimpse the display case. My heart softens for a few beats as I smile at the little girl, her pigtails poking out of a pink knit cap, before it hardens again for the man holding her.

At least Bill has the decency to look uncomfortable, wincing as he casts a smile my way. His lips move almost imperceptibly—a curse, no doubt; he's worried I'm going to cause a scene—as his shifty gaze flickers over to his partner in crime.

She's biting her bottom lip as she watches the exchange.

She knew about me.

She damn well knew what part she was playing in all of it.

"Excuse me, ma'am, have you decided on your flavors, or

should I move on to someone who's ready?" the server behind the counter asks, raising her voice a touch, nodding at the line of people waiting behind us in this sweaty, rammed hellhole.

The one helping Bastard Bill is closing up his box, which means he'll be leaving shortly. The absolute last thing I want to do is run into him on the sidewalk. I need to stall.

"We'll take one of everything, please," I order as calmly as possible.

The worker tips her head in disbelief. "*Every*thing?"

"Justine!" Mom's mouth gapes as she surveys the display cases in horror. Beyond the cannoli is a vast selection of cookies and other delectable pastries.

I plaster on a saccharine smile. "You should get a bigger box."

Chapter Two

"Dɪᴅ you hear anything about that order for the Simpsons?" Ned calls out, his focus on his daily crossword puzzle, his light Scottish brogue laden with skepticism.

"Uh-huh," I answer around a mouthful of amaretto cannoli.

"Oh?" He peers over his reading glasses. We've been chasing after the company's distribution center for a week since they missed the original delivery date. "Good news, I hope?"

A nod is all I can manage while I struggle to chew.

"You know, you could always take smaller bites."

I finally swallow. "Where's the fun in that?" Mom sent me back to Polson Falls with everything from Sam's Pastry she couldn't freeze. My expensive plan worked—I avoided a direct run-in with Bastard Bill—but I may die from a ricotta overdose before the week is through. "Here. Help me out." I hold the Tupperware container toward Ned.

"Oh no, I've had two." He pats his trim belly. The man is tiny —only a few inches taller than me, and slight in stature, perpetually drowning in his winter coat. I worry he isn't eating enough. "So, the fridge? What's the scoop?"

"It's on its way."

"Is it certain, though? I can't tell Josie that if it's not certain."

"Oh, it's certain." By my fourth call—and my promise to call every hour on the hour until I had an ETA—the girl got off her ass and tracked down the exact location. "The fridge is on a truck from Pittsburgh as we speak. I got the truck number, the driver's name and cell number, his underwear size—"

Ned snorts.

"Delivery is set for tomorrow morning."

His shoulders sink with relief. "Thank goodness. They've been waiting an awful long time for that thing. Josie was none too happy with me when she called."

Josie Simpson is lucky she didn't physically come into the store to chew Ned's ear off, or I might have returned the favor. I've only known Ned for about six weeks, but I've grown protective of him. "Hey, you warned her. She could have had any of those"—I gesture toward the row of floor models that fill the back right corner of Murphy's—"within days, but *no*, she had to have the fancy special-order retro fridge, and that means waiting."

"I suppose." More quietly, and bitterly, Ned adds, "Bet they wouldn't give Home Depot the runaround."

"Nah." I wave off his grumbling, though I can't say the distributor would leave a big-box store hanging like they did us. Murphy's Appliances may be a staple family business in Polson Falls, but it doesn't bring in a fraction of the revenue that one of those big chains does. That, coupled with higher prices because we can't negotiate the same bulk discounts, and any talk about our competitors leaves my kindly old boss in a bitter mood. "Bet Home Depot doesn't send out Christmas cards and shortbread every year." A tradition his late wife Trudy always took care of until her passing last year. My first weekend as a Murphy's employee was spent in Ned's kitchen, elbow deep in butter and flour.

The door chimes, announcing a customer, the first one today.

I spin on my heels, ready to greet the newcomer, until I see the hulking man sauntering along the aisle, his snow-covered boots leaving tracks on the runner. "*Oh, it's you.*"

Dean Fanshaw grins. "Good to see you too."

I've always liked the quiet and easygoing firefighter, even if he's a hound when an attractive woman is within fifty yards. "I meant you're not going to buy anything."

He stops a foot away from me—a wall of impressive muscle beneath layers of winter gear. "Not today. Here to pick up that chest freezer for my neighbor."

"Yes! Tony called and said he was sending you in. It's all ready to go around back. Let me get the paperwork for you." Ned shuffles toward the office as quickly as his slight seventy-six-year-old body can carry him.

"Just out there, saving Polson Falls folk, one fire or appliance delivery at a time, huh?" I tip my head back to admire Dean's face. There's no denying he is stunningly attractive. I have the urge to drag my finger along his cut jawline every time I see him, but especially now that it's emphasized by the black beanie pulled down to hide his blond hair.

"It's who I am." His baby-blue eyes drift from the box of sweets I left on our front counter, back to me, to my mouth. "You have a little something ..." He taps the corner of his bottom lip with his finger, a secretive smile growing wider by the second.

It has to be cannoli filling. If we had customers, I'd be professional and grab a tissue. But Ned is in the back office, and every interaction Dean and I have had since we met has been laced with sexual innuendo, so why stop now?

"Right here?" I make a show of slowly dragging the tip of my tongue along my bottom lip until I catch the sweet cream. "Did I get it all?"

Dean tracks the move, clearing his throat. "Yeah."

He knows it's all an act. At another time in my life, we would have found ourselves tangled in bedsheets by now. I know he'd be game. But, while flirting shamelessly with Dean has become a favorite pastime, the last thing I want in my life is another wandering dick—especially when it's attached to a guy who happens to be best friends with Scarlet's soulmate.

Platonic friends with the big, sexy meathead, I can do. In fact, I appreciate it.

"Looks like you're settling in well here." His gaze snags on a grill in the corner—the one I've been begging Scarlet to go halfsies on for the house.

"Can't complain. Thanks again for the hookup." Dean's the one who mentioned Ned urgently needed a reliable hand after his only employee stopped showing up. We figured out later the jerk got a job at Home Depot.

"Glad it worked out."

"I hope Ned thinks so. I've heard him use the word 'eccentric' once or twice in reference to me. 'Dramatic' too. But not 'insane,' so I think I'm in the clear." I'm only kidding, of course. Ned is nothing but smiles when I show up in the morning and is always chuckling. He seems to appreciate my antics. In truth, I think he's been lonely. "Speaking of working out, what happened with that gorgeous brunette you were dry-humping in the corner of Route 66?" They were all over each other at this year's New Year's Eve party and ghosted a minute past midnight.

Dean shrugs. "Nothing much."

"Really? I was *so sure* there was something there." I struggle to keep my composure.

His eyes narrow. "What did Beckett tell you?"

"Nothing." I pause a few beats. "Except that you and Abuela hit it off."

Dean's head falls back with a groan as I burst out with laughter.

"I had *no idea* her grandmother lived with her, okay? She never mentioned it."

"Sounds like you gave a senior citizen one hell of a Happy New Year's eyeful, though." I look downward, which is what dear Abuela did when Dean strolled into the kitchen buck naked in search of a glass of water. According to details Shane wasn't supposed to repeat, she got a solid five-second look at his morning wood and then chased him out of the house with a

13

rolling pin, screaming at him in Spanish for defiling her grand-daughter.

"What's it like standing naked on a front porch in January?"

"Embarrassing, and cold."

"Or embarrassing *because* you were cold." I hold up my hand and pinch my index finger and thumb close together. "Even big boys have to hide sometimes." Which is what happened to Dean. It wasn't too long before his one-night stand realized what her grandmother had done and let him back inside, but it was long enough to shrink more than his ego.

His cheeks flush. "I can't believe Shane told *you*, of all people."

"Of course he did! I'm his favorite. Here." I reach into the pastry box and collect a profiterole. "Open wide."

With a smirk, Dean obliges, and I pop the treat into his gaping mouth.

"All set!" Ned ambles out from the office, waving the paper-work. "Why don't I help you load up from the dock?"

Dean doesn't need help loading, especially not from a man who complains about his creaky, aching bones at least twice a day, but his mouth is too stuffed to say anything.

"I've got it. I need to salt the exterior." The temperatures climbed long enough to melt snow before dropping below freezing again. It'll be an ice rink out there and dangerous for potential customers. I pat my boss's shoulder. "You stay in here where it's warm."

Ned shakes his head. "I'm one lucky son of a gun to have you here, Justine."

"And don't you forget it." I grab my jacket off the hook. "I'll meet you out back, Fanshaw. Don't keep me waiting." I flash a playful wink before strolling toward the loading dock, feeling Dean's attention on my back the entire way.

———

"He needs to think about retiring. Enjoy his life while he can." Dean's powerful jean-clad thighs flex as he stands in his truck's bed, shifting into position the small chest freezer he just lifted in. Scarlet says he's too muscular. I disagree.

I hug my body to ward off the cold as I lean against the brick wall, admiring the view. "He's mentioned it a few times, in passing." Usually while he's glowering at the sales reports. "I don't think he can bring himself to do it yet. He likes the routine and seeing people every day. Plus, he has no one to take over." His father opened Murphy's seventy years ago and passed it on to Ned. But Ned and Trudy's only son died tragically in a skiing accident at twenty-two years old. His Little League baseball pictures still grace the walls. "There is no one to keep the family legacy going."

"I hate to say it, but maybe it's time for the legacy to end." Dean pauses to survey the back of the old brick building that is in sore need of a facelift. A rare somber expression fills his face. "Real estate on Main Street is worth a ton. He could make a killing on this location. And business is not gonna get better. I heard talk of more competition coming. Good luck finding anyone crazy enough to want to compete."

A sour taste fills my mouth. According to Ned, ever since the west end of town exploded with new development, his revenue has dropped by forty percent. Sure, born-and-bred Polson Falls residents still show their loyalty and appreciation for his customer service, but the new families don't hold the same nostalgia for the town's history. They want a good deal, and they want it now.

I hate to admit it, but Dean's right. Murphy's days are numbered, regardless of having someone to pass it along to. "You know what'll happen, right? This place'll end up becoming another dental office." I counted five when I was in search of one to fill a cavity. "Or a bubble tea shop." I don't have any skin in this game—I only moved here a few months ago, and I can't see myself staying forever—but I know it's Ned's heart and soul, and that alone makes me want to see Murphy's survive for years to come.

Dean grimaces. "I tried that bubble stuff once. Couldn't stand the texture."

A sly smile curls my lips. "Are you saying you don't like the feel of balls on your tongue?" Sometimes he makes it too easy.

"Jeez, MacDermott." He hops to the ground.

The back door to the butcher shop in the building next door creaks open. A lanky, bundled body emerges, dragging a bag of garbage toward the dumpster, sliding around in his customary white New Balance sneakers that offer no traction against the ice.

"Thank God you're home. I'm in withdrawal!" I holler by way of greeting. I had a pleasant routine started, heading to Todd's every day at lunch for a bowl of the daily soup and an earful of town gossip. But then Todd closed shop after Christmas with little warning to his customers or us—a move that stunned Ned.

Todd said he needed a rest.

The forty-five-year-old lifts his head to peer out from beneath his hood, showing off a tanned complexion. "Oh hey, Justine. Happy New Year!"

"Where'd you run off to?"

"Jamaica."

Explains his chipper mood. "Why didn't you tell me? Or better yet, take me with you? I thought we had a bond."

"Uh … yeah, sorry, it was kind of a last-minute decision." He laughs nervously. "I've got a pot simmering. Your favorite."

"Potato bacon?" I mock whisper, though I'll take anything that comes out of that magical vintage red Crock-Pot. His recipes have been passed down through generations, and they all have bacon —my kryptonite—in one form or another. They're like nothing I've ever tasted. I've accused him on more than one occasion of sprinkling cocaine in to keep me coming back, because I'm addicted.

He grins. "I used the good stuff. Twice smoked, thick cut."

I let out a loud moan. "I love it when you talk dirty."

Even in the cold, Todd's blush shows on his cheeks. "Well, uh…" He skids a few steps over the ice as he tosses the bag. "It should be ready in half an hour."

I check my watch. "It's a date! Can't wait to fill you in on the New Year's gossip." I jerk my head toward Dean, who groans.

"Sounds good." Todd ducks back inside.

"Is there anyone in this town you don't flirt with?" Dean asks.

"A question like that coming from *you*?" I smack his arm. "It's fine. Todd knows I'm kidding around. He's a good egg." Third-generation owner of Dieter's Meat Shop and Delicatessen, another staple family business that's persevering against the test of big-box store development. When Dieter Junior died of a heart attack, he left his family legacy in the hands of his only son, along with the two-story building it resides in, which includes four store-fronts, the apartments above, and a sizable lot.

"Todd's in love with you."

"Well, yeah. Who isn't? Besides Bastard Bill."

Dean takes a few steps closer to tower over me. His voice softens as he asks, "Heard you went to Boston to see your family last weekend. How was it?"

"Just peachy." I hid behind the heavy brocade curtain all night, spying on the house next door while gorging on cookies and cannoli.

"Things getting any easier?"

Everyone knows about my ugly breakup. I'm sure Dean's heard the worst of it. After all, Shane had a front-row seat to my Christmas Day drunken meltdown, thanks to Fireball and an unsanctioned visit to Bill's Instagram account. They were sitting in front of *my family*'s Christmas tree.

But I'm tired of talking and thinking about and crying over Bill. I need to put it all behind me. "I didn't start the year naked on a porch, so … things are looking up?"

Dean's gaze roves over my features, and I see undiluted interest. Maybe one unrestricted night with this guy would dull the distracting ache that stirs every time I think of Bill. It wouldn't mean anything to either of us and wouldn't scratch our superficial friendship. Dean's the kind of guy who stays friends with everyone, right down to his one-night stands.

I shake that crazy thought out of my head. Dean also slept with Scarlet's mom. Granted, Dottie is a siren and Dean was so drunk, he can't remember anything, but still …

He's a literal motherfucker.

"Here. You'll need this." I press the paperwork for the freezer against his chest, using the moment to step back and put distance between us. "Enough chitchat. I've gotta get everything salted so I can get to my soup."

Dean folds and tucks the paperwork into his back pocket. "See you at Route 66 this Friday?"

"Will Abuela be there? I think she'd like one of my custom-made T-shirts."

"I'm gonna kill Shane."

"Please don't. He's so good at fixing things around our house. And besides, it's bingo night at Bonny Acres, and I hear Nancy has some weird rash they can't diagnose, which means *I* could be chosen to call the numbers. Do you know how big a deal that is?" I've been volunteering at the assisted living center since November, which, fair enough, is a far cry from the ten years that Nancy's been there, but she refuses to relinquish the role of number-caller to me or anyone else. I think they'll have to pry those bingo balls from her cold, dead hands.

"So? Those things don't run late. Come after," he coaxes softly.

"Don't beg. It's unbecoming. But fine, I'll consult my jam-packed social calendar and get back to you."

He flashes a crooked grin over his shoulder on his way to his truck. If Scarlet's going, I'll be there, and he knows it. "See you Friday."

I watch Dean pull away before I slam my fist on the loading dock door button and dive back inside. Warmth envelops me as I trudge through the store, aiming for the front door and the container of salt. My stomach is growling in anticipation of lunch.

"Excuse me, do you work here?" a raspy male voice calls out.

"I do, but if you can hold on a minute, Ned'll be out to help you." It's too early for his afternoon nap, which he takes in his little office. "He's just in the ..." I trip over my winter boots as I spot the man.

He flashes a dimpled smile. "Hi."

"Hi," I echo, momentarily dumbfounded. Who is this god, and where did he come from? Certainly not Polson Falls stock. Not that there aren't gems in this town—Shane and Dean are living proof of that—but this guy looks like a big-city import in his tailored wool trench coat and herringbone-patterned scarf.

His smile widens, showing off perfect, straight white teeth.

Abandoning my task, I saunter over, thankful I wore my cute red beanie instead of my oversized trapper hat with the flaps down the side. "Is there something I can help you with?" A litany of dirty thoughts tag onto the end of that question, but I bite my tongue. Ned gives me a lot of leeway, but he'd draw the line at propositioning his customers for a quickie in the storage closet.

"I'm sure you can." Rich brown eyes cast a curious glint as they search my features, as if he can hear my unspoken thoughts. "I need a fridge. This one's nice." He smooths a manicured hand over the mint-green '60s retro-style model. But I note the scabbed-over cut on his index finger and the callus on his thumb. So, he gets his hands dirty, but also knows how to get them clean. My dream combo. As is the fact that he towers over me and wears a sexy, thin layer of scruff over a square jaw. His entire look is curated, from his loosely styled chestnut-brown hair down to his gray suede Chelsea boots.

"Yeah, this one draws a lot of attention."

"Why do I feel a 'but' coming on?"

"*But*, it's seven grand, plus taxes and delivery."

He lets out a low whistle. "More than I wanted to spend on an appliance today."

I scan the guy's outfit. He doesn't mind spending money on

clothes. "Also, it'll take four to six weeks to arrive, from recent experience."

He grimaces and somehow still looks gorgeous. "I just need something basic and cheap. Even a floor model would be fine."

"We have a few of those. I can also show you options that will come quickly." *Like I would with this guy's hands on me, I'm sure.* I duck to hide my smile as I shrug off my coat and toss it onto a nearby stove. Scarlet is going to die when I tell her this story later.

Hot Guy's gaze drags over the length of my fitted sweater and wool leggings, down to my adorable Sorels, before rising again, a secretive flicker dancing in his eyes. One of attraction and dirty promises, the same kind inundating my thoughts.

My insides flutter. Bill was the only one who could stir this feeling in me with just a look—until now. "I'm Justine."

"Garrett."

"Nice to meet you. This way." I nod toward the cluster of refrigerators.

He falls into step beside me, his stride long and leisurely.

I catch a hint of his cologne—a warm medley of cloves, orange, and vanilla. It's masculine and yet soft, and it's my new favorite scent.

"How long has this place been here?" he asks, studying the twenty-foot-tall ceiling.

"Seventy years. Family owned since day one."

"Wow. Gotta say, don't see too many independent stores like this anymore." He pauses. "How's business?"

"Great!" I lie. "Murphy's is well established."

"Seventy years," he echoes.

"Exactly. And local folks take pride in supporting their own. This entire block on Main is made up of long-running businesses. Well, except for the cupcake store. She's new." I drop my voice. "And not going to last long, if you ask me." Bethany's notorious for mixing up orders and, according to Todd, never pays rent on time. "Dieter's next door? That's been there since the 1920s. It's the longest-standing business in Polson Falls. Isn't that wild?"

Garrett whistles. "Gotta love history like that."

"Right? Here, this one's very basic, and it's twenty-five percent off." I make a spectacle of presenting the Maytag fridge, Vanna White–style. "And you can take it now, if you have help, or we can set up delivery for you. We have a guy." Does Garrett know many people in town? "Say, when did you move to Polson Falls?"

"Still in the process." He opens the fridge door and peers inside. "How do you know I'm not from around here?"

"'Cause I've never seen you, and I would remember." He hasn't been to Route 66 on a Friday or Saturday night.

"Is that so?" His smile is crooked. "When'd you leave Boston?"

I grin. Though mild, my accent is a dead giveaway. "At eighteen. But I've been in New Jersey for the last twelve or so years. Newark, mainly."

"I know Newark." He acknowledges with a nod. "I grew up in Manhattan."

"That explains the vibe."

He leans against a nearby side-by-side, folding his arms across his chest, as if he's settling in for a conversation. The heavy wool material stretches, highlighting cut biceps. "What brought *you* to Polson Falls?"

"My best friend. She lives here, and I needed a change after I caught my now ex-boyfriend with his pants down, so to speak." Perhaps too much information, but I'm an oversharer, and I've just announced to Garrett that I'm single. "What would make *you* leave New York City for this little Pennsylvania town?" There's only one explanation I can think of. "Wife? Girlfriend?" I check his ring finger. No band.

He smiles, noticing my not-so-sly fishing expedition. "Neither. My uncle. He's getting *up there*, and he wants my help, so I'll be in between a few places for a bit."

"That's very ... sweet of you." And unexpected.

He waves it off. "I like the atmosphere here so far. Way more

21

relaxed." He pauses, his gaze drifting around the quiet store. "So, I'm guessing you're not a Murphy?"

"No, I'm a MacDermott. No relation."

"How'd you end up working in an appliance store?"

"Is that judgment I hear in your voice? Did my mother send you?"

He lifts his hands in surrender. "I'm just trying to fit a woman like you into a place like this."

I shrug. "Ned is one of the sweetest men I know, and he was looking for reliable help. And frankly, you've never met a woman like me before."

He leans in. "I'll admit, I am intrigued."

"Yeah?" I sense myself edging closer to him, my voice dropping into a more playful lilt. "So am I."

Garrett opens his mouth but falters, a wry smile curling his lips.

"Justine? You out there?" Ned calls from the direction of the office, making me jump. It severs our bubbling tension.

I step back and clear my voice. "Here! What's up?"

"Boy, that Kirk Bodin likes to talk. He just called and said he spoke to you about finding a good plumber and electrician—oh!" Ned startles as he comes around the corner and sees Garrett. "I'm sorry, I didn't realize you were with a customer. How are you today, sir?"

Garrett abandons his leisurely stance, pulling himself up to his full height. "I'm fantastic. You must be the owner."

"That's me. Been puttering around these walls since I was six years old. Though, lately, I feel like Justine here might be running things." Ned caps that off with a wink that tells me he's teasing. "I'm sure she's taking good care of you."

"She is." Garrett frowns. "But I'm interested in hearing about this electrician. I'm having some work done, and I may need one soon."

"Well, we've been using Bobby Dunlop for years. I've known him since grade school! But Kirk said you told him not to call

Bobby, Justine?" Ned's face pinches with confusion. "Why'd you do that?"

"Bobby retired last fall," I remind him gently.

"Oh, that's right. Who is it that …" Ned's brow wrinkles in thought. "Jimmy, his son, he's taking over."

"Yeah, except I heard from two reliable sources that Jimmy shows up high to all his job sites." Those guys at the firehouse gossip worse than anyone I've ever met, but it's good for intel.

"Oh dear. That's not good."

"No, and your old plumber, Richard, spends half the year in Florida."

"So many changes around here." Ned scratches his chin. "I guess we do need some new names to send people's way, then. I'll make some calls, have some conversations—"

"I'm on it, Ned. I'm gonna get a whole list together, not just of electricians and plumbers but people who do drywall and tiling, a general contractor or two. Some good locals you can trust."

Ned waves a dismissive hand. "We don't need all those people."

"We do, trust me. Customers who are buying new appliances are also people looking to get the bathrooms renovated and their kitchens refreshed. Like Garrett here, who's getting work done." I gesture toward him. "You want him coming to us for that information instead of the *other* guys, right?"

Mention of our competitor seems to spark a small fire in Ned. "When you put it like that, I guess it can't hurt. That's a lot of work, though, Justine."

"It's nothing. Interrogating tradespeople is my jam. I could talk about copper pipes and Sheetrock all day long. You sit back and relax."

"Okay, then." Ned turns to Garrett. "See? What'd I tell you? Who's the boss around here? So … can we help you decide on something today?"

"I've decided." Garrett reaches out to tap the only fridge I showed him. "This one, as long as I can pick it up on Thursday."

"*Really?*" I can't hide the surprise in my voice. "You don't want to see a few other options?" This is the cheapest, most basic one.

"I like the option in front of me." A playful glint flashes in his eyes as they draw across my features, flickering to my mouth.

"Are we still talking about kitchen appliances?" I mock whisper, my pulse stirring with excitement. This guy couldn't be any more obvious.

"I don't know," he whispers back. "But I need somewhere to put my leftover pizza and beer."

I press my hands to my chest. "Be still, my beating heart! You keep checking off future husband boxes every time you open your mouth."

"You young folk ..." Ned turns and moves toward his office, chuckling. "I'll be at the counter, getting your paperwork started. Come on over when Justine's done asking for your hand in marriage."

Garrett wears a secretive smile as he watches Ned disappear around the corner. "How do you know so much about copper pipes and Sheetrock?"

"I don't. I just talk a big game. But I do know about hiring tradespeople. It's what I did for years after college."

His eyebrows arch in surprise.

"I needed a job, and my uncle needed someone who wasn't an idiot."

"You don't say." He regards me. "You here every day?"

"Every day that we're open. It's just me and Ned."

Garrett surveys the closest wall where pictures of three generations of Murphys hang—all of them similar to Ned in their slight stature and kind eyes. He bites his bottom lip in thought. "Hey, you think he'd ever consider selling this place to me?"

My mouth drops. It's the second time this guy has thrown an unexpected curveball. "What do you mean? Like, sell *Murphy's* to you?"

"Yeah."

"You have aspirations of running a small-town *appliance* store?"

He shrugs, looking around. "I aspire to own something of my own, and I like the feel of this place."

"Did Dean put you up to this?" We were just talking about this out back.

"Dean who?"

"Never mind." I sigh. "I don't know if Ned would ever entertain the idea. He doesn't know you from Adam." One of my Gramp's favorite sayings, and one of the few that doesn't include offensive language.

"But he knows *you*."

"Yeah, what's your point?"

"So, you could put in a good word for me."

I bark with laughter. "*I* don't know you from Adam either."

"But I thought I was your future husband?"

"A contender. We'd have to date first." Dating may be the wrong word for what I want to do to this guy. "You do know this place would cost a lot more than that $7000 fridge you *didn't* want to buy, right?"

"At least a few of those." He smiles. "But would you stay and work for me?"

"You want to buy Murphy's *and* hire me." This conversation is getting stranger by the minute. "Wouldn't that make you my boss, though?"

"I guess it would." He frowns in thought. "Is that a problem?"

"Only if you have an issue with marrying your employee."

"Can't say I've been in that situation before. Might be worth finding out."

He's a thirty-something-year-old man who didn't hightail it out of here at the first mention of the M word—joke or not. I decide I like this guy. A lot. "And what if it turns out that I'm *a very bad* employee?" I've slipped into my lower, teasing voice that I always used on Bill. "Unruly. Doesn't listen to a thing you say, does whatever I want?"

Heat sparks in Garrett's eyes. "I think I could find a way to keep you in line."

My heart races again. Who *is* this man? He must be all talk. If he had the kind of money and know-how to buy Murphy's, he'd be smart enough to *not* do it.

Through the front window, I see a woman slip on the sidewalk and barely catch her footing. *Shit.* As much as I could stay here and flirt with Garrett, I better get out there and do my job before someone hurts themselves and Murphy's goes down in a flaming lawsuit. "Good luck with your business endeavors. I'll see ya around." I head for my coat.

"Wait a minute!" Garrett hollers. He's standing with his arms out, a bewildered look on his face. "That's it?"

"What do you mean?"

"Was all that sweet talk just to get me to buy an appliance?"

"Maybe." I steal one last glance over my shoulder. "You know where to find me if you need something *else*."

Chapter Three

"HONEY! I'M HOME!" I hang my coat on a hook and kick off my boots, leaving them on the rubber doormat for the snow to melt.

"That story about Abuela was supposed to be a secret!" Shane's voice carries from the back of the little house.

"It is! A secret among friends." I follow the delicious scent of sautéed onions and garlic. "Dinner smells amaz—" My words die with a gasp as I regard the mechanical massacre on the kitchen floor. "What have you done to Stuart?"

Shane kneels in front of the dismantled dishwasher in his typical uniform of jeans and a well-worn band T-shirt, a streak of dark grease across his forehead. "I was trying to fix him one last time, but he's finished."

"But he's a classic!" Right down to the faux-wood panel and metal buttons. A 1970s original and hideous, but he works so well in this shabby chic kitchen of butter-yellow cupboards, festive mosaic tile backsplash, and avocado-green appliances.

"We'll get a new Stuart," Scarlet murmurs without looking up from the stack of tests she's grading at the kitchen table. "Are there any good deals at Murphy's?"

"Through me? Of course."

"Good, 'cause you're paying half."

"What kind of landlord are you?" I drop the bag of pretzel buns I picked up at Todd's on the table, then swipe a handful of chocolate-covered raisins from the bowl in front of Scarlet and shove them into my mouth.

She snorts and pushes the bowl out of my easy reach, knowing I'll devour them before dinner. "The kind who has never asked for rent from my squatting best friend."

"You cannot put a dollar value on the gift of my daily presence," I manage, the words garbled. The truth is Scarlet owns the house outright, thanks to an inheritance. I cover half the utilities, but she'd never let me pay rent if I offered. She gets so much joy out of calling me a squatter, though. I can't take that away from her.

Shane eases himself to his feet. "I guess I'll haul this outside, babe?"

Scarlet pries her attention from the stack of papers to flash a smile at him. "Thanks for trying."

He offers a crooked grin. "Anything for you."

I stifle my groan and throw my hands up in the air. "What about for me?"

"Dean's waiting for your call."

"I'm not his type. I don't have my seniors' discount card yet. Or a rolling pin."

Shane's head falls back with a bark of laughter.

"I warned you, she will not let that die." Scarlet pokes the air with her red pen, aiming it at Shane. "You can't tell her things like this."

"You kidding? That's why I told her. Fanshaw needs his ego checked." He lugs the detached dishwasher door out, his arms tensing under the weight.

Scarlet's gaze trails him, a yearning look in her blue-purple eyes.

"Will you be staying next door tonight, or shall I wear my earplugs?" Nights when Shane isn't working and he doesn't have his son tend to get noisy around here, with Scarlet's bedroom above mine. Thankfully, they usually stay at his place.

She gives her head a little shake, as if she caught herself in a lustful daze. "How was work?"

"Oh, no big deal. You know, other than meeting the next love of my life." I flop into an empty chair.

Scarlet purses her lips. She's trying to figure out if I'm serious or if I'm just being ... well, *me*. "What's his name?"

"Garrett."

"Garrett what?"

"I don't know. Just Garrett." Ned isn't the greatest at paperwork when the customer pays cash. That's all that was on the handwritten order in the office. His first name and a phone number. Nothing else—no last name, no address, nothing I could use to ferret out more information about my budding obsession.

"I don't remember any Garretts growing up." She frowns in thought. "I wonder if Shane knows him."

"Doubtful. He's from New York. He's moving here to help out his aging uncle."

Her sharp but feminine features slacken. "That's so sweet."

"I know. Came into Murphy's to buy a new fridge." I give her a thorough description of his physical magnificence.

"And so ... what now? You're going on a date?"

"If he plays his cards right." I throw my feet up on an empty chair and regale Scarlet with the details while Shane filters in and out, collecting pieces of Stuart and catching bits of the sordid inner dialogue that ran through my head all afternoon.

"So, you guys didn't exchange numbers or anything?"

"Well, not yet. I'm playing hard to get—"

Scarlet snorts.

"Shut up!"

"Ice-cream cones last longer on a scorching July afternoon than your resolve when you get something—or someone—in your head."

"I can play hard to get." Though I never have, preferring to chase after what I want. But look where that got me with Bill. It's time I take a different approach. Besides, I'm still reeling from that heartbreak and hesitant to serve myself up on a platter to the next guy. "Garrett's coming on Thursday to pick up his fridge and profess his undying love to me. You just wait."

She opens her mouth to speak but pauses, a serious look passing across her face.

"What?"

"Nothing! It's just ..." She sinks into her chair. "Three days ago you were texting me from behind your mother's curtains, contemplating which knife to use to slash Bill's tires."

"I would *never*."

She cocks her head with a challenge.

"I would never, *again*. That was years ago." I drop my voice to hiss, "And it's *still* a secret." Bill suspected me, but he could never prove it, just like I suspected he cheated on me with the Starbucks barista, but I never found hard evidence. Given all that's transpired about his character since, I'd say the tire incident was merited.

"What's a secret?" Shane strolls in, pulling on his work gloves.

Scarlet pretends to fasten her lips with her fingertips and tosses an imaginary key over her shoulder.

"Yeah, yeah. Double standard." He uses the dolly to haul the dishwasher out, leaving us with a gaping hole beneath the counter.

I mock sniff. "Poor Stuart. Just left out in the cold after giving the humans so many good years of service."

Scarlet rolls her eyes. "My point is, I'm glad there's this new prospect, but don't pin *all* your hopes on this one guy you just met. I know you, and I know what you're like. You're *already* hooked, and I don't want to see you get hurt."

"I got hurt, remember? By the last guy I thought would ever do something like that to me." My voice grows husky, forcing me to clear it. "I'm just goofing around. If nothing else, this guy will be a fantastic rebound. I mean, you should see him." I arch my eyebrows to emphasize my claim.

"Dean would be a great rebound!" Shane hollers from the hallway before the front door slams shut.

Scarlet holds up her hands. "I'm just looking out for you."

"I know. That's why I keep you around." I lunge forward and snatch a handful of raisins from her bowl before she can react.

Chapter Four

"HOW COULD THIS HAPPEN TO ME?" I squeal, using the reflection in the washer door to inspect the inflamed pimple on the tip of my nose. I felt it coming, but I never could imagine it would turn into *this*. Not even concealer could hide it this morning, it's so ripe.

"What are you going on about now?" Ned looks up from his crossword puzzle. That and the weekly obituaries in the local paper are the two sections he never misses.

I stalk over to him and gesture at the angry red pustule.

He adjusts his reading glasses to get a better look. "Oh, that's a doozy. Must be all those sweets you've been gorging on this week."

"See?" I throw my hands up in the air. "I knew this was somehow Bastard Bill's fault."

Ned grunts. He's heard all about my cheating ex and is not a fan. "I remember when Raymond got those. Some real nasty ones too."

"When he was a pubescent boy, right? *Not* a thirty-year-old *woman*, waiting for her future husband to arrive." Which is any minute now, based on Garrett's phone call to ask if he should come to the back of the store for pickup.

"Men don't notice pimples."

"It's changed the shape of my nose!" I can see it through my peripheral vision. "How am I supposed to flirt with this guy when he's staring at it?" Or worse, averting his gaze to be polite? Which kind of man will he be? A gawker or an avoider? Both are equally bad. The more I imagine this exchange, the more my panic grows. "I can't be here for this."

"Why don't you go for a walk, then?" He pats the air, trying to calm me. "I'll take care of this order and message you when he's gone."

"Yeah, good idea, wingman." The first thing I did when I started here was teach Ned how to text. I'm so glad for it now. "I'll head to the drugstore to get poison for it, and then I'll hide next door. Just"—I grab a pen and scribble my phone number down —"tell him I died, but he can call me later if he wants."

Ned watches me jam my feet into my boots and grab my coat. "For someone with so much confidence, you sure are fussing over such a tiny little thing."

"It's practically a boil!" I charge for the front door.

"Careful out there. It's slippery."

"Good. If I fall flat on my face, maybe it'll burst."

Todd's soup had better be good today.

———

I inhale as I push through the butcher shop door. Dieter's smells delicious as always—a medley of garlicky homemade sausages, fresh bread delivered by truck each morning, and a flavorful chowder simmering in Todd's vintage red Crock-Pot. It's become a daily comfort, and it stirs pangs of hunger.

I open my mouth to announce my presence by demanding to know what the flavor of the day is when a familiar voice stalls my tongue.

"… parked around back, but I could use your help hauling that fridge in. I think the two of us could manage."

My heart skips a beat at the sound of Garrett's deep and raspy timbre.

But wait—he knows Todd?

"I've moved an appliance or two up those stairs over the years. Yeah, no problem, just let me finish writing this order, and then get Dillon to cover the front." The sound of pages flipping carries through the otherwise quiet shop.

What are they talking about? Move the fridge *where*? Upstairs? As in, to one of the apartments?

"You didn't mention anything to them about our arrangement while you were there, right?" Todd asks, a touch quieter.

"*No* way. The fewer people who know, the better."

"Good." Todd sighs heavily. "I'm telling you, my dad has to be rolling in his grave. Grandpa Dieter too."

"They'll settle down when they see the shiny new butcher shop you're running on the other side of town."

I frown. *Wait, what?* I shift closer toward the deli counter, using the shelves of sauces and spices for cover as I eavesdrop, thankful for my short stature and the depth of the store—they didn't seem to notice anyone enter.

"How much longer before it hits public record?" Todd asks.

"They're stalling the paperwork as long as they can. Another month, at least. Just long enough for me to get all the permit approvals in place." There's a long pause and then Garrett offers, "Don't worry about it, man. It was a smart move, and you have every right to do what you want with your property."

"Yeah, but there are some Polson Falls folks who are gonna be bent out of shape over losing this building."

"There'll be some noise, sure. There always is, but it'll blow over once they see what I'm replacing it with."

A sinking feeling hits me as I grasp what I'm hearing. Todd sold his building. Everything Dieter left him—the butcher shop, the other storefronts, all the apartments above, the sizable plot of land …

To Garrett?

Who the hell is this guy?

"In any case, I wouldn't hold your breath with Ned. He's old school. You'll need a miracle or a body bag to get him to sell that place to a developer."

My jaw drops.

"I guess we'll see. I just handed him an offer in writing with some decent zeros on it. I don't think it'll take too long for him to figure out what's best. Hopefully, that cute employee of his can help me convince him of that."

"Who, Justine?"

My ears burn, hearing my name.

"Yeah. I was hoping to talk to her today, but she wasn't there. She left her number, though. I'll work on her until she helps me seal the deal."

"*Work on me?*" The words explode from my mouth as I storm around the corner.

Both men stand still, shock filling their faces.

"Is that what you were doing the other day? *Working* on me?"

Todd's eyes flicker from me to the clock to the Crock-Pot. "Justine. You're early."

"Actually, I think I'm right on time today, *Todd*," I snap, spitting his name out like it tastes bitter. "So, Jamaica, huh? What, were you celebrating something down there? A recent cash windfall?" He's wearing his usual Tommy Bahama button-down; today's version is a black-on-gray tropical print. It might be the only brand of shirt he owns, and it has become a running joke between us. But today, nothing is funny.

His tanned face pales. "Let me explain—"

"Not interested. And *you* ..." I scowl at Garrett, who's dressed in jeans and a Patagonia jacket, but no less attractive, save for the serpent's tail I missed before. "What, you thought you could come into Murphy's, woo me, and then *use* me to get Ned to sell his place to you?"

He flinches. Good. At least he's uncomfortable having his slimy plan thrown back in his face.

"What's wrong? Not so flirtatious today, are we?"

"It's not like that—"

"Bullshit. I heard what you said, and it's *exactly* like that! And a body bag? *Really?*" I stab the air with my finger, aiming my anger at Todd again. "You should be ashamed of yourself, talking about him like that. He's been like family to you since you were in diapers."

"I didn't mean it that way, but you know it's true," he mutters, his sheepish look oozing regret.

"What *I* know is that you went and sold your family's building to some *developer*"—I glare at Garrett—"and then thought you could hide it from the rest of us. You spineless coward."

"*Us?*" Todd throws his hands in the air in exasperation. "You just moved here! You don't even pay your friend rent!"

"So what?" I've told Todd far too much about myself during our daily soup and gossip sessions.

Garrett takes a step forward. "If you'll just let me explain—"

"Explain what? How you're going to rip down one of the oldest parts of Polson Falls? You think the town's going to let you do that?"

"The town council is eager for this development—"

"But the people of Polson Falls aren't." Not all of them.

Garrett sighs, and when he speaks again, his tone is calm and cool and nothing like the playful version from the other day. "I'm sorry to say, there's nothing those people can do. The deal is done, and this is happening whether they like it or not."

"We'll see about that." I fold my arms. "And you're not getting Murphy's." As if I have any control over it.

Garrett slides his hands into his pockets. "Murphy's would have been a nice-to-have, but I don't need it for this project." His gaze settles on my nose.

I suck in a sharp breath, suddenly remembering why I was avoiding a run-in with Garrett in the first place. "This isn't over." I spin on my heel and rush out before he can see my cheeks flame. "You'll never get away with this!"

The sidewalk in front of Murphy's needs more salt. I slip and slide, barely avoiding a car using the laneway between our buildings as I charge toward the front door, plowing through it with a huff.

Thankfully, the store is empty of customers.

Ned leans against the counter, wearing his reading glasses. "Oh, Justine. He came and left. I forgot to text you," he mumbles, focused on the page within his wrinkled hands. "I gave him your number like you asked. He said he'd call."

"If he has a death wish." I march forward. "Is that the offer to buy Murphy's?"

"It is." He frowns. "You knew he was going to do this?"

"No, I didn't." I thought it was a joke. I sure as hell didn't know who he was. I still don't.

"It's a decent offer." He pauses. "Harrington ... where have I heard that before?"

"Garrett Harrington? That's his name?" Not that it matters, but it's good to know your enemy before you set out to destroy him. "When he gave you this decent offer, did he happen to mention that he bought Todd's building?"

"What?" Ned slides his glasses off. "Todd sold Dieter's building?"

"Yeah, except he's trying to hide the sale as long as possible because he knows people are gonna be pissed when they find out this Garrett guy is tearing it down."

Ned's face pales as he studies the memo in his hand. "Wait. Does that mean ... but he said he liked my store."

"Of course he said that, because you'd never sell to him if you knew he wanted to tear this place down too. Garrett's trying to hustle you." And hustle me into helping him.

"He can't tear this place down." Ned peers around the space, shaking his head. "It's been here for seventy years. It's my life."

"You're right. It is. Can I see that?"

With a dazed look, he hands me the paper.

I don't bother reading it before I rip it into pieces.

Chapter Five

"I'm sick and tired of these men getting away with whatever they want." Shirley arranges her cards in her wrinkled hand, the crimson paint of her manicured nails contrasting against the matte-black deck. There are two things this spirited firecracker never misses—her weekly appointments at the hair and nail salons.

The first time I walked into Bonny Acres and noticed the copper-haired resident sitting by herself at a table, I didn't think twice about strolling up and taking a seat. I remember the way her hands paused on her round of solitaire, and her chartreuse eyes narrowed on my face as she hissed, "What the hell are you doing here?"

Of all the residents, I had to pick the belligerent one who hates people. No one warned me.

But I was already seated, and I like a good challenge, so I said the only thing I could think of: "My ex and I broke up because he's a cheating bastard, and I'm here to play cards. Do you know rummy?" I held my breath as seconds passed like slow-pour honey, and then the woman's head fell back with a loud cackle. There were audible gasps nearby. Apparently, Shirley laughing is like witnessing a volcano erupt—equal parts mesmerizing and terrifying. She folded her game and expertly dealt our hands, and we played several rounds while she interrogated me about every last one of Bastard Bill's faults. It was therapeutic.

When I got up to leave, she warned me not to sit at her table again without smuggling in a treat from Confetti's, the bakeshop across town. "Something with pistachio. And none of that diabetic, sugar-free crap they feed us in this prison." It turns out Shirley has an unruly sweet tooth.

The director of Bonny Acres stopped me in the hall that night on my way out, flabbergasted. Shirley is the longest-standing resident at the home and a royal pain in Harper's derriere—her words. Never in all her years had Harper seen Shirley tolerate anyone for that long, let alone smile while doing it.

It seems I'm a unicorn, and I've made a very unlikely friend.

Since that night, I always veer to Shirley's unofficial table—no one else sits there as no one wants to deal with her icy glares and acerbic tongue —with a small pastry box, and she is always ready for a few hands of rummy while we take turns griping about Bastard Bill and other grievances, usually related to the quality of food at the assisted living center.

"Can they? Get away with it?" I swap my cards. Rummy was my Gramps' favorite game, and he taught me young. I think it's one of the reasons I love visiting places like this—it gives me a chance to feel like he's still sitting across the table.

"Harrington Group has its dirty fingerprints on most of the new commercial development. Some of the residential too." Shirley trades a card from her hand with a fresh one from the deck.

"Harrington." As in Garrett Harrington.

"And don't expect any help from the town. Make no mistake, it's all this hotshot mayor and his council want. Ferris Gump. What kind of name is that? His momma didn't love him, that's for damn sure. They've been wooing big-city money and passing ordinance changes left and right, so these money-hungry developers can come in here and do as they please without taxpaying citizens having much say.

"Seven years with this fool, and you can tell who matters and who doesn't. That park at the end of the block? A lot of Bonny Acres' residents like to head over there for a change of scenery. It used to be a nice place, with the big trees and the water fountain and the playground for grandkids. But several of the oaks got wilt, the playground is unsafe, and the fountain hasn't worked for years."

It's not the first time Shirley's complained to me about that park's disarray. I've heard grumblings from other residents too.

"We've been hounding them to take some pride and fix it for everyone. Does Gump listen, though? Nah, he's too busy approving big-city plans. If he had his way, Polson Falls would be all concrete and condominiums. You know, last summer they changed building height restrictions and the density bylaws from two stories to three? And Brillcourt's owner was looking to convert that place to condominiums, but the council voted against that one. Not enough low-income housing in the area." She waggles her pencil-drawn eyebrows. "Seems awful suspicious to me that the building burns to the ground not six months later."

Brillcourt is the low-rent apartment complex Scarlet grew up in and her mother lived in until just a few months ago. The building has been condemned, fenced off, and the property sold. No one knows what'll go in there, but we all suspect it won't be affordable housing for single-income families.

While I doubt the cause of the fire (a space heater coupled with a smoke alarm system that was all for show) was intentional, it does sound like prime pickings for someone with money and ambition to jump on.

"But he's talking about tearing down one of the oldest blocks on Main Street. I know it's the run-down side, but there's history there." A painting of Polson Falls Main Street circa 1927 hangs on the walls of Dieter's, showing Model-T Fords parked outside. "There's a freaking picture of JFK buying a Reuben sandwich at the deli counter." Dieter Junior and Dieter Senior smile proudly in the background.

Shirley collects a shortbread cookie before nudging the little pastry box toward me, but I decline, not wanting to feed any new horrors on my face. The last one is still healing and hidden by concealer. "I remember that day. Clear blue skies and cherry trees in bloom. JFK's motorcade came through Polson Falls on their way to the big car manufacturing plant over in Springfield. That kind of history doesn't matter to a lot of folks around here these days, though. Didn't you know? Old is out, new is in."

I can't guess at her age, and I don't dare ask, but I know she's getting up there. Still sharp as a sliver of glass under your thumbnail.

"I'm sure Gump would sell *this* place if he could get his hooks into it. Us wrinkly old birds don't fit with the town aesthetic. Probably why he won't spend money on the park either. Who knows what he's got planned for that land. Can you imagine what a developer could do with it?"

I survey the large common room of Bonny Acres—designed to look like an old-fashioned parlor of dark wood and floral wallpaper, and with plenty of nooks and crannies where wing chairs and ornate tables wait for residents to trickle in for game night. Volunteering at this place to keep me busy was one of the first decisions I made when I moved here, and I haven't regretted it once.

My focus lands on the prominent portrait of the Bonnys above the stately fireplace—a wealthy couple who owned the original Victorian house that serves as the face of the center. They had no children but plenty of friends and this big old house. Once several of those friends began facing minor health issues, the Bonnys invited them to move in, hiring a nurse and a cook to provide care. I think they just didn't want to spend their days alone.

Eventually, the Bonnys passed away, but the younger generation of relatives and friends was tasked with keeping the place alive. It's expanded considerably over the years, with an enormous addition behind the original house that offers studio and one-bedroom suites for married couples. All in all, there are fifty-four residents living here today.

Shirley draws a card and tosses an unfavorable one. "All these new folks flocking here from the city are saying they want nicer and newer, and that's who they're catering to. Not us old farts who'll be dying off soon enough."

While she may be cynical, anyone who's been watching the flood of change would see she's not entirely wrong. "But can they get away with this?"

"They *think* they can." She holds up her index finger, the lengthy nail filed to a trendy point. "Gump and his minions are waiting with scissors, ready to cut all kinds of red tape. That little weasel has been caught skipping steps more than once to push things through."

"Garrett said he'd have his permits approved before people even found out about the sale."

She drums the tabletop with her fingers. "What is this developer of yours planning?"

"I don't know. And he's not *mine*."

"That's because you're no fool. I don't waste my time with fools."

It's the closest thing to a compliment Shirley's paid me. "It better not be one of those blasted condominiums. Can you imagine one of those ugly concrete things right in the heart of our town?" Her face pinches with anger. "Like I said, Gump's been changing all the bylaws for density and height. That's zoned for mixed use right now. If there's no rezoning involved with his plan, then there's no need for the public meeting. No announcements, no chance for the public to have their say and appeal the town's approval." Shirley scowls at her cards before swapping out another.

"Which means no way to stop it." Just like Garrett said. He probably got a kick out of my tantrum as I stormed out.

"Oh, we're going to stop it, don't you worry. Or at least become a festering boil on their asses." Shirley winks at me.

"There's a reason they're trying to hide this project. You see, a lot of towns and cities don't protect historic buildings. They just give them a nice little label, and then they let the owners do whatever the hell they want. But Polson Falls is different. The historical committee, which I'm a voting member of, made sure of that."

"Sounds like I'm talking to the right person about this." I had no idea she was part of such a thing, but it makes sense, given how fired up she is and how often she complains about the significant changes Polson Falls has seen in recent years.

She peers over her glasses at me. "It's not all aquatic aerobics and card games around here. A few of us keep up to speed with what goes on in our town. Hold town council members' feet to the fire, so to speak, so they know we're watching every move they make." She sets her cards on the table, pausing the game. "I've been on it for years, ever since that idiot mayor Wilson allowed a developer to tear down the town's first bank to put in a parking lot. What a beautiful building that was. There was a two-hundred-year-old elm beside it that went too. Developer stood in that town meeting and promised to save it, then turned around practically the next day and cut it down. That's how these guys work. They'll tell you anything you want to hear, make all kinds of promises, offer to pay for things, all to get what they want. Slick as sin. All liars, every last one of them."

"Don't I know it." I've seen it firsthand.

"We got rid of Wilson for that. The next mayor, Benjamin Orly, he was a good fellow, rest his soul. He cared about protecting the town's heritage. We worked with him to establish local historic preservation ordinances and install a heritage commissioner. Of course, when Gump came in, he tried to replace her with one of his cronies and water down those bylaws to nothing. We got the state preservation office involved. Shut him down."

"I knew you were a badass, Shirley."

She chortles. "I don't like losing, that's for sure."

Neither do I, and it feels like that's all I've been doing. "Okay, so what's the plan, then?" The hefty, helpless weight that settled on me when I saw Garrett's true colors and watched Ned deflate with the news is noticeably lighter.

"Passing a historical designation using the town's ordinances takes time we don't have, and if they take a wrecking ball to it before our clock strikes twelve, this is all moot. That's how these guys get away with it."

"It sounds like that's what Garrett was hoping for."

"I'll call the commissioner first thing in the morning to get the bug in her ear. I have her personal number, after all." Shirley says this with pride, as if it's a special gift bestowed upon her and her alone. "Our ordinance states that if the commissioner flags just cause to claim historical landmark status before permits are approved, the town must pause its permit process for up to six months while a decision on the building's status is made."

"And if we get Todd's building—well, Garrett's building now, I guess—"

"Shame on that boy for selling off his family's history like that." A subdued look passes across her face. "I knew Dieter. Ned too. Good men, both of them, and that's a rare breed. I can understand this being hard on Ned, having these developers come in and erase everything he's known his whole life."

Yesterday afternoon at work was quiet and somber. Ned left early to go home, saying something about needing to rest. I think he needed alone time to deal with the news that an era—what he's known for his entire life—is coming to a definitive end. "So, if we get the building designated as historical, they won't be able to tear it down?"

"It'll be a lot damn harder, that's for sure. Like with everything else, there are loopholes." Shirley twists her lips. "We also need to make noise. Harrington Group can't demolish anything until the tenants are out. You go and find out what they know. And head down to the library. There's something about that building's history ... I can't put my finger on it, but I remember it having a colorful past. Anyway, tell Alice Grant I sent ya. She'll help you go through all the newspaper archives. I'll bet you find some nuggets in there."

"I'm on it." It's a great way to keep my mind occupied. I have no idea where the library is, let alone have a library card, but I keep that bit to myself. Shirley would be disappointed by my ignorance.

She puckers her lips, picking up her hand again. "We need to let the people of Polson Falls know what that weasel Gump is up to."

"You really don't like him, huh?" Or most men, for that matter.

"He's a smug man who acts as though there's a crown on his head. But it's election year, and Gump won't want a bunch of noise."

"Who are you picking a fight with now?" Harper saunters past. She has a stack of papers tucked under her arm. It feels like she's *always* here, working.

"Oh, just the sniveling mayor." If there's anyone else Shirley tolerates in here besides me, it's the director. Even if she still gives the poor woman grief.

"Lord help him." Harper notices the pastry box but ignores it, shifting her attention to me. "Don't you have somewhere better to be on a Friday night?"

"You kidding? What's better than checking bingo cards and getting hit on by Roger?" Route 66 doesn't come to life until ten, anyway. I lean back in my chair. "Hey, so what's the scoop on Nancy and her undiagnosed skin condition?"

"It's no longer undiagnosed, and it's not contagious, so she'll be in soon."

"Oh." My shoulders sink, unable to hide my disappointment.

Harper regards me with chocolate-brown eyes, so soft compared to her stern demeanor. "What, you thought a rash would keep her out so you could call the numbers?"

"I was hopeful."

Harper guffaws. "That woman was hit by a car and rolled in

the next week in a wheelchair, wrapped in casts. There ain't no minor itch that's gonna keep her away."

"Don't you think some variety would be good for the residents?"

"Might keep us alive longer. Good for your bank account," Shirley quips. I can't blame her. Nancy's voice is monotone, her energy flat. She's not friendly either. She annoys easily. Within five minutes of meeting her, she declared that I'm not the right fit for Bonny Acres, and she insisted on training me on how to distribute bingo cards and daubers.

Shirley said she overheard Nancy petitioning Harper to fire me, but I can't tell if that's the truth or just Shirley stirring trouble.

Either way, I'm a fucking volunteer.

The only interesting thing about Nancy is her attire—themed home-knit monstrosities that make the ugly Christmas sweater tradition a year-round affair.

"Look, I know Nancy can be a bit prickly, but she's been a dedicated volunteer for nearly a decade, and bingo is her thing. If you want to call the numbers, you'll need to negotiate that with her." Harper flashes a wicked smile and strolls away.

"She's liable to put arsenic in your tea," Shirley warns.

"Yeah, I got that vibe." The last time I dared suggest to Nancy that we swap roles, her glower burned holes in the back of my head all night.

Peering over her shoulder to make sure Harper's gone, Shirley pops another shortbread into her mouth.

Chapter Six

"WHAT ABOUT THIS PLUMBER, CURT SHAPIRO?" I shout over the live band, the female singer covering a Stone Temple Pilots song.

Shane shakes his head. "Notorious for overcharging and replacing things that don't need replacing. Do not recommend him."

"So, no to Curt Shapiro." I mark an X beside his name, along with the reason, and accept a fresh pint from the Route 66 waitress, mouthing my thanks. She didn't have to bother taking my order when she saw me slide into the booth—I'm predictable when it comes to beer.

"You know, you could've just stayed working for your uncle if you were going to be vetting tradespeople," Scarlet notes. "Way better pay."

"This is just busywork. And Ned needs me more."

"How's he doing?"

"He's sad."

"Of course he is." Dean watches the TV screen above, absorbed in the Flyers game while still carrying on a conversation. "There's a whole life of memories there. He and Dieter weren't just business neighbors, they were good friends. Todd and Ned's son were close in age. They grew up together."

"But he had to know this was coming. The town just spent all that money upgrading the sewer lines. Everything else around here is changing. Look at *this* place." Shane nods around us at the chalky-black, board-and-batten walls and industrial lighting. "It was Luigi's for decades and when he died, people fought to keep the family restaurant going. But someone new came in, and they turned it into what the town needed, and now it's packed every weekend."

"So, you're saying you're on Todd's side? That selling to a developer was a good thing?" There's a challenge in my voice.

"Relax. I'm saying that building's seen better days. Remember that call we got a few years back?" He looks at Dean. "The man we had to carry down those stairs?"

Dean grunts in answer.

"That apartment was a dive. Nothing's been updated in decades. They're barely up to code, and Todd hasn't invested anything. How many renters does he have up there now?"

"Just one. Death Metal Dawn." She plays rage music at all hours of the day and night.

And Garrett, if I am to believe his lie about moving in, which I don't. Though I don't understand the whole refrigerator act. That's rather elaborate if he's lying.

"See? Three apartments sitting empty, because they need work that Todd doesn't want to bother with. And, for as many people that you think don't want change, there are five times as many who've been pushing to revitalize for years. That end of town needs it."

"Revitalize, fine. Bulldoze, though?"

"It's like they're completely erasing everything this place was," Dean says.

"Yeah. Exactly." I smack him across the shoulder. "See? He gets it. It's like …" I search for an example I can relate to. "Sam's Pastry. I've been going there my entire life with my family. It's tradition. I can't imagine if it was suddenly gone."

Shane shrugs. "It'll happen eventually."

I glare at him.

"We know you're loyal to Ned, but you have to admit, Polson Falls could use a few cute little shops and cafés on Main Street," Scarlet says gently. "It's kind of pathetic right now."

"I know. I just feel so bad for him. He lost his wife last year, his business is in the shitter, and now he gets to watch the demolition of his best friend's building." I slump. It's not just my loyalty to Ned that's bothering me. My anger with Garrett is a splinter under my skin I can't ignore. And, if I'm being honest, I'm embarrassed. There I was, fawning and flirting, oblivious. I should have seen through his act. I'm smarter than that.

But on that day, I was a brainless housefly, buzzing straight into a strip of yellow tape.

Scarlet taps her fingers on the table's surface. "I was driving through Dover the other day, and did you know they have a bubble tea shop now?"

A grin splits my face despite my mood. "You hear that, Dean? Balls on your tongue. Your fave."

He shakes his head. "She is relentless."

"Speaking of relentless, my bladder is about to burst. I need to pee." Instead of waiting for Dean to shift his massive body out of the booth, I take advantage of my size and climb over his lap.

"Here, let me help you." He seizes my hips and gives a little squeeze before sliding me across. I'm no fool. The move isn't necessarily inappropriate—given I've climbed onto him—but it burns a distinctive feeling into my brain of what it would feel like to have Dean gripping me like that from behind.

Say, in my bedroom.

Undressed.

The sly look on his face when I glance back at him confirms he knew what he was doing.

"Well played. One point goes to the sexy big lug." I hold up a finger. "But fair warning, I never lose at this game. Ask Scarlet."

"She does not." She punctuates that by toasting the air with her drink. "And she doesn't play nice."

Dean holds his arms out to either side, palms in those giant hands upraised. "Bring it, tiny tiger."

"Wait. I'm coming with you." Scarlet sets down her glass and stares at Shane, waiting.

He's the picture of relaxation, his one hand wrapped around his beer and his other arm slung over Scarlet's shoulders. There was a period where they hid their relationship, given Scarlet is Shane's son's teacher, but the secret's long past out. "Did you want to just ..." He gestures at his lap.

She glares at him for even suggesting she repeat my move. While people may know they're dating, I'm sure there are parents here tonight, and if Scarlet cares about anything, it's her reputation.

I, on the other hand, couldn't care less what people think of me. Scarlet calls it my superpower.

With a teasing grin, Shane acquiesces, sliding out and standing, stretching his arms over his head in the act, attracting more than one female gaze in the vicinity. I have no problem admitting my best friend's boyfriend is gorgeous.

What makes him even more so is that he only has eyes for her.

Together, Scarlet and I weave through the waitresses and tables, heading toward the back where the band plays and a crowd loiters by the bar. "It seems busier than usual, doesn't it?" Route 66 is always lively on Fridays, but tonight it feels like it's bursting at the seams.

"Nobody wants to travel all the way to Philly in January for a night out."

"Guess not." Though it's been like this since I moved here last fall. Maybe Shane has a point and Polson Falls needs more places like this. What's that movie line? If you build it, they will come?

I'm surveying the crowd—a healthy mix of barely legal to empty-nesters—when I spot a familiar head of perfectly styled hair.

"*No way.*" It couldn't be ...

But it is.

"What?" Scarlet frowns.

"It's him." Garrett is seated in a booth at the back with an older man, cutlery lying across their plates to signal they've finished their meals.

"*That's* the developer?" Scarlet's eyebrows climb halfway up her forehead. "*Damn.* Okay, I get it."

"That's because you can't see his reptilian scales from here."

"Right." Her face sours. "What a waste."

The restroom door is to our left. I keep moving past it, my bladder's needs temporarily forgotten.

"Justine … what are you doing?" Scarlet asks.

"Probably something stupid. Catch up with you in a bit." I weave through the crowd. Garrett and his companion are in such intense conversation, they don't notice me marching toward them, my jaw set with determination.

"Look who it is!" I drop myself into the narrow space on the bench next to him.

Garrett, mid sip on his beer, jumps a touch, surprised by my bold interruption. "Justine," he manages around his swallow. After a beat, he shifts over to give me more room.

"Good idea. Wouldn't want me sitting on that tail of yours," I say loud enough for only him to hear, capping it with a toothy grin.

His forehead wrinkles. "Huh?"

The man across from me watches our exchange with curious blue eyes. He's distinguished-looking and attractive, everything about him shaped tidily, from his steel-gray hair to his cuff links. I know I've seen him before—that thick gray mustache makes a statement. I just can't place him yet.

"Garrett, are you going to introduce your friend?" he finally asks.

"I'm Justine." I throw my hand across the table, gripping his in a firm shake.

His face softens a touch. "It's nice to meet you. I'm Richard, Garrett's uncle."

"*You're* his uncle?" My mouth gapes.

"Why do you say it like that?" Another flicker to Garrett. "Were you expecting someone different?"

"Actually, the way Garrett described you … yeah."

"Oh?" He cocks his head at his nephew. "Do tell."

"I don't know what she's talking about." Garrett's wearing a black button-down shirt, the sleeves rolled up to show off cut forearms. The muscles in them cord as he grips his pint glass.

"Sure you do. What was it you said, *exactly*? Oh, right." I snap my fingers. "You were moving to Polson Falls because your uncle was aging and needed your help." This man in front of me is in his early sixties—at most—and from the looks of his shoulders and his upper body, is nowhere near ready for a room at Bonny Acres.

"Is that so?" Mixed with amusement, I catch the faintest hint of displeasure in Richard's tone.

Garrett's jaw tenses. "That is *not* what I said."

It's exactly what he said, and my ire flares that he would dare paint me a liar. But if he wants one of those, he's got it. "He asked for names of assisted living facilities in the area. I gave him a few recommendations, including the one I volunteer at, Bonny Acres. Great place, but between you and me, I don't know why he'd think you belong in one of those."

Richard clasps his hands in front of him, leaning in a touch. "I'd love to hear his answer to that."

Garrett falls back against the bench, muttering something under his breath that I don't catch. "Richard, Justine works next to the Revive project location. She's recently learned about it and isn't thrilled."

"*Ah*, I see." Uncle Richard says that like it all makes perfect sense. "And you grew up in Polson Falls?"

"No, she's only been here a few months," Garrett answers for me. "I don't know why she's taking it so personally."

Because you made it personal when you made me like you, asshole. I force a smile. "*Actually*, what I'm not thrilled about is your nephew coming into Murphy's, feeding me lies while flirting with me, all under the guise of getting me to convince my boss to sell the building to him."

"Inaccurate." Garrett shakes his head to emphasize his claim.

"So you *didn't* ask me to stay on as an employee if you bought Murphy's? You *didn't* tell me you had ways of keeping me in line if you were my boss and I was being *bad*?" I let a tinge of sultriness slip into my voice as I lean toward him.

Annoyance flashes in Garrett's eyes as they scan my face, along with something else I can't confirm. A heated challenge, perhaps. I'm so close, I can pick out the curved pattern in his brown irises and the heavy ring of hazel circling his pupils.

A throat clears, pulling our attention across the table.

Uncle Richard's bushy eyebrows arch into a "What the hell is going on?" position. "Which building is this? I don't recall us discussing any other development projects for HG."

Garrett sighs. "It's not for HG."

His uncle's lips twist as he stares down his nephew for one … two … three seconds.

And I wait with bated breath for the dust to settle on whatever secret of Garrett's I just unearthed.

But when Richard speaks, his voice is calm and collected. "Justine, I apologize for any miscommunication that may have taken place between you two. It was certainly not on behalf of HG. We would never condone such behavior as what you're describing." A sharp glare cuts to Garrett. "As far as Revive is concerned, I can assure you I have every intention of adding to the charm of Polson Falls rather than detracting from it. The last thing I want to do is lose the small-town feel that everyone appreciates. I myself have recently purchased a home in the area because of this charm. But I can understand your apprehension. Perhaps seeing the new building design may ease your worries."

It seems I'm sitting across from the *real* boss. "You have the plans handy?"

"I don't." He looks to Garrett.

"Still a few final touches to go before I'm comfortable sharing them broadly."

"I wouldn't call myself 'broad,'" I air-quote that word with my fingers.

"I'll bet you're louder than a town crier," Garrett mumbles under his breath.

"I'll leave it to your discretion. You are spearheading this project, after all." Richard wipes his mustache with a napkin, though it was clean. "It was nice to meet you, Justine. I'll keep you in mind when I require the name of that assisted living center, though I suspect it will be quite some time. Garrett, I expect a phone call within the hour." That last part is delivered as an order more than a request.

With that, Richard slides from the booth, collects a wool jacket hanging on a hook, and strolls out, offering a casual wave to a few tables on his way past.

"You are unbelievable." Garrett slumps in his seat.

"Thank you. I get that a lot from the men in my life." I move to sit on the vacant side of the booth. "So, your silver fox uncle is the developer, huh?"

"He owns the company, yes."

I pick a cold fry off his plate and pop it into my grinning mouth. Yes, it could be considered gross, but I've had far worse in my mouth, and the pint of beer I have waiting for me will wash away his germs.

"What are you so happy about?" Garrett regards me warily, as if waiting for me to do something rash, like throw this empty pint glass at his head.

"*Someone's getting in trouble,*" I deliver in a singsong voice.

"I'm not getting in trouble." He tugs at a shirt cuff. "What I manage for HG and what I invest in on my own are two different things."

"HG ... I've seen that around town."

He smirks. "You mean on billboards for *development* projects?"

"Your uncle's the one who's been playing with Polson Falls

like it's his own personal Lego set. I knew I'd seen that mustache somewhere." In the local newspaper.

"Harrington Group has helped bring to life much of what the elected officials envisioned for the future of this town," Garrett answers coolly.

"Wow, did a politician coach you on that answer?"

He smiles with his teeth and there's nothing jovial about it. "Is there something specific you needed from me tonight, or did you just come here to embarrass me in front of my boss and ruin my evening?"

"You've ruined Ned's whole week. His weekend, too, so I figure repaying the favor is the least I could do."

A look flickers across Garrett's face but vanishes in the next breath. "If you want to make me the bad guy for buying Todd's building, go ahead. It doesn't change anything."

"*You* didn't buy it. Your *uncle* did."

"Your point?"

I shrug. "No point, other than that's almost like your *daddy* buying it for you."

His jaw tenses. "I work directly under my uncle and, like you heard, I'm leading this project."

"So you're a baby developer."

He pinches the bridge of his nose.

"Why do you want Ned's place?" Because clearly that's not part of HG's plan.

"I want to own it."

"So you can tear it down?"

"I didn't say that."

I wait for him to elaborate.

He sighs. "Property value around here has gone up ten to twenty percent year over year for the past five, and it's not going to stall. There are two more residential developments in the works on the south side of town, and they're about to announce the extension of the rail line, connecting Polson Falls to Philadelphia. When that happens, there's going to be a flood of commuters looking for more affordable housing. Buying commercial real estate on Main Street now is a smart move for the long run."

"You don't even feel the least bit guilty about trying to hustle a sweet old man?"

He huffs. "I was not trying to hustle him—"

"Stop bullshitting me."

Garrett folds his arms. I can't help but track the move, the way the shirt's material stretches across hard muscle. I don't want it to be flattering. I hate him.

I pick at another fry to distract my thoughts.

"Help yourself." He pushes the plate across the table toward me.

"That fridge you bought from us. Who was that for?"

"For me, like I told you."

"And why did you need Todd's help to move it upstairs?"

"Because refrigerators are heavy."

I pause mid bite. "Wait, you're telling me that you're *living* in one of those apartments?"

He runs his tongue over his teeth as if deciding how to answer. "For the next few months, while I'm getting the project up and running, I might want a place to crash on occasion while I'm in town. This is convenient. Besides, the apartment's vacant, so why not?"

"Those places are shitholes."

"Not as bad as the closest motel. Like I said, it's temporary, and I'm not that picky."

"Yeah, I can see that." My gaze drags over his shirt, the silver chain around his neck, his watch, and the wool coat and cashmere scarf hanging on the hook beside him. I'm no expert, but none of them look like department store specials. I'll bet his shoes don't have a speck of salt on them. And his hair ... are those salon highlights? They seem too perfect to be gifted by the sun. I never noticed that before, too enthralled with the entire package to pick it apart.

Disappointment pricks my heart, remembering how easily he

made me feel good that day—how he made me forget—but I steel my resolve. I like being single, anyway. "This Revive Project ... what is it?"

"A mixed residential and commercial building. Storefronts and two floors of condominiums."

"Condos on Main Street? They're not going to allow that."

"You mean, the town council? They've given preliminary approvals."

"No rezoning requirements," I mumble, more to myself. I have to share these details with Shirley. She'll lay an egg when she hears about this.

The corners of his mouth curve upward. "Were you hoping for a public meeting?"

"Why would I want that?" I feign casualness.

He shrugs. "Some people get it in their heads that they can stop a project from happening."

"And what? You're saying people's opinions don't matter?"

"No, I'm saying that if a town council wants a project to go through, they'll find a way to make it happen."

"And if residents don't want a project to go through, they'll find a way to stop it."

"Like what?" Amusement laces his tone.

I shrug.

"What could it be? Let me see." He steeples his fingers in front of his face. It's an obnoxious move. "Of course, there's the town historical building ordinances."

"Valid for a building built in the early 1900s."

"That *hasn't* been deemed a historical landmark to date, which is an extensive process. A building with no real special historical, cultural, or aesthetic value."

"Not to *you*."

"This project is going forward because it's what's good for the town." There is no waver in his voice.

"We'll see." I bite my tongue against the urge to bring up Shirley and the heritage committee.

We get caught in a staring contest that would make the average person cagey, his eyes boring into mine as if he's mining for private and intimate secrets. If he thinks I'll yield, he will be disappointed. I'm the type who will sit in my car in a parking lot just so the person who honked for me to hurry up and pull out won't get my spot.

I make a point of unzipping my hoodie.

It works as a suitable distraction, Garrett's gaze dropping to my chest and the fitted custom-made T-shirt adorning it. "Did you make that just for me?"

"You think *that* highly of yourself? No, I had it made for every jerk with a penis I come across. Never expected it to be applicable to so many."

"Classy."

"Hey, *you're* the one gawking at my breasts," I say loudly, earning a few looks from around us.

"Glad you're not the bitter type." He waves down his waitress, making a signature sign for her to bring his check. "I don't understand why you're so upset about us replacing that eyesore. It's not like you have long ties to the place."

"It's not the eyesore, it's the people you're hurting in the process and your callous methods."

"Did you see the offer I made to your boss?"

"Before I tore the paper in half for him? Nah, didn't bother reading it."

His lips twist. "There's another home improvement store coming to Polson Falls."

I falter over the sudden change in direction. "You mean besides Home Depot?"

"Yeah. That new construction over on Maple Drive. It's going to be another chain store."

"How do you know?" Everyone's been speculating which retailers might be moving in there, but no one knows for sure.

He gives me a flat look.

Of course, developers know.

Shit. It's bad enough we have to compete against one big-box store but *two*? Ned's going to be upset by this news.

"I know business is bad, and Ned's struggling," Garrett says as if reading my mind. "He's owned that property outright for decades. He has no liens on it, and no one to leave the business to." He pauses. "Unless *you* were hoping it would go to you. Is that why you're working there?"

My jaw drops, his suggestion flaring my rage. "I'm not the one out there swindling the elderly," I snarl. I'll bet Garrett's been pumping Todd for information. He probably knew all the answers before he came in that day to ask the questions. "I started at Murphy's because Ned needed reliable help."

"Well, you'd be helping your boss out more by convincing him to sell to me than what you're currently doing."

"And what am I currently doing?"

"Obstructing a sound deal and being a royal pain in my ass."

"What can I say? It's what I'm good at."

Brooklyn arrives with the bill, along with a "Hey, Justine," for me and a playful smile for her customer that he matches. One look at this exchange, and any fool could tell they've been flirting all night. Who can blame them? She's an attractive brunette college student with dimples, and he looks like *that*.

"Don't waste your time on this one," I warn her. "He may have a shiny platinum exterior, but it's all cheap metal underneath. You know, the kind that gives you a bad rash and turns your finger green."

"Ignore her. She's upset it's not going to work out between us." Garrett slides out a matte black credit card that looks as sleek as he is, leveling me with a smirk.

"It's more extreme disappointment. I'm sorry, but any woman who told you she was satisfied with *fifteen seconds* was lying to you. We have needs. Also, missionary? Expand your moves. There are books."

.

A mixture of irritation and amusement burns in Garrett's gaze as his cheeks flush.

I smile, challenging him to spit out whatever rebuttal he's holding between gritted teeth.

But he quietly hands his card to Brooklyn with a murmured thanks.

"I'll be right back." Brooklyn spins on her heel and hightails it away from the table.

"You are petty and childish." Garrett reaches for the phone and key fob on the table, giving me a sneak peek of a jutting collarbone and padded muscle just below.

"Thank you! You know who else could be called childish? That twenty-one-year-old waitress. She must be *at least* a decade younger than you." How old is this baby developer?

"At least." He smiles, not taking my bait. "As fun as this was, I think I'll head back to New York now. I have a lot of work to do before I flatten Todd's building."

He's trying to get under my skin. I won't bite. "Sounds like it. And by the way, thanks for the investment tip."

He answers with a blank look.

"You know, about all the new housing and that train station extension. Ned's building will be worth a ton if he sits on it for another few years instead of selling now. Think of how much *more* someone will have to pay if they want it."

"He'll also lose money month over month once Lowes comes in."

"Like you said, he owns the building, so his carrying costs are low. Even if he shuts down Murphy's, I'll bet he could lease it and make great money in rent. Especially with that shiny new condo building next door. How long will that take to build? Thirteen months? Fourteen?" I think back to contract lengths for the trades-people I placed working on small condominium projects. "I mean, that's assuming there aren't any delays, which I'm guessing there will be. Major ones."

The muscle in Garrett's jaw twitches. "You really are a pain in my ass."

"I'm only just getting started." I slide out of the booth and stroll back to my people.

――――――

It's after two a.m. when Scarlet saunters into the kitchen, her flannel pajama pants swirling around her ankles, her hair in disarray from rolling around in bed with Shane for the past hour. "Do I want to know what you're up to?"

"Probably not." I inhale a gulp of water to help quash the impending hangover, and then refocus on my laptop screen.

"You've been in a mood since running into that guy."

"Have I?" That guy being Garrett John Harrington *the Third*, according to the Google search I conducted the second I settled back into my booth. *Of course* he's a third. Because he's not obnoxious enough just being Garrett. The first and second of his name were high-profile lawyers, the first earning the rank of attorney general for the state of New York. Clearly, the third went in another direction than his namesake after graduating from Harvard, following in his real estate developer uncle's footsteps instead.

Garrett never mentioned his stint at college when he brought up my hometown of Boston. He had a good run there from the looks of it, too, as captain of their rugby team. Based on what I found, he'll be thirty-five in May. A Taurus. Too bad for him, I'm a Leo. We were doomed from the start.

Scarlet leans over my shoulder. "Polson Falls Citizen Bulletin? When did you join that?"

"Thirty-eight minutes ago." The admin for the town's Facebook group accepted my request immediately, and since then I've been scouring the page to familiarize myself with the town and the types of things the ten thousand members are posting. "How are you *not* on this? It's a gold mine of information."

"Really? I heard it's mostly people complaining and weird stuff."

"Oh yeah, there's definitely that." Today alone, a man is asking for opinions about a bite on his arm—festering pictures included —and another man dressed as Pennywise is offering his services for children's parties. A woman went on a rant about the plow that cleared the snow in front of her house leaving too big a drift for her sedan to manage and how it's the mayor's fault.

Most people who complain find a way to name and blame the mayor, and if not him, then unruly teenagers.

But there are also plenty of helpful posts—recommendations for small-business owners, "free to good home" offers, questions about upcoming events, and volunteer opportunities.

What I came here for were the people concerned about how much Polson Falls is changing for the worse—subdivisions running from one end of town to the other, farmland being sold off and rezoned, old homes being torn down and replaced with mini mansions that eat up the lot and ruin the aesthetic of the quiet street, excessive traffic, and constant power outages because the town is running on outdated infrastructure.

I found them.

They're noisy, and at the root of their fury is the lack of support from the council to protect Polson Falls' identity.

These are Shirley's and Ned's people. These are the ones we need on our side.

"I'm going to bed," Scarlet says through a yawn.

"Give Shane a good-night blowie for me. Oh hey, do you know where the library is?"

"Yeah … Why?" Caution lingers in her voice.

"Research. Can we go on Sunday?"

"Sure." She pauses. "Just … don't bring my name up in *whatever* it is you're up to. I have a career to protect."

"You'll stay squeaky clean, promise." I crisscross my chest with my index finger, but she's already on her way up to her room, the stairs creaking beneath her feet.

If anyone's about to get dirty, it's Garrett John Harrington *III*.

I crack my knuckles.

Chapter Seven

Shirley tracks me as I march through Bonny Acres' common room toward her customary table on Monday afternoon, notebook in hand.

"Well? What'd you find? Anything worthwhile?"

"Three-story building. Condominiums on top of storefronts."

Shirley scowls as I download what I learned on Friday night while antagonizing Garrett from across the booth. I don't mention how firmly entrenched in my mind the man has become despite my anger, how the thought of my next run-in with him has my pulse racing with excitement about the verbal sparring session.

"So it's official. Tearing down history for condominiums on Main Street. And no need for rezoning." She shakes her head with disgust. "Did you do that research like I asked?"

"I did." I pull out my list of notes. Four hours at the library yesterday with a lesson in microfilm from Alice Grant proved fruitful. This building's past has more colors than Joseph's Technicolor dream coat. "Have you ever heard of the Stavro brothers?" They were the original owners, pooling their money to buy the empty lot on the tail end of Main Street. They'd come from the city to live a quiet country life—or so they claimed—living in the apartments upstairs and running a popular diner for years.

"Yes!" She snaps her fingers, her eyes lighting up with recognition. "That was their name. Criminals, right? What was it they were into again?"

"Bootlegging." A robust Prohibition-era operation out of the dank, dark basement, distilling and shuttling their product from New York to Philadelphia, and everywhere in between. The police were paid off to look the other way, and so they thrived in Polson Falls for years, until one snow-coated Sunday morning, all four were found shot to death in the basement among empty crates and smashed gallon stills, caught in the middle of a poker game. The articles I found pointed toward a Mob hit, but the killers were never caught.

Dieter Senior had opened his shop six months prior to the murders, having no clue who he was renting space from—or so he said. When the building went up for sale, he purchased it for a steal, given its dark connection.

"I don't know if a Mob-style hit is grounds for preserving the building, but it's notable, right?"

"Damn straight. What else you got?"

"A few things. Did you know that Dieter's has served not only JFK, but a whole bunch of famous people?" I list off dozens of names—governors, senators, house members, along with three Hall of Famers who visited regularly.

She scratches her chin in thought. "That might work."

"Other than that, I pulled together a list of businesses that have been in there." Over the years, the other storefronts were home to a wide range of businesses supporting Polson Falls—a cobbler, a tack shop, an accountant, an art gallery, a coffee shop, and a small law office for a young attorney who years later became famous for a high-profile murder case.

"Can I have that?" Shirley points to my notes. "I want to pass it all along to Colin. He's the editor-in-chief at the *Tribune*. He promised he'd put out a story for us, and this'll speed things up."

"Sure." I tear out the pages and hand them to her. "What about that heritage commissioner?"

"Michelle?" Shirley's lips twist with displeasure. "She said she'd look into it, but she's not sure how many people will care."

"Oh, you mean, *these* people?" I pull up the Facebook group on my phone. "Haven't you seen this yet?" I spent an hour crafting my concerned citizen message last Friday night, including as much history about the businesses in this building as I could dig up from the internet, lacing it with nostalgia and peppering in some *support local* rah-rah before I hit Post and crawled into bed.

I woke to a hundred new notifications and anger. From there I just sat back and watched it grow legs of its own all weekend. Some people dared to suggest a new building might be nice, and the proud Polsonites squashed their opinions with snarky "Go back to the city where you belong, then!" reactions. The demands I was hoping for, though? That the building be preserved, that HG restore the current structure rather than tear it down?

There were dozens of those.

Shirley adjusts her glasses, squinting to try to read my screen. "Where is this from?"

"The Polson Falls Citizen Bulletin group on Facebook."

Her face screws up as she waves it off. "No time for that."

"You should make time. These are your people." I start reading through the comments out loud. "'If Mayor Gump spent more time listening to his constituents and less time rubbing elbows and who knows what else with these developers, destruction like this wouldn't be happening.'"

Shirley snorts.

"'I knew Gump back when he was failing ninth grade math. Which of you morons elected him to run our town?' Ouch. Surprised that one didn't get taken down."

"It's the truth!"

"Either way, your editor friend needs to see this. Same with Michelle." If they're not already in the group, lurking like the majority of the ten thousand members do. "There are hundreds of people who don't want this condo going in and others who don't care about the condo but don't want the building torn down."

"Just you wait. I used to babysit Colin, and I got him that job at the paper. He writes whatever I tell him to. *I*'ll write the damn article if I have to." She thumps the table surface with her fist. "By the time we're through, *everyone* is going to know what HG and Gump tried to get away with."

"You ever watch those nature channel shows?" Harper is suddenly hovering over our shoulders. "Where the killer whales work as a team to knock the seals off the ice shelves so they can get at them? That's what this feels like"—she waggles her finger back and forth—"the two of you with your heads together." She tucks her file folder under her arm. "What are you doing here, Justine? It's not Friday."

"Just visiting. No big deal." I smile sweetly.

"No big deal, huh?" She studies us. "I'd say you're plotting world domination."

Shirley folds the page of notes and tucks them in her cardigan pocket. "Not the world. Just Polson Falls."

"Did I tell you that I *really* like that new color on you?" I nod toward the earthy lipstick shade, a stunning complement to Harper's golden-brown skin. "Who are you dressing those luscious lips for?" Rumor has it Harper takes extra coffee breaks when Philip from the maintenance company is here to fix leaky pipes and clogged toilets.

Her nostrils flare. "*My*self."

"*Good* answer. We dress for ourselves, not for men."

"Don't you be trying to butter me up. I wasn't born yesterday."

"I wasn't trying to butter you up, I swear!" I hesitate. "But if I started coming in more than once a week, do you think I could get a crack at calling the—"

"No."

"It was worth a shot," I grumble.

"And *you*. I heard what you've been up to." Harper's attention shifts to her resident, and there's a tone of reprimand hanging in that statement.

Shirley opens her mouth but stalls when Harper's finger comes up.

"I got the scoop from Gladys. Between you fussing about the chicken and this mess with Saul, you were busy over lunch with your pot and your stir stick, weren't you?"

"You can't blame me about the food. You take away our salt, sugar, red meat, caffeine … May as well give us shovels and let us start digging our own holes out back."

"If I fed residents based on what you wanted, they'd all be dead from heart attacks and diabetic comas. And don't think I don't know about all those sweets Justine's been sneaking in here for you." Harper saunters off, leaving my card partner's lips twisted in a smile.

"What kind of trouble did you stir up now?" I ask.

"Nothing, I just shared the truth. I heard Saul sneaking out of Gertie's room last night. *Late.*" She flashes me a knowing look.

My mouth drops with a gasp. "Doesn't Saul have a thing with Shelly Ann?" They take their daily walks together, holding hands the entire way. It's heartwarming to see, given the two of them moved to Bonny Acres after losing their spouses.

"They did, *and* Gertie and Shelly Ann are supposed to be friends." For a woman who hates everyone, Shirley still makes it her business to know all.

"What did Shelly Ann say?"

"She's out of the picture. Moved to the manor last week."

"Oh." My shoulders slump. "*Oh.*" Bonny Acres is perfect for those who need a little help—with medications, putting on shoes, washing—but are mostly independent. Once there are any signs of real decline that raise safety concerns, such as confusion or falling, the residents are required to move to Hampton Manor, a posh name for a nursing home that Shirley claims she'd rather die than step foot in. "So, what happened at lunch?"

"Liz and Charmaine had it out with Gertie for stabbing their friend in the back." She nods toward one corner where Gertie sits alone, her chin held high, pretending to ignore the two white-haired ladies glaring at her from a few tables over. "But turns out Saul *also* asked Susan out to a movie the other day."

"I can't keep up. Susan who?"

"A woman from the third floor. She's new. Always bragging about her knees and hips being her own. *Nobody* likes Susan." Shirley waves a dismissive hand. "When she heard about Gertie and Saul's little romp, she confronted Saul. That's how Gertie heard about the date and got mad. She and Saul have been visiting each other's rooms *for months*."

My jaw drops. "They were going behind Shelly Ann's back all this time?" I know all too well how a discovery like that feels. "I hope she's handling it."

"Saul says it was never exclusive. Anyway, I'm surprised he had the nerve to show his face after that." She nods to where Saul sits pretending to be engrossed in the newspaper while he steals furtive glances around. "It's never this busy on a Monday night, but everyone came down hoping for round two. Most excitement we've seen here since Frank Stucato took a bunch of Viagra and passed out in the common room with a teepee in his pants."

I snort-laugh. "Hey, you may not have sugar or salt or caffeine, but at least they haven't taken dick away yet."

"I'd rather have cake." Shirley's head tips back with a boister-ous, smoky cackle that turns nearly every head in the common room. "Now, why don't you show me how to use that Facebook thing."

Chapter Eight

I NOTE the strange yellow smear on the front window of Dieter's Meat Shop as I push through the door. I haven't stepped inside in two weeks, instead slowing in front of the shop every day at lunch hour, long enough to make eye contact with a wary Todd through the window before turning my nose up and storming past.

But today I'm caving, mainly because the fridge at home was empty, but also because my curiosity trumps my resolve.

Inside smells of the usual delicious medley—garlic, meat, and a warm, spice-infused broth. Does that scent waft upstairs to the apartments above? Which apartment has Garrett claimed as his dirty crash pad when he's too tired to drive home? I've only seen a sleek black SUV parked out back once since this fiasco began, but I haven't had the displeasure of running into him. I think he's avoiding me, a thought that makes me smile.

Todd looks up from the counter, the sparse blond hair on top of his head standing on end as if statically charged. When he sees me, his face falls.

"Well, that's not a friendly greeting." Today's Tommy Bahama shirt is in a burnt orange. Normally I'd make a teasing comment.

"Are you here for soup or to give me more grief?"

I check the chalkboard: chicken noodle. "How about a little of both?"

He reaches for a Styrofoam bowl without another word. Unusual for Todd, who thrives on chattiness.

"Have you ever thought of using something more environmentally friendly?"

"I'd have to increase costs."

"I'm sure your customers wouldn't mind paying an extra quarter if it saves the planet."

"Cut the act, Justine." He swirls the ladle around to collect a decent amount of meat. He knows I'll complain otherwise. "I saw what you posted in that Polson Falls Facebook group."

"All *I* did was share information about upcoming changes to Main Street with my fellow residents. I felt they had a right to know before a bulldozer shows up." I wondered if Todd was a member. "Why? Have people said something to you about selling this place to a developer?" I ask innocently.

He huffs. "My regular customers are accusing me of betraying my late father and grandfather's memories."

"Ouch."

"Donald Ackers told me he'd rather eat regurgitated dog feces than give me another penny of his money."

Eww. My face pinches. "Points for creativity?"

"I never asked my dad to give me all this." He waves his free hand around. "You know, I didn't even want to be a butcher! Sure, I did all the training because he wanted me to, but I went to college for advertising. Had a job lined up and everything!"

"*Really?*" I can't help the doubt in my voice, my attention darting to the eight-and-a-half-by-eleven sheet of paper tacked to the wall with Todd's own messy handwriting in Sharpie, listing this week's deli specials. Pastrami is spelled wrong. He never mentioned this career path in our daily chats.

"Figured he'd sell the shop when he was ready to retire and collect rent. Or sell the whole building and enjoy the money. I didn't care! But next thing I know, I'm spending my days carving carcasses, chasing Bethany the cupcake lady for rent money, and refereeing fights between Yvonne and the renter above her over that bloody music."

"Dawn's music can be a bit much."

"And now people are telling me I can't sell what's mine to sell? What am I supposed to do? Just give it away? Let it crumble? My dad wouldn't like that either!" Bewilderment fills his face.

This frazzled version of Todd is new to me. A twinge of guilt stirs in my belly, but then I remember that the public's reaction would be the same whether they found out now or later. "If you had gone about the sale differently, instead of trying to hide it, people wouldn't be so mad. You completely blindsided your tenants."

I visited the other stores on the block to glean whatever information I could. Bob from the CornerMart ranted for twenty minutes, waving the letter that stated the building was under new ownership and his lease would not be renewed once it expires on March 31. He's run his convenience store from that location for thirty-four years. Yvonne, a small woman with wiry gray hair and horn-rimmed glasses who owns the sewing shop, was planning on closing at the end of this month and had given her notice, but she was still distraught at the idea of demolition. Bethany from the cupcakery wasn't the least bit put out, but Todd never made her sign a lease. It didn't take too much prodding to learn Garrett had dangled a check to compensate her for her move.

"As if that would have made a difference. And how was I gonna tell Ned, huh?" Todd throws a hand toward Murphy's. "He was so happy when I told him I'd keep the shop going. I knew this would crush him. You don't think I feel bad?" He picks up the *Tribune*. "And now *this*. I can only imagine how many more customers I'll lose."

I don't have to ask what he's talking about. The paper landed on Murphy's doorstep an hour ago. Ned and I hovered over it, devouring the front-page spread about the sale of the building and the "rumored" plans, with the headline, "Polson Falls Likely

Landmark Set To Be Demolished After Hush-Hush Deal." Aside from the rundown of historical significance (using my library research), the Polson Falls Historical Committee is quoted often, naming and blaming Todd for trading his family legacy for dollar signs, local government for not protecting Main Street from greed, and Harrington Group for having the audacity to name a project Revive when what they're doing is killing the town's quaint character with a three-story blemish.

In a nutshell, the article is scathing, and the historical committee has confirmed they are working with the commissioner to have the building designated. They end it with a plea to the town's citizens to call their councillors and the mayor's office—the numbers are listed.

"I can't believe you sicced the granny gang on me, Justine!"

"*Wait,* who?"

"Oh, come on. You know who I'm talking about."

"The historical committee?"

"Shirley *is* the historical committee. She runs the damn thing. And half her minions live at Bonny Acres."

"She has minions?" She doesn't like anyone there.

"They're at *every* public meeting, causing problems and stirring up trouble. I know you know them, so don't lie. You volunteer there."

"A *granny gang*?" I snort. "Look, I may have told Shirley about you selling the business, but I didn't sic any *gang* on you."

"Do you have any idea the trouble they cause? That plaza out near the county road, with the bakery that makes the delicious egg bread you keep bugging me to bring in here?"

"Confetti's?"

"That one. The granny gang stalled that project for an entire year with a bunch of appeals about a ravine and beavers, and I can't remember what all they threw at the council."

"You're lying." That's the bakery Shirley insists I bring her treats from.

"I'm not. Look it up. The last time they got a bee in their

bonnets, they stirred up so much noise for Wilson, they cost him reelection."

"The guy who let someone demolish the town's first bank? Sounds like he did that all by himself."

"By the time the granny gang was through with him, people were convinced he was taking kickbacks, even though there was no proof."

"Wow. I had no idea she had that much influence." I *really* did pick the right person to play cards with.

"You don't have to look so happy, huh?" He scowls. "It's like Shirley's got some kind of grudge."

"If she holds a grudge about anything, it's the incompetent men like Gump who keep getting voted in. And why do you care about any of this? You got your cash out. You don't own the building anymore."

"That's not the point. I'm supposed to be moving to the other side of town."

"You're upset with *me* because people are upset with what *you* did."

"Upset with me?" He throws a hand at the window. "Someone egged me last night and now it's frozen to the glass. Do you know how hard it is to get frozen egg off glass?"

"I don't, but I imagine it sucks."

"I ran into Phyllis Kent at Weis the other day. She's a longtime customer who's been coming here since my grandfather was still running things, and she let me have it."

I whistle. "She must be getting up there."

"She's ninety-four and needs a walker to get around, but she *still* comes in here every Tuesday afternoon to order pork schnitzel." He shakes his head. "When she saw me at the grocery store, she flipped me the bird!"

A bark of laughter at the mental image escapes before I can help myself.

"Oh, that's hilarious, is it?" Anger and frustration twist Todd's features. "You know what? You'll have to go somewhere else from now on. I don't want your business anymore."

My mouth hangs open as I watch him dump the soup back into the Crock-Pot and toss the bowl into the trash. Is he serious? "What is this, an episode of *Seinfeld*?"

"No, this is my life, and there's nothing funny about what you're doing to it."

"*I* didn't do this to you. *You* did this to yourself!"

"Don't let the door hit you on the way out." He storms into the back, leaving me in shock in the quiet store.

Is that it?

Is our friendship over?

My stomach growls, as if voicing its displeasure for this unpleasant turn of events. I've been looking forward to this meal *all morning*.

I tend to do impulsive—dumb—things when I'm hungry.

And angry. I'm definitely that, even though shame lingers closely behind. Todd has always been good to me.

Stealing a quick look to where Todd disappeared, I round the counter, grab a fresh container, and ladle myself a bowl. Sealing it shut with a lid, I slap down a ten-dollar bill next to the cash register. It's far too much, but I stop myself from going into the register for change. I do have *some* boundaries. I swipe a bag of pretzel buns to cover the balance instead and rush out the door.

Chapter Nine

A BRISK WIND cuts through my coat as I dart outside to toss trash in the dumpster, the last task before I lock up Murphy's for the night. Ned's gone home, and Dean is supposed to be here any second to pick up our new dishwasher.

"You make a lot of noise for someone so small."

My head whips around at the sound of Garrett's voice, and my heart skips a traitorous beat. It's been weeks since our Route 66 run-in.

He's perched in the driver's seat of his SUV. One leg hangs out as if he paused halfway between either climbing in or climbing out, his dress pants hiked up to reveal a striped sock. The town paper is folded in his gloved grasp.

"Your building's been getting a lot of press." I can guess what page he's on—the latest article featuring Yvonne and her sewing shop. She's closing her doors to customers this Friday for the last time ever, and Colin made it sound like she was not doing it by choice.

Sure, she was retiring, anyway, but the focus was about her views on a developer coming in to tear down the place where she's watched Polson Falls' children grow for over three decades, selling yarn to grandmothers knitting blankets, vibrant cottons to be crafted into costumes, and silks worn down aisles at weddings. Colin also managed to blame the craft chain store across town—and, by extension, HG, who built and owns the building—for her need to close her doors five years sooner than she'd once expected.

The emotional piece was capped off with two pictures—one of the first day Yvonne opened, and another of her last week, a sweet little grandmotherly lady with a sad look in her gray eyes, even when she's smiling.

"Hey, I had *nothing* to do with that." But I'll give it to Shirley for knowing how to pull puppet strings. Colin seems to chase a story in any direction she points him in.

"Why don't I believe you? Oh right, because these articles reference a bunch of information that no one outside the project group knew about—except you." Despite the accusation, there's no hint of anger in Garrett's voice.

"I guess you shouldn't have blabbed, then." Curious where this verbal sparring match might lead, I saunter over, huddling against the cold. Todd's truck is gone, so I don't have to worry about an awkward run-in with him. "I may have opened the gate, but I have no control over which wily beast pops out." And this wily beast despises condominiums.

Garrett shrugs. "Whatever. It's a fluff piece, nothing more."

"Really? Because it seems to me like more than a few people aren't on board with the way you want to *revive* Main Street." According to Shirley's contacts, the mayor's office has been flooded with calls.

"A small group who will move on soon enough. No big deal. I've seen it all before."

"In your extensive years of property development?"

He smirks. "In the end, it won't make a difference. This week, it's *this*." He holds up the paper before tossing it onto his dash. "Next week, the paper'll be singing the project's praises."

Not if Shirley has anything to do with it. "The heritage commissioner will demand a stay on any demolition until the building's significance can be determined." Shirley's confirmed that Michelle sees the merit and conversations are in the works.

"You think an illegal business and a quadruple homicide is grounds for landmark designation?"

"Prohibition era is quite the buzzword. Can you imagine a speakeasy in that basement?"

He snorts. "Have you seen that basement? Besides, the town can't support a business like that. Not yet." Garrett slides out of his seat, a faint waft of that smoky citrus cologne swirling in my nostrils.

"You have to admit, the JFK sandwich is pretty important."

"Right, of course. There's your clincher. Speaking of sandwiches." He leans in to grab a paper bag.

"Nice car." I can't help but admire the tan leather interior and the fully loaded *everything*.

"A perk with the job." He smirks. "Even as a baby developer."

"You get a fancy ride, but not a hotel room?"

"I don't see any hotels around here, do you?"

"There's one out on the interstate. Only thirty minutes away."

"The one with cameras in the smoke alarms?"

"Oh, a Garrett peepshow. *Fun.* But I thought you weren't picky." My smile is wide and fake. "I guess you'll just have to build a hotel, then."

"Maybe I will." He towers over me, standing too close, his dinner nudging my thigh. It's distracting. "You going to try to stop that too?"

"Depends. Did you find more elderly people to hustle out of their land?"

He snorts but doesn't have an answer.

Headlights shine across the back of Murphy's as Dean maneuvers his truck to back into the loading dock. "As thrilling as this time spent with you has been, I have better things to do. Enjoy your stay. Hope you like death metal." I saunter back to Murphy's as Dean throws his truck into park.

He slides out, pulling on work gloves. "Who's that?" He nods toward Garrett.

"The pretentious asshole who's trying to tear down the building." I say it loud enough to carry.

He frowns. "What's he doing here?"

I steal a look to see Garrett hauling a duffel bag out of his back seat. He slings the strap over his shoulder and heads for the stairs to the apartments. "Crashing. Can you believe that? Harvard grad rolls up in a luxury SUV to squat in an empty apartment."

Dean drops his tailgate. "All any guy needs is a mattress and a fridge."

"I know he has the fridge." *I hope it breaks down.* I watch Garrett balance his meal in one hand while struggling to unlock the door to the apartment above Todd's shop. Finally, he gets it and disappears inside. Dim lights fill the room through the window, illuminating old kitchen cupboards.

What on earth does this guy think he's doing? Just drive the two hours back to New York. Or rent a room in Philly. It's only an hour away, and there are plenty of hotels to house his pampered ass there.

"Let's get this show on the road. I've got places to be." Dean slaps the button to open Murphy's loading door. It crawls up its chains, groaning in protest.

"Yeah? Where do you got to be that's more important than being with *me*?" I tease.

"A date."

I inhale as he passes me. "No wonder you smell so good."

"Do I?" He hops onto the concrete pad.

I watch him drop the ramp down to his truck and check the straps around the dishwasher, testing their strength. "Haven't you dated all the women in this town?"

"Most. Not all … yet." He looks pointedly at me before maneuvering the appliance down with a dolly. "Heard you're going to Boston this weekend."

I sigh with exasperation. "Yeah. My brother's been bugging

me to meet his new girlfriend for weeks. I'm going just to shut him up."

Dean hops onto his truck bed. "Not worried about a run-in with the ex?"

"Nope. I told them I wasn't coming if he was going to be in town, and Joe promised it's just us." Mention of Bill causes a sharp prick in my chest, but I promptly cut off the pain and box it up. It's done. We're over. I'm moving on. "Scarlet's coming for moral support, on the off chance I get drunk and emotional."

"You? *Never.*" Dean uses his powerful thighs to shimmy the appliance into position.

"Careful with thrusting those hips of yours into Stuart the Second. Save that for your date."

"Why did you name your dishwasher?"

"Because he's a hardworking employee and deserves to be recognized. So is Kevin the refrigerator and Carl the oven. Jerry's about to retire."

"And Jerry is—"

"Microwave."

Dean mumbles under his breath. "About your trip to Boston, you know, I'm around for moral support too."

"Is that what the kids are calling it these days?" I quip.

"I mean it, Justine. As a friend." He pauses, draped over the box to peer at me, his eyes earnest.

It swells an unexpected knot in my throat. "Thanks. I appreciate that." But Dean and I don't have that kind of friendship. We have the lighthearted, superficial one that doesn't talk about feelings, and I need to keep it that way. "Do you wait until after dessert to make your big move? Or are you more of a between-dinner-and-dessert kind of guy? Or do you just call it 'dinner,' but you're going over to her house to fuck?"

"Shut up." His chuckle carries into the quiet night.

Chapter Ten

"Your daughter has picked a fight with the town's biggest developer." Scarlet grins into her red wine.

"Oh?" Mom sticks a thermometer in the beef tenderloin she pulled from the oven. In a dish next to it, the roasted potatoes sizzle. Somewhere else in the kitchen, a homemade Caesar salad with extra Parmesan and bacon waits to be tossed. It's her favorite meal to make, and she only makes it for the most special of occasions. "What do you mean by 'picked a fight'?"

"I'm standing up for those who feel they don't have a voice, while trying to save a historic landmark."

"Justine found out about the developer's plan to tear down a building on Main Street and replace it with condos. No one else in the community had heard about it yet, so she put them on blast. Now people are calling town council and there have been several front-page articles published in the newspaper, trying to stop it from happening. The heritage commissioner is involved."

"Oh dear. Does that seem wise?" Mom turns to me. "These people have a lot of money tied up in those kinds of things. I doubt they'd take too kindly to someone causing them problems."

I wave her worries away. "I'm not afraid of this Harvard grad."

"You should see him, Kitty." Scarlet gives my mom an arched brow while handing her the oven mitts, knowing Mom forgot where she set them down and was about to frantically search for them. Twelve years of family dinners at the MacDermott household has made my best friend as comfortable in this kitchen as anyone who grew up under this roof.

"*Oh.*" Mom titters as she slides the meat back in a little longer. "I'm not sure aggression is how you're going to win him over, dear."

I roll my eyes. "Trust me, I'm not trying to win him over." Not anymore. "He's a dick."

Mom opens her mouth, no doubt about to reprimand me for my language when suddenly, she freezes, listening intently as a door creaks open elsewhere in the house.

Joe's boom of "Is that beef I smell?" carries.

"They're here!" Mom hastily sheds her apron, uncovering a new red silk blouse, and fluffs up her hair with her fingers. It's even feathered today, like TV Kitty's, and she probably has no clue. Joe is going to lose his shit when he sees her.

"Come, Justine! And don't be so crass. No need to scare Sara away." Mom squeezes my wrist before rushing to the front of the house.

"I guess it's showtime." I stretch on my tiptoes to try to sneak a peek, curious about the woman who's hooked my brother's heart. The only other woman who's had him so enamored is Scarlet, and that was one-sided.

"Don't be an asshole," Scarlet warns.

"Funny, Joe said the same thing." Along with begging me not to embarrass him too much.

"Can't imagine why." Scarlet smiles through a sip of wine.

"A patient made it for me." Sara holds up her dainty wrist to show off the string of pink beads encircling it, her blue eyes twinkling. "She was one of our oncology patients who was released just last week. Clean bill of health."

"Gosh, I don't know how you do it, working with all those sick kids." Mom presses a hand over her heart.

"I'll admit, it's not easy. But so many of them walk away healthy and happy, and that makes the tough cases a little easier to handle."

It's not enough that old-money Sara, who doesn't have to work a day in her life, is a nurse. She's in pediatrics.

My mother was right. She's fucking delightful. Everything about her, from her honeyed voice to her wide smile to the way she locks gazes with you when you're speaking—as if you're the only person in the room—is soothing.

Personality aside, she's classically beautiful, with dimples and delicate features, framed by silky ash-blond hair that reaches halfway down her back. There's no heavy-handed makeup routine on this one. She gives off a simple but elegant girl-next-door vibe.

And looking at Joe now? At how he can't peel his gaze off her, can't stop grinning like an idiot, like he's got a secret?

I can't help but smile. I've never seen him this happy. "So, Sara, how did you get roped into a date with my schmuck brother?"

Joe tosses a pea at my forehead in answer.

Mom heaves a sigh and Dad shakes his head.

"All he had to do was ask." Sara winks at him. "My hospital was hosting our annual charity event, and Joe happened to be there."

"The agency bought a table. Ten grand a pop."

Dad whistles. "Hope you at least got a good meal for that."

"It's top notch. Sara quarterbacks the event, and she's got great taste." He reaches over to squeeze her hand.

She flashes a toothy grin. "Between the dinner tickets and the silent auction, we bring in much needed money to support the pediatrics wing. Anyway, Joe and I were introduced, and ... here we are."

"Hear that, Scarlet? An auction for children. Just like what Shane does." I waggle my brow.

Sara turns to Scarlet. "Is that your boyfriend? Does he run a charity event too?"

"Not exactly." Scarlet shoots me a warning look mid sip.

"He headlines it," I offer.

"Headlines?" Sara frowns.

Scarlet spears me with a side glare. "Shane's a firefighter, and they have this yearly auction for emergency workers in town. It's totally appalling and outdated, but it raises money for a children's charity around Christmastime."

"Don't forget to mention the calendar," I mock whisper.

Sara's eyes widen. "There's a firefighter calendar?"

"Oh yes, and Shane's the centerfold. Here, let me show you—"

Scarlet wrestles my phone out of my hand, her cheeks flushing. "Maybe later, huh?" More quietly, she adds, "Asshole."

"Sara, did you ever find a condo?" my dad asks, changing the subject. "The last time you were here, you were looking for something closer to the hospital."

"I *did*. Thanks for asking, George." She shifts her focus, seeming delighted that he remembered. "It's a rowhouse. I close on it next weekend, but I want to have a few things remodeled before we move in. Nothing major. One of the bathrooms is dark —all black tile." She scrunches her nose. "Floral wallpaper that your son isn't particularly fond of ..."

Joe catches my attention, distracting me from the conversation. He cocks his head in question.

"What?" I mouth.

"Well?" he mouths back, subtly nodding toward Sara.

I roll my eyes, but I know what he's asking. Joe and I have always been tight, and while he despised the idea of his best friend and little sister hooking up at the start, once he got over the awkwardness of the idea, our bond grew even stronger. I've met every single girl he's ever dated, and I've never faltered when sharing my opinion. He always complains I'm too harsh, and yet that never stops him from asking. Deep down, I know he cares what I think.

I can see it now, the way he bites his lip. I'll bet his leg is bouncing beneath the table.

"She's *way* too good for you."

His shoulders sink with relief. "I know." He lifts his wineglass and reaches across the table to toast me.

I can't stop myself from asking as I carve into my meat, "So, what's Bastard Bill up to tonight?"

Mom chokes on her wine, shooting me a glare.

"He's in Montego Bay."

"What is it with cheaters and liars going to Jamaica this year?" I mutter.

Sara and Joe share a quick look.

"I thought we had a no-Bill rule for tonight." Joe watches me. "And do you care what he's doing?"

I know *who* he's doing. "Just making conversation."

"Okay, well, since you need something to talk about, we have some news we want to share." Joe grins at Sara, collecting her hand in his and pressing it to his mouth. "I asked Sara to marry me."

Mom's cutlery hits her plate with a clang as Sara slips the tucked necklace from her sweater, revealing a diamond solitaire ring dangling from the end. "I said yes!" She squeals.

Shocked excitement erupts around the table, with exclamations of "A wedding!" and "Congratulations!" and "When did this happen?"

Meanwhile, my jaw is still hanging.

Joe? Getting *married*?

Before me?

He's never kept a girlfriend for more than a few months, and here we are at, what, the three-month mark? And he put a ring on her finger?

"Have you two talked at all about the big day?" Mom's hands are clasped and pressed against her cheek in adoration. "Any early plans you want to share?"

Sara and Joe share another look.

"We have made some, yeah." Joe nods slowly. "The wedding's going to be May 1."

"May 1," Mom echoes and then she gasps. "Wait a minute, as in *this* May? As in ..." She strums her fingers on the table, counting. *"Four months from now?"*

"More like three. January's almost over," my father corrects.

It dawns on me. Suddenly, this makes sense. "Oh my God, you knocked her up! I'm gonna be an aunt!"

"No." Joe whips another pea at my forehead.

Sara's cheeks flush. "Friends of our family own Cliffside. It's this hotel in Newport, Rhode Island, and, well, it's *amazing*. Old and historic and right on the water. We've had all our family events there growing up, my debutante ball ... anyway, there's a two-year waiting list to book an event, but they *just* had a cancellation, and so we thought, let's grab it before it's gone." She throws her hands up. "So we did!"

"That sounds ... *lovely*. Just lovely. Did you hear that, George? Our son is getting married *this year!"* Mom exclaims, but I catch the nervous twinge in her voice. She must be thinking the same thing I am: Who's picking up the tab for this hotel by the ocean in Filthy Richville? Knowing my parents, they've socked away some funds to help out with the reception, but they weren't expecting their child to marry into a dynasty.

"We know it's tight timing, but we're not worried." Joe settles his arm over Sara's shoulders. He can't stop touching her. "This one's a wiz when it comes to pulling events together."

Sara waves his compliments off with a giggle. "It's my mother who's the expert, but I've learned a lot from her. Between the two of us, it'll be no big deal."

Not when money's no issue.

"It's all about the ring, the venue, and the dress, right? We've got the first two nailed down, and Sara could wear burlap and look stunning." Joe chuckles.

"I guess this can come out of hiding now." Sara giggles as she slips her necklace off, sliding the delicate diamond ring on. The band is slender, the jewel unpretentious, its setting simple but elegant.

Like Sara.

"Your mother and I couldn't be more thrilled, son. Just thrilled." Dad slaps Joe on the shoulder. "Do Craig and Molly know yet?"

"Nah. I made Bill promise to keep his mouth shut until I told you guys."

"So he *is* capable of keeping a promise." Bill knew about Joe getting married before I did.

But no one pays any heed to my bitterness, too excited about the welcome news. No one except Scarlet, who gives my shoulder a gentle squeeze.

Dad turns to my mother. "What are they doing tonight?"

"I didn't ask. This was going to be an intimate dinner."

"We should invite them over for dessert so we can share the wonderful news!"

"Oh, that's a good idea. Say, in an hour?" Mom dabs at her mouth with her napkin and then slips out of her chair. "Excuse me for a moment. I need to send off a quick text to Molly to see what they're up to."

If I had a quarter for every time I've heard my mother utter those words …

Dad pats his chest as if searching for something within his pocketless shirt. "I wonder if I have any more of those Cohibas."

Joe grins, leaning forward to slide three cigars from his back pocket. "I got us covered."

Pain sparks in the back of my throat as I watch everyone around me bustle with exhilaration over my brother's upcoming nuptials. I'm overjoyed for him, too, really, but … after all the time

I put into Bill—the *years*—this was supposed to be me and knowing that leaves me feeling empty.

"Hey, Justine?"

I peel my attention away from my brother to meet my future sister-in-law's anxious gaze.

"I know we just met like an hour ago, so this might seem crazy fast—"

"Crazy. *Yeah.*" I grunt as Scarlet's sharp toe catches the side of my ankle. "But congratulations. It's amazing."

Her shoulders sag as her head bobs. "Thanks. I'm so excited. I've kissed a lot of frogs in my years. I never thought I'd meet a guy like him." Her eyes flitter to my brother, shining with adoration.

"Yeah, he's pretty special." I'm sure I used to look at Bill like that. But Joe's nothing like Bill. His biggest fault is his loyalty to his best friend.

"So are you, from everything he's told me. I mean, you're larger than life. He talks about you *all the time*. Everything is Justine this, Justine that. I was so nervous to meet you tonight." She giggles as she tucks a strand of loose hair behind her ear. "And I know this is rushed, but the wedding is kind of around the corner. My parents are throwing us an engagement party in a couple weeks! And I wanted to ask you in person, I don't know when I'll see you again ..." She's rambling. "Joe and I talked, and we would really"—she folds her hands together as if in prayer —"*really* love it if you would be one of my bridesmaids."

"Uh ..." The surprises keep on coming. I mean, I shouldn't be surprised that Joe would want me in the party—I'd threaten bodily harm if he didn't. I just figured I'd know the woman he's marrying for more than a minute before I was asked.

An insidious thought strikes me, and my body chills. "Who's his best man?" I already know the answer.

Sara winces. Clearly, Joe has filled her in on the adventures of Justine and Bastard Bill.

Another swift kick against my foot has me jumping and shooting a glare at Scarlet.

Only she's firing one back at me, and I can practically hear her scolding voice in my head. *This is your brother's wedding, dummy. Of course, you're not going to let Bastard Bill stop you from being in it.*

I force as wide a smile as I can muster, thankful that Sara still can't read me yet to know I'm faking every second of my joy. "I'd be honored."

Chapter Eleven

It's after five p.m. on Sunday when Scarlet and I push through the door and drop our bags on the hardwood floor, the five-and-a-half-hour drive seeming like it took twice that.

"*So* good to be home," I moan.

"Uh-huh."

"Still *so* hungover."

"Uh-huh." Scarlet falls back against the wall with a thud. "I'm too old for this shit."

Dessert with Molly and Craig turned into celebratory cannoli and shots of Drambuie, which turned into a game of Twister, followed by drunken karaoke. Neither Scarlet nor I remember getting to bed, but we woke up in our clothes, cringing from pounding heads and smacking our parched tongues.

A sharp curse sounds from the kitchen.

We share a frown. "Shane?" Scarlet calls out.

"Yeah." Frustration bleeds from his voice.

We drag ourselves to the kitchen, to where Shane attempts to install the new dishwasher, his face flushed despite the chilled air. An announcer drones over the radio, calling a football game.

"What's going on?"

"Nothing. It's just a weird design, and I think it's missing an attachment." He tosses a tool into his bag. "Hank's going to come over and take a look, see if he can figure it out."

"Is he a legit plumber? 'Cause I need a good plumber for Murphy's list." I flop into the chair, though I long for my bed.

"You're still working on that?" Scarlet molds herself into Shane and he responds instantly, wrapping his arm around her slender body, pulling her tight against him. "Missed you," she purrs, burying her face in his neck.

He kisses her forehead. "How was your weekend?"

"Good. Joe's getting married this May, and Justine's in the wedding party."

"May? Like *this* May?" Shane's eyebrows pop. "Four months away?"

"Three. It's February tomorrow. Which reminds me." I flip the page on the ugly feet calendar I got Scarlet for Christmas. "Look at those bad boys."

She grimaces. "The toes look like thumbs."

"Didn't your brother just meet this one?" Shane asks, still hung up on my family news.

"Yeah. In November."

He lets out a whistle. "Odds that they'll make it down the aisle?"

"Oh, they'll make it." I snort, picking at the bowl of chocolate-covered raisins, though I'd kill for a greasy burger to soak up the last of the alcohol fermenting in my belly. "My mother called it. She's perfect for him. She's perfect, period." Sara kept up shot for shot with us and had no qualms about busting out an atrocious rendition of Stevie Nicks' "Edge of Seventeen" before offering backup vocals for me singing Heart's "Alone." The clincher for me was when she sabotaged Joe by sticking her tongue in his ear during our game of Twister, giving Scarlet and I the win.

She's a keeper.

But the best thing about last night was that I was able to ignore the six-foot-three-sized hole in our celebration. It won't be so easy to forget Bastard Bill exists come the day of the wedding when he's standing across from me, but I have three months to prepare myself.

If that's possible. God, how am I going to enjoy that day?

"Joe picked a good one. Justine lucked out with her future sister-in-law." Scarlet nudges a wayward hose with her toe.

"I'm sorry, babe. I wanted to have it done and cleaned up before you got home."

"That's sweet of you to try." She treats him to a full-mouth kiss as if I'm not sitting right here.

He responds with a deep groan that I feel in my belly. I know where this is heading—me, sitting here alone while they take off next door so they can have loud sex.

"What's Dean doing?"

Shane peels himself away from Scarlet's mouth. "Watching the game somewhere. Why?"

"Because I think I need to get laid." Maybe that'll help with this odd, weighty feeling I can't seem to shake.

Shane grins. "Give him a call."

"Would that be wrong? To use him like that?"

"It's Dean. You know how he rolls."

"True." No risk of catching feelings from that one.

"He slept with my mother," Scarlet reminds me.

"Also true. Dottie and I can compare notes after." I slide my phone out of my pocket. "How do I word it? 'Hey, Dean, wanna fuck?'"

"I like it. Straight to the point. Hold up." Shane makes a show of checking his watch. "Let me time how long it takes for him to dial your number once you hit Send."

I'm tapping out the message when my phone rings, startling me. "How did he know? I haven't—oh, it's just Joe." As rough as Scarlet and I felt this morning, there were no signs of life from Joe's room when we left. I know why he's calling. He wants to hear what I *really* think of Sara, now that I'm not drunk and telling him how much I love her through hiccups. "I guess my booty call will have to wait." I answer with my usual, "Yo, bro."

"You made it back to Hickville." Joe's voice is croaky.

"Yup. Gonna hook up an IV now." After I proposition Dean.

"Same." He groans like he's in pain. "Listen, you got a minute?"

"Not really. I was about to call a potential fuck friend over."

He mutters something under his breath and then, "How did you turn out like this?"

"What do you want? I told you. Sara's way too good for you, but I'll make sure she shows up at the church or hotel or wherever you two are getting hitched. I'll tie her up if I have to. Also, I don't know who Sara's maid of honor is, but I'm bringing so many oiled-up strippers to the bachelorette, fair warning."

"That's what I wanted to talk to you about."

"Sara's bachelorette?" I frown. "Oh, she's having one whether she likes it or not."

"She doesn't know if she wants to yet, but if she does, it'll be small and classy—"

"You are *not* banning me from going, Joe. What happened at Darlene's was *not* my fault." Though our cousin still blames me for it years later. "Even the cops said—"

"Relax, that's not what this is about." He sighs heavily. "I told Sara not to mention anything last night because I wanted you two to get to know each other before you flipped out. *Don't* get mad at her, okay?"

The little hairs on the back of my neck rise. "Mention what?"

"It's about Sara's maid of honor."

Chapter Twelve

"How am I supposed to be in a wedding party with *not only* Bastard Bill *but also* the woman he cheated on me with? Like, it wasn't bad enough that my ex-boyfriend is the best man?" I pace in front of the washing machines.

Sara and Isabelle are best friends.

Isabelle is the one who introduced them at the charity event, which I now know is the real reason Joe and Bill reconciled so quickly.

Isabelle is Sara's maid of honor.

Ned scratches his chin as he watches me stomp around his store. "Seems to me they should have told you about this situation *before* asking you to be in the wedding party."

"That's what I said!" I throw my hands in the air toward Ned. "See? You get it. Scarlet gets it. Even Dean gets it!" He showed up with Hank to help Shane install Stuart the Second and was treated to an hour of my ranting.

But, if I'm being honest, not telling me was probably the smartest move. I wouldn't have given Sara a fair shot otherwise, and it would have ruined the night.

"And what did Joe say to that?"

"That I didn't have to be in the wedding party if I didn't want to, but it would make him really sad if I wasn't." My shoulders sink. "What am I supposed to do? Sit behind my parents and suck on sour grapes?" Cast an ominous cloud over the whole event?

"They should be choosing you over their friends. You're family."

"I wish it were that easy." According to Joe, Isabelle and Sara have been best friends since they were five. They're the female version of my brother and Bill. Forcing them to make that choice doesn't feel right, as much as I would love to wield that power.

And Bill's never going to bow out on my behalf. That would require integrity and empathy. The fact that he cheated on me in the first place—and the way he did it—proves he has neither. "Besides, they're keeping the party small, only three on each side, and the bastard and the thief are the only friends. The rest is family." Skewed toward Sara's side. The only people Joe cares to have standing alongside them are his best friend and his little sister.

I could hear the struggle in his voice when he was laying it all out on the table: how Bill may be Joe's best friend, but he's always been terrible at relationships; reminding me—again—how Joe never approved of us hooking up in the first place; and how he warned me not to get back together with Bill after he split with Debra, but I didn't listen.

How, as much as I might not want to hear it, Bill and Isabelle fit. Like, marriage and babies fit.

I've never wanted babies. Never felt the urge. Bill always said that was fine, that he had Rae, so he was satisfied. And now he's talking about marriage and babies with another woman?

No, I did not want to hear that.

"These types of situations aren't my specialty." Ned adjusts his reading glasses to refocus on his puzzle. "Whenever someone upset Trudy, she'd put on a nice dress, hold her chin up and smile, and pretend they didn't exist. Said she always felt better." He chuckles. "She wore a lot of nice dresses over the years around me. Boy, that woman sure had a temper."

Hearing Ned speak about his late wife always stirs conflicting emotions of warmth and sadness. They were married for over fifty years. What's it like for him to go home to an empty house every night? I think it's why he spends so much time here.

"So you're saying I should bring the hottest date I can find to the wedding, and I damn well need to look better than the maid of honor."

"Yeah, something like that," Ned says absently, frowning at the front window.

I follow his gaze. Sun shines down over the pickup parked on the street. "Who's that?" A work truck, based on the scaffolding and tools filling its bed and the two men in soiled clothes and construction boots stomping along the sidewalk, their arms laden with rollers and paint cans.

"I don't know, but they should be parking in the back if they're doing work in the building. They're blocking spots for customers."

"Why would they work on anything in there? They're bull-dozing it."

"Who knows? Can't take down the building until Todd's moved to his new location, and that's not until April. That was part of the deal."

What deal? "Did Todd tell you that?"

"Yeah. He swung by on Saturday to chat for a bit. Brought me a steak."

"While I was in Boston." *Coward*.

"Anyway, who knows what that developer's got planned for that space. Yvonne cleaned the last of her things out yesterday."

I wander closer to the window to get a better look. Garrett is there, talking to his uncle, a stack of paper tucked under his arm, a coffee gripped in his hand.

Despite my loathing for the man, a spark stirs at the sight of him—the broad collar of his wool coat lined up against his jawline, his hair swept off his forehead in a wave. A dimple creeps into his smile. "Why must the prettiest ones be the biggest assholes?"

"Sorry, didn't catch that?" Ned reaches up to adjust his hearing aid.

"Nothing. I'm going to see what's what." The door dings with my exit.

Melting snow and ice drips in a steady stream from the eaves, thanks to an early February thaw. I step around the puddles in the pavement as I stroll next door.

"… meeting with them at one to go over the drawings—" Garrett cuts off abruptly when his brown eyes land on me. "Hello, Justine." The simple greeting drips with caution.

I force a wide smile—the kind I imagine Ned's Trudy would plaster on when facing her enemies. Except I'm not in a fancy dress, and I can't pretend Garrett doesn't exist. I'm very, *very* aware of him. "*So* good to see you again, neighbor." I shift my focus to Richard Harrington. "Uncle Richard, glad to see you still looking fit and mobile."

His responding laugh is soft and melodic and seems genuine. "You should be wearing a coat, young lady. It's not spring yet."

"Ah." I wave off his protests, casting a wink. "I'm cold-blooded, as I'm sure your nephew has told you."

"No, but he has mentioned how you're keeping him on his toes." If Richard is at all concerned about the public uproar over tearing down the building and his company's name being dragged, he doesn't reveal it. But I guess you don't become as successful as he has by getting ruffled over controversy.

"I can't take all the credit for that."

Garrett snorts.

I ignore it. I have a specific purpose for this confrontation. "What's going on here?" Now that I'm in front of the building, I see the workers draping sheets and setting up ladders in Yvonne's. Another is papering the window, shutting it from street view.

"Just a little refresh," Garrett answers vaguely.

"Why? You're planning on tearing down the building in … May?"

Richard opens his mouth to answer, but then, thinking better of it, turns to Garrett, waiting for him to address the question. He *is* spearheading the project, after all. I guess he wants to give his nephew practice in dealing with unruly townsfolk.

"We'll be using it as a temporary sales center beginning next week until our new HG office is open across town. Our schedule is already tight, and I can't waste valuable time," Garrett answers smoothly. "Also, I think the sooner people see how we're *improving* Main Street rather than listen to rumors circulating, the better for everyone involved."

Better for Garrett and HG, surely. "Next week, huh? *Wow.* You're just trucking along."

Garrett steps back. "I'm sure you were on your way to something important. Don't let us keep you." He gestures toward the butcher shop, clearly trying to get rid of me.

"Todd's angry. He cut me off his soup." I steal a peek through the window—the egg yolk has been scrubbed clean—but Dillon, his employee, is behind the counter. I wonder if he's been instructed not to sell me anything too.

"Angry with you. Can't imagine why," Garrett mutters.

"I know, right? It's unfathomable."

"If you two'll excuse me, I was just popping in between meetings, but I'm on my way back to the office." Richard taps Garrett with a paper roll. "Give me an update later. Justine, don't catch a chill." Richard marches toward an idling black Lincoln, the hem of his dress pants tapered perfectly to his ankles. He slides into the back seat.

"He has a driver," I say out loud as the car pulls away. Of course, he has a driver. The man drips money. *And* he knows my name. I don't know if I should be flattered or concerned. My mother's warning about getting on powerful men's bad sides rings in my ear.

"Richard's a busy man. Why waste the hour commute back to Philly? Speaking of wasting time ..."

"*Ouch!* You know, I kind of miss flirty Garrett. He was a slime-ball, but at least he wasn't a complete asshole."

He sighs. "I'm just under a lot of pressure—in part, thanks to you—and I don't have the energy to deal with whatever shit you want to fling at me because you're in your man-hating phase."

"I don't hate *all* men. Just liars and cowards and cheats."

"Then there's no reason for your issue with me."

I bellow with fake, obnoxious laughter. "Oh yeah? No reason? How's that fridge I sold to you working out? Remember that day?"

"So you're admitting your anger has nothing to do with HG buying this building and *everything* to do with you thinking I led you on?"

"*Hustled me.* And Ned. Because you're a *hustler.*"

"You really like that word."

"If it walks like a duck …"

"Whatever game you're trying to play, you *aren't* going to win. So find something else to put your energy into. Something positive." His eyes flicker downward. "And put on a coat."

"I'm fine."

"You're cold." He shifts his attention to a worker edging past us, nodding in greeting at him.

"Oh, you mean because of *these*?" I raise my voice, gesturing at my nipples, pebbled and no doubt prominent through my thin cotton shirt. "I'm not cold, I'm just happy to see you."

The worker steals a glance over his shoulder and barks out a laugh.

The corners of Garrett's mouth twitch. "Still classy, I see."

"Not everyone can be as sophisticated as you, Garrett John Harrington *the Third*," I taunt.

His eyebrow arches. "Looked me up, did you?"

"Know thy enemies and all that." I jerk my chin toward the building. "Get your guys to park in back. You have a giant lot and that way you're not taking spots from customers."

Garrett makes a point of looking around. "Which customers would those be?"

"The ones you're blocking." My carefree veneer is fading, my annoyance peeking through. "Show some respect to the business owners you *haven't* driven out of town yet."

His amusement sours. "Always a pleasure, Justine."

"Eat a dick." I storm back to Murphy's.

———

"Forty-two," Nancy drones in her monotone voice, tossing the used ball into a basket. Tonight she's wearing a blue sweater vest with a giant groundhog knitted into the front, in honor of last week's Groundhog Day. The brown in it matches her bowl-cut hair perfectly.

"Did she say fifty-two?" Mimi looks around, searching for confirmation. The lady is sweet as pie but often forgets her hearing aids.

"No, forty-two. *Winnie the Pooh* forty-two."

"*Forty*-two," Nancy emphasizes, spearing me with an annoyed glare for embellishing.

Mimi grins. "My grandson loves that little bear."

"So do I," I mock whisper, before continuing my weave around the room, replacing daubers and pointing out called numbers on cards—despite Nancy's protests that it's cheating—until the hour creeps toward nine p.m. and someone shouts a resounding "bingo" on the final round.

The residents start shuffling out of the room with good-nights, leaving me to collect their game pieces.

"Justine!" Shirley waves me over with a sharp nod. "Come here. Need to fill you in."

She's sitting with another human, which is enough reason to abandon my task. "You have more juicy Bonny Acres gossip for me? What's Saul been up to, that dirty dog?"

"Better. I don't think you've met Vicki yet." She gestures to the other person at her table—a tiny, pinched-faced woman with round glasses and cropped white hair that has been sprayed into a helmet. I've seen her around before, her face always buried in a memoir or autobiography, but we haven't spoken. "She's been helping me with some historical research."

"Are you part of the granny gang?"

"Shirley told me about that. What a silly name," Vicki scoffs, her voice high and reedy.

I hold up my hands in surrender. "I did not come up with it. But I can have T-shirts made in a range of colors."

She titters with laughter.

"Vicki, this is Justine, *our* in-house spy. She's the one who first tipped me off about Dieter's building."

"Such a shame what that son of his is letting happen. He was a good man." Her face falls with distress.

"That's what I keep hearing. Ned, my boss, speaks highly of him. I work with him, over at Murphy's."

Mention of Ned erases the woman's frown. "Oh really? How is he doing?"

"Good. Lonely, I think, now that Trudy's gone."

"You know, I went out on a date with him once. He took me to the Galaxy Drive-In." She smiles wistfully. "Such a gentleman. But then he met Trudy soon after—she was from a different town—and that was that."

"You should come into the store and say hi. I'd bet he'd like to see an old friend."

Her mouth curves, as if pondering that suggestion.

"More important things, about this research ..." Shirley's eyes sparkle. "You ever heard of the poet Hugh Whitman?"

I shake my head. "Poetry's not my thing."

"I don't care for it either, but he's Polson Falls' claim to fame. He grew up here and won a Pulitzer for his work. That new school they're building? They're naming it after him. Anyway, Vicki had it in her head that she remembered a story about how Hugh Whitman moved back to town for a stretch and was living in one of Dieter's apartments. So she started asking around and—"

"My old neighbor's cousin's aunt knows his family," Vicki cuts in. "They started digging through boxes of photos and look what they found." She holds up a black-and-white photo. "That's him with Dieter Senior outside the butcher shop."

I peer at the storefront and the two men standing on either side of the door—one, a young man in a butcher apron whose face I know from pictures on the wall, and another, a much older man with wild hair and a cigarette burning between his fingers.

The next picture Vicki holds up is a moody, professional shot of Hugh Whitman sitting on a chair, gazing out a tall window, a guitar cradled in his lap. "Recognize that place?"

"That's Dieter's building." The curved head and grille pattern is unmistakable.

"They used that picture in a national magazine article. She also found an old Christmas card from Dieter to Hugh, saying how much he'd miss having him as a tenant."

"He was living in that apartment when he wrote his Pulitzer Prize–winning work. Probably drunk for most of that time, if rumors are true, but that's beside the point." Shirley raises a finger. "If that's not a notable figure to the town's history, I don't know what is."

"You think this will be enough?"

"We'll see what the commissioner says. Now, about that sales office." Shirley's gaze narrows. "You hear any more on that?"

"Nothing yet. The windows are still covered with paper." An hour after my little fit, the workers moved their trucks to the back. They've been coming in and out all week. "From what I saw, the painters are done. A flooring truck was there yesterday." To have that kind of cash to burn … "But Garrett did say they'd be opening next week."

"Then we need to get to work." A sparkle ignites in Shirley's eye.

The trouble-making kind.

Chapter Thirteen

"Do you guys have anything bigger?"

"Bigger. Than *this*." I gesture at the chest freezer. "It's 24 cubic feet. You can fit entire human bodies in it. Several. You want me to prove it?" I lift the lid. "Come on, you and me'll climb in here right now. I've already done it once." When I first started at Murphy's and saw the massive freezer sitting on the floor, I couldn't help myself. It was too tempting.

Mike's round belly shakes with his jovial laugh. "I don't need to fit humans in there. I need to fit a whole cow. The meat's coming tomorrow, and my chest freezer gone and died on me."

"Well, how much meat is that?"

"Four hundred and twenty pounds."

My jaw drops. "*Who* needs that much beef?"

"A cattle farmer who's not about to pay supermarket prices." He lifts his camo baseball hat off his brown mop of hair before putting it back on. "So, this is the biggest you got, huh? What'd you say? 24 cubic feet?" He peers up at the rafters, mumbling numbers to himself. "Yeah, that'll work. What's the warranty on it?"

I run through the standard Murphy's spiel.

"Okay, sold."

"Perfect. I'll get started on the paperwork."

"I've got it, Justine." Ned shuffles out from the office, a hot tea in his grip, and heads toward the counter. "Mike! How's your dad?"

"Still kickin'."

Ned chuckles. "Aren't we all. So, the freezer?"

"Yes, sir. Not something I was planning but don't have a choice."

"But you had a choice about who to come to, and we appreciate your business." Ned caps that off with a kind smile before settling into handwriting the bill of sale.

"What's the latest on next door?" Mike nods toward Todd's building. "I've been hearing tons about all this development. Nothing good. I got three hundred acres right outside town. How long before they come knocking on my door?"

"It could happen," Ned murmurs. "They've been knocking on mine."

"There ain't enough money in the world." Mike snorts. "Haven't had a chance to give Todd a piece of my mind yet."

"Get in line for that. Better yet, head over to HG's sales center and let them know what you think. They're opening up in the old sewing shop any day now." It's comforting to see a middle-aged man taking issue with all the development. Shirley keeps lamenting that only people collecting their old-age checks care, but that's not true.

"Is that what that is? They were peeling the paper down on my way in here."

"Really?" I dart to the window, but of course, I can't glean anything from this angle. "Ned?"

"Go on," he waves. "Go on and see what you need to see."

Rushing into my winter things, I dart outside.

Sure enough, HG's makeshift sales office is fully lit and finished, a crisp white and red HG banner affixed where Yvonne's Sewing Nook sign used to hang. The remodel itself is nothing fancy—freshly painted white walls, installed golden wood floors, and some new lighting—simple, but crisp and clean, far nicer than the cluttered, dated sewing shop.

Inside is sparsely furnished, with a sleek desk in the far corner for a computer and a few chairs. Most of the space is reserved for large wall prints and easels holding designs for what I assume is the new building.

Garrett and a curvy blond woman in a blue suit hover around the computer. Probably a staffer brought in from Philadelphia to sell the condo units. She has "sales" written all over her—her hips pulled back with confidence, her chin held high. Has Garrett ever whispered about methods to keep her in line if she's been bad?

My stomach curls, feeling stupid for ever playing along with him. But, as Shirley would say, that's beside the point.

As if sensing me on the street, Garrett's head snaps up and he zeroes in on me. He's dressed in simple black pants and a white button-down shirt, but everything's tailored to perfection. His eyebrow arches in question as if to say, "What is it now?"

I blow him a kiss.

He says something—I doubt it's flattering—and then strolls toward the door, his steps measured, his expression controlled. The glass door swings open with a push of his splayed hand. "Did you need something, Justine?"

"Why *thank you* for the invitation. I think I *will* come in!" I squeeze through the narrow space before he can utter another word, brushing past his solid body, catching that now familiar spicy scent.

The woman in the suit offers me a warm smile as she closes the distance, her heels clicking on the gleaming hardwood. She's beautiful, her suit tailored to flatter her wide hips, her sleek platinum blond bob-cut settled at her shoulders. "Welcome! I'm Morgan. You must be here to learn more about the exciting Revive Project?" She aims her French-manicured fingertips toward the easels with a flourish. Is she trying to impress me or her boss?

"I *am*!" Now that I'm standing inside, I can see the wall art for what it is—a montage of projects in the area over the last seven years. "Wow. HG is responsible for *all this*. I knew they had their hands in a lot around Polson Falls. I just didn't quite realize how much." There's an aerial photograph before and after of the town limits. In just ten years, the town's urban center has doubled. "Look at all that farmland, just paved over and gobbled up by development."

"Development that your town craved and sorely needed," Garrett responds. "Not everyone who inherits a farm wishes to keep it running."

"And how did those deals happen? Did you put on overalls and drive up their lane on your John Deere, flirt with the farmer's daughter, and tell them you've always wanted to herd cattle?"

The corners of Garrett's lips twitch, but his tone remains even, unruffled. "All of these landowners were paid handsomely, and now all those new families have moved into the area, both their tax dollars and disposable income supporting the local economy."

Morgan's bright blue eyes flicker between the two of us. She must be able to sense the cloying tension in the space, that I am not a prospective buyer she'll be able to entice. Without a word, she slips back to her desk to feign acute focus on her computer screen.

Designs for what I assume is this Project Revive sit on easels— various schematics showing the building from different angles, both interior and exterior.

"So?" Garrett settles beside me. "What do you think?"

I'll admit, the new building looks nice, albeit almost double the footprint of the current. It's not the concrete block that Shirley was worried about, the exterior a mixture of brick and stonework and decorative cornices. The storefronts are all sleek and black, and uniform. Sketches of the condos show modern one- and two-bedroom residences with high ceilings and upgraded fixtures.

I would live in one of these places.

But that's also beside the point.

"Oh look. A tree!" I tap the single oak sketch.

"Yes, where there wasn't one before." Garrett's brow furrows. "You have a thing against trees too?"

"Let me guess, you're going to market it as 'added green space.'" I air-quote. "All you guys love that big catchphrase. Throw in a patch of grass in the boulevard for Fido to pee on and suddenly, you're environmentally friendly."

Garrett's exasperated sigh ricochets off the crisp white walls. "Something tells me nothing will impress you. If you don't mind, we have a lot to prep before tomorrow's opening."

"It's tomorrow, huh?"

"Yeah." His eyes narrow. "Why?"

"No reason. I'll let you get back to it. Great to meet you, Morgan! Good luck working with this one." I cast a wave on my way out.

She answers with a tentative smile. She's dying for details.

I slide my phone free and punch out a text to Shirley.

Justine: Operation Goliath is a go for tomorrow.

"They sure know how to arrive in style." Ned and I watch as the oversized steel-gray van with the Bonny Acres' logo pulls into the parking spot in front of Murphy's. First Shirley, then Vicki ease out with the help of the center's driver, a burly man with a big smile. Vicki finds us in the window and waves, her smile zeroed in on Ned.

He squints as he offers a hesitant wave in return. "Is that Vicki Morley?"

"It's Vicki. I don't know her last name."

"Gosh, I haven't seen her in ... how long has it been?" he muses, scratching his chin. "Fifty-five years? She and I went out on a date once. Lovely gal. I heard she married Gus Sullivan."

"He died a few years ago. She lives at Bonny Acres now." All information I learned during our Sunday arts and crafts session.

"You should come with me one Friday. I'll bet you have a few friends there to catch up with."

He waves off my offer. "More people to miss when they're gone."

Six other residents from Bonny Acres pile out, all bundled in winter gear. Shirley spares me a chin jut before marching to the back of the van, instructing the driver to open it with a wag of her finger. All business, that one.

"It's cold for this, isn't it?"

"Nah, they're prepared. It'll only be for an hour or so." Long enough for Shirley to hatch her plan. "You gonna join us?"

"Someone needs to hold down the fort here, but I'll pull up a chair and cheer you on from the window."

"I thought as much. Wait here a minute. I've got something for you." I tug on my mittens.

———

"Save our small town! Protect our history!" My voice joins the fray as our little band of protesters marches back and forth in front of HG's sales office, the signs we made on Sunday held high for passersby to see as they ease along Main Street.

But it's not just me and the Bonny Acres clan. Shirley put the call out last night, and locals have answered. The sidewalk in front of the storefront is packed with business owners, family, and friends. Two officers from the police detachment arrived to "keep the peace"—one of them, Shirley has known since he was toddling around in his parents' backyard, buck naked, a fact she made sure to announce before giving him a hug.

I pause for a moment, gripping my "Stop Greedy Developers" sign, and take it all in, and smile. The turnout is better than I ever could've expected.

Garrett can't so easily dismiss this.

I hazard a peek over my shoulder. He's pacing inside his little sales center, his phone pressed against his ear, his jaw tense.

Who's he talking to? If I had to guess, Richard. He hasn't dared come out and address the crowd, though.

What's he going to have to say to me after this? The thought of our next altercation has my adrenaline pumping.

"There's Colin." Shirley nods toward a balding man with black earmuffs casting a look both ways before trudging across the street. "Your developer friend called him to do a piece on his condominiums." Shirley's cackle is downright wicked. "We'll give him a piece, all right."

Colin stops in the middle of the street and lifts his camera, the lens aiming directly at me.

So I do the only thing I know how to do well—smile wide.

Chapter Fourteen

"I CANNOT BELIEVE YOU!" Scarlet howls with laughter, unfolding the local paper to get a better look. "When was this?"

"Tuesday."

"You were protesting on Main Street on Tuesday and *didn't* tell me?"

I stretch out on the living room couch. "Oops. I forgot."

"Bullshit. You knew this was coming, and you wanted to shock me!" She playfully kicks my leg before her attention returns to the page. "'David Takes On Goliath.' I take it you're David?"

"Yeah, making me the poster child was *not* the plan." At least not *my* plan. Colin showed the pictures to Shirley the night of the protest, and she insisted on the close-up of me for the front page. According to her, it'd be more impactful to see a young face fighting for Polson Falls' identity than her sour old one. "Read the article. It's pretty good." It stretches across pages two and three, with plenty more pictures, including one with Ned, sitting alone in Murphy's window, the "Please don't erase me" sign I made gripped in his fists, his face somber as he looks on.

It's a gut-punch of a shot. Colin has skill.

"They must have rushed this to print."

I watch quietly as Scarlet reads.

"'Rather than utilize the historical bones of a building that has fed, clothed, and housed Polson Falls families, including Pulitzer Prize winner Hugh Whitman, for a century, HG is rushing to flatten it without public input, resident Justine MacDermott claims.'"

"I practiced that one a few times."

Scarlet keeps reading. Her eyebrows pop. "'Polson Falls mayor Ferris Gump acknowledges that while property development group HG is working with the town planning office for their building design, permits have not been issued. Residents' response to these plans have not gone unnoticed, and the council will be meeting with the heritage commissioner next week to discuss.' Oh my God, does that mean they might stop the build?"

I offer a one-shouldered shrug. "Shirley says it's political doublespeak and they're just buying themselves time until things settle down. But she also said it's an election year, and Gump's going to run again. The last thing he wants to do is piss off the people who come out to vote."

"Wait, our mayor's name is *Ferris Gump*? How did I not know this?"

"You're not the only one. All these young families moving into these new homes? They may want development, but they get their news off social media headlines, not the *Polson Falls Tribune*. They're not following this stuff. They don't come to town meetings." But Shirley and her crew do. "Gump may use the heritage commissioner as an excuse to delay approving building permits until after the election for fear of losing votes."

"But they'd risk pissing off a developer who's investing a ton into this town?"

"The town will blame the historical committee and noisy residents." Like me. "It's probably just lip service, but it has to be making HG sweat." I know for a fact Garrett reads the local paper.

"Listen to you." Scarlet studies the article another moment before tossing the newspaper to land on my head. "We're framing that, you anarchist."

"Damn straight. It's one of my best pictures yet."

"In fact …" She grabs her phone and types out a message.

"Who are you texting?"

"Shane. I asked him to go find as many copies as he can. We're sending a copy to your parents, and to Joe."

"Speaking of which, ugh." I groan, smoothing my hands over my face with the reminder. "Joe texted me the invitation to their engagement party next weekend. They wish to seek the pleasure of my company at the Waltons' residence on the thirteenth of February in the eve," I recite in a mock British accent that conflicts with my Bostonian twang. "On Valentine's Day weekend. Like hell I'll be there."

"You're *not* going?"

"Of course I'm going," I mutter. "I'll put on a dress and pretend I don't care, and hate every second of it with a big, fat smile."

Scarlet's face pinches with sympathy. "You could say yes and then bail. Say you're sick."

"And miss out on such an important night of my brother's life because of Bastard Bill? I skipped Christmas. No way am I skipping this." Even if every bone in my body is warning me against subjecting myself to the torture. "*He* can skip it." As if that'll happen.

"Okay, well, don't forget that I can't be there for moral support this time. It's Shane's grandparents' anniversary. We're going out to dinner with them and Cody."

"Fine, but you better be coming to the wedding." Joe promised she's on the guest list, and if she's not, she'll be my plus-one. But her mention of moral support has me thinking. "Is Shane off shift that night, or is he taking the shift off?"

She scowls at the ceiling as she mentally maps out Shane's schedule into next weekend. "Nope, that's a day off."

"Perfect. I think I have a backup, if he hasn't found someone to bang yet."

Reaching for my phone, I fire off a text to Dean.

Chapter Fifteen

"HAVE A GOOD NIGHT, VIN!" I call out.

The owner of Vinnie's, a middle-aged man with a shiny bald head and a unibrow, pauses building a row of pizzas for delivery orders to smile at me. "See ya around soon, hey?" He winks. "And keep givin' them hell."

It seems *everyone* has read the David and Goliath article, and, in the case of Vinnie, a long-time Polson Falls business owner who has had to contend with three big pizza chains setting up shop over the last five years, he's happy to see someone putting up a fight.

"What else do I got to do, right?" I hip-check the door, two steak sandwiches wrapped in paper dangling from my fingers. They're nowhere near as good as the ones from our favorite diner back in Jersey, but at almost ten p.m. on a Friday, they're perfect for a night of loafing in front of the TV with Scarlet.

Few cars ease along Main Street toward their destinations, their headlights glaring against the wet pavement. The Corner-Mart lights cut out as I'm passing. I see Bob's silhouette at the window, switching off the open sign. It seems early for a convenience store to shut down—the ones around our old apartment were open all night—but Bob's business relies on foot traffic, which is virtually nonexistent in the winter. He's lucky to get two customers after seven. Most people drive the extra five minutes to the Rite-Aid.

I wonder what Bob will do now that he's being evicted. He closed his store for twenty minutes to join the protest. When I asked him if he'd found a new location yet, he laughed sadly. It would cost him too much to set up elsewhere, and rent prices are double what he's been paying Todd up until now.

The HG sales center is cast in darkness but as I'm coasting past, a glow in the very back catches my eye. I slow my car to a crawl.

Garrett is there, leaning against a wall, his hands folded on top of his head. I haven't seen him since the day of the protest. Morgan has manned the sales office every day this week, and his SUV was gone from its usual parking spot.

On impulse, I pull into a parking spot and hop out. Darting up the sidewalk, I reach for the door ... and find it unlocked.

So I saunter in.

"You should lock your doors. Never know what might crawl in from the street at night." The muffled sound of death metal music carries from the apartment above.

"Just what I need ..." Garrett's arms drop. "I'm *really* not in the mood for this tonight." There's not a hint of humor in his voice as he stares up at the ceiling, his Adam's apple jutting.

"Having a bad week?" That protest and article might have had more of an impact than I guessed.

"Something like that." His chest heaves with a sigh and he pulls himself up to full height. "This is the first project my uncle has handed off to me to manage end to end, all decisions. It's not even a big one, compared to some of HG's work. It was supposed to be simple and straightforward, and a way to prove myself to him as he plans succession for his company. Do you understand what that means? *Running* HG. Because Richard *is* getting older, and he *did* ask me here to help him." His jaw tenses. "It's not my fault you misunderstood what I said that day."

I snort. "Don't even try. You misled me."

"Well, now he's getting involved, because I can't handle things." He paces, his body rigid with tension. "I don't know what game you're playing, but this is my livelihood, Justine. My future."

"You seriously want to talk about livelihood? Go talk to Bob." I fling a hand in the direction of the darkened convenience store. "Or Ned, or Vinnie across the street, who've all been hurt by HG's development projects in this town. I'd say talk to Yvonne, but she's already gone."

"That's life. Communities grow. Old businesses close, and new ones open. Some thrive, and some don't. And did you even know Yvonne? Did you *ever* step foot inside this store?" Garrett's voice rises in challenge.

"That's not the point."

"What *is* the point, then? Because, for all the people you lured out to protest, there are ten times as many in town who *want* to see someone investing money in Main Street. I've had plenty of interest in these condos and the commercial spaces."

"Then you have nothing to worry about." I meant to say it flippantly, but it comes out sounding like a challenge.

He opens his mouth to say something but catches himself, as if thinking better of it. "You know, you're like some sort of …" He struggles for words as he stares down at me, his eyes roaming my face. "Tiny, beautiful *menace*, plotting my downfall."

"You think I'm beautiful?" My tone is patronizing, but I don't miss the way my stupid heart skips. I heard him call me *cute* when I was eavesdropping on his conversation with Todd. Cute is fine, but cute is forgettable. *Beautiful* is harder to dismiss from a man's thoughts, especially when I'm making his life hell.

"You *know* you are. And despite what you've convinced yourself, none of that day was an act. But now I wish I'd never stepped foot inside that store. Never met you," he says more to himself, his focus flittering to the easel where his project design sits.

It really is a nice-looking building.

A small part of me—a minuscule part—feels guilty. Maybe he's right, and the town does need this. Maybe my fight is a selfish one. But I've never been one to back down, and it's too late now. The granny gang has made me their damn poster girl.

The song above us—if one can call it that—shifts, and the volume escalates.

"Sounds like it's going to be a long night for you."

"It is, so if you don't mind …" He takes a step forward, into my personal space, his eyes locked on the door. I hold my stance for a few beats, listening to him draw breaths, chest lifting with each intake, to see what he'll do, how he'll respond.

Finally, his gaze falls to meet mine.

I'm excellent at reading people's eyes, but I can't read what's in his. They're cold and yet blazing.

God, he *really* is a magnificent creature—the symmetry in his face is astonishing. The anger and hurt over his hustling antics still burn inside me, but it's competing with the way he makes my blood race.

He glances down at my lips, and his throat bobs with a hard swallow. "This isn't going to end the way you want it to. Or the way *I* want it to, frankly."

"I guess we'll see."

He takes a step back. Then another. It's a dismissal. He wants me out of his hair.

"My sandwich is getting cold." Spinning on my heels, I saunter out the door, as if unaffected by the way my pulse thumps.

———

Ned peers at me from above his glasses. "You've been checking that thing every two minutes. Between that and the pacing, you're sure going to be exhausted tonight."

I slide my phone into my back pocket and continue dusting the stoves. We haven't had a customer walk in since eleven this morning. "I'm *dying* to know what happened." The heritage commissioner was meeting with the town council at one about Todd's building.

It's almost three.

Ned shifts his attention back to his accounting report. "I'm sure Shirley'll call as soon as she has news to share."

"I have this bad feeling." It's lingered in my thoughts ever since my run-in with Garrett last Friday, when he promised things wouldn't go how either of us wanted. What did he mean? Which way could it go, if not one or the other?

Between all this Polson Falls drama and Saturday's engagement hell party, I'm a live wire.

The door chimes, drawing my attention to the bundled form.

"Shirley! I thought you were going to call."

"That was the plan, but I was at my nail appointment. Figured I might as well stop by." She sees Ned and her hard expression softens a fraction. "Good to see you still living life on your own terms."

"I'm trying." Ned chuckles.

As much as this little reunion is sweet, I'm dying for an update. "Have you heard from Michelle?"

"I did." Shirley's face tightens. "Those weasels found their loophole."

————

The glass door to the HG temporary office flies open as I plow through. "Where is he?" I demand, not bothering with pleasantries.

Morgan is sitting at her desk with a couple. She cuts off midsentence. "Uh …"

"Garrett. Where is he?"

"Excuse me for a moment." Rising from her seat, she smooths her hand down the sides of her black pencil skirt and approaches me slowly, as if preparing herself. "He was at a meeting with—"

"Yeah, I know where he *was*." In a town office boardroom ten minutes before a closed- door session with the town council, Michelle on one side, Ferris Gump, Garrett, Richard Harrington, and the town's building inspector on the other. A row of suits, armed and ready.

According to Michelle's recounting, Garrett and Richard sat quietly while Gump explained that the town's inspector was scheduled to do a routine inspection of several buildings, including Dieter's. The exact date of that inspection was to be determined—it could happen anytime. It could happen today, at which point the inspector was certain he would find an issue worthy of condemning the century-old building and forcing the current tenants out immediately.

Richard then calmly explained that if this were to happen, HG would not be willing to invest the funds to reverse the decision, regardless of how trivial, which would then force the town to issue an order for demolition.

Michelle immediately saw this for what it was—HG and the mayor taking advantage of a clause in the town's historical ordinances that states a condemned building can't be classified as a historical landmark.

Of course, the mayor played into it, asking Michelle if she wanted to be responsible for a resident and several business owners thrown out into the cold suddenly.

Of course she didn't.

That's when Garrett stepped in, playing the good cop to his uncle's bad. If Michelle backs off on trying to stall the permits with this historic claim, HG will fix any issues that come up *should* the inspector visit the property in the coming weeks. Beyond that, in a show of goodwill, HG would see what they could salvage of the original building as part of their new build. No promises, though.

Except for the unspoken one—that the town was ready to condemn the building at any point, as needed, permanently blocking the path to landmark designation.

It's done. It's over. HG has won, and Garrett knew it when he was squaring off against me.

"Where is Garrett *now*?" I push.

She flinches, like she's not sure she should answer this deranged woman who stormed in. "He left for New York. He won't be back until next week."

"Good. When you talk to him next, tell him the longer he stays away, the better for him."

Chapter Sixteen

Icy air nips at my bare legs as we traipse down the sidewalk, dodging other pedestrians. The five blocks from Dean's friend's place to the engagement party didn't seem too far a walk when I was stalling to get here. Now I'm wishing we'd taken Dean's suggestion of a taxi—the solid line of yellow crawling along the street would have bought me more time *and* kept frostbite away.

According to my GPS, the Waltons' building is on the corner ahead—a boxy, fifteen-story structure with tan-colored facade and decorative iron grates covering the windows of the first floor. There are countless buildings like it along this street, but also ones far taller and more elaborate, all with condos valued at no less than five million and in many cases, several times that.

This is Sara's world, the one she grew up in. And, by default, it's about to become my brother's world. The guy whose favorite meal is canned spaghetti on buttered Wonder Bread.

It's a jarring thought, but the only one I can focus on is that I'm about to face Bill and Isabelle, and there isn't a store of pastries to hide behind. I've been dreading this moment since I climbed into Dean's truck this afternoon.

I swallow against my nerves and cling tighter to his brawny

arm. "My code word for tonight is *sucker punch*." It's what I'd pay money to watch someone deliver to the bastard.

Dean's face splits with a wide grin. "How the hell are you going to work that into a sentence?"

"You doubt me?"

"If there's one thing I don't doubt, it's you when you set your mind to something." He adjusts the collar of his charcoal wool jacket with a leather-gloved hand as if it were bothering him.

"You clean up good, you know that?"

He flashes a crooked smile that shows off a dimple. "*You* knew that. Remember the auction?"

I hum with agreement. He *did* look good in head-to-toe black.

"You're not so bad yourself." His gaze drops, but the provocative cherry-red, V-slit maxi dress I bought for tonight is hidden beneath my black wool trench coat. "I like those shoes."

These five-inch gold stilettos might kill me before the night is through, but there was no other option. They were always Bill's downfall when I strolled into the bedroom wearing nothing else. "Not so bad? *Please*, I saw your pants tent the second I stepped out of the bathroom." Which I hogged for nearly two hours while getting ready.

His cheeks, already red-tinged from the cold, flush a shade darker. "Come on, you can't blame me. No man's going to be able to look away when you stroll in. Especially when you're in man-eater mode."

I bark out a laugh that catches a nearby pedestrian off guard and makes them stumble a step away. This is why I brought Dean with me. Besides moral support, he always boosts my ego. Plus, there's nothing that says "I'm over you" like strolling in with a gorgeous firefighter on my arm, even if I'm still a work in progress. "Just remember, I gave you permission to put your arm around me, but don't get any other ideas. You're keeping your big dick on the couch with you tonight."

"If you say so." His lips twist in a secretive smile, like he knows something I don't.

I'll bet Shane told him he was a second away from getting a booty call before Joe dropped his bombshell. Or he's figured out the same thing I have—that depending on how badly tonight goes, I might need a night of no-strings-attached sex with a good friend to help me drown my misery.

And that's what Dean is becoming to me.

The streetlight changes, prompting us to cross the intersection. Any second, my phone will chirp with a "you have arrived at your destination" prompt.

The sudden urge to turn around and run back to our home for the night hits me. "How do you know Drew?" When I asked—did *not* beg—Dean to be my plus-one to this soiree, he suggested forgoing a hotel and crashing at his buddy's. The one-bedroom apartment is a closet, but it's free, and Drew handed us the keys before heading to his girlfriend's.

"Through a friend of a friend." Dean's focus lands on the doorman ahead, waiting beneath a green awning for tenants and their guests. "So, your code word ... what's it for?"

"High risk of a humiliating breakdown, overwhelming urge to cause bodily harm ... the usual. Just get me out of there if I drop it."

"Got it."

"Good evening." The doorman dips his capped head as we approach the ornate front doors, the masonry surrounding its frame molded into a floral design. He's in the full fancy getup—double-breasted black jacket with gold piping and chunky white buttons. "Which residence will you be visiting this evening?"

"The Waltons'. My brother is marrying Sara."

He offers a polite smile that says he doesn't give a fuck who's marrying who while he stands out here, freezing his balls off, before reaching for the handle with pristine white gloves. "Check in at the desk ahead."

"Thank you." I pull my shoulders back and stroll in.

———

"Joe, what are you getting yourself into?" I feign nonchalance as Dean and I pass through what the coat check attendant in the foyer next to the private elevator called the "gallery room"—a long, wide hall with a dozen paintings, sculptures, and chairs that could double as their own art pieces—toward the buzz of voices and soft music. A grand staircase clad in glass and an exotic wood finish I've never seen before coils upward several floors on our left.

What am *I* getting myself into?

My heels click against the pristine black marble floors. "Do me a favor and don't collect any numbers tonight. It's not a good look for my date." I don't need anyone pitying me any more than they already do if they've heard the gossip.

"I wouldn't do that."

I spear Dean with a doubtful look. "*Please.*" It's a game between Scarlet and me when we're at Route 66: How many random women will slip napkins and business cards into Dean's pockets in one night? The only time we ever saw fluster cross his face was when one of them tucked a business card down the front of his pants. *Way* down.

He flashes a wry smile. "My pockets are closed for the night."

"So chivalrous of you."

My heart drums in my throat as we round the corner into a large, high-ceilinged room banked by windows that overlook the city. Any sizable pieces of furniture have been removed to make way for at least fifty well-dressed guests, plus a small army of servers in black-and-white tuxedos, carrying trays of champagne flutes and appetizers.

"So this is how the one percenters live." The lavishness of the entranceway extends here, with an array of sculptures in corners and extravagant finishes for the walls, floors, and lighting. There isn't a single detail that could be considered basic, and while art deco might not be to my taste, I admire the detail.

As if sensing my trepidation, Dean slips a warm hand on the

small of my back and leans down to whisper in my ear, "How do your tits look so damn good in that dress?"

I snort, seeing the crude question for what it is: a distraction more than a come-on. "Two words: *boob tape*."

Genuine surprise fills his face. "You can tape those things?"

"You expect me to believe that with all the breasts you've fondled, you've *never* come across boob tape?"

He frowns in thought. "None that I noticed."

"Play your cards right tonight, and I might let you help me peel—"

"Justine! Oh good, you're here." Mom's interruption sounds breathless, as if she ran across the room to get here. She probably did. "I was beginning to worry you'd changed your mind about coming."

"I honor my commitments, Mom. You know that. But I'm here for a good time, not a long time." A few drinks and a couple of key hellos—just enough to stroll out with my head held high.

"That's fine. Joe and Sara will understand." After a brief kiss on my cheek, she collects my hands within hers. "Gosh, look at you. You look *stunning*." She raises her eyebrows at me in a way that says, "But that's a lot of skin, dear."

"Nowhere near as stunning as the mother of the groom." I can't remember the last time I've seen her in anything more formal than a blouse and trousers. Probably Bill's wedding to Debra.

Ugh. Everything in my life seems to tie back to him.

"You picked out a good one for me." She beams as she strikes a pose in her royal blue satin dress before her curious gaze shifts to the looming figure beside me.

"Dean, this is my mom, Kitty." There's no point using her actual name. It'll get lost within minutes. "Mom … Dean."

She tips her head back. "It's so lovely to meet one of Justine's new friends."

Dean flashes his million-watt smile, sending her into a fit of Kitty-esque titters.

"Okay, settle down. Where's Dad?" I search the room. But it's not him I'm looking for. The sooner I locate Bill, the sooner I can avoid crossing paths with him.

"I left him over there, talking about cigars or some other nonsense with Clive, Sara's father." She waves it off before dropping her voice to whisper, "This place is something else, isn't it? I thought your father was going to test the picture frames for gold on our way in."

A warm hand catches my elbow and my attention. "Beer, Justine?" Dean has spotted the penguin suit behind the full bar and needs a drink that doesn't come in a dainty flute.

"In this dress?" I scoff. "A Negroni, please."

He turns to my mother. "Kitty, can I get you something?"

"Oh, I have a champagne going somewhere. On a table, I think. But thank you. That's very sweet."

"Yeah, that's Dean. *Sweet.*"

He flashes another brilliant smile, and Mom bursts into another round of titters, one that turns a few heads.

"Stop that." I jab his side with my index finger, meeting hard muscle. "She's not Dottie, *comprende*?"

He strolls away, parting the small crowd with his size .

"Who's Dottie?" Mom asks.

"Scarlet's mother. Dean got drunk and banged her a few years back."

A strangled sound escapes Mom's mouth. She knows nothing of Scarlet's siren mother or the scenario that could have led to that outcome.

I'm too preoccupied with my own worries to enlighten her. "Are *they* here?" I don't have to specify who.

It takes her a few beats of blinking and swallowing to regain her composure. "Yes, they've been here all night. The last I saw, they were going out onto the terrace with Craig and Molly. They have heaters set up."

"And where is this terrace?" So I can avoid going anywhere in the vicinity of it. It shouldn't be too hard. This place is huge.

"Far left. Come, we should introduce you to Sara's family." She collects my arm.

But I plant my heels on the patterned hardwood floor. "I'd rather have my drink and my big, beefy crutch with me before I dive in."

Mom gives me a look that's half pity, half admonishment. "I know the situation is far less than ideal, but this isn't you, Justine. You don't cower. You charge in headfirst, like a bull."

"Olé." I sigh, her words cutting deep. "I know. You're right." I guess Bill broke something in me.

"It'll be like a Band-Aid. The sooner you get it over with, the sooner it's done. Come." She gives my arm a gentle tug forward, whispering, "Just tone down the crass words and talk of *banging*. We want to make a good impression on Joe's future in-laws."

"So, *don't* be myself?" She just finished complaining that I wasn't.

"Be you, but a more refined version. And please, for the love of all that's holy, don't cause a scene that will embarrass your brother."

"Moi? *Never*." I force a smile as Mom prattles in my ear and we meander through the throng of guests. They're all from Sara's side, from what I can see, or a side of Joe's life I'm unfamiliar with.

"Sara's parents' names are Audra and Clive, and they are as lovely as she is. Honestly, I've been so nervous all week, wondering what they'd think of us. But Audra has been nothing but gracious since we arrived. I can see where Sara gets it. And your father seems to be hitting it off with Clive and the others ... a few of Sara's uncles are here. I can't remember their names, so make sure you lead with the introduction. Her sister's named Katrina, and her brother is Kent. They're twins, and they're both in the wedding party."

A towering form in a black suit blocks our path, his back to us.

After a glance around for another route and then a moment of hesitation, Mom chirps, "I'm so sorry, could we squeeze by you?"

The man turns …
And my jaw drops. "What the fuck are *you* doing here?"

Chapter Seventeen

GARRETT and I stare at each other, his face plastered with the shock I'm feeling.

"Honey, do you know this gentleman?" Mom's eyes flitter nervously between the two of us and the few people around who heard my outburst.

Well, obviously. I bite my tongue against that snippy response as I process seeing my enemy in the last place I expected.

Garrett gives his head a small shake. "Who are you here for?"

"Joe's my brother." I blurt. "Who are *you* here for?" In his stylish black-on-black tieless ensemble, the buttons of his shirt unfastened far enough to reveal the hint of collarbone, he somehow looks both casual and elegant.

His cheeks puff with his exhale. "Sara's my cousin."

His cousin. As in family. "All you rich people are related," I mutter, feeling my mom's sharp glare boring into the side of my face. God, but this means Garrett's going to be at the wedding too. It isn't bad enough I have to deal with seeing Bastard Bill and Isabelle, now I have him to contend with too?

I knew I should have stayed home.

After another awkward beat, Mom thrusts her hand forward,

taking over the conversation. "I'm Justine's mother, Joan, but *everyone* calls me Kitty."

He shifts his glass and collects my mother's invitation. "It's very nice to meet you, Kitty. I'm Garrett."

"Garrett." She looks to me, waiting for an explanation.

"Garrett *Harrington*. From HG."

Vague awareness flickers in her expression, but she's not connecting the dots yet.

"The developer who's tearing down the building next to Ned's. Well, his *uncle* is the developer. Garrett works for him. He just had his training wheels taken off." It's basically what his admission last week alluded to.

"That's an interesting interpretation." I catch the amused twinkle in his eye. Of course, his sour mood is gone, now that they've played dirty and won.

"Oh ... *Oh. I see.*" My mother's eyes widen. When I sent her the online link to the newspaper, she called me immediately to warn me off causing trouble for *those* kinds of people—the rich and powerful sort. Turns out *those* kinds of people are going to be related through marriage soon. "What can I say except Justine is very passionate when she finds a cause she believes in." There's an apology in her voice.

"Passionate." Garrett nods slowly. "That's *one* word for it."

"He called me a terrorist."

"Menace. Though she has been terrorizing me."

"My apologies. A menace." A tiny, beautiful one. A jolt of awareness skitters along my spine. He's only ever seen me in my Polson Falls habitat, which comes with snow boots, sweaters, and offensive T-shirts. I pull my shoulders back, suddenly more thankful for the extra time and effort I put into my appearance tonight.

But what does he think of this version?

Garrett sips on his drink—bourbon? Whiskey? Something amber colored and no doubt hard—while his eyes slip down the V-neck that exposes my well-taped cleavage, and farther, to where the two slits on either side of my dress cut all the way to the tops of my thighs. Eyes sliding back up, his gaze seems to snag.

"I thought staring at a woman's rack was beneath you?"

"Gosh, where is that drink of mine?" Mom caps that off with nervous laughter, looking around for an escape. I didn't get my barge-into-trouble-like-a-bull demeanor from her.

"Allow me." With the lift of one finger, a penguin suit with a tray of champagne flutes appears out of thin air. Garrett collects one and hands it to my mother, before collecting another, his gaze steady on mine as if daring me to take it.

Dean is still waiting in line for our drinks and chatting up a stunning woman with black hair and tawny-brown skin. That guy is a magnet for conversation. As attractive as he is, he's approachable. Maybe it's his "I'll rescue your cat from a tree before we go test your mattress" vibe. Twenty bucks says he's trying to find a way around his no-number pact.

"Why not?" I accept the glass, my fingertips grazing Garrett's in the process. I can't ignore the way my skin grows hot with the feel of his touch. But I do my best to drown it by tipping my head back and pouring the entire serving down my gullet in one shot.

"*Justine*," my mother quietly admonishes.

"It's okay. Garrett knows I have no class. Right?" I wink at him. "By the way, is Uncle Richard here? I want to make sure I say hi." Nothing about that sounded friendly.

"I believe he's over there." He nods toward the other side of the room. "And I'm sure he'd *love* to learn about this turn of events."

Wait. "There's no *turn* of events. Polson Falls is Polson Falls. Different world and circumstances."

A wry smile touches his lips before he smooths it off. "Kitty, you must be excited about the upcoming wedding." His question is for my mom, but his focus lingers on me before shifting.

"Oh, we are *thrilled*. Sara is a dream come true. I've never seen Joe so smitten."

His features soften. "My cousin is the best of the lot."

"I can wholeheartedly concur." I tap my empty glass against his.

"That's bad luck." He slides it from my grasp, his fingers slipping over mine a second time, and trades it with a fresh one from the nearby penguin. When he hands it back, his grip lingers an extra beat before releasing.

"Trying to get me drunk?"

"I have a feeling you're going to do that all on your own."

"I will not take that bet. But don't get your hopes up. I have my lay for the night lined up."

"Justine," Mom hisses.

"What? I didn't say 'bang.'"

"I'm going to check on your father." She ducks away.

"It's a good thing I don't have abandonment issues." I suck back half the glass in one gulp.

Garrett shakes his head. "It's refreshing to see that you're like this with everyone."

"What, charming?"

"Obnoxious."

"*Charmingly* obnoxious, though."

"If you say so."

We stare each other down as if waiting for the other to speak. When I stormed away from Morgan yesterday, I was certain that the next time I saw Garrett, I would struggle to not choke him. But here we are, and I find myself falling back into this inevitable push and pull of attraction and distrust.

Those lips that so deftly spin lies. They're like … pillows.

Kissable pillows.

A familiar laugh catches my attention. I follow its sound, and my breath hitches.

Bill just slithered in from the terrace. He's wearing his mink-brown hair longer than usual and combed back. His suit is new, customized to fit his lanky frame. I'd always bugged him to invest in tailoring, but he was too cheap.

Isabelle is in tow, his arm roped around her willowy frame.

I hadn't realized how tall she was. The top of her head reaches his cheekbone, her long legs peeking out from beneath a calf-length, one-shouldered black cocktail dress. I envy women who can wear that precise length—my legs always look stubby.

They're talking to another couple, people I've never met, but who Bill seems to know well based on his casual stance. Whatever Bill says makes the other man roar. I'm not surprised; he has always been good at drawing laughter, his wit razor-sharp and never missing a beat. Isabelle sees it, too, the way she gazes adoringly at him, her hand settled on his trim waist.

This is the woman Bill left me for.

And that day that I discovered what was happening, when I stood in our apartment, tears streaming down my face, demanding to know how he could throw away such a great thing, he looked at me with pity—with pity!—and asked what, besides our hyperactive sex life, was such a great thing? He wanted *more* than just a good time. He wanted a wife, and he didn't see me filling those shoes. Joe was right, though. They do fit together, at least by appearance. And he's well on his way to building a life with her now, one that doesn't include me.

Do they know I've arrived? Does Bill even care that I might be standing back and watching this? That he's hurting me?

A sharp, painful ball swells in my throat.

"Justine?" Garrett's voice pulls me back. He's frowning. "You okay?"

"I'm fine." My voice is suddenly hoarse.

He follows where my line of sight hovered a moment ago.

"Look, this has been a slice, but I should go make my presence known. I have places to be tonight." Quiet places, where I can scream in private. Turning back, I scurry in the opposite direction that my mom went, as fast as my five-inch heels can carry me, snatching another glass of champagne on the way.

———

"Took you long enough." I dive with both hands for the Negroni in Dean's grip. The three flutes of bubbly have gone to my head but have done nothing to numb the dread in my stomach.

"You didn't make it easy." He surveys the high walls of floor-to-ceiling bookcases and the spiral staircase that leads to the second floor, all constructed in that exotic lacquered wood used elsewhere in the penthouse. The dim lighting and rich wood tones cast a mood. "Are we supposed to be in here?"

"Didn't you know? Rich or poor, *everyone*'s welcome in a library." I veered down a narrow hallway, thinking I'd find a powder room to hide my impending implosion. I found one, but it was occupied, so I kept wandering until I landed here.

"Did you see your brother?"

"Not yet. I needed to take a detour."

"You ran into your ex?"

"Ran *before* I could run *into*, so to speak." I savor the bitter taste of licorice root and herbs on my tongue. "Who was the woman by the bar you were getting chatty with? She was stunning."

Dean pauses, likely seeing my question for what it is—another detour away from my current shitty situation. "Meera. A doctor at the hospital where Sara works."

"*Ooh.* Think of all the weird things she could do with your prostate."

He grins. "She's not that kind of doctor."

"Please. It's med school 101. Everyone's that kind of doctor."

"Really? In that case, I knew I should have gotten her number."

"There's still time. And let's be honest, I have enough disasters to deal with tonight. I'm not going to add sleeping with my moral support to the mix. Seriously, you should grab her number." So my miserable night can be complete.

His head tilts. "Is this a test?"

"I don't play those games."

Dean barks out a laugh.

"Okay, fine, I play *those* games. But tonight's already gone to hell, so what does it matter if my date is picking up another woman?"

The door creaking open interrupts his response.

I spin around to see Garrett stroll in, a fresh tumbler in hand, along with a flute of champagne. "Double fisting. Who's classy now?"

"Still not you." He surveys Dean, then the drink in my hand, before setting the flute down.

"If I didn't know better, I'd think you came looking for me," I tease, but my heart stirs with the idea that he didn't dismiss me from all thought the second I scuttled away like Cinderella at the stroke of midnight.

"Your brother and Sara are wondering where you are." He lifts his glass to his lips, his gaze settled on me. It's such a casual move, as if he's saying, "So what if I *was* looking for you?"

"They'll find me. You two did. And, *boy,* am I lucky." I wink and toast the air. "Speaking of double fisting ..."

Garrett chokes on his drink, coughing a few times. "Is she *always* like this?"

"Some days are worse than others. She's in fine form tonight."

I waggle a finger. "Don't even try. You *love* it."

Dean offers a hand and introduces himself as a friend of mine.

"*And* boob tape remover." I point to my breasts. "You've earned it, bro."

Garrett returns the handshake. "I'm Sara's cousin."

"*Also* the guy who paid off a town inspector and is tearing down Todd's building and destroying a part of Polson Falls history. Don't forget to mention that part."

"Huh. No shit ... small world." Dean sips on his beer as he studies first Garrett, then me, then the champagne flute sitting on the table. He's doing simple math, and a thoughtful expression passes across his face when he feels he has the answer. "Listen, I need to hit the can. You good here, Justine?"

"Only if you go and get that proctologist's number."

"Won't let you down." His chuckle fades as he disappears beyond the door, pulling it shut behind him.

Garrett's footfalls are slow and measured as he closes in. "You show up to this engagement party looking like *that*, and then hide in the library?"

"I'm not hiding. I'm perusing my next read." I scan the titles closest, a smile of triumph catching me as I reach for *Moby Dick*. "My favorite. For *obvious* reasons."

"You think I can't see through your act?"

"What act? Ocean, check. Giant sperm—"

"I met Joe tonight." Garrett pretends to study the books along with me. "They've been together for, like, two minutes, but ... seems like a good guy."

I shove the book back on the shelf, my natural defenses sparking. "That's because he *is* a good guy."

"Except for his taste in friends." Garrett's pace is slow as he drags a fingertip along the spines, not a speck of dust showing. "The ex you caught with his pants down, that's his best man, Bill. Isn't it?"

"It's Bastard Bill to you." I swallow against my rising dread. Garrett has reason to want to hurt me, and now he has the perfect knife to stab me with if he so chooses. One hit is all he'll need to take me down. "I take it you met him too?"

"Isabelle introduced us earlier."

"You know Isabelle." *Great.*

"Of course I do. She's been Sara's best friend since childhood."

"You're that close to Sara? Man, I couldn't pick my cousins' friends out of a lineup if my life depended on it."

"I spent every summer in Newport with Sara, growing up. Izzy would visit a lot too." He pauses, studying me. "You have no idea that they asked me to be in their wedding party, do you?"

"Oh my *God*." My groan fills the silent space. Joe mentioned that the party was stacked with Sara's family. I was so hung up on Bill and Isabelle being there, I didn't bother to ask who else specifically. Not like it would matter if I had. *Never* could I have imagined *this* connection.

He smirks. "Don't contain your excitement on my account."

"I won't. Promise." I focus on inhaling my drink.

Garrett leans against the frame of the bookshelf. "I remember Sara saying something about a sticky situation with the best man and Joe's sister when she asked me but I wasn't paying attention. I've had way too much on my plate these past few months."

"It's sticky, all right." A retort involving Bill's semen builds on my tongue, but I let it die there. There's nothing funny about my predicament. I drag my fingertip along the book spines as Garrett did, heading in the other direction, holding my breath, waiting for his punch line.

"It's shitty what he did to you. What *they* did to you." There's no hint of amusement in his tone to suggest he's getting perverse joy from my misery.

"Do you even know what they did?"

"I can guess, if Izzy's involved."

"Not a fan?"

"It's not that. It's just …" His words fade.

I peer over my shoulder to see him frowning at the carpet in thought. "It's just what?"

"She might not have set out to go after a taken man, but she'd also convince herself it's okay if he's the one who instigated it. In the end, it's about what she wants being more important than anyone else. She can be selfish like that."

"Are you speaking from experience? Because you seem like you've given this a lot of thought."

"She had a big crush on me for years, but I was never interested, if that's what you're asking."

"Why not? She's beautiful."

"She's bland, and she has no sense of humor. I'd be bored."

That she didn't win Garrett over brings me a wave of relief I didn't expect. "I don't understand how Sara can be best friends with someone like that. She seems so sweet and kind."

"She *is* both of those things, and she accepts Isabelle, faults included. Isn't that what a best friend does?"

"I guess." Scarlet has my back, no matter what. And, as much as I am Team Shane, if she decided she didn't want to be with him anymore, if she got drunk one night and fucked around with another guy, I'd still be her best friend. I'd tell her she's an idiot, but I wouldn't leave her corner. "Chicks before dicks?"

He smirks. "For the record, I know she gave Izzy hell when they first hooked up."

"Yeah, Joe punched Bill and cut him off for two weeks, until that charity event they were all at." I snort. "Hard to hold a grudge when that person introduces you to the love of your life, right?" I smile sadly. "I used to think Bill was the love of my life."

"He's not."

"Well, that's super obvious now." I swallow the lump, feeling Garrett's eyes on me as I scan the book titles without reading any. "But hey, if they hadn't hooked up, I wouldn't have moved to Polson Falls. We wouldn't have met, and I couldn't have been a huge thorn in your ass."

"On second thought, I *hate* Bill and Isabelle." He sucks back a gulp of his drink.

I laugh, despite the conversation. "I guess it doesn't matter who instigated it. They're together now."

"But you're not over him." It's a statement rather than a question.

"Believe me, I am *so* over him. If he came in here on his knees right now, groveling to me, I would *never* go back." I mean it, but I also know it'll never happen. The way he's going about his life with her in his arms? I'm the furthest thing from his mind anymore.

Garrett's eyebrows arch with doubt. "Then why did you bolt? You don't seem the type."

"Because I'm not over how much it still hurts." How my heart both aches and feels hollow at the same time. How hard it is to digest that my life has veered in an entirely new direction, and I had no choice in the matter. "Our lives have always been so intertwined. I mean, look where I am." I throw my hands out beside me. "I can't get away! Plus, it's all too fast, you know? We broke up in October, and everyone expects me to just *suck it up*? I thought we were going to get married. Sure, he was a bit gun-shy when the topic came up, but I figured it was because of his ex-wife, *Debra*." I've never been able to say that name without it sounding sour. "Turns out it wasn't her. It was me. *I'm* not enough. The years I put into that relationship, all the history between us … none of it was enough." I didn't expect to blurt out that vulnerable truth so easily, and to Garrett of all people.

Oh no … my bottom lip is wobbling. I tip my head back and down the rest of my drink in one gulp, hoping it will quell the threatening tears.

Garrett swaps my empty glass for the champagne.

"See? I knew you were trying to get me drunk. You think you can make me like you."

"I *know* I can make you like me." He smiles, but I don't miss the sympathetic frown.

I waggle my finger at him. "Like I said, we may have this New York connection now, but Polson Falls is another world."

He sets my empty glass on a coaster. "Can we call a truce on all the development stuff? You know, clock out for the night?"

"Like Ralph Wolf and Sam Sheepdog?"

Garrett's face screws up. "Who?"

"You know, the wolf and sheepdog? 'Morning, Sam. Morning, Ralph.'" I deepen my voice to imitate the two characters.

His blank look tells me he has no idea what I'm talking about.

"The Looney Tunes cartoon. God, what is it with your generation? No appreciation for the classics. But I knew that about you." I cap that off with a wink to soften the dig.

"My generation, huh? And you're, what, two years younger than me?"

I gasp and slap his chest, my hand landing on hard muscle. "I am beyond insulted. Five years, Garrett. I'm only thirty." Thirty-one this year, but who's counting?

He smirks, looking down at where my hand lingers. I don't pull away, and he doesn't step back. "I'm sorry, there wasn't a readily available bio for you online."

"Shocking." But that means he looked.

"It was! I was expecting at least one picture of you doing a keg stand with a skirt around your armpits."

"Those are only available to my dearest friends on Facebook. Please respect my privacy." Reluctantly, I move my hand.

His soft chuckle is like music filling my ears. "Come on. Let's go." He jerks his head toward the door.

"I can't. There are too many books to look at in here." I sweep my hand around the room. "I think I'll stay here all night."

"Don't you have a date to entertain?"

"Who, Dean? Trust me, he's fine out there on his own. And we're a hundred percent just friends." That last part, I felt compelled to add.

"You know you'll have to go out there eventually."

"Eventually, yes. But my plan is to not remember *any* of it. Just please, don't let me fall over. With these slits as high as they are, I had to forgo certain undergarments"—I drop my voice—"and that could get awkward."

His gaze drops for one … two … three beats before he sucks back the rest of his drink. "If you insist on hiding, there are plenty of other places in this penthouse."

"Such as?"

A devilish twinkle ignites in his eyes. "Follow me."

Chapter Eighteen

"QUICK! GO!" Garrett rushes me into an elevator, our drinks sloshing in his grip, my giggles trailing us. "Hit three."

I fumble with the buttons. He wasn't kidding about places to hide. We've skittered along hallways, snuck up and down staircases, through a staff room, a gym, a movie room, a dining room that seats eighteen, and a bustling kitchen with staff who stole suspicious glances at us.

The elevator doors close, and Garrett sinks back against the wall. "Close call."

"Why? Who saw you?"

"My father and Richard were waving me over, but I ducked out when they weren't looking. Here." He hands me my fresh Negroni and then licks the spilled liquid from the back of his hand, between his thumb and index finger. "Licorice, huh?" The simple move is intoxicating.

Or I'm intoxicated.

Either way, watching his tongue smooth over his skin—imagining it on *my* skin—quickens my pulse.

But it's his casual demeanor and the way he seems to enjoy playing hide-and-don't-seek with me that's drawing me closer to admitting I like Garrett Harrington. At least, this version of him.

"What's that?" He frowns at the appetizer in my hand.

"Bacon-wrapped fig. A penguin suit passed by, and I grabbed two. Here." I hold it up toward his mouth.

He leans in and pulls it off the toothpick with his teeth. The satisfied moan as he chews stirs something deep in my belly.

"This is why I'm suffering without Todd's soup. He puts bacon in *every* recipe."

The elevator doors open into pitch-black and Garrett leads me out.

"Is this where you end me like I'm a Stavro brother?"

"I would never do that in here. Wouldn't want to ruin it for myself." He flicks a switch.

I let out a whistle, taking in the all-glass walls of the rectangular room in the dim light. It's small compared to the rest of the penthouse—kind of like a top hat to cap off a perfect outfit—and empty of furniture, save for a Peloton bike and treadmill in one corner. "Nice place to work out."

"Morning sun hits here." He strolls toward the terrace off the far end, leading me through the doors. Outside is a sitting area with a fireplace. A faux vine wall separates the space from view of the terrace below, where low voices murmur and the waft of cigars rise.

I cock my head, studying the sculpture in the corner. "What is that giant rock supposed to be?" Sara's parents are clearly art collectors. The penthouse is littered with pieces, each one worth more than everything I own.

"A giant rock." He wanders to the glass railing, leaning his forearms against it. "I've always loved this view."

Cold nips at my bare skin, but I welcome it, following Garrett to the edge of the glass railing to look out on countless buildings. From far below, a steady stream of cars and honks carries. Whether it's two in the afternoon or two in the morning, I doubt it changes much—this city buzzes at all hours. Even living in Jersey felt different. "This place is insane."

"Yeah, the Waltons are filthy rich."

"And what are the Harringtons?"

He grins. "Slightly less filthy."

"Where's your home?"

Garrett leans over the railing and points. "Eight over, but you can't see it from this angle."

I whistle and say in a singsong voice, "Someone's got a trust fund."

He chuckles, unfazed by my teasing. "Almost lost it after I dropped out of law school."

"*Dropped out?*" My breath hitches. "Wikipedia neglected to mention this life event. Harvard?"

"Yeah. My dad wasn't too happy about the move. You know how it goes."

"Trust funds and Harvard? Oh yeah, totally get it. We are on the same wavelength, you and me." The way things are going, I'll be paying for a degree I'm not using until I'm shopping for my own room at Bonny Acres.

He flashes me a sheepish look. "He came around, when he saw how hard I was working for Richard."

"Why'd you want to make the switch?"

"To property development?" His focus drifts over the rooftops. "Buildings make a statement. There's nothing conceptual in them. All the time and effort you put into your job turns into a pile of brick and mortar. It's satisfying."

I bite my tongue against the urge to ask how satisfying it is to tear down an old building. "Where does Uncle Richard live?"

"You know you can just call him Richard, right?"

"I should. I'm not a big fan anymore." When Garrett said the man was stepping in to deal with the mess I'd made of his project, I should have known our cause was already lost.

"He has a penthouse a few blocks from here, and a penthouse near our Philadelphia office. And then there's the house outside Polson Falls that he's having renovated. It's up on a hill and has a barn for horses and everything. He plans on retiring there."

"Really? When he could be out in the Hamptons?"

"He's not a fan of the ocean. Prefers the quiet, small-town vibe."

"But not *that* small."

"Everyone benefits from the added amenities." Garrett peers around us. "You know, some of these buildings are the original prewar era?"

He's shifting the conversation away from Polson Falls, but I don't resist. It's nice to take the night off from our feud. "I did not, but it doesn't surprise me."

"Yeah. This one is over a hundred years old—1913. There are only twenty-six units." Light from the sconces catch his eyes, and I see the sparkle in them as they drift over the exterior walls. "Obviously, they've gone through extensive remodels and upgrades. All the units have been modernized. Well, except for 10-D. The woman who owned it spent a fortune in the '80s on a French neoclassical designer. There's even a ballroom. She died a few years ago, and they've had a hell of a time trying to sell. Everyone loves the architecture, but no one wants to live in it." He snorts. "Not my taste, but I have to admire it."

"So you *do* care about history."

The muscle in his jaw ticks.

I lift my hands in surrender, still gripping my drink. "You're right, Sam. We haven't clocked back in yet."

"Which one's Sam again?"

"The sheepdog. I'm the wolf."

"Why do you get to be the wolf?"

"Because wolves are generally sexier, and *well* ..." I wave my free hand in front of myself, as if making a presentation.

"Point made." He sucks back a gulp of his drink. Bourbon, I learned. That's his third one since I met him. How many does it take before he's not in control of his inhibitions? Because I think I'm getting close to reaching my "whatever happens, happens" threshold.

"Earlier, in the library, what did you mean when you said I showed up to this party looking like *that?*"

His gaze glides over me, his mouth working on the answer as if weighing whether to give it. "Like you dressed to kill a man."

"I'll take that as a compliment." I smile through a sip, as my pulse races.

"Good, because it was meant to be one." A flare of heat flashes in his eyes.

When I strolled in here tonight, my wish was to watch Bill crumble with regret, but now I'm far more interested in my new victim.

A shudder overcomes me, the cold finally winning the assault on my bare skin.

Garrett's hand is on my shoulder in an instant, guiding me inside, his warm touch sending electricity through my limbs.

The glass room is quiet, the air somehow thicker than when we first arrived. There aren't any couches or chairs up here. Nowhere to get comfortable. I swallow. "Where to next?"

He looks around. "We're running out of places to hide. All that's left are the second-floor bedrooms."

"They would *never* find us in there."

"My thoughts exactly." His playful grin reminds me of the first day I met him, when I was mentally picking out the perfect outfit for our first date—and inevitable sleepover.

But guilt pricks at my conscience. Joe called my phone a bit ago, and I ignored it.

As much as I'd like to test each mattress's springs—with Garrett beneath me—I've stalled the inevitable long enough. Plus, I promised my mother I wouldn't embarrass Joe. Getting caught playing R-rated Goldilocks with the bride's cousin might fall under that umbrella. "I should show my face. Can we take the long way down to the party, though?" Hopefully by the time we reach it, I'll have found my nerve.

"If you insist." His eyes dip down my dress before he offers me his arm.

"Gosh. Put on a red dress, and suddenly everyone's a gentleman."

"I've never been anything but."

My heels click on the marble stair treads as we slowly descend to the second floor.

"The main staircase is on the other side." He settles a palm against the small of my back and leads me down a hallway banked by doors and decorated by abstract artwork. I don't balk at the contact. If I'm being honest, I'm hoping he'll take it further, to a move that can't be mistaken as gentlemanly.

The elevator ding sounds.

"… it's been months. What else do you want me to do? I apologized to her. More than once."

My feet stall dead at the sound of Bill's voice around the corner. He must have come up in the elevator.

And there's no doubt he's talking about *me*.

Months? It's only been *four* months. And he thinks an apology for cheating on me is sufficient?

"It's not like her to disappear like this," Joe says.

"She didn't leave. Her date and her coat are still here," Sara offers.

Great, she's here too.

"Okay, let's just find her and face this like adults. Have it out if needed, away from the party."

They're coming closer, and there is more than one set of heels clicking. I'll bet Isabelle is with them.

I was having such a good time with Garrett, I'd temporarily shed my dread, but now a fresh wave washes over me with the idea of all four of them coming. This feels like an intervention. My head begins shaking of its own accord. "Nope, not ready yet," I whisper, peering up into Garrett's eyes, silently pleading for him to save me. I don't trust myself not to burst into tears, and I'll die if that happens.

Hooking a hand around my waist, he pulls me through a door, shutting it quietly behind us, throwing us into pitch-dark.

"Where are we?" I inhale. It smells like fresh laundry.

"Linen closet." His voice is barely audible. "I used to hide in here when we were kids. *Shhh.*" He pulls me closer to him until our bodies are pressed together, the heat of him a comfort against my skin.

I can sense his heart beating.

"Maybe she's on the third floor?" a female voice I don't recognize says from right outside the door.

"Good idea. Okay, Izzy and I'll check it out." That's Sara. "Be back in a few minutes." Two sets of heels click away.

I'm acutely aware of Garrett's breaths skating across my forehead as we wait for them to move on. The best thing now would be for me to make it down to the party room, pretend nothing is amiss, and avoid whatever "facing this like adults" entails.

"Don't let her ruin your night, man," Bill says.

"She's not ruining anything. I feel bad. This was too much to expect of her."

"Okay, well … you want me to bow out? You want to find another best man?"

My head bobs up and down. *Yes, that would be the noble move.*

"Don't put this on me. I'm still pissed at you. Remember when I told you not to date my little sister? But you did. Remember when I *told* you not to break her heart? And what happened?"

"I know! I get it! I should have ended it the day me and Isabelle connected. I wish I had. But Scarlet was moving, and Justine was already depressed about that."

That doesn't change the fact that you cheated on me, you asshole! Rage erupts, vibrating through my limbs.

"I still love her, you know that. It's just … it's not the same. Not like I feel about Isabelle."

I swallow against the bitterness of that truth pill. That's what he said to me the day we broke up, after basically telling me I'm the girl you fuck, not the one you marry.

"Don't worry about it. She's gonna turn up soon," Bill says in a softer tone. "This is Justine. You know how she is … She loves attention. What better way to get it than to have the bride and groom hunting for her."

My jaw drops. This isn't about earning attention. It's the exact opposite. I want to be invisible.

I'm a split second from popping out of the closet to scream at Bill, when Garrett's arms bracket me tighter, his hand fumbling in the dark, sliding over my shoulder, into my hair, around my nape. I sense him leaning forward, his lips skating across my cheek as he searches for my ear. "Get a hold of yourself, Ralph," he whispers, his mouth a hairbreadth away.

I snort, the reference so unexpected coming from Garrett.

"*Shhh.*" But his body is shaking against me with silent laughter.

"Did you hear that?" Joe asks suddenly.

Shit. It's one thing to be wandering around the Walton penthouse. It's something else entirely to get caught hiding from my ex in a closet. Unless …

My adrenaline spikes as I reach up, and curling a hand around the back of Garrett's neck, I yank him down. My mouth lands on his jaw at first, but it's not hard to find his lips from there.

They're even softer than I imagined, and they don't hesitate—not for a millisecond—to pry mine apart and slide his tongue inside. The potent taste of his bourbon combines with my lingering licorice root, but I don't mind the mixture as our mouths work languidly against each other, coaxing and prodding and exploring, our heads tilting for better access.

Dear God.

I am kissing the baby developer, the hustler, the enemy.

I'm kissing Garrett, and my knees are threatening to buckle from the raw pleasure of the experience.

I've gone rogue.

What would Shirley have to say about this?

I peel away with my hands pressed against Garrett's hard chest and pause to listen. Joe's and Bill's voices are moving down the hall. The threat of them yanking open the closet door and catching us in here is gone.

"Why did you do that?" Garrett whispers.

"Because getting caught making out in a closet is way less embarrassing than getting caught hiding from Bill."

"Really?" A few beats pass, and my ears catch Garrett's hard swallow. His breath skates across my lips, his only inches away "You know they're around, right?"

"You mean, they could still catch us?" The sexual tension in the air within our blackened little closet is palpable, a static electricity standing my body hairs on end. The fact that I can't see him only adds to the charge.

Because I can *feel* him.

"Definitely still a threat." His hands glide over my body, one cupping my neck, his fingertips settling behind my ears on either side. The other lands on the small of my back, pulling my body closer to his. "I wouldn't want you to be embarrassed tonight."

"No, we can't have that." My pulse hammers in my throat as I toss my purse haphazardly to the floor, freeing my hands. It lands with a soft thud just as Garrett and I collide.

Where the first kiss was delicate and unfrenzied, this one is altogether different—desperate and hungry, as if we've been lusting for this moment for weeks and aren't going to waste a second of it.

My hands scour his arms, his shoulders, his columnar neck as we cling to each other's mouths, a messy concoction of lips and tongues and nibbling bites. His body is solid, his flesh hard and curved in all the right places, and the feel of him beneath my fingertips sends an acute need rippling through my body.

"This is one hell of a dress." His lips leave my mouth to trail along my jawline, sliding down. He bends his towering form until his mouth finds the exposed flesh down the plunging neckline.

"I picked it just for you."

His soundless laugh breezes across my skin. "And you call me a liar." His tongue dips beneath the material of my dress.

"Don't mess with the girls. They're in perfect position."

"The boob tape."

"The *glorious* boob tape. It'll take me forever to fix them if you mess them up, and I didn't bring extra."

He pulls away. "Okay." The hand at my back slides lower, gripping one of my ass cheeks with a tight squeeze. "Anything else off-limits?"

A delicious burn ignites between my thighs. "Consider me your playground."

With a soft curse, he pulls himself upright to meet my mouth again, sinking us into a passionate kiss that turns our breathing ragged and my need spiraling out of control.

My teeth catch his bottom lip, earning his growl.

"Quiet, unless you want this to end prematurely," I warn, dragging my tongue across his jutting Adam's apple. It's a tie between that and sharp collarbones surrounded by muscle for my favorite part of a male body.

"You mean, within fifteen seconds?"

My face splits with a wide smile as I smooth my hand over the front of his pants, palming his rock-hard erection. "I've heard rumors floating around at Route 66 about that. Not sure who started those."

"I should find that person and make sure they stand correct-ed." His grip on my ass loosens, his hand shifting around to a slit in my dress. Warm fingers coast over my bare skin as they trace a path up over my hip.

He sucks in a sharp breath.

"I warned you, this dress isn't designed for modesty." Or underwear. But it has its advantages where easy access is concerned.

"It was designed for you." He releases my nape to curl his fist around my hair, giving it a gentle tug back, until I'm peering up into nothingness. But I can feel him staring down at me in the darkness, his shallow breaths kissing my skin.

He leans in to find my ear with his lips. "Speaking of play-grounds, I always liked the seesaw best." His hand shifts from my hip, inward.

I gasp as his index finger finds my slick center, glides along it. "Why is that?"

"It was so simple, and yet so much fun. Two people climb on and take turns, going up"—he slips his finger inside me—"and down." He pulls it out, before sliding it back in. "Over and over again." His nearly inaudible whisper in my ear is intoxicating, stalling my tongue and my brain for long seconds as I revel in his touch.

But I'm desperate to touch him too. "I remember seesaws not being very fun when one person got off too soon, though." I tug at his belt and pants until they come undone. The cotton of his boxer briefs is thin, granting me easy access to wrap my hand around him, to test his size. I groan with a mixture of relief and delight as I discover another reason for Garrett to be so arrogant.

My fingertips are inching beneath the elastic waistband when he stops me.

"You should wait a few minutes."

"Why?"

His ragged breathing fills my ear. "Because you feel too good, and I wouldn't want to feed into those inaccurate rumors."

Having a man like Garrett explode in my hand within fifteen seconds would make me feel powerful, but we can boost my ego later. "As you wish." I occupy my hands with his broad chest and my teeth with his earlobe as my arousal pools, his deft fingers working magic, his thumb circling my clit while two fingers stroke in and out. He catches that perfect spot every time, like a musician hitting every high note with precision. My body responds as if he's tethered a string to my impending orgasm, and he's drawing it out. I can't recall the last time a man other than Bastard Bill brought me to this place, and it took me months of training him.

"Who taught you how to do that?"

"Why?"

"I need to send them a fruitcake." If he's this good with just his hands, I can't imagine how skilled he is with his other tools.

He snorts. "Just to be clear, is that considered a gift or a punishment?"

My eyes roll back in my head as the throb in my lower belly intensifies. "The *best* gift," I moan.

"Shhh. You're getting loud."

I press my lips together and bury my mouth in the crook of his neck, a lack of inhibition taking over as my body winds tighter beneath his skilled hand. Now that I'm here with Garrett, I never want to leave.

Garrett must sense the pending explosion because he speeds up his tempo, and his hand squeezes gently around my nape. "Come on, let me have it."

I grit my teeth against the anguished sounds that threaten to sail from my lips. Garrett's body bends with mine, keeping me upright as wave after wave of intense pleasure rockets through me.

When it's all over, my legs wobble.

"Fuck, that was so hot." His hand slips away from my sensitive flesh. "I wish I could have watched it."

"Next time." The second the words are out of my mouth, I'm scolding myself. *Next time?* This is the *only* time. Which means I need to make the most of it. "Your turn." My lips land on his as I fumble with his pants, pushing them down his thighs. My fingertips hook around the elastic waistband of his underwear—

"Have you tried her phone?" Sara asks, suddenly on the other side of our door. So preoccupied with chasing this high, I never heard the footsteps.

"Not for a while. Let me try again."

Garrett and I freeze, our mouths still pressed against each other as my body goes rigid.

"Fuck," I whisper-hiss.

"Where is it?"

"In my purse." Which is on the floor. Somewhere.

I drop to my knees, blindly searching. My fingertips catch the edge of the silky material just as it trills. I dig it out and shut it off.

My heart thunders as deafening silence takes over.

Long seconds go by where nothing happens. I guess it wasn't as loud as it seemed.

I reach for Garrett's thighs to steady myself so I can get to my feet again. Maybe they didn't hear—

The door flies open, flooding the closet with light.

I can appreciate what this looks like—me, on my knees in front of Garrett, his pants unfastened and hanging halfway down his thighs—to an audience of not only Joe, Sara, Bill, and Isabelle but also Mom and a beautiful blond woman in a sleek black cocktail dress.

"Oh my God." Sara gasps, her hand flying to her mouth.

"Jesus Christ, Justine." Joe shakes his head, his expression torn between laughter and exasperation.

I wait a beat for Mom to complete the trifecta and take the Holy Mother Mary's name in vain, but she remains speechless, her jaw hanging.

At least Sara doesn't seem horrified to catch her cousin with his pants down. Sure, her eyes are averted, but I see the pursed smile. "Aunt Blair, this is Joe's sister, Justine. Justine, this is my aunt Blair. Garrett's mom."

His mother. Fantastic.

Blair, for her part, seems to be fighting the urge to laugh. "It's a pleasure."

"Likewise." I was wrong—this *isn't* less embarrassing than simply getting caught hiding in a closet. And it's more awkward, given I'm still on my knees and Garrett isn't rushing to pull up his pants.

I do the only thing I can think of. Climbing to my feet, I smooth my palms over my dress and tuck my purse under my arm. With a regal chin dip and greetings of "bastard" and "thief," I stroll out toward the elevator, hollering over my shoulder, "Thanks for the tour, Sam Sheepdog!"

Chapter Nineteen

"You did not." Scarlet gapes at me before her head falls back with a howl of laughter. Of the many things I love about my best friend, possibly the most important is that she doesn't ever judge me for my antics.

"Whatever. I went back down to the party, introduced myself to Clive and Audra and the twins, said bye to my parents, and took off with Dean." We grabbed a pizza and hung out on his friend's couch in our pajamas, playing Spider-Man on the PS5 until I passed out. When I woke up, I was tucked into bed, alone and relieved that I'd made it through the engagement party without crying.

"What about Garrett? Did he come talk to you or …?" She leaves the question hanging.

"I didn't see him again. Then again, I didn't stay long." I can't imagine how the conversation between him and his mother went. What do you say to your thirty-five-year-old son after catching him in a closet with a woman?

"What did Joe and Sara say?"

"About my disappearing act? Or my classy closet incident?"

"Both."

"They didn't seem to care. They were too busy being *in love*."

Joe called me on our drive home today to apologize for not being more considerate of what I was going through, facing Bill and Isabelle like that. Even he admitted how big a selfish dick Bill can be sometimes. I couldn't avoid his soft reprimand for the name-calling, though. Apparently, that wasn't mature. I disagreed. I thought the delivery was eloquent.

But really, he—and Sara, who was chirping in the background—was more interested in what's happening between Garrett and me. I'm sure they think my moving on would solve their problems, that all I need is a new man in my life to forget how terribly Bill treated me.

They're in for a rude awakening. I can hold on to a grudge like it's a lifeline.

Scarlet bites her bottom lip. "You should have at least gotten his number."

"For what?"

"I don't know. You could have gone out tonight."

"Yeah. 'Hey, guy I've been tormenting except for the one night we made out in the closet, you wanna be my Valentine's date?'"

"When you put it like that." She folds her arms over her chest, the move pushing up her cleavage in her little black dress. "You sure you don't want to come out to dinner with me and Shane?"

"Just the three of us at a candlelit dinner? Romantic."

"Call Dean. You know he's hiding tonight."

"Nah. He's had his fill of me. I'd rather stay home. And it's your first Valentine's with Shane, dummy." I take a bite from my chicken nugget. I need to start eating better.

Her nose scrunches up. "As long as you're not going to stalk Bill's Instagram all night."

"I've deleted him."

"You didn't! Good for you …" Scarlet's words fade, her eyes narrowing. "Because you've made a fake account to follow Isabelle's stories."

"She's far more active with her posting." And her account isn't locked down. Foolish.

Scarlet pinches the bridge of her nose. "So … what happens now with the developer guy?"

"Nothing. I'm back in Polson Falls. We've clocked in again. Ralph Wolf and Sam Sheepdog are on duty." Though there's nothing more that can be done. HG won, and the building is set to be demolished. Shirley's warned me that gestures of goodwill never pan out with these guys.

Would it be so bad to give in to temptation again?

Scarlet arches an eyebrow. "Looney Tunes? Really?"

"See?" I wave a fry at her. "This is why we're best friends."

———

"But that's why I bought the extended warranty." Helen Oates waves the pamphlet in the air as if to prove she has it. "The dishwasher is only two years old, and it keeps flooding."

"Because you've been putting regular dish soap in it," I say slowly. "You admitted to it."

"It's cheaper! And soap is soap. It shouldn't matter."

"Except it does." Did she not notice the excessive suds?

Helen's lips purse, her fingers clutching the handles of her chunky purse. "Ned said the warranty would cover me for five years, so I would like a new dishwasher. Thank you." Those last two words come out snippy, as if to say, "We're done here. Do as I ask, minion."

My patience is running thin, and I'm not getting anywhere with this woman. "Have you called the manufacturer?"

"Yes, and they were even less helpful than you." She lifts her pointy chin. "I'd like to speak to someone who understands these things. Where's Ned?"

I glue on the widest smile I can. "I'll get him for you."

I find Ned in his office, savoring the last of his traditional peanut butter sandwich. "Helen Oates is insisting to speak to you about a warranty on the dishwasher that's not working properly because she is using dish soap. She's not getting the answer she wants from me."

"Mrs. Oates ..." He nods to himself. "That one takes 'the customer is always right' to a new level. Trudy hated dealing with her."

"Trudy and I have some things in common."

He tosses the crusts into the garbage can.

"I'm sorry. I tried. I don't know how you're gonna make her happy."

He rises slowly from his chair. "Don't you worry. I've been selling appliances for sixty years now. I've seen and dealt with it all."

"Okay. Well, I'll just hang out here for a bit, so I don't club her over the head with her own purse."

"Now *that*, I haven't seen yet." His soft chuckles trail behind him as he shuffles out.

I linger in the office, using the time to boil the kettle for herbal tea and tidy up loose papers, my mind wandering to the engagement party, as it has repeatedly. There's been no sign of Garrett's SUV in the parking lot next door. As far as I can tell, he hasn't been back to Polson Falls since the meeting with the mayor, and that was more than a week ago.

Have thoughts of me crossed his mind?

Does he regret what happened between us?

Because I'd be lying if I said I did.

On impulse, I rifle through the receipts in the filing cabinet until I spot his name in Ned's scrawl. His number is below. Without thinking too much about it, I punch it into my phone's Contacts. "Never know when you may come in handy."

The door chimes with a new customer—or one less, though something tells me Mrs. Oates will pin Ned down until closing if it means she gets what she wants.

I collect my steaming mug and saunter out to the showroom floor.

Speak of the devil, and he shall appear.

My heart skips a beat at the sight of Garrett. He's in refrigerator alley again, inspecting the inside of a mid-range model. He has no coat on today, which makes me think he walked over from next door. His gray dress pants and fern-green crewneck sweater hug his body in all the right places, highlighting those broad shoulders and sculpted torso I admired beneath my fingertips.

I creep up behind him, ignoring the itch to touch him again. "When I hexed the fridge I sold you, I didn't think it would work so fast."

He spins around, his eyes bright and full of humor. "Justine. Good to see you."

"I know." I take a long sip of my tea.

He watches me intently before reaching up to check the tag dangling down, his fingertip skimming mine. "Licorice root. You like that flavor, huh?"

"I was that kid who fished out every black jelly bean, even though no one else would eat them."

He hums, as if my answer says something about me he'd guessed. "You didn't stick around."

I assume he's referring to the engagement party. "I'd say I made my presence known."

"That, you did." He grins. "How was the rest of your night?"

"Uneventful. No closets. You?"

"I didn't stay long. The night got boring very fast."

Interesting. Would he have stayed had I? But I shouldn't be asking questions like these. It'll cause confusion. "So ... what brings you to refrigerator alley again?"

"Well, first, *this*." He holds out a small brown paper bag.

With a curious frown, I collect it and peer inside. "Todd's soup." A inhale confirms it. I would know that blend of secret spices anywhere. I can't keep the soft moan from escaping, earning Garrett's smile.

"You said he cut you off."

"Completely uncalled for." I think Todd's been hiding from me ever since, pushing Dillon to man the counter and take out the trash. Or it could be the angry customers he's hiding from. *Everything* isn't about me. "Does Todd know this wasn't for you?"

"I neglected to mention that part."

"I see. Smuggled soup, then."

"You're opposed?"

"Absolutely not." I try to ignore how my chest fills with warmth at his efforts. "What was your other reason for coming?"

He holds up a beige folder tucked under his arm. "I have a business proposal for your boss."

Apprehension slides down my spine. "*Another* one?" Is Garrett coming back around for another attempt to buy Murphy's so he can close it down?

"No. Not like that at all. The condos going in next door will need appliances. Everything. Washer, dryer, oven, range, refrigerator"—he points to the one he was inspecting—"and I'm hoping I can work out a contractor deal with you guys to supply them."

"*Us*?" This was unexpected. "But you're HG. You must have connections with the manufacturers. Why wouldn't you go to them?" Or frankly, Home Depot or any other big chain that would give him a better rate given their buying power. And on that many appliances, the difference would be significant. "What are you up to?"

He snorts. "Suspicious much?"

"When it comes to *you*? Always."

"I thought we were past this."

"Why would you think that?" I steal a glance over my shoulder. Ned's still handling Helen Oates. Just in case his hearing aid is dialed up, I lower my voice. "What? Just because we fucked around I'm suddenly going to trust you? Think you're a good guy?"

"I *am* a good guy." He sounds offended. "I spent all night helping you hide."

"No, you're just good at a few key things." *Very* good.

He bites the inside of his cheek in thought. "It's just a gesture of goodwill on behalf of HG to the surrounding community. Plus, I figured Ned might appreciate the business."

Ned's jaw will drop at this opportunity. He was just complaining the other day about profits. But the goodwill part ... does Garrett think I'm a fool? "Let me guess, you buy all those appliances through Ned and then Ned—and by extension, me—can't say anything bad about your project without looking like a giant hypocrite."

A slow, smug smile unfurls on Garrett's lips. "In your case, I think that ship has sailed, don't you?"

"Au contraire. The ship is coming back around to pick me up. I warned you, what happened in New York stays there. Wait, is this why you were so nice to me? Was *that* a gesture of goodwill too?"

"This is business. You and me, we're *not* business. We don't have to play this game anymore."

"There is no 'you and me.' And I'm not going to be a part of your community outreach program." I can't believe he thinks I'd fall for this!

The bell chimes as Helen Oates exits, whatever arrangement Ned made with her seemingly satisfactory. He moseys over, a curious look furrowing his brow. "I see the big developer is back. Is there something we can help you with today?" I don't think Ned's capable of kicking someone out of his store, but he isn't his usual cheerful self with the greeting.

Garrett studies me another long moment before shifting his attention. "There is." He holds up his folder. "I have a new proposition for you that I think you might be interested in."

"Is that so." Ned's soft gray eyes flicker to the folder, studying it a moment, before they shift to me. "Are we going to like it?"

This decision is up to Ned. I can't dictate how he runs his business. "I don't know, but *I'm* going to take out the trash. Seems this place has become too welcoming for the *rats*," I throw over my shoulder.

"Enjoy the soup!" Garrett hollers back.

Chapter Twenty

"LuAnne Phillips got caught doin'" the hokeypokey with the owner in the back of his paint store. If you know what I mean." Dottie waggles her eyebrows as she brushes clippings off her six-year-old customer's neck.

With Dottie, there's only one thing it could ever mean. I know it, her boss Ann Margaret knows it, and by the disapproving scowl on the mother whose son is getting a haircut, she knows it too.

I laugh around the Tootsie Roll pop I fished out of the kids' treat bowl. "It's my favorite dance. Almost did it myself a few weekends ago."

"You should be doin' it *every* weekend at your age." Dottie drags the black cape off her customer, shaking out the last of the trimmed hair. "Okay, Benny, you are all done, and boy, do you look handsome. You're going to be a real lady-killer when you're older. Go on and get yourself a lollipop." She taps his nose before he hops down.

If Scarlet were here, she'd grumble about how her mother makes *everything* about physical appeal and sex. I can't blame her. Having Dottie as a mother, with all the drama that came along with her, couldn't have been easy. She had Scarlet when she was just fifteen—a knockout even back then, based on old pictures. And she used those good looks and charm to lasso plenty of men around town over the years. Some of those men had gold bands on their ring fingers.

But Dottie isn't my mother, and I find her sordid humor, morally gray life choices, and her complete lack of inhibition refreshing. She's not a mean-spirited woman; she just focuses more on what she wants, rather than what's acceptable by society's standards.

I miss having her around the house for those brief few weeks after Brillcourt burned down and before she moved into her new apartment. It's why I make a point of stopping by the little hole-in-the-wall hair salon every so often.

"So, how are things going with the fire chief?" According to Scarlet, Dottie's never been good at any sort of relationship, short or long term. It's been years since she had a meaningful one, too preoccupied with keeping her seat warm at the local pub. But her barfly days seem to be waning. The Route 66 bartender was worried enough to ask Scarlet if something had happened to her. He hadn't seen her around town.

Turns out, something did happen: sobriety, and a kindly widower who treats her better than any of the other men she's invited into her life.

"Oh, they're going." She winks, smoothing her hands over her fitted leopard-print skirt. It's a rare thing to see Dottie in anything that doesn't hug her curves and show off some cleavage. "What about you? I read that article in the newspaper. You're locking horns with that big developer, huh?"

We almost locked other body parts, but I know not to utter a word about that to Dottie—it'd be spread across Polson Falls by nightfall.

The doorbell chimes before I can answer, and in strolls Shane's eleven-year-old son, Cody, and his mother, Penelope.

More aptly named the Red Devil, not only for her gorgeous mane of red locks but for the many years of hell she put Scarlet through. It's only been a few months since she's eased up, after her jealous rage over Scarlet nearly cost her everything. Things have been awkwardly civil since then, and Scarlet has made me promise not to provoke her with my flippant remarks.

"Well, look at what the cat dragged in! Did you grow since I last saw you?" Dottie's sultry smile softens, her eyes tentative as they flicker between Cody and Penelope.

Cody's cheeks flush as he pushes a hand across his forehead. "I dunno. Maybe?"

"I think you did. And it looks like you could use another haircut."

"Yeah, I liked how you did it last time, when my dad brought me."

"Shorter on the sides, though," Penelope says in a crisp voice. *Oh*, she must have hated hearing that Shane brought Cody here, to the woman who so long ago had an affair with her father.

"*Mom.*" Cody scowls at her. "Even Dad said it looked better how she did it. I want it like that again. Just like *that*."

"As long as your father approves." Penelope huffs. "Fine. Let's get this over with." *So we can get out of this dive,* she doesn't have to say out loud. Her sneer at the '80s perm poster on the wall says it for her. I will give her credit, though—the fact that she brought Cody here, to the woman she spent decades blaming for her father's infidelities, shows she can put her son's wishes over her bitterness, even if she's going to bitch about it.

Kind of like I am willing to stand up for my brother at his wedding, despite having to look Bastard Bill in the eye.

"Hey, Justine." Cody smiles shyly at me on his way to the chair.

"Hey, kid." I've never gone out of my way to spend time with anyone's child, but this one, I like. "When are we going to have a Spider-Man rematch?"

Cody grins. "Next weekend?"

"Good, 'cause I've been practicing with Dean, and I'm gonna kick your ass."

He giggles. He *always* giggles when I curse in front of him, which, according to Scarlet, is way too much.

"He's *eleven*." Penelope shoots me a pointed glare before heading to a chair in the waiting area.

With her back to me, I mouth a quick prayer while pretending to sprinkle holy water to expel the demon, earning Dottie's snort-cough.

"Speaking of that developer, he came by here the other day." Ann Margaret, the owner of Elite Cuts and a saint for putting up with Dottie, collects her customer's hair between two fingers before snipping at it. "I can't recall his name."

"A silver fox with a full mustache?" I may no longer be a fan of Uncle Richard, but I can appreciate a well-aged man.

"No. Younger fellow, *very* handsome."

"Garrett?" *Here*?

She snaps her fingers. "That was his name."

"Where was I?" Dottie sounds offended that she missed him.

"At lunch."

"Well, dang. I'm always up for meeting the attractive new man in town." She winks at Cody as she collects her scissors.

"What'd he come in for?"

"A trim."

My eyebrows climb halfway up my forehead. There is no way that guy would let a no-frills Polson Falls salon take scissors to his hair. Or so one would think. "Are you sure it was Garrett?"

"Can't forget a name like that. Classy, ya know? Like Rhett Butler or Beau Bridges."

"Yeah, that's him. Classy." Fingering women in linen closets.

"I think he also wanted to introduce himself and do a bit of damage control after all that hubbub in the paper. I heard he's been in and out of half the businesses in Polson Falls, buying everything he can to support the locals."

"Sounds familiar." To say Ned was flabbergasted by the proposal Garrett made would be an understatement. Ned told him—and me—that he'd have to think about it. Business is business, and if he's going to have to contend with a year of noisy construction beside him, at least he can benefit from it in some way.

"You sure he isn't runnin' for mayor?" Dottie chuckles. "Wouldn't that be nice. Get rid of that frumpy Gump and have an attractive politician in town again." It's a delayed reaction, but I see the moment her words play back in her head and her eyes dart toward Penelope.

Whose father was the mayor of Polson Falls when he fell into Dottie's amorous arms.

Penelope peers up from her phone to spear Dottie with a flat glare before smoothing over her expression with practiced skill. "He's trying to make friends around town so when his project goes to the council for approval, the public won't gang up against him." She offers the bit of information as if dangling scraps in front of a dog.

I'm the dog, and I'm begging for scraps. "What do you mean? I didn't think there was going to be any approval process."

"There wasn't supposed to be." She smirks, clearly enjoying being the holder of valuable information. "A friend in the permits office told me that the engineer's drawings needed a revision that puts the height six inches higher than the town ordinance allows. So now HG needs to file for a height variance, and *that* needs to be approved by the council."

"In a council meeting." That the public can attend. The hamster inside my head speeds up on its wheel. "Are there any loopholes? Ways they can get around it?"

"Nope. Not unless they completely change the design of the building." Penelope shakes her head with certainty. She was the mayor's daughter, after all. She knows these things.

A slow smile stretches across my face. "So it's not over yet."

Penelope laughs, a rare sound. "I wouldn't get too excited. The council wants this development to go through. They'll approve it."

And when they do, there is a hundred percent chance that Shirley will rally the troops for an appeal to jam them up.

This is big—huge!—news. I need to pass along the information, stat.

A thought strikes me. "When did you hear about this?" Was it before or after Garrett spent a Saturday night ingratiating himself with me?

"A few weeks ago."

Heat flushes through my body. "That son of a bitch. Goodwill, my ass." I knew there had to be more to that generous appliance deal for Ned. Who knows how else he's going to try to buy the locals.

Cody giggles.

If I weren't already burning inside, Penelope's glare would set me on fire.

Chapter Twenty-One

"WHAT ARE you in the mood for tonight? Shepherd's pie or chicken cacciatore?" Scarlet scans the grocery store receipt from the passenger side of my Hyundai as I take Main Street toward home.

"Neither. Both those need an hour to bake. It's frozen thin-crust pizza night. Twelve minutes."

"Oh right." She frowns at the clock on my dash before stretching her arms over her head with a groan. "Or we could go to the firehouse. Shane said they've had a huge vat of Chief Cassidy's franks and beans recipe simmering all day."

"Hanging out with a bunch of grown men who stuffed themselves with beans and sausage. Sounds like fun. Besides, you just want to sneak into the gear closet with Shane to play with *his* frank and beans."

"Speaking of fondling people in closets." She gives me a knowing look.

"That's not happening again. At least, not with Garrett."

Scarlet shakes her head. "Justine, come on! You don't even care if they tear down that building, do you?"

"That's not the point. It's the principle."

"No, it's your stubborn Irish blood and need to win. That

building is brown and ugly and old. There's graffiti all over the side."

"All cosmetic."

"You've seen the proposed design. It's *nice*. It might even bring this side of Main Street back to life."

"Yeah, fine, it is," I admit. The *Tribune* finally reported a positive piece on the Revive Project, with concept pictures. Shirley was furious, declaring Colin dead to her and refusing to so much as glance at the article. "But I can't just let it go."

"Why not?"

"Because ... because ... *then* what?"

"Gee, I don't know. Then you hook up with the rich, hot property developer who's totally into you?"

"I mean, what do I tell Shirley and Vicki? I can't be out there petitioning and plotting with them one day, only to wave the white flag the next. Especially now that we know it's not over yet. They need me." I pause, a thought striking. "Unless it's a feigned retreat." I've been sitting on the news I learned from Penelope for days—unsure of how to approach Garrett the next time I see him, whether I want to play clueless or confront him. But a third option is forming in my mind: toying with him, letting him think what happened between us in New York is bleeding into Polson Falls, that we *can* separate business from pleasure, and then, wham!

He finds out he's being played.

That's not a bad plan either.

"The fact that you're referencing war tactics is slightly alarming. And all for *that*." She throws her hand toward the windshield as we approach the brick building, dim except for the CornerMart and the dull glow of lights from two apartments above.

Including the one above the butcher shop.

Garrett's here.

My pulse races as my adrenaline kicks in.

I make a last-minute hard left, cranking my steering wheel toward the laneway between Todd's and Ned's buildings. The back end of my car slides on the slick pavement. Scarlet squeals as we regain traction seconds before plowing into a snowbank. "*Are you crazy?*"

"I just need to make a quick pit stop." I park beside Garrett's SUV, leaving the car running. "Be back in two minutes."

"Where are you—"

Scarlet's question cuts off when I slam the door shut and rush to the stairs. They're wooden and slippery, and I nearly wipe out as I scramble up them.

With a deep inhale, I knock and hold my breath.

Heavy footfalls sound on the other side, and a second later, Garrett fills the doorway. "Justine." He pushes a hand through his mane, sending it into sexy disarray. "I wasn't expecting you."

"Most people aren't," I croak, my tongue suddenly parched. He looks casual tonight, in a plain white T-shirt that frames his collarbone and neck and gray track pants that hang low on his hips, highlighting the asset hiding beneath.

That closet fiasco may have been the dumbest thing I've ever done.

I edge into the apartment without an invitation. My shoulder brushes against his torso on the way past, sending an electric current through my limbs.

Dean and Shane weren't exaggerating about the sad state of these apartments. The original golden wood flooring is worn down to unfinished, gray in spots, several kitchen cupboard doors hang off only one hinge, and the light fixtures are all naked bulbs. The cheap white fridge I sold him looks out of place simply for the fact that it's new and clean.

"Love what you've done with the place." I kick off my winter boots, shed my coat, and stroll to the living room on the other side, as if welcomed in. It's a large space and marginally better on this side, a plush charcoal futon and a live edge coffee table in the center of an otherwise barren room. In the far corner, a small flat-screen sits on a stand, playing tonight's NHL game. From here, I have a clear view into the bedroom. It's empty, save for the few shirts and pants that hang in the closet and a leather duffel bag on the floor.

Everything is temporary and portable.

"It does the trick when I'm too tired to drive home."

"Which Stavro brother lived here, do you think?" I eye the window ahead. Was this the unit that inspired the Pulitzer Prize winner's drunken prose?

"No idea. Never gave it any thought."

Loose papers are scattered across the coffee table, and a bottle of beer sits next to his laptop. "Burning the midnight oil?"

He checks his watch. "It's only seven, but I'm sure I will be." He slides past me and slaps his laptop shut.

"Hiding something?" Like an application for a variance approval?

"I have nothing to hide."

Liar. I watch him collect and shut file folders, his T-shirt clinging to the web of muscle across his back.

"Are we clocked in or out tonight? 'Cause I have to admit, I'm having a hard time keeping up with Justine and Ralph."

"Let's call it a dinner break."

"In that case, there's a cold beer in the fridge if you want."

"I have somewhere I need to be. But thanks." Now that I'm standing in the same room as Garrett, I could take pleasure in finding ways to poke at him all night, but Scarlet will kill me if I leave her in an idling car for too long.

He drops his body into the futon with a groan, leaning back. "You say truce, and yet why do I feel like you're here to bust my balls about something you think I've done?"

"Guilty conscience?"

"I have nothing to feel guilty about." He takes a long swig of his beer, his focus on the game. "Is Ned still considering my offer, or did you somehow convince him it'd be a bad idea?"

"Ned's a grown man who can make his own decisions. You can ask him. If you have time, that is. You know, given you're so busy, running around town, ingratiating yourself with everyone.

Getting cuts from the local '80s hair salon." I sidle up behind the futon and comb my fingers through his hair—because I can't help myself from touching him. It's as soft as I remember it. "Ann Margaret did a decent job."

A deep hum sounds in his throat. "That feels good."

"What, this?" I rake my fingers through a second time.

"Yeah. Keep doing that. Just like that." He sinks farther back, his legs splaying, giving my imagination a mouthwatering view. "How did you know I went there?"

"People talk."

"And what'd you say? Wait, let me guess … how I'm not such a bad guy after all." He tips his head to meet my gaze, his Adam's apple jutting out. "How you're too stubborn to admit you like me, but you know you do."

"Is that so?" Unable to stop myself, I reach down to trace the sharp point in his neck with my fingertip.

It bobs with a hard swallow beneath my touch. "And how many times you've caught yourself thinking about that Saturday night."

"About how good I looked in that red dress? Trust me, I think about that *all the time*." I drop my hands to his shoulders, taking a moment to admire their shape before my thumbs dig into his tense muscles, kneading at the knots. I used to do the same for Bill after a tough day. It always ended with me straddling him, sans clothes.

Garrett groans, and I feel it inside.

"Oh wait, I remember now. You mean, when you took advantage of a drunk and vulnerable woman."

"*You* kissed *me*, remember?"

"I had no choice. It was life or death."

His chuckle stirs my blood. "Okay, Justine, if that's what you need to tell yourself. But *I* remember every second of that night. I remember the sounds you made, and how you felt."

"Oh yeah?" I lean forward, sliding my hands over his torso.

Angling my lips just close enough to brush against his ear, I whisper, "And how did I feel?"

A long exhale slips from his lips. "Soft ... tight ..." His voice has turned husky, and there's a noticeable ridge in his pants. "Wet."

I swallow against the surge of adrenaline his words are stirring. I had a half-baked plan when I stormed up those wooden steps—to taunt and fool him into thinking I was coming around on this business versus personal relationship, only to hit him where it hurts—but it's backfiring. The smell of his cologne and feel of his body is kicking my hormones into overdrive. Now all I want to do is climb over this furniture and straddle him, a move that won't hurt either of us.

I need to get out of here before this harebrained plan goes askew.

"I know about the height variance," I whisper, nipping at his earlobe.

A sharp hiss sails from his lips.

"And about the town council meeting." I trail the tip of my tongue along his jawline, just below his ear. "So does the granny gang." The news gave Shirley her second wind.

"Ralph lied. This isn't a dinner break."

"They're planning their attack. I've ordered them matching T-shirts." I make to pull away, but Garrett seizes my wrists, holding me in place.

"Justine." He turns to meet my gaze, fire burning in his. "It's a minor variance. Six inches." His lips brush against mine. Neither of us moves closer or farther away. "They're going to approve it."

"Probably, but then we'll appeal, and it'll have to go through the process. That could take months. Longer. And there aren't any loopholes to avoid that."

"So this is how we're going to play now. Okay." His jaw tenses but then he smiles—a devastating, full-dimpled smile—and his hands smooth over my arms. "You are so goddamn sexy when you're picking a fight that you and I both know you can't win."

He begins drawing circles around the inside of my wrist with his thumb, reminding me of that night in the linen closet, when he was exploring other parts of me.

Gooseflesh erupts over my skin. "What can I say, I'm naturally scrappy."

"Every time I think of you now, I picture you in that red dress. But you know what I haven't been able to get out of my mind since that night?" His voice has turned gravelly.

"My unprecedented wit, my giant brain ..."

He pulls me down until I'm bowed over the back of the futon and his lips can reach my neck. "What it felt like to have you come apart from the inside out, without making a sound."

My cheeks flush from want. I see what he's doing—trying to flip my seductive game around on me. "Too bad I couldn't return the favor."

"You did. All I needed was that memory and a bathroom." He releases my arms, sliding one hand down to rest on his thigh, inches away from the prominent ridge. "It's come in handy a lot."

I curse, unable to move. Watching Bill pleasure himself was one of my favorite foreplay activities. It's as if Garrett knows.

My fingers coil into fists, his T-shirt bunching beneath them. I claw at the cotton, tugging it upward, uncovering a well-defined pelvic V and cut torso that I desperately want to drag my tongue along. "Don't let me stop you now." My voice sounds hoarse, needy.

"Is that your thing?"

"It's one of my things. I have many."

Garrett's breathing is shallow as he slides a hand down into his waistband, pushing his garments aside.

For the second time since knocking on this apartment door, my mouth goes completely dry. "Jesus Christ," I whisper, unable to hide my admiration. He's perfect in *every* way.

"A six-inch building variance, Justine." He grips himself at his base and begins lazily stroking. A bead of pre-cum leaks from the tip. "Less than this."

Not even close. I've seen my fair share of naked men and have been everything from wildly impressed to supremely dissatisfied.

Garrett wins every award in the penis department.

"So? What do you think?" he whispers.

"I don't want it to fall off," I mumble, my breaths ragged, my body humming with need. I can picture climbing onto that. I can almost feel it inside me.

A car horn blasts.

Shit. Scarlet! "You need to hurry this up." He has to fall apart in front of me, to be vulnerable like I was that Saturday night.

His laughter is dark. "Sorry, I can't rush these things." His hand continues its languid pace. He may be teasing himself, but he's torturing me.

Fuck this. "I can." I clamber over the futon and drop to my knees in front of him. Shoving his hand aside, I wrap mine around his shaft, reveling in the delicious contrast of velvet-soft skin and rigid flesh against my palm.

He shudders beneath my touch, his gaze turning molten.

Garrett curses as I take him into my mouth fully, the tip of him hitting the back of my throat, the faint taste of saltiness coating my tongue.

On my way back up, I release him long enough to smile. "Did I forget to mention that I have no gag reflex?" And that I enjoy giving head? My mouth surrounds him again, and I focus on my task, gripping his base as I suck hard. Normally, I would tease him. I would slide my tongue along his underside, swirl it over his tip. I might even let it slip down into places most are too timid to venture.

There's no time for that now.

"Holy fuck," he hisses, as I drag primal sounds from him with each pass of my mouth. His fingers tangle in my hair as his hips begin to rock, sporadically at first before falling into a steady rhythm, until he's fucking my mouth in this ramshackle apartment above the butcher shop.

And I am relishing every second of it.

"Coming," Garrett chokes out a second before he spills into my mouth. I swallow everything he gives me, savoring the feel of him pulsing against my tongue as I wonder what's next for us.

Another series of angry horn blasts has me scrambling to my feet. Scarlet's fist is slamming against my steering wheel. She might leave me here.

"That's my ride. Gotta go." I rush out, grabbing my coat and jamming my feet into my boots on the way.

———

"I thought you were mad at him."

"I *am*."

Scarlet blinks several times. "You left me in the car to give the guy a blow job."

"It wasn't the plan! It just kind of happened. I went up there to toy with him, but then *he* started toying with *me*."

Scarlet smirks. "And his dick accidentally slid into your mouth?"

"Ralph's mouth."

Her lips pucker. "Looney Tunes role-playing, huh? Kinky."

"You were honking the horn like a madwoman, so really, this is all your fault." I toss a throw cushion at her.

She ducks out of the way, escaping to the kitchen where the timer for our frozen pizza dings, her laughter carrying. "Two or three pieces? Or are you full?"

"Hardy har har." I pull my phone out to check the email from Sara that came in while I was preoccupied with her cousin. It's not long before I'm groaning for another reason. "This is a nightmare!"

Scarlet emerges with a plate loaded with pizza, setting it on the coffee table before curling up cross-legged on the couch beside me. "What are you on about now?"

"The bridesmaid dress that Sara and *Isabelle* chose." I hold up my phone to show her the picture.

Scarlet cocks her head. "Okay. It's not *the worst* dress she could have chosen."

"Actually, it is."

"The lace may be a bit much, but the sage hue's nice?"

"If I want to look like a corpse." With my olive skin tone, the only shades of green I can pull off are vibrant. "But that's not the half of it."

"Okay ... what else is wrong?"

"Nothing. If you're five foot ten and willowy like Katrina and *Isabelle*. I'm five feet tall. The high neckline will make me look all boob, this hemline guarantees I have stubby legs, and what the hell is with the flared sleeves?"

Scarlet giggles. "I'm sure she wouldn't mind you having the hem shortened when you have it altered."

"Oh, that's right, it gets better. Sara says the dress doesn't come in petite sizes, but a seamstress should be able to make it work. You know why it doesn't come in petite sizes? Because no petite woman in her right mind would ever choose this dress!" I shake my phone to emphasize my annoyance. "Do you know what it'll take to alter this? The *entire thing* will need to be taken apart and put back together. It's going to cost as much as the dress itself." Which is outrageously expensive. "Plus, it's lace. That's even harder to adjust!"

"You know, my mom's a pro at altering clothes," Scarlet admits, never keen on praising Dottie, even where it's due. "She's been doing it all her life."

"Really?"

"How do you think her dresses mold to every curve on her body like they're a second skin?" She snorts. "She could make this look good on you."

"Done." A small wave of relief touches me, but bitterness follows. "I swear, this is all Isabelle's doing."

"Come on ... She's already taken Bill. Why would she go out of her way to sway Sara to pick an unflattering dress?"

I hold up the picture. "So I look like a sickly garden gnome."

Chapter Twenty-Two

"Nah. We don't need all them bells and whistles. Something like this is what I'm looking for." The man ambles to the end of the aisle to inspect the electric coil stove.

"*Psst.*" His wife hangs back, angling for my attention, waving me closer to her.

I edge over. "Yeah?"

She steals a glance his way. "I don't care about the stupid stove. I need a microwave. Can you please convince him they don't cause cancer?" she whispers. "His mother put that idea into his thick skull, and I can't beat it out, even after fourteen years of marriage. He won't let me have one."

Let her ... My teeth grind. One of *those* men. "Then buy one yourself and bring it home."

"You don't think I tried that? My parents gave me their old one. It was gone by the time I got up the next day, out on the curb."

"I would have put him on the curb along with it," I mutter before I can bite my tongue.

"Believe me, I was ready to. If we didn't have kids ..." She shakes her head. "I'm at my wit's end."

"Honey? What do ya think?" he calls out, bending over to peer into the oven. "Big enough for your roasts?"

I think I want to kick him in the ass.

"I'll see what I can do," I whisper and then stroll over. "It's standard size, so it should cover all your needs. Both yours and your wife's. And you know what goes well with it? *That.*" I point to the range-microwave combo a few units over. "That's a popular model."

He follows my finger, and scowls. "Oh, we don't need one of those."

"But didn't you say you were shopping for a range hood too?"

"Yeah, but we don't want a microwave."

"They save counter space. *Super* convenient."

"Until you got a tumor the size of a melon in your head."

I smile politely. "Sir, microwaves don't cause cancer."

"That's what these manufacturers all want us to think. Biggest money-maker out there, those radiation boxes. That and them TVs."

"You don't have a TV?"

"'Course we have a TV." He frowns. "Who doesn't have a TV?"

"Who doesn't have a microwave?"

"*We* don't, that's who." He jabs himself in the chest with his thumb. "I'm telling ya, there's been studies, back when these things first came out. But the government doesn't want anyone to know. It's all marked classified."

"Oh, you mean like the alien files."

His eyes widen. "See? You get it."

"I'm starting to." This guy is a nutjob.

The door chimes with another customer. *Thank God.*

"I'll let you and your wife discuss your decision for a few minutes." I mouth, "I tried," to the poor woman before exiting the aisle.

And plow into a solid body with an *oof.*

"I'm so sorry, I ..." My tongue stalls when I look up into Garrett's handsome chiseled face. "Oh. *You*." I take a step back to appraise him in a crewneck sweater and dark-wash jeans. Still expensive, but far more casual than his usual city chic.

The corner of his mouth kicks up. "Hi, Justine. How long has it been?"

"Can't recall." Four days, sixteen hours, thirty-six minutes since I had him in my mouth.

He studies my lips, and I know what he's imagining, because I've caught myself replaying his guttural moans and trembling body more than I'd like—while in bed, in the shower, at work. Basically, all the time.

We've crossed a forbidden line where we've both unraveled beneath the other's touch, and there's no turning back.

I clear my throat. "What are you doing here?" There's a thick manila envelope in his clutch. Ned warned me that he was taking the deal.

"I have a commitment letter and a draft contract for your boss to review."

"Don't you guys wait until closer to the end? Or at least until you have permits?"

Garrett shrugs. "Peace of mind for Ned and shows him I'm serious."

"Especially since your variance and building permits aren't approved yet."

"Yes, of course. You've caught on to my wicked plan."

He's mocking me. "Just so you know, I'll be going through that with a fine-tooth comb for any employee gag order."

"I'd expect nothing less from you. But don't worry. In this case, it's a straight-up contractor pricing contract. No gagging involved." Again, his gaze drops to my mouth. "Though that wouldn't be a problem for you."

I swallow. This is not a side I've seen of Garrett yet. I'm the crass one. He's always been so prim and proper in public.

Normally, I'd see his lewd comment and raise him tenfold, but I can't seem to find the words. "Ned's in the office."

Garrett's eyebrows furrow with concern. "You're off your game."

"I'm *not* off my game." I *so* am. "I'm just not playing *your* game." The one where we get into a verbal sparring match that ends in us meeting in the apartment upstairs over my lunch break to fuck, because things between us are escalating quickly.

"Excuse me, ma'am?" The microwave-hater peers around the corner. "We've got a couple of questions."

"Be right there." I smile at Garrett. "If there's nothing else, I need to try to sell a radioactive death box to a conspiracy theorist."

"Have fun. Wait"—he holds up a finger—"there is one thing. I'm looking for a good plumber. Do you have anyone you can recommend?"

"What for?"

He leans in as if to whisper a secret, his lips inches from my ear. "To fix a broken toilet in the temporary office."

It's the most unsexy answer, and yet a shiver runs down my spine. "Curt Shapiro."

"Curt Shapiro," Garrett repeats, watching me closely. "Nah, I'm getting to know how you work, and that was too easy. What's wrong with him?"

With a reluctant sigh, I admit, "He overcharges and fixes problems that don't exist."

He chuckles, my attempt to steer him wrong not upsetting him in the least. "Okay, do you have another name you could offer? A good one. I'd appreciate it."

With another—louder—sigh, I say, "Hank Lazarro. He's the best in the area." Turns out Shane was right—there was a clamp missing from Stuart the Second, and the manufacturer said it was on back order, so Hank built a perfect replica and had the appliance running in under an hour. "His number's on the list pinned to the wall. Go on back there and Ned'll give it to you. And make sure you tell Hank we referred you."

Garrett smiles. "That wasn't so painful, was it?"

"Excruciating."

He moves for the office, but stalls. "Oh, by the way, I negotiated a truce with Todd on your behalf."

"Why would you do that?"

He falters on his answer. "Because I'm trying to fool you into thinking I'm a good guy, so you'll back off this variance issue."

"Clearly. It's a good thing I'm not easily fooled." Again.

"Right. Either way, you're allowed to go back in there, just so long as there's no more talk about the development or him selling the property. No more guilt trips. That's his rule."

"I don't want to go back there." My stomach growls in protest.

Garrett shrugs, his back to me as he walks away. "He mentioned something about double-smoked bacon."

———

The usual garlicky fragrance is absent in the butcher shop today, replaced by a mixture of something less pungent and decidedly sweet.

I inhale as I edge in, savoring the aroma, my apprehension growing. Maybe this is a joke and Garrett is setting me up to be kicked out again.

Todd is at the counter, ringing up a customer. I can just make out his sparse, electrified hair through the spaces in the condiments.

"When's the big move to the new location?" The graying man slides his wallet from his back pocket.

"Next month. Right before the summer grilling season takes off. We'll be shut down for about a week to get everything set up."

Dieter's is moving next month? I've only been coming here since December, but it's funny how quickly routines can form and a person can cling to them. Soon, Murphy's will be by itself on the block, surrounded by construction.

"Make sure you take a flyer so you have all our new info. Store hours and all that. Might even have a website."

"Gonna be a big change for ya, after being in this place for so long."

Todd nods. "Yeah, a lot of memories here. But I sure am excited about the new refrigerators and back room."

I lurk at the corner of the barbecue sauce shelf, still unseen. "Aren't they all the same? Saws and meat hooks?"

Todd's eyes flash to me, and there's no mistaking the wariness in them. "The one here's got steps going down to it. My doctor says my forty-five-year-old knees can't handle doing those a hundred times a day anymore."

"Bet you've got the butt of a twenty-year-old, though, huh?" I quip.

Todd's face turns beet red.

"Have a good day." Waving the paper-wrapped package in the air, the customer heads out, chuckling.

"It smells different in here."

"Does it?" Todd busies himself with replenishing the stack of butcher paper. "Must be the egg bread. Bakery brought me some." He points to the far side, where a rack of the braided loaves sits.

"You brought in egg bread." Only after I harassed him for months. I wander over to get a closer look. "Are these like the ones from Confetti's?"

"Better."

My mouth makes an *O* shape. "That's a *bold* statement."

He shrugs, but I catch the way the corner of his mouth twitches. "I hear Ned's gonna supply HG with their appliances for the new condos."

"Sounds like it."

"That's not a bad thing."

Todd specifically said there was no talk of HG. Is this a test?

I take my time strolling along the perimeter of the meat counters, feigning interest. I've never given his meat display much attention. "What's that?" I tap the glass in front of a bucket of yellow sauce.

"Chicken breasts in a spicy mango marinade."

My feet falter. Scarlet loves mango, and after I left her in the car that night, I owe her one. "You know what? I'll take two of those. And a loaf of that egg bread."

Todd's eyebrows pop, but he quickly smooths them over. I've only ever bought soup and pretzel buns from him. "Coming right up." He slides on fresh gloves and grabs a plastic bag. "What's new with you?"

"Not much. Let's see ..." What's happened since he kicked me out that day? "My brother's engaged. The wedding's in May, and Bastard Bill and his new girlfriend are in the wedding party."

His hands pause mid-scoop.

"So is Garrett. Turns out he's Sara's cousin. So that's going to be a fun day."

"Sounds like it." He shakes his head. "You still volunteering over at Bonny Acres every Friday?"

"Yup. Same old there. Shirley complaining about her starved sweet tooth and Nancy being Nancy."

"She still not letting you call the numbers?"

"Not even once! What is it with her?" I let my frustration bleed into my voice. Todd and I have had *many* conversations about my Bonny Acres rival. He's the only one who's tolerated my rants for this long. As a longtime Bonny Acres volunteer, he's convinced she feels somehow threatened by my presence. "I am, like, the least intimidating person in the world."

He chuckles, and the sound chips away at my shield of caution. "She's just particular. Always has been."

"Thirty-six," I drone, mimicking Nancy's lackluster voice as my eyes skim the sign on the wall. Potato bacon. Garrett wasn't lying.

Todd notices where my attention has landed. He rests his

hands on the top of the display case. "Would you like some soup today, Justine?"

"I mean, I guess I may as well. Since I'm here."

"Yeah, since you're here." He sets to filling a Styrofoam bowl, ladling extra bacon for me.

I stifle a sigh of contentment.

All is right in the world again, even if only for a little while.

Chapter Twenty-Three

I ACCEPT a strip of clear tape from Harper and stretch to affix the string of four-leaf clovers to the corner of the ceiling. The common room of Bonny Acres bustles with residents tonight. According to Shirley's intel on my way in, it's been a busy week. Roger from 2-A smuggled in a quart of whiskey on Tuesday night. They found him naked and passed out in a wing chair on Wednesday morning. And then Crystal in 3-F accused Natasha of trying to steal away her husband, Donald.

Everyone's down here to see what happens next.

"Don't you go falling off the ladder now," Harper scolds, moving in with her arms out as if to catch me.

"Um, have you met me? I'm a pro at ladders. Comes with the territory of never being able to reach anything."

"So was my grandpappy, until he tumbled backward off one. Broke his neck right in front of me."

"That's a *fantastic* story to share at this exact moment." I shoot her a mock-severe look. "One more piece should do it."

She tears off another strip of tape and hands it to me. "So? Big plans for this weekend?"

"Sending out bridal shower invitations. My brother's getting married in May, so my mother is hosting a shower for our side of the family in Boston." The invitations are via email and a formality more than anything. Kitty called every aunt, cousin, and family friend to save the date, given the tight timing.

"Weddings in the family are always nice."

"There are exceptions."

Harper frowns. "What's wrong? Rotten brother?"

"No, amazing brother. Rotten best man. He's my ex." I stretch on one foot to slap the last piece of tape on. "And the maid of honor is the woman he cheated on me with."

Harper's frown deepens. "If that isn't a raw deal, I don't know what is."

"Tell me about it. But I survived the engagement party, and she's not coming to this shower." When my mom gave me the date, she confirmed that Isabelle very conveniently has a work function she can't get out of. "And I will be otherwise engaged and unable to attend Sara's family's shower. So that just leaves the bachelorette party and the wedding." And Christmases, for the rest of my life.

Nancy marches through the door then, hugging the wire bingo ball basket against a St. Patrick's-themed monstrosity—a green sweater smattered with clovers and leprechauns and rainbows. "She really did make one for every occasion."

"She knits them all herself."

As if sensing my attention, Nancy's gaze veers to me and narrows, except it looks more comical than threatening, the thick lenses in her glasses magnifying her eyeballs. She mutters something under her breath that can't be flattering.

The most baffling piece about her hatred for me is that I've never been outwardly mean. I've never done anything wrong.

"Back to your ex, for what it's worth, he's a damn fool for letting go of someone like you."

"See? I knew there was a reason why I liked you, Harper. You're *so* smart."

She winks.

"And kind, and beautiful, and—"

"I'm not giving you Nancy's bingo duty."

"But it would make me feel *so much* better about my breakup."

She chuckles, shaking her head.

"Fine. What about a resident vote? I think that'd be ..." My words fade as Garrett strolls into the games room of Bonny Acres. "What is *he* doing here?" Flutters stir in my insides despite my confusion.

"Who?" Harper follows my gaze.

"Garrett," I hiss, as if afraid to say his name out loud. He's got a giant white cardboard cake box in his hands.

"Oh, him. Yeah, he called earlier to see if he could visit tonight to speak to some of the residents."

"And you said yes?"

"I did." Indignation raises Harper's voice. She doesn't like being questioned. "People around here like to know their opinions matter."

"Not when that opinion is about the lackluster meal plan," Shirley chirps from a nearby table, eavesdropping. "Hurry up, Justine. We're running out of time to play."

Residents came down for some Friday night excitement, and they just might get it. What is Shirley going to do when she realizes who just walked in here? She's shrewd. What if she figures out I've crossed enemy lines? She'll turn on me like she turned on Colin. This is not good. Polson Falls and New York could collide.

I drop my voice. "He's the enemy. Pure evil."

Harper gives him a head-to-toe once-over, admiration flickering across her expression. In his plain dark-wash jeans and crewneck sweater, he could pass for any loving son or grandson coming to visit their loved one. "Don't look too evil to me."

"That's all part of the act. He loves to play the good guy, swooping in to help people. Like some sort of fairy-tale prince, saving the damsel in distress who's hiding in a library. Only the next thing that damsel knows, she's on her knees, bobbing for his apple. And what did Snow White learn about apples?"

Harper's eyebrows crawl halfway up her forehead.

I'm flustered. "Okay, I may have butchered that analogy. But I'm telling you, he's up to no good. He's here to try to buy them off, like he's been doing all around town." There's no reason for him to be here otherwise.

Garrett strolls toward us with a broad smile, earning many curious glances. Though, that may be more to do with the circumspect box in his hands. "Hi, I'm Garrett Harrington. Are you Harper?"

"That's me. It's good to meet you." She gestures toward me, still perched on the second rung of the ladder. "Sounds like you and Justine are acquaintances?"

"You could call us that." He turns to me, a wide smile taking over his face. "I had *no idea* you would be here tonight."

"Uh-huh." Todd must have told him.

His gaze flickers downward, to the fitted green sweater I chose to match the St. Patrick's Day theme tonight, then meets my eyes again. I see the humor in his.

The challenge.

"What's in the box?" I ask.

"This? Just some treats from one of my favorite bakeries. I thought the residents might enjoy them." He shrugs as if to say, "It was nothing."

"You brought a *giant* box of sugar for a room of elderly people to enjoy. Do you know how many people in here are diabetic?" My voice drips with reprimand.

His smile never wavers. "Which is why there's an assortment for various dietary needs, from celiac to diabetic to lactose intolerant."

My expression sours. "You thought of everything, haven't you?"

"That *is* very thoughtful of you, Garrett," Harper says. "But we follow a strict menu here. I'd need an ingredients list—"

"Let us live!" Shirley squawks from her spot, pounding the table with her fist.

Harper shakes her head at the outburst.

"I figured as much." Garrett sets the box on a table and fishes a printed paper from his back pocket, stretching his sweater across his fit upper body. He hands it to Harper. "Here's the full list of ingredients."

What a perfect little Boy Scout.

Harper cocks her head—a sign that she's impressed. Not much impresses her. "Well, okay then. Let me grab my glasses so I can go through these, and then we can dish some out before Shirley wages war."

He chuckles, as if that's not a plausible outcome. "Sounds good."

Harper marches away.

He looks around the room. "So this is where you spend your Friday nights before you accost innocent people at Route 66."

I climb down the ladder. There are too many ears perked and hearing aids cranked up for this conversation. "Follow me."

But he doesn't, instead wandering toward Nancy and her atrocious sweater. "Is it bingo night?"

She tucks a wayward strand of hair behind her ear. "Yes. Every Friday is bingo night."

"Oh man … I used to go with my grandmother to the bingo hall when I was young. Every Tuesday. She loved it. That was so long ago now." He pauses. "They'd let me call the numbers sometimes. That was fun."

I snort. It is *so* obvious what he's trying to do. I'm going to kill Todd.

Nancy studies Garrett, then the bingo ball cage, then Garrett again, biting her bottom lip in thought. "If you want to … I mean, if you're still here when we start …" She gestures toward the ball cage.

My mouth drops with a gasp. "Are you kidding me? I've been asking for *months* and in walks Pretty Boy, and you melt into a puddle?"

She scowls, her face burning. "You help everyone cheat. You don't take it seriously."

187

"That is incorrect. And he has never played a round of bingo in his life." I jab at Garrett's chest with my index finger. "He doesn't even have a grandmother."

Garrett laughs, as if my suggestion is absurd. "*Of course* I have a grandmother. At least I did. She passed away a few years ago."

"Oh yeah?" I step in closer until I'm forced to tip my head back to meet his stare. His delicious cologne wafts in my nostrils, but I ignore it. "How many bingo halls are there on the Upper East Side?"

A devious spark flashes in his eyes. "What's wrong? I thought you'd like having me check out this place that you recommended for Richard."

"I see what's happening here." A lie for a lie. Payback for me embarrassing him in front of his uncle and boss. He's going to sabotage my connection to Shirley.

"I don't know what you're talking about." But everything about his expression says he finds this game hilarious.

And I sense attention on us. No doubt eagle-eye Shirley is watching the showdown.

"This little act of yours?" I swirl my index finger in the air, aiming at the cake box. "Another goodwill gesture? It won't work. You can't buy these people with vegan squares."

"I just want to have a genuine conversation to hear concerns. They are Polson Falls residents, after all, and their voices matter."

I barely stifle the eye roll. "You want a genuine conversation? Really? Okay. Hey, Shirley." She's the only one he's here to see. "HG wants to hear your opinions on everything they're doing to Polson Falls."

She pauses to scrutinize him from head to toe before turning back to her cards. "Let's see those desserts first. Then maybe I'll talk to the harbinger of destruction. *If* I feel like it." She's negotiating like a prisoner being pumped for valuable information.

Folding my arms, I smile wide at Garrett. "You heard the lady. Let them eat cake."

———

Shirley sets her cards down in front of her, her sharp gaze dissecting Garrett across the table. "A run and a set, deadwood equals two."

"Nice." Garrett tosses his hand into the pile. "Have to say, I haven't played rummy in a while."

"I can tell. You stink." She collects and shuffles.

The fact that Garrett had any clue how to play in the first place shocked me. By the way Shirley's pencil-drawn eyebrow arched when he asked her to deal him in, it surprised her too. They've played five rounds, Garrett listening quietly while Shirley won each game in between mouthfuls of cheesecake and berating him for all that's wrong with the direction Polson Falls is heading, including his project.

I've sat quietly, the enthralled spectator.

"I know what you guys did, taking advantage of a loophole. You and Gump. How much did it cost you to grease that inspector's pockets?"

"I assure you, there was no greasing of any pockets," Garrett says calmly.

"Everything Gump touches is greasy," she mutters. "And you've got buckets of money to spend on that sort of thing."

He leans back in his chair, folding his hands on the table in front of him. "Between you and me, I don't like the guy, but your town elected him, so I need to play nice. It benefits me to do that. But it also benefits you."

She deals another hand, throwing his cards at him. "How do you figure?"

"Because I can be an ally."

She snorts. "Is that what you call being an ally? Tearing down our history? No, thank you."

"We have a fair amount of influence, which means there are things we can do." He collects his cards, studying his hand. "Like that park, for example. You said you've been asking the town to improve it for years and they've done nothing?"

"Gump claims they've got no money."

"Like you said, HG has buckets of it." He smirks. "So what if we revitalized it?" He swaps a card out and collects a fresh one. "Replaced the trees and park benches, put in a better playground. Add a few gardens and walking paths. And a plaque to honor your local poet. Hugh Whitman, is it? How does that sound?"

Shirley tosses away a card. "That sounds like a bribe."

"It's only a bribe if there are strings attached."

"I've heard this song and dance before. A developer pulled the same stunt over in Rottersburg. Promised to replace an old bridge people been complaining about for years and got approved for their big condominium project because of that promise. The condo's been finished for five years, and guess what's not fixed yet?"

"The bridge. RGI Corp. Yeah, I heard about that one." Garrett shifts his cards around. "That's not how HG operates."

"That's how all you guys operate. You see wrecking balls and dollar signs, and you get erections." She slaps a throw-off card onto the table. "What about your Revive Project? No strings tied to that town meeting?"

"None. I'm there to request approval on a small variance. Barely six inches"—his gaze cuts to me, reminding me of the last time we had this conversation—"and the council will approve it."

"There are some things Gump can't squirm his way out of, and you and I both know it. Due process and all. Isn't that why you've been out, kissing babies and enticing people with park benches?"

The corners of Garrett's mouth twitch, but he schools his expression. "Like I said, this isn't a bribe. I'm going to revitalize that park, anyway."

"I'll believe that when I see it," she mutters.

"You *will* see it. And you've seen my plans for my building—"

"Haven't, and I'm not interested." She smiles at him, like she's about to tell him something she knows he doesn't want to hear.

"An appeal from the public will stall your project for months, maybe more, depending on how hard we fight. And I've got a lot of fight left in me. Condominiums do not belong on our town's Main Street. End of story."

His jaw tenses, the first sign that he's frustrated with her stubbornness. "An appeal isn't ideal, no. Not for me and not for the town's residents, who will be looking at a boarded-up building, or worse, a fenced-off hole in the ground, for longer than necessary. I don't think that's what you want for your town either."

The two of them stare at each other over their respective hands, one measuring the other as a viable adversary.

I can't help but admire how Garrett is handling himself.

"Five minutes until bingo," Nancy drones, shaking her cowbell five times.

Shirley folds her cards. "I think that's enough politicking for one night. I'll see you at the meeting, developer."

He sets the cards neatly on the pile, taking this for what it is— a dismissal. "Thank you for giving me some of your valuable time."

She grunts in answer but then after a moment adds, "The sweets were a nice touch, I'll give you that much."

He smiles, climbing from his seat. "I can't take all the credit. That was Justine's idea."

My jaw drops at his blatant lie. "It was *not*. You little—"

"Have a good night, ladies." He strolls away.

I meet Shirley's probing look. "I had no idea he was coming tonight," I say, before darting across the room. I catch up to Garrett before he slides out the door, grabbing hold of his arm. "You've turned Todd against me. Congratulations." I mentioned Shirley's sweet tooth to him more than once.

Amusement crinkles the corners of Garrett's eyes as they drift over my features. "What are you talking about? You and Todd are on speaking terms again because of me."

"And what was that bullshit you shoveled back there? A plaque to commemorate the poet? *Really?*"

"I thought it would be a nice touch." He mock frowns. "Unless you think memorializing four murdered bootleggers in a family park would be more appropriate."

"Your plan won't work. You can't buy Shirley off."

Sincerity smooths over his features. "I'm not trying to buy her off. That park is a two-minute walk from my project, so it benefits the residents for HG to invest and make it a selling feature. But more importantly, I'm trying to show Shirley that HG doesn't have to be the enemy here, and that if we work together, we can do good for the community. *You* should help her see that."

"Me?" I snort. "Do you realize how stubborn she is?"

"Almost as stubborn as you?"

"*Way* worse."

"I don't think that's possible." His eyes roam my face. "She seems to like you a lot, though."

"Because up until now, she thought I wasn't an idiot, and that's rare." I dare steal a look back over my shoulder to where Shirley sits, watching us. She's going to have questions about this. My stomach rolls at the idea of being grilled by her, of having to admit that, yes, in fact, I am an idiot.

"In case you were planning on stopping by the apartment tonight—" Garrett's voice suddenly so close to my ear startles me, causing me to jump back.

"I wasn't."

He smirks, pulling himself up to his height again.

"This is my turf. You can't just come in here and stir things up like this."

"Two minutes!" Nancy rings her cowbell twice.

"Oh hey, Nancy," Garrett calls out. "Unfortunately, I need to drive home tonight, but it means *so much* to me that you offered." His grin is pure smugness. "More than you could ever know."

My teeth grind.

She ducks from my glare and busies herself with handing out the last of the bingo cards.

"You're taking your buckets of money and big-dick energy

back to New York, are you?" A flicker of discontent stirs that he won't be around tonight for me to spar with later.

Not for any other reason.

"Yeah. And then I'll be tied up with meetings in Philadelphia. You won't have to deal with me *stirring things up* for a week or two, *at least*."

A week or two, at least? My disappointment swells, but I swallow against it. I don't want to feel this way for him. "Don't rush back."

"Maybe I will. This is turning out to be a lot more fun than I expected." Reaching up to give my shoulder a squeeze, he steps around me and strolls away.

I hand out the bingo daubers in a daze until Shirley beckons me over with two fingers. "You're getting to know that developer well." Her shrewd gaze dissects me. "What was that about over there?"

"It's just a game we're playing."

"A game?"

"He likes getting under my skin."

"Huh ..." Her eyes narrow, as if she doesn't believe me. "Handsome fellow."

"I hadn't noticed," I lie, earning her derisive snort. He's not just handsome. He's consuming my every thought.

And now his words linger. "That offer to spend money and fix up the park, though, that sounds like a sweet deal."

"Don't buy any of that." She waves off my words. "It's all smoke and mirrors. I can see right through him. Remember what I said about these guys saying and doing whatever it takes to get what they want."

"Slick as sin, I remember."

"That's right. Fools fall for his type. And you are not a fool."

"I am not a fool," I echo.

Something flickers in her wrinkled expression. "One bastard in your life was enough, right?"

I realize what that was—worry. The prickly Shirley is worried about me getting hurt. That makes me smile. "Don't worry, I see through him too."

"Time to start," Nancy drones, spinning the bingo balls.

Shirley yanks the lid off her bingo dauber. "So, who's winning this game between you two, anyway?"

"I am. Naturally," I say with as much confidence as I can muster.

Though I'm not sure I believe it anymore.

Chapter Twenty-Four

"COME ON, give it to me raw. Can you make this better?" I stand in our living room with my arms held out, the sage lace horror hanging from my body in all the wrong places.

Dottie twists her lips in thought as she circles me, pinching the fabric here and there. The outfit she arrived in—leggings, baggy heather-gray sweater, and messy bun—is far more casual than her usual formfitting dresses, stilettos, and coiffed hair, but this toned-down version is refreshing. "I can't make it worse. You're wearing a doily."

"Oh *God*," I wail, throwing my head back. When Sara handed me the dress bag at the bridal shower and waited for me to open it, it took every stitch of decency within me to feign excitement. It helped that my mother stood behind her, spearing me with a warning glare that promised disownment if I dared speak the truth.

"*Mom.*" Scarlet scowls from her spot on the couch, a stack of math tests to grade.

"What? She asked for the truth." Dottie collects my hands in hers. "But don't you worry, my darling. By the time I'm done with this, you'll be turning more heads than the bride."

"I don't think that's the look she's going for." Scarlet shifts back to grading.

"Well, that's the only look I know how to do." Dottie winks at me. Sliding on a stylish pair of glasses, she begins tucking pins along my shoulder seam with the same ease she takes scissors to hair. "When's this wedding?"

"Four weeks. Is this doable?"

She waves a dismissive hand. "Plenty of time to get this dress perfect. Are they ready for their big day?"

"They're getting there. It sounds like Sara's got it all under control." Most of the conversation at the shower was about the planning. The invitations went out right after the engagement party, they've picked their meal, and booked their honeymoon. A string quartet will play for the ceremony, and they booked the live band that was supposed to play at the wedding that canceled and vacated the spot Sara and Joe nabbed.

When I brought up the bachelorette party, Sara informed me it would be in two weeks in New York, and that Isabelle had taken care of it. I just need to show up, i.e., I've been cut out of the planning. Then she patted my knee, her eyes twinkling as she whispered, "The guys are doing this sophisticated sommelier-guided tequila tasting throughout the city, and Garrett will be there."

I bit my tongue against the urge to tell her that the sommelier is a frat-boy named Matt whose expertise was earned over many years of passing out drunk at bars, and that the only tequila they'll be tasting will be while watching women get naked, because that's the only type of bachelor party Bill would ever plan. At least, that's the Bill I knew. Has Isabelle changed him that much?

And as if I care that Garrett will be there.

"Guess what their wedding favors are." I pause. "Boxes of macarons flown in from Sara's favorite patisserie in Paris."

Dottie whistles. "Someone's not countin' pennies."

"Yeah, they deal in hundred-dollar denominations. You should see her parents' penthouse. They're art aficionados. They have rocks that are worth more than my entire existence."

"Any single, rich relatives I need to meet?" Her eyebrows waggle.

"I'm pretty sure her uncle Richard is—"

"*No.*" Scarlet glares at me.

"Oh, honey, of course I'm only kidding. I would never do that to Griffin. He's such a sweet man." More quietly, Dottie adds, "But in case it doesn't work out with him, who's this rich uncle?"

"The silver fox HG developer I picked a fight with."

Dottie frowns. "Wait, the HG guy is Sara's uncle?"

"And Garrett's, the one Justine's pretending she doesn't want to screw," Scarlet says.

"Scar!" That's the last thing I need cycling around town, and with Dottie on the seat, the pedals move fast.

"What? You've been a bear since he left."

"That's not true."

Scarlet gives me a flat look.

Okay, it's mildly true. Last week wasn't so bad. This week has dragged, though. I took a lot of trips to the dumpster behind Murphy's—to toss an apple core, one Styrofoam soup bowl, a candy wrapper—and each time I looked out on the empty spot in the parking lot, my frustration ballooned.

He teased the idea of coming back, just for me. Philadelphia is only an hour away. Why couldn't he come back to Polson Falls even once? The truth is, he could have if he wanted to. That reality sank my mood lower each time, and Shirley's warning echoed in my ear. This is all a game for him, a means to getting what he wants in the end.

Dottie gasps. "Has something happened between you two?"

"*No.*"

Scarlet grunts.

A hard knuckle wraps on the door, interrupting this dangerous conversation. "Excuse me, did someone call about a fire?" Shane strolls in wearing full firefighter gear. Every time he's in the area, he makes a point of stopping in. I think it's to witness Scarlet's cheeks redden when she sees him in uniform.

I jerk my chin toward her. "That one's loins are burning. Better come quick."

Dottie barks with laughter at the double entendre as Shane crosses the room to plant a kiss on Scarlet's lips. "Hey, babe. Was in the neighborhood."

Dean lingers at the door.

"There he is. How's my big boy doin' tonight?" Dottie winks at him.

He grins, his cheeks flushing. "Hey, Dottie." His gaze shifts to me. "That's … uh … not like the other one."

"No shit. It's terrible."

"Not for long," Dottie hums as she keeps pinning.

"Hey, did you give that doctor a call?" Dean was waffling the last time I bugged him about it.

"We've talked a few times." Nothing about his tone hints at any excitement, but that's Dean. He's casual about *everything*.

I school my expression. "Did you ask about your prostate?"

"Oh, you need that checked out, love?" Genuine concern mars Dottie's face. "Because I know a thing or two—"

"Oh my God," Scarlet groans, covering her face with her hands.

Dean laughs, his cheeks flushing again. He's so fun to embarrass. "I'm seeing Meera on Saturday."

"*Oh.*" Dottie clues in that this is not a medical concern. "I'm sure she'll give you a thorough once-over."

Their radios crackle with dispatch, beckoning the men.

With a quick kiss against Scarlet's forehead, Shane peels away, and the guys head out.

Dottie sighs wistfully, moving to the next seam, murmuring more to herself, "What a night that was."

Chapter Twenty-Five

WARMTH from the sun grazes my cheeks as I step out the back door of Murphy's. Spring officially landed in our ugly feet calendar, and temperatures have soared since, reaching into the low seventies. The smell of thawed soil and mud permeates the air.

I hop over puddles, intent on my forgotten wallet in my car, until I spot Garrett's SUV. My pulse quickens, even as I temper my excitement with the reality that he's been gone for weeks, that he didn't rush back for me.

An oversize white truck is parked nearby, and someone's propped open the heavy door that leads into the basement. Male voices carry up from the depths.

I trudge closer to the gaping hole, the wooden steps leading down narrow and steep.

"… shoring there, there … all over there."

"But it's doable?" Garrett asks, his raspy voice stirring my nerves.

"The way this place was built? Definitely."

"How much extra are we talking, ballpark?"

"Gotta run numbers, but if I had to guess …" The man's voice trails as he peers up to see me standing in the doorway. "Hello?"

Another man steps into view, and a second later, Garrett is there.

My heart skips a beat. "Don't mind me. Just here to see the murder site."

"I'll give you a call later, John." At least Garrett doesn't sound angry that I interrupted them.

With firm handshakes, the burly man and his lanky sidekick climb up the steps, clipboards tucked under their arms.

"*Bye*, John."

He gives me a tight-lipped smile on his way past to the truck.

Garrett stands at the bottom of the stairs, peering up at me, a curious but unreadable expression on his face. Dark shadows linger under his eyes, as if he hasn't slept much.

"I like this look."

"What look is that?"

"You, beneath me."

A slow, wry smile spreads across his lips, and I hold my breath, waiting for him to make the lewd retort I set him up for. "You're here to pester me, so you may as well come down and check it out."

"Not playing along today, huh?" I ease down the stairs. They're steeper than I expected, and I accept Garrett's hand until my shoes hit the dirt floor with a thud.

I immediately feel the sense of loss when he lets go, but I push it aside. "Who were those guys?"

"The general contractor for the project, and my numbers guy."

"Did they know they're disturbing a crime scene?"

"From a century ago?"

"What, you don't believe in ghosts?"

"No."

"Me neither. But maybe John does." I wander into the vacuous, stone-clad space. It's the length of four storefronts above us, and poorly lit between a few naked bulbs and scattering of windows, too small for even a child to fit through. It smells like any musty old basement, but there's no hint of water anywhere.

"Have you told them about the delays yet?" Shirley is adamant she's not backing down at that town meeting. Her argument? The detrimental effects of having a condominium towering over the other Main Street buildings, as well as the fact that the town changed their zoning a year ago and HG should conform to our needs, rather than the other way around.

And she's putting all her poker chips in. She may have fought the need for a Facebook account, but she has since infiltrated every town's group within a thirty-mile radius of Polson Falls, gathering granules of intel that might help her cause.

Garrett smirks. "Funny, I wasn't aware of any yet, and I'm the one running the project."

"What does that mean? What do you do all day, besides flirt with me and try to buy off old ladies with bakery sweets?"

He trails behind me as we sink deeper into this building's undercarriage. "Good question. Let's see ... between dealing with architects and engineers, getting permit approvals, managing general contractors and their tradespeople, sales and marketing, financial lenders, investors, the community, legal, accounting ... not much."

"Didn't think so." That's *a lot* of balls to juggle. I won't admit that I'm impressed, though. "You were gone a long time. Must have had an awful lot of meetings."

"What's wrong, you missed me?"

Yes. "Missed annoying you." I smile over my shoulder. "Makes my days more interesting."

His eyes slide downward to my backside, which these jeans flatter. "Your current job isn't challenging enough?"

I let the ogle go without comment. "It's never been about the challenge." It was about something stress-free and new, but most of all, it was about feeling needed.

"How long do you think you'll stay there?"

Until Ned doesn't need me anymore. That's the answer I gave my mom when she asked the same question. But does it mean when Murphy's doors close for good? Or when Ned isn't around anymore to run it? The latter puts me in a sad mood just thinking about it. "Until you open up the speakeasy down here," I say instead. "I have the perfect flapper dress. It's *really* short. Shows off my legs." I break into a mock Charleston dance that I perfected one Halloween. I spin around. "What do you think?"

"I think you'd make a terrible employee." But he's grinning.

"Good thing you know how to keep me under control, huh? So, where were the murders? You ever find out?"

"Behind all that." He juts his chin toward the wall of crates in the back.

It's at least ten degrees colder down here than above ground. I wrap my arms around my body to keep myself warm as I move toward them. "What's all this stuff?"

"Old junk from way back in the day."

"You mean, you haven't looked yet? *Someone's* looked." The lid on the nearest crate sits askew. Hooking my fingers around the edges, I lift it …

A small gray mouse scurries past my fingers.

With a shriek, I let go of the lid and hop back, crashing into Garrett's body as a loud bang ricochets through the hollow space.

Garrett bursts into a choking laugh.

I elbow him in the stomach, earning his grunt. "You knew that would happen."

"Here. Use this." He reaches for an old crowbar resting nearby and pries the lid up again. Pausing to give any more critters time to run out, he pushes it off the rest of the way with his arms.

I pull out an amber-colored glass bottle, running my thumb over the ridged, dusty surface to uncover a marking: the letters *S* and *V*. It clicks. "Do you realize what this is?" I hold it up for Garrett to see. "S.V. is for *Stavro*." I drag out the syllables. "This is their distillery stuff. I can't believe it's still here!"

Garrett lifts a few bottles. They're identical in design. "Todd said whoever killed the brothers took the full crates of booze and ingredients, and then trashed the operation so no one could pick up the business. But they obviously didn't destroy everything."

"And it's just been sitting here the *whole time*?" I stroll past a stack of whiskey barrels two high. "This is the coolest thing I've ever seen. Like, legit history, right ..." My words fade as I round the makeshift wall and come face to face with a small square table, playing cards strewn over its surface, a thick layer of dust coating everything. An ashtray sits at one corner. Four chairs surround it, one tipped over.

"Is this ... is that ... Oh my God." The cards are aged, but those brown smears can't be from time.

Garrett sidles up beside me. "Cops take the bodies and any necessary evidence. The rest, they leave behind for someone else to clean up. Dieter Senior was superstitious, so he just left things the way they were. No one ever comes down here."

"He was superstitious, but he bought a building where four men had been murdered."

"Guess he also knew a good deal when he saw one."

A surreal feeling washes over me. "This is ... *crazy*."

"This is what you came down here to see, isn't it?"

No, I came down here to see you, fool. Is he waiting for me to admit it out loud? "I didn't expect an *actual* crime scene."

"It was a bit jarring the first time I saw it," he admits. "It preserved well. This basement was built properly. Good drainage outside, mortar in the stonework."

Something I overheard John say triggers in my thoughts. "Hey, why were you talking about shoring this up when you're demolishing it?" I duck. "Is this place about to cave in on our heads? Is this how I go?" Maybe that inspector wasn't wrong.

"Demolishing it *was* the plan." Garrett's lips pucker. "Richard wants to rework the design to keep the old structure. I've been with the architects and engineers day and night for weeks. They hate my guts."

My jaw drops. "Why the change?"

"Makes more sense, given the revisions the town engineers are requiring."

It's a vague answer, but it's not what matters. "What does that mean?" It sounds like Richard has taken over the project from Garrett. That can't be good.

"Besides a ton of rework and not enough time to do it?" He looks around the ceiling. "They don't build them like they used to. This place has strong bones, so we're going to expand on them. We can keep the building's face, with some significant embellishments and tie-ins for the overall design. The interior will be gutted. A lot of it's been patched and modified over the years. There's nothing worth saving."

His words sink in. "But you're going to save the building." We won. Sort of?

He watches me closely. "Some of it. Probably not enough to satisfy Shirley."

Right. Shirley. "What about the height variance?"

"Still there, and still needs approval, so if you can put in a good word with her, I would appreciate it."

"She's not going to care about this. It's the condos on Main Street she takes issue with. Plus, she thinks everything you say is bullshit. Lip service that'll never pan out."

"Yeah, it's all bullshit." He holds out his arms, as if the answer is within these old stone walls. "Glad to see you *still* don't trust me."

"You didn't start off on the right foot."

He nods slowly. "Actually, I think I did. It was the next foot that did me in."

I laugh. "Stepped right into a manhole."

"Stepped in *something*." He chuckles, and it's such an easy laugh. But it dies quickly, his attention lingering on my face as if trying to read me.

Is he wondering what I am—how much of this thing between us is an act?

Have I been completely wrong about Garrett all this time?

"So, we're keeping this for our speakeasy, right?" I hover my hands over the table. "How do we preserve this until the place opens?"

He shakes his head but grins. "Sometimes I can't tell when you're joking."

"Oh! I have the perfect name!" I pause for effect. "Stavro Bros."

As if in answer, the light bulb above the table flickers.

I freeze, the hairs on the back of my neck standing on end. "Did you see that?"

"I did, but—"

It flickers again.

I dive into Garrett's side just as a small pop sounds, the filament inside burning out.

I sink with relief, still clinging to him.

"I thought you didn't believe in ghosts."

"I do when they talk to me."

Roping an arm over my shoulders, he pulls me around to face him, our chests against each other. "And what did they say?"

"They like the name, but my choice of business partners is questionable ..." My words drift as his hand slides around my nape, tipping my head back to meet his warm brown eyes.

"What am I going to do about you, Justine?"

"Is that a rhetorical question?"

His gaze traces my lips. "I did miss you."

My breath hitches at the frank admission. "Not enough to come back." I hear the vulnerability laced in with the challenge.

"I knew I wouldn't get any work done if you were nearby, distracting me." His thumb caresses behind my ear.

I sink into him as I revel in his touch. "Sorry to interrupt your busy baby-developer life."

"Why? I'm not sorry." With a hard swallow, he leans down to brush his soft lips against mine.

I can't help the sigh that escapes as I slip my tongue past his parted lips, the tip of it teasing his. The last time we kissed like this, it was pitch-black and he tasted like bourbon. Now, I devour the spearmint taste of his mouth while admiring his face so close to mine. My fingers grasp at his biceps, drift over his collarbones, tease his warm skin.

With a groan, he guides my head to another angle, granting us both better access that we seize with abandon, our tongues taking turns plunging and exploring, coaxing each other further with each pass. My body sinks into his, delighting in the hard press of his erection against my stomach. I've thought about that delightful feature of his often over the weeks—how good it would feel thrusting in and out of me.

I rope my arms around his body to pull him in tighter. As much as I want into his pants, I'm enjoying his mouth too much.

"Damn, how tall are you?" he whispers.

"I'm a giant." I stretch on my tiptoes to help erase some of the glaring height difference. I was in five-inch heels when we were caught in the linen closet. His neck must be hurting.

Releasing my nape, he seizes my waist and hoists me up until our faces are aligned. "Better?"

"Not quite." I wrap my arms around his shoulders and my legs around his hips.

His hands come around to span across my ass without shame, supporting my weight with little effort.

I flex my thighs around him as I grind against his groin. "There. That's perfect."

"Fuck," he hisses.

"That's the plan." Our mouths descend into a flurry of hasty tangled kisses, our breathing ragged, our teeth catching against each other. If we weren't in this dirty murder basement, I'd be tugging at his clothes, but it's not ideal, so we make up for it with an aggressive assault on each other's mouths, and neither of us seems to want to yield.

While I cling to him like a spider monkey, his fingers press into the crevice between my thighs, toying with my most sensitive spots through my jeans, stirring a flood of warmth and desperation. I *need* him to touch me there again.

"Upstairs, *now*," I demand in a hoarse whisper, tossing all caution aside. My lips feel bruised.

"My thoughts exactly," he manages between kisses, before turning toward the door.

His feet falter, his hands growing lax.

I pull away to see what made him put on the brakes.

Todd is at the base of the stairs, slack-jawed. "I was just taking out the trash and …" His words drift.

I let go of my vise grip of Garrett's body and land on my feet on the dirt floor. We step apart.

"… saw the door sitting open."

Garrett clears his throat. "I was meeting with my general contractor, and Justine interrupted me."

"Yes, I interrupted." With my tongue.

A stupid grin spreads across Todd's face. Today's Tommy Bahama shirt is purple with pink pineapples. It's annoyingly cheerful.

"How's the move coming along?" I ask, my voice loud and forceful, as if that'll erase the memory of what he witnessed. I've resumed my daily soup visits since Garrett negotiated our peace treaty, refraining from accusing Todd of betraying my Bonny Acres secrets. I didn't want to risk another feud, and besides, I deserved that payback. "What is it now? One week away?" Bob and Bethany are long gone, as is Death Metal Dawn.

Todd's the last man standing, his shelves growing bare from inventory-reduction sales. It's cheaper and easier than moving it across town, he claims.

"A week and a half. I close doors next Saturday."

That's Sara's bachelorette party. Could this be my excuse for skipping it? The end of an era. Small-town solidarity and all.

An awkward silence grows.

"So, does the granny gang know about *this*?" Todd asks, and there's no need to press him on what he means.

About me falling hard for the slick-as-sin developer? Hell no.

Am I a complete fool for letting this happen?

"You mean, all this Polson Falls history"—I wave a hand at the crates—"that you've been hoarding in your basement instead of giving it to the museum? No, I can't see how they would."

Todd folds his arms, not cowing to my challenge. "They can have whatever they want, but it's not mine anymore. They'll have to ask HG for it."

"I'll pass that information along. I should head back to work now." I steal one last look at Garrett, to soak in his physical perfection until we can deal with *whatever* this is that's happening between us. "Don't even think about throwing any of this out. It *all* needs to be saved."

"Even the murder table?" Garrett hollers after me.

"*Especially* the murder table."

"See you tomorrow," I offer, charging past Todd.

"No lunch today?" There's humor in his voice. I'm discombobulated, and he knows it.

Shit. Lunch. My wallet. That's why I came outside in the first place.

"See you in ten."

Chapter Twenty-Six

I STARE at Garrett's number programmed into my phone. Never in my life have I hesitated texting someone before, and yet for some godforsaken reason, I'm too nervous to do it now. Is it because he never gave me his number? Or because it's going to cross some weird relationship threshold—having his dick in my mouth is one thing, but calling him? Whoa, *slow down, Justine.*

Or is it because that little voice in my head is warning me to stay back? That despite telling myself I can keep it physical, I'm not sure I can.

I toss my phone onto the couch beside me and listen to myself breathe.

Is the house *always* this quiet? Scarlet went next door after dinner. I won't see her until the morning when Shane leaves for work and she comes home to get ready for school.

Hugging a throw pillow, I flick through Netflix, unable to find anything that grabs my attention. Probably because my attention has been hung up on Garrett since stumbling out of that basement.

That kiss today … My fingertips skate over my lips. It was different from the other times. Still electric, but somehow *more*. I want to chalk it up to the intensity of the moment—that creepy basement, the lights flickering, my senses on overdrive—but I'm not sure I believe that. It's more likely that I'm seeing Garrett as someone other than the cold-hearted jerk I convinced myself that he was.

But did he feel it too? That unspoken shift between us?

I had every intention of cornering him after work—in the sales center, in his dive, wherever I could find him—but he was gone, back to Philadelphia, according to Morgan. Who knows for how long this time.

He didn't even stop by to tell me.

That's a sign, isn't it? Even though I don't want to believe it, that's a sign that this is all just fun and games.

But that's what I'm good at, according to Bill.

With a groan, I drag myself off the couch and wander into the kitchen to turn on the kettle for tea. This is ridiculous. I'm thirty years old. I should just message Garrett and ask him what kind of psychopath leaves without finishing what he started.

No … that's a little accusatory. It needs to be something clever, playful.

I focus on April's foot on the wall—seven toes, two of them missing nails—and an idea strikes me. With a laugh, I dart back to the living room. Yanking off my sock, I snap a close-up of one foot. I attach that to the message and without any other intro, hit Send just as the kettle whistles.

I've barely turned off the element when my phone chirps with a message.

Garrett: *Which Stavro ghost is this?*

Flutters stir in my stomach. How did he know it was me? I never gave him my—oh, I did. Ned passed it along for me, on that fateful day. Which means Garrett must have programmed it into his phone.

I don't dwell on that little nugget, punching out a response.

Justine: *Vern.*

Garrett: *Vern has sexy feet.*

I bite my bottom lip, waffling over my response. Something I never have to do. But I can't remember feeling this surge of nervousness, at least not for an eternity.

The three dots bounce on my screen before I have a chance to respond.

Garrett: *Where are you?*

Justine: *Home. You?*

I busy myself pouring hot water into a cup and dunking my tea bag, watching the cloud of yellow seep out.

Anxiously awaiting his answer.

The minutes drag with no response. He must be in a meeting or at the gym or—

A knock sounds at the front door, startling me. We rarely have visitors—only Shane, Dean, and Dottie. Occasionally Becca, an old friend of Scarlet's.

But never this late.

I leave my tea in the kitchen to open the door and see who it is. My breath catches at the sight of Garrett standing on our porch. "Morgan said you went to Philly."

"I did. And then I drove back here."

To see me. I hear those words, though he didn't say them. I hear them because I want them to be true.

He's in his gray track pants and a clingy, long-sleeved shirt, his hair in sexy disarray. It's like he threw on whatever he could find in his rush to come over. He must have done so, because my last text to him was eight minutes ago, and it's a four-minute drive. "Eager much?"

He steps in without invitation, forcing me back, his body towering over me as he shuts the door and flips the lock. "I have a thing for feet."

"Oh well, in that case, you are in luck, because I have the perfect calendar ..." My words die as his cool fingers wrap around my nape again, like he did earlier today. Every inch of my body comes alive, in anticipation of those hands roaming wherever else they want to on me tonight. "How do you know where I lived?"

Minty breath skates across my cheek as he steps in closer. "Sara."

"She just gave you—"

"I asked."

"So, about earlier today …" I peer up into the molten eyes locked on my face, and my breath hitches at the raw desire shining there. "You too, huh?"

His jaw tenses. "Oh yeah. Me too."

I can't say who lunges first. In the next instant, our lips are crashing into each other as he lifts me up and my legs curl around his waist, his hands gripping my hips as he holds me. It's as if we're resuming where we left off, only now we've had hours to simmer in lust.

We bump into the small console table on our way to the wall, toppling the candlesticks and framed picture. The sound of glass cracking makes me wince, but I quickly forget, distracted by the feel of Garrett's hard length pressing against my apex.

My fingers grasp at his shirt, tugging at it. "Need this off," I manage with our mouths still tangled.

He pulls away for a second, using his hips to pin me to the wall while he yanks his shirt over his head in one move, casting it aside.

"*Oh my God, why must you be so perfect?*" I groan, admiring the canvas of hard ridges and sculpted muscle beneath my hands.

With an arrogant smirk, he dives back in, his mouth landing on my jawline as his fingers fumble with the buttons of my pajama top. I push the silky material off my own shoulders, exposing my skin to the cool air.

Garrett's arms flex as he lifts me higher, his mouth landing on my pebbled nipple, his teeth scraping across my flesh, stirring a prick of sharp pleasure before he sucks.

I moan out loud, the back of my head thumping against the doorframe. This is what I was missing that night in the closet. "I'm never wearing boob tape again." My hands weave through his hair before gently fisting it as I arch my back, giving him better access.

"Where am I taking you?" he whispers against my flesh.

Right here, against this wall, is fine by me, I want to say. But on the off chance that Scarlet comes back for something, that's not wise. Every go at Garrett has ended hastily because someone interrupts us. If it happens one more time, I might die. "Bedroom. Through the kitchen." With that command out, I capture his lips with mine again, my hands cradling his jaw. The faint stubble against my skin is intoxicating.

Garrett's feet pound along the hardwood as he carries me down the hall, through the kitchen, slowing only to fit us through the narrow doorway and kick the door shut behind us. The bedside lamp is already on, casting a dim, moody glow.

"I can't get enough of your mouth." He sets me down.

"That's because you haven't had the rest of me yet." I shove my pajama shorts and panties off my hips, letting them fall to the floor.

His eyes flare as they rake over my naked form. "I believe you." Hooking his thumbs around his waistband, he sheds his track pants.

"Your turn for commando tonight? I guess that's only fair." My breathing is ragged as I move backward toward my bed, both to lead him there and to get a better head-to-toe view.

Garrett Harrington naked is a vision.

He simply stands there a moment, allowing me to admire him as I perch myself on the edge of my bed. The sharp V cut of his pelvis is like an arrowhead carved into his body, pointing down-ward to my toy for the night—jutting upward, tall and proud.

While I gawk at him, his own gaze traces my every curve, jumping between my heavy breasts and where my thighs join and back again, as if unsure where to focus.

Then, as if some switch gets flicked, some decision made in that beautiful brain of his, he stalks forward, guiding me until I'm on my back, my thighs falling apart.

He curses under his breath, getting his first real look at the part of my body he made sing once not so long ago, in the dark. "It's a good thing I couldn't see anything in that closet," he admits roughly.

"Why is that?"

"I wouldn't have been able to stop myself." He drops to his knees. Peering up at me through thick lashes to show me the desire burning in his eyes, his mouth seals over my center.

A sound of intense pleasure climbs out of me, his tongue even more skilled than the hands that grip my thighs, pushing my legs apart to grant him access. I angle my hips, my fingers weaving through his hair as he laps at my core with teasing swirls and hard sucks. Bill was the only one who could ever coax an orgasm out of me this way, and it took forever. He'd often get frustrated, and then I would get frustrated, and we'd end up fucking before he went back to finish me off.

But with Garrett, things are happening and fast, a shiver building along my spine, my body opening itself up fully to him again. Where I had to be silent in the closet, now I release every sound without remorse or shame, my hips rolling as I chase the looming explosion.

It arrives in a rush, surprising me, tremors coursing through my limbs and my hips arching off my mattress, as uncontrollable cries wrench from inside. Pleasure consumes me in waves that Garrett prolongs with his tongue until I'm shaking from the intensity.

"No more," I gasp, shrinking away.

He releases me, leaving me delirious, floating on a cloud of ecstasy that I never want to come down from.

I don't know that I ever came that hard with Bill. I do know that it never happened that fast. Not with him, not with anyone. "That has to be a record for me," I murmur, my eyes half-mast.

"Too fast?"

"No, just right. Because you have time to do it again." Ten more times.

I feel his chuckle between my legs, even though he's climbing onto the bed, kneeling before me, rolling on a condom.

"Not a fan of missionary, right?" He seizes my calves and lifts my body until it lines up perfectly with his rock-hard erection, leaving my lower back resting against his thighs.

"You take a lot of notes when I talk, huh?" I arch my back and hips, teasing him. I'm helpless in this position. "It's fine if you don't know what you're doing."

"You haven't been with the right person."

I'm not about to bring up my sex life with Bill, which was robust and healthy. "That's not it. I just prefer—" I cry out as he pushes into me without warning.

"Prefer what?" Garrett smiles. He knows how much pleasure he can bring a woman with that beast. What a smug bastard.

"Other things," I manage around a gasp. God, he's only halfway in and it's overwhelming. "Dirtier things." Dirty, by some people's standards. I claim no judgment about anyone's sexual proclivities.

He pulls out to the tip, only to sink back in.

"You don't waste time." I've never taken anyone his size before, and it's making me pant.

"Gotta make these fifteen seconds count." The slight strain in his voice betrays his calm bravado. He pushes, sliding all the way in, drawing another moan from me as he pauses to let me adjust.

My legs fall to either side of his arms. He's gripping my thighs so tight, I can't move, anyway.

His chest heaves with labored breaths—not from exertion, but from a struggle for control, for patience. "I can't wait to uncover all your little secrets. Dirty and otherwise."

I look up to find him gazing down at me, a curious look on his face. Does he even mean that, or is it something you say when you're balls-deep inside a woman? Where does Garrett see this going?

Those aren't questions I'm supposed to be asking of a guy I'm casually fucking.

If that's what this is.

"I like this angle." It gives us both prime viewing for where we're joined, but even better, I get a delightful view in the full-length mirror attached to the back of my door. I can admire the web of muscle across his back, the tight, hard mounds of his ass, his thick thighs. It's the best of both worlds.

I shift my hips, earning his groan.

He finally begins to move. My body slowly stretches for him, welcoming him more with each new rolling thrust. The illicit view of his flexing muscles and where we're joined builds my arousal quickly. Soon, my bedroom fills with the intimate sounds of flesh against flesh and uninhibited moans.

He shifts, adjusts his angle a touch, and suddenly he's hitting that perfect spot inside me with each stroke. I cry out as my body bows, that feeling in my lower belly coiling tighter.

"There you are," Garrett murmurs, and his tempo speeds up, his muscles tensing as his grip on my thighs tightens. My metal bed frame creaks noisily, his hips pistoning in and out of me at a new, punishing rate. A thin sheen of sweat coats both our bodies. I revel in it, stealing a glance in the mirror. The sensual image reflected pushes me over the edge. I explode, my inner muscles squeezing around Garrett with each wave that crashes in, my cries loud and unabashed.

His head falls back with a groan that sounds more like a growl, his muscular form going rigid. Seconds later, I feel him pulsing inside me as my body keeps rocking against his, chasing the last of that high.

Releasing my legs, he flops down halfway on top of me, his skin hot, his chest heaving, his heart pounding against my shoulder. We lie naked and splayed for long minutes, our ragged breaths mingling together the only sound in the house.

"Is someone ready to admit she was wrong?" Garrett asks into the silence, his voice raspy.

I brush my lips over his ear, teasing him as I whisper, "I think you're getting way ahead of yourself." I cap that off with a tongue-drag along his lobe.

He shudders a sigh. "I'm not. You should make a public announcement."

"In the *Tribune*?"

He snorts. "Exactly. Polson Falls hasn't heard enough about HG."

Talk of the *Tribune* and Polson Falls drags back the reality of our current dynamic. We're adversaries. He lied to me and tried to use me. I've been plotting against him since January, working doggedly to stall his big project.

How the hell did we end up here?

Maybe it was inevitable.

But now that we *are* here, I'm not willing to let it go yet.

I weave my fingers through his silky-soft hair. "Stay." The word comes out without any planning, but as soon as it does, I know I mean it.

His eyes meet mine, a questioning look in them.

"Just for the night." I smooth my hand down to where we're still joined. "I'm not finished playing with you yet."

He leans in to press a kiss against my lips. "Okay."

———

I wake to a low, repetitive hum. It takes a split second and my mattress moving to remind me I'm not waking up alone this morning, that the heat against my back is from an exquisite male body lying next to me, that the delicious ache of my thighs is from a night I hope I never forget.

"You set an alarm?" I ask, my voice croaky. "That's criminal." The last time I looked at the clock, it said four a.m.

Garrett groans. The mattress shifts again.

I roll over to see him perched at the edge of my bed, his bare back a span of muscle, his head hung as if he's struggling to get his bearings. "I have a meeting in an hour, and last night, I did not finish what I needed to for it."

"Garrett Harrington the Third did not complete his home-work? Why ever not?"

He smooths his hands over his face to rub the sleep out. "Because of you and that trap between your thighs."

A rough cackle escapes me. "I guess I've found my new strategy."

"To destroy my career? I think so." But I hear the amusement in his voice.

"Oh, shut up. You weren't complaining last night." Not through several rounds of mind-bending sex in various positions, until we ran out of condoms. But it didn't end there. He earned himself a good-night blow job, and the way he gripped my hair as he lost himself in my mouth and groaned incoherent things ... no, he had no complaints.

"Remember what I said about getting distracted if I stayed in town?"

"Vaguely. You should skip the meeting."

"It's with the town planning department."

"You should *definitely* skip it, then."

He chuckles, the sound vibrating in my belly. "I can't, Justine."

"Fine, lie back down with me, just for a minute."

"I'm not falling for that." He peers over his shoulder to show me tired eyes. "We're meeting to go over my proposal for the park redesign."

My plans to mount him the second he was within reach shift to the background. "You're actually doing that."

"You sound like you don't believe me."

"Because I don't." Do I?

He stands with a long reach-to-the-ceiling stretch.

My mouth goes dry as I watch him fish his track pants off the floor. *That* was all mine last night. "Are you?"

"Am I what?"

"Going ahead with it?"

"Yeah. I want the proposal ready in time for next month's town meeting."

"The same meeting as the one about the variance?" How convenient.

"It happens to be the same, yes. But the sooner I can show Shirley that I'm not like RGI Corp., that I'm good for my word, the better." He yanks his pants up, tucking my new toy into his waistband.

I pout. Though I still have the top half of him to appreciate.

"I don't like it when people question my integrity."

I'm not sure who that warning is directed at. I've not only questioned Garrett's integrity but I've pissed all over the idea of it. "Then you should give them reasons to take you at your word."

"That's what I've been trying to do." He pauses. "Any advice, as far as Shirley goes?"

"Are you asking me for insider intel on the granny gang?"

"Yeah, I guess I am." He lingers at the end of my bed, waiting.

I falter. Am I betraying her confidence by helping Garrett?

God, I can't think straight with him in nothing but track pants, fucked-all-night hair, and swollen lips.

Staring at me.

I sigh with reluctance. "Shirley doesn't like people thinking they're smarter or know more than she does. So … think about running those park plans by her. Make her feel like she's a valuable part of it." Sometimes I wonder if all the fuss Shirley kicks up comes down to needing to feel useful.

He smooths a hand through his hair, though it does little to tame the wild. My fists did a number last night. "I can pay a visit to Bonny Acres again one Friday night. Would she be agreeable to that?"

"She'll give you grief. That's just the way Shirley is." I hesitate. "Sneak her in something from the bakery. Nothing vegan or healthy. She loves pistachio."

"Pistachio," he echoes.

"But there can *only* be one pistachio thing in a selection, or she'll know I tipped you off."

He laughs, as if this is amusing. "Got it."

"And *this*"—I wave a finger between him and me—"stays out of it. She can't know about this." She'd call me an idiot, a fool. It would bother me to disappoint Shirley like that, and I'm not used to caring about what other people think.

He smirks. "And what exactly is this?"

The best sex I've ever had. "I am taking advantage of your finer assets, while you are trying to get in my good graces in hopes that I don't create any more obstacles for your project." Do I believe that anymore?

"Right. Of course. That's what this is." He smiles, but there's a hint of something else behind it. "I'm heading to Philly after my meeting, and I'll probably stay there because, well ..." He waves a hand between us.

"Yes, this deadly snare of mine."

"Exactly." His gaze drags over the blankets I've burrowed under. "Should I expect more nudes while I'm gone?"

Is that his way of asking me to text? "Never know." I slide my foot out from beneath the covers, flexing my toes in the air. "Any idea when you'll be around again, so I can plan my next attack on your career?"

"Not sure. I've got a lot of meetings over the next few days."

"What about all those Polson Falls babies you still need to kiss?"

Rounding the bed, he leans down and lays a soft kiss against my lips. "There. Done."

I smooth my palm over his stubbled jaw, remembering the delicious burn of it scraping across my inner thigh. I don't want him to leave.

"Really gotta go, Justine."

"Fine. Just let me see my toy one more time ..." I tug at his waistband, stretching it out to get a good look down his pants—and groan—before letting it snap back in place.

His abdominal muscles clench in response. "Message me later. If you want."

"We'll see. I may be too busy cleaning." There are used condoms strewn all over the floor. "You left your DNA all over this place. I could frame you for murder."

He frowns. "With my semen?"

"A crime of passion. You sick bastard."

"But then you wouldn't be able to enjoy my finer assets."

"Conjugal visits could be fun. Imagine all that pent-up frustration."

"Conjugal." His eyebrows arch. "We're back to talk of marriage, are we?"

"We've come …" I draw a circle in the air to finish my sentence.

He laughs as he heads for my bedroom door.

"Hey, don't you want to know how I got your phone number?"

"Either Sara or the fridge receipt. Knowing you? The latter." He smirks as he opens my door.

Scarlet is on the other side of it, in the kitchen, dressed for a day in the classroom, sipping on her coffee as Garrett strolls out, shirtless.

"Good morning," he offers before veering down the hall to where the rest of his clothes wait on the floor.

"Morning," she murmurs, her eyes trailing after him with interest before shifting back to peer at me lying in my bed.

Moments later, the front door opens and shuts.

"Good night?"

I yank a pillow over my face and scream into it.

Chapter Twenty-Seven

NED SURVEYS the porcelain bunnies and bouquets of tulips that adorn the Bonny Acres' reception area. "I can't believe I've never been in here before."

"I can't believe it's taken me four months to convince you to come with me."

"I don't know if *convince* is the right word."

"Convince, harass—we're splitting hairs. The important thing is that you're here."

"And Vicki knows I'm coming?"

"I mentioned the possibility to her, yeah. And she was excited."

He reaches up to touch the half Windsor knot with his free hand, his other gripping a small pot of pansies. "How is my tie? Is it straight? Trudy always used to fix them for me."

I smile. I've only ever seen Ned in sweater vests and beige trousers, but it's clear he's chosen something nicer for tonight. "It's perfect. You look dashing, young man. Stop fussing." I offer him my arm, which he gingerly takes.

The common room is already half full of the usual Friday night social butterflies. Shirley is at her customary table, alone, playing a riveting game of solitaire. In a table by the far corner, Vicki huddles with a book. But she must have been watching the door because she looks up as soon as we walk in and waves at Ned.

"Justine!" Harper calls from the opposite side of the room, beckoning me over with a chin jerk.

I lift my finger to tell her "one minute," but Ned pats my hand down.

"I can make my way over there. I'm not shy." He shuffles across the room, slowing to greet several residents on his way past. It seems he knows more people at Bonny Acres than he realized.

Harper waits for me with an odd smile on her face.

"What's up? You need help with decorations?" I look around. Easter eggs and bunny streamers hang from the ceiling. Everything seems set already.

"I do need help, but not with that. Nancy called me an hour ago to tell me she has a nasty bug, *so* tonight is your lucky night. The night you've been pestering me about for months." She gestures toward the bingo ball, dragged out from the closet and waiting.

"*Seriously?*" I throw my arms in the air in victory. "Yes! Finally!"

Harper shakes her head. "I don't understand you sometimes."

"But you're happy for me." That's what that little smile was.

"I'm happy I won't have fifty-four residents with diarrhea this weekend."

"Two things to celebrate, then."

She snorts. "Also, pure evil is back. Guess we'll need plates and napkins again." She juts her chin toward something behind me.

I spin on my heels and watch as Garrett strolls across the room toward me, arms laden with a white bakery box. I can't help the wide smile that erupts over my face. "What are you doing here? I thought you said you had something in the city tonight." We've been texting daily. Casual, superficial messages. Mostly playful barbs at each other. A few feet pics for fun.

"I moved things around."

"You should have warned me."

"I like surprising you." His eyes drop to my red tunic and leggings. "You look *really* good tonight."

My pulse races, my fingers itching to reach out and touch him again. It's been days, and my body instantly throbs at the sight of him.

"And *you* can't look at me like that here," I warn, acutely aware of the attention on us.

"Right." He sets the pastry box down. Already, several residents are out of their seats and flocking toward us, all smiles for Garrett. They don't care if he's the harbinger of destruction for their beloved town. They want to know if he brought any of that lemon pound cake.

"So ..." He reaches for the folder tucked under his arm, stealing a covert gaze over my shoulder. "What's my move here? Do I just walk up to her?"

"Empty-handed? *No.*" I emphasize that with a headshake.

"Good thing I brought this, then." He holds up a small white paper bag with a grin.

"Okay, follow me. And remember, this was *not* my idea and I have no part in it." I lead Garrett to Shirley's table.

"Hello again," he greets her cordially.

She pauses in her game and examines him up and down, stalling on the folder under his arm and the small bag in his hand. "Are we playing or not tonight, Justine?" Irritation laces her voice. She hasn't taken that tone with me since the first day we met.

A rash of anxious butterflies stirs in my stomach. This does not bode well for me. "Sure. We can play." I drag a chair out.

"Do you mind if I sit?" Garrett asks.

"Something tells me you're going to, anyway," she mutters.

He sheds his jacket, throwing it over the back of a chair, sending a faint waft of his cologne toward me. I inhale.

And, I swear, Shirley's sharp eyes zero in on my flaring nostrils.

Garrett takes a seat and sets the bag beside her. "It won't meet Harper's guidelines."

She watches it a moment as if expecting lizards to crawl out, before cracking it open. "Pistachio. However did you guess?" The sharp glare she throws over her glasses is not aimed at him but at me.

This common room suddenly feels too hot.

"I'd love your opinion on something, if you don't mind." Garrett moves quickly, opening his folder and pushing it in front of her. "This is a preliminary design for the town park at the end of the block that we were talking about. I had my people address all the issues you've mentioned, as well as incorporate a few new features. I wanted to know what you thought, if you had suggestions."

She adjusts her glasses and peers down at the colorful schematic. "Water park." She harrumphs.

"They're very popular for hot days. And the playground is twice the size."

"Too many children for my liking. All that noise."

He smothers a threatening smile. "Which is why we added this seating area on the other end." He drags his finger across the page. "*Way* over here. Next to a garden that the town would maintain in their budget. We also thought it'd be great to incorporate a few of the more popular ideas from other parks, like community vegetable plots and a trash can art program where resident artists are tasked with creating art pieces. You might like that, seeing as you're a supporter of the arts."

"Whitman Park," she reads the name out loud.

"After Polson Falls' prized poet. He's important to you, right?"

"He was a drunk. He doesn't deserve a school *and* a park."

Garrett falters. "Well … we could go with Justine's suggestion and honor the Stavro brothers instead?"

Shirley grimaces. "The booze smugglers?"

"I did not suggest that. I didn't suggest *anything*." I kick his shin under the table.

Silence drags on at the table, until finally, she taps the page with her manicured fingers. "What do *you* think about these plans, Justine?"

"Uh …" I can't get a read on her mood, but that feels like a trick question. "This is the first time I'm seeing this. I have no thoughts."

"No thoughts at all." She sounds disappointed.

I struggle not to squirm in my chair. "I think you should tell HG how to spend their money. You'll get what you want, and it's good for the community."

"Is that so?" Her eyes thin on me, and I'm not sure if that was the right answer.

"Nancy has diarrhea," I blurt.

"That's wonderful news," she deadpans.

"It is, because it means I'm calling bingo tonight. So I need to go and prepare." I slide out of my chair.

"Prepare?" Her face pinches. "For what?"

"Prepare myself mentally." I dart away, abandoning Garrett to her wrath.

———

"Let's procreate, seventy-eight!" I bellow, and the room erupts in chatter and laughter as several people dab their cards and others throw jabs at nearby friends.

"Did she say eighty-eight?" Mimi calls out over the buzz, searching for someone to confirm the number. It's far livelier in here tonight than usual.

From their little corner table, Ned points out the number on Vicki's card for her. They've been in that spot all night, talking and laughing nonstop.

It makes me smile, seeing him this happy.

That takes some of the edge off given Shirley is angry with me. She tolerated Garrett until bingo started, and then got up from the table and walked out. On which note—sour or slightly less so—

they ended things, I can't say, but she refused to so much as look at me on her way past.

She feels like I've betrayed her, and that has left my insides twisted in a knot I'm doing my best to ignore.

Garrett lingering against a wall in the corner helps. Every time my attention sweeps that way, it gets hooked on his smile, on his dimples, on him. I could stare at that face for hours.

"What's the next one?" Someone hollers.

"Oh, right." I reach into the cage and pull out another ball. "Did you score, twenty-four!"

"We all know Saul did," someone chirps, earning snorts.

Saul is nowhere within earshot tonight. Neither is Gertie.

I give them time to search out their numbers and for the chatter to die down before I reach into the cage again. "Oh, this one's my favorite ..." I pause for effect, until I have everyone's attention. "Your place or mine, sixty-nine!"

A roar of laughter erupts as everyone searches for the number.

Garrett arches a curious brow, and I wink before dragging my eyes down the length of him. The mental image of his body beneath those clothes still burns bright in my mind, and that memory stirs other memories. Ones I shouldn't be having right now.

"That's bingo!" Roger waves his card in the air, distracting my lustful thoughts.

Garrett catches my gaze long enough to cast a lazy salute before ducking out.

I frown. Where's he going? Will I see him again tonight?

"One more round?" someone calls out, stopping me from chasing after him.

"Just one!" someone else yells, followed by, "Encore!"

Nancy never gets an encore, I think with smug satisfaction. "Yeah, why not." I drop the used balls back into the cage.

Chapter Twenty-Eight

THE LAMP in Ned's front window casts a dim light in the modest brick bungalow when I pull my car into his driveway. "As promised, door-to-door service."

Ned lingers a moment, staring out at the house. "I still remember the day Trudy and I walked through that front door for the first time. It was the summer of '67, and she was wearing a yellow dress, bright as a canary."

I smile. "I'll bet you have a lot of memories here."

"*Lots* of memories," he agrees. "Lots of laughs, lots of tears." He pauses. "I talked about her a lot tonight, but Vicki didn't seem to mind. She had a lot to say about Gus too. I think we both needed to talk to someone who understood."

"It's a good thing you listened to me then, huh?" I nudge his arm with my elbow. "You should come with me again next week. You and Vicki can talk about Trudy and Gus some more. I'm sure they would be happy you two are doing that." Finding some comfort in these lonely after-years.

"You know, maybe I will." His mouth curves in a frown. "What was Garrett Harrington doing there tonight?"

"Trying to win over Shirley with a town park redesign that he's willing to fund."

"Did it work?"

"Doubt it."

He chuckles. "That is one tough bird. But good for him for trying."

"Yeah, well, now I think she's mad at me for helping him. Or just talking to him." Or because she sees the chemistry between us that I was stupid enough to think I could hide. That guilty feeling hasn't gone away.

"She'll get over it." He waves my worries away. "Todd told me HG is relooking at saving some of the original building. That might be a nice compromise."

"That won't change her mind. Plus, who knows if it'll happen. HG could just be saying that to appease people, like that developer who cut down the two-hundred-year-old elm tree."

"Oh, I remember that one. Boy, were people mad about that. But they moved on. It's what we all have to do." Ned leans in a touch. "Todd also told me what he walked in on in the basement the other day."

I groan, my cheeks flushing at the thought of that conversation. "Todd has a big mouth." There's no point denying it anymore, though.

"He'd say the same thing about you." He twists his lips. "You know, it's okay to admit you were wrong about Garrett."

"Was I, though?"

"I think you know the answer to that." He reaches out to pat my wrist. "But that's just my two cents. What do I know? Have a good night." He eases out of the car and trudges up the steps to his front door.

I wait until he's safely inside before I dig out my phone to text Garrett.

There's already a message from him waiting for me.

Garrett: *You named your dishwasher Stuart?*

Scarlet's cackle of laughter greets me as I push through the front door and shed my coat and shoes. "I can't decide if it's better or worse than last year's calendar."

"What was last year's?" Garrett's voice stirs my blood.

"Fornicating bugs." I step into the kitchen to find them both lingering with a bottle of beer in hand, Garrett studying November's webbed foot.

"Where do you even find something like that?"

"You'd be surprised. Comfortable much?" He's changed into track pants and a T-shirt, and looks ready to settle in for the night. I'm thrilled, but this was unexpected.

"I am. Thanks for asking." He leans back against the wall, taking a long sip of his beer, his eyes never leaving me.

"How long have you been here?"

He frowns at Scarlet. "What, about half an hour?"

"Yeah. About that."

"So you just let strangers into the house now?"

"You mean, the half-naked man I met a few days ago?" Scarlet hands me a cold beer from the fridge. "How was bingo tonight?"

I grin, momentarily distracted. "Did he tell you?"

"That they let you call the numbers? He did, yes." She shakes her head. "I can't imagine what you came up with."

"I was good! Right?" I coax Garrett. "I was good?"

"Impressive."

"See? It's all about the delivery."

"I'll bet. Will they let you do it again?" Scarlet brings her bottle to her lips.

"Are you kidding? Once Nancy hears about the encore I got tonight, she will wear a diaper and shit herself before she ever lets me near her bingo balls."

Scarlet chokes on her mouthful of beer and leans over to spit it into the sink so she can battle a coughing fit.

Garrett shakes his head at me.

I shrug. "What? She knows me."

Setting her drink on the counter, Scarlet fakes a big yawn, stretching her arms over her head. "Well gosh, look at the time."

I frown. "It's nine thirty."

"Exactly. Time for bed. Night, guys." With a wink at me and a whisper of "I'll wear my earplugs," she ducks upstairs.

Leaving Garrett and I staring at each other from across the tiny kitchen.

I take Scarlet's spot near the sink. "You're full of surprises tonight."

"Too many? Should I go?" He points toward the door and moves a half inch, feigning.

I shake my head, earning his smile. "How'd things go with Shirley?"

"She didn't spit on me." He takes a giant gulp.

"That's a win." I watch his throat bob, remembering the feel of that sharp jut beneath my tongue. "I think she's mad at me."

"She wouldn't touch those." He nods toward the bag of sweets sitting on the counter.

My stomach sinks. "Oh man. That's serious."

"It bothers you this much that she's upset with you?"

"Yeah. She doesn't like *anyone*, but for some reason, she likes me. *Liked me.* Knowing that made me feel special, I guess. And I respect her. She's smart, and tenacious, and does not take life lying down."

Garrett studies me quietly for a moment. "She'll get over it."

"That's what Ned said, but I don't know about that. She still isn't talking to Colin after he published those plans of yours, and they've known each other for decades." She doesn't like losing, but I think what she really doesn't like is feeling disregarded. Polson Falls and everyone in it is moving on without her. "If you haven't noticed, she's stubborn."

"Sounds like someone else I know." He sets his empty down. "Ralph and Sam should clock out on all this development talk."

"But aren't you at all concerned?"

He cocks his head. "About what?"

"Shirley's done with me. You've lost your inside man. *This*"—I wave a hand between us—"won't help your cause anymore."

"You're saying I've neutralized you as a threat to my project."

"Exactly. So there's no need for you to keep trying to win me over."

He hums. "You could still go to that town meeting and object to the variance."

"On my own, without the granny gang? I suppose I could." I have zero passion for it anymore. Garrett has won after all.

"Then, clearly, my work here *isn't* done." He pulls his body off the wall to saunter toward me. "Because I don't trust *her*." He points to the front-page *Tribune* cover affixed to the fridge, of my close-up.

"She *is* quite the anarchist."

"She *looks* sweet, but she's caught me off guard a few times, giving me whiplash." He grips my waist and hoists me onto the counter, fitting his hips between my thighs. "I need to keep a close eye on her. She's probably plotting to sabotage me right now."

I struggle against a grin. "She needs constant distraction."

"That's the plan." His lips skate across my jawline, and I utter a soft moan.

"I wouldn't let her out of my sight if I were you."

"That's why I can't go home this weekend." His hands settle on my ass, gripping tightly. "I have to stay here and distract her from doing anything … irrational."

"*All* weekend?" A flutter stirs in my belly. But he must be kidding.

"Definitely. She's too unpredictable." He pulls me flush against his body.

I sigh with the hard press of him against the apex of my thighs. "Can you handle her all weekend?"

"It'll be exhausting, but that's how important this project is to me." He dips down to clamp his teeth over my pebbled nipple, heat from his mouth searing through my sweater.

I tip my head back, reveling in the sharp pinch mixed with

pleasure. "Did you know that the brown antechinus can have sex for up to fourteen hours in a day?"

His mouth stalls. "I don't know what that is."

"A marsupial mouse. The male will mate as much as possible, but all that sex kills his immune system, and he usually dies."

He pulls himself back up, peering into my eyes. "Where did you learn something like that?"

"Came across it while I was searching for Scarlet's bug sex calendar. There was also one for mammals. It was enlightening."

"Are you saying I might die after this weekend?"

I don't think he's kidding about staying. My adrenaline rushes. "You should be fine. You're not a brown antechinus. Just don't set any alarms. Those make *her*"—I point at the clipping on the fridge—"irrationally angry."

He smirks. "Where *is* this bug calendar?"

My hands smooth over Garrett's chest, admiring the hard curves. "I set fire to it. Long story. Not important."

"You're right. You know what is?" He lifts me off the counter, his hands gripping my hips, holding my body flush to him as he heads toward my bedroom. "This favorite number of yours."

———

"You should think about wearing fewer clothes."

Garrett smirks as he checks his shirt collar in my full-length mirror. He arrived on Friday night, and it's Monday morning now, and aside from the five hours on Saturday when I was at Murphy's and he was in the sales center next door doing whatever it is project developers do, we haven't been apart.

For much of that time, we *really* haven't been apart. Scarlet left the house on Saturday morning when Shane got home and hasn't been back until this morning, leaving us to our depraved activities. I've never been so engrossed with another human body in my life. There isn't an inch of him that my tongue hasn't touched. My thighs ache from being stretched for so long.

I miss him, and he hasn't even left yet.

Garrett collects his duffel bag off the floor.

"You're like a nomad."

"I have a home base. It's just not in this state." Garrett leans down to plant a long, sensual kiss on my mouth. "I have a ton of meetings and work to get done this week. It's best if I stay in Philly."

A pang of disappointment stirs in my chest. "That's fine. I'm sick of you, anyway."

"Same." He leans in again, this time teasing my lips with the tip of his tongue.

I take the bait, stretching for more contact.

He pulls away with a knowing smile, stalling just out of reach unless I pull myself up. "What's your plan for next Saturday?"

Next Saturday ... I groan at the reminder. The bachelorette. "I don't want to go." I've never *not* wanted to go to a bachelorette. And Scarlet can't make it because of some charity event the firehouse is running that she's helping with, which means I'm facing forced pleasantries with Isabelle all on my own. It's not my strength. In fact, it might be my number one weakness—pretending I'm someone I'm not. I'm dreading this.

"Okay." Garrett shrugs as if it's no big deal.

I groan a second time, throwing my arm across my forehead. "But I *have* to go."

He smiles. "If you need a place to crash for the night, I'll send you my address."

"To your trust fund palace?" What does that side of Garrett's world look like? I only got a glimpse at the engagement party. Aside from that, all I really know about Garrett is that he works nonstop and has the sexual stamina of a bull.

"More like a loft, but yes."

I frown. "Will *you* be there?"

His eyes narrow. "Do you want me to be there?"

I want you to be everywhere. Another Saturday night with Garrett? That invitation sends a thrill through me. "Okay?"

"Okay. Thanks for the weekend." He steals one more kiss before he's out the door, offering a goodbye to Scarlet on the way past.

I throw on a T-shirt and boxer shorts and venture out on wobbly legs, sneaking a glimpse of my wild mane in the mirror. "Oh, I have sex hair. Nice."

"You're alive. I wasn't sure." Scarlet smirks around a sip of coffee.

"He asked me to stay with him next Saturday in New York." Or at least, casually offered it. "You know, because of the bachelorette."

"That's good, right? Isn't Joe and Sara's new house in the middle of renovations?"

"Yeah. And Joe's condo will be crowded." But is this what we're doing now? Spending weekends together?

She frowns. "Why am I sensing an issue here?"

"I don't know. I guess I'm confused. How did I go from liking a guy, to hating him and plotting his professional demise, to letting him bang my brains out? How did this happen?" Did I ever hate him, though? Or was I just hurt and allowing my spiteful side to take over?

She shrugs. "You're Justine. Things like this happen to you."

"True. But what even are we?" There's this ongoing little game of ours tied to the Revive Project. We're clearly best fuck friends. But spending an entire weekend here … the way he kissed me goodbye … it's beginning to feel like more.

And *more* comes with all kinds of problems—namely, heartbreak.

"Maybe you two should talk about it?"

"*No.*" I scoff. "The sex is *way* too good to risk ruining it."

"Right. Of course." She takes another sip. "Hey, by the way, what's it called when a squatter brings in her own squatter?"

I pour myself an extra-large cup of coffee. "I don't know, but at least *my* squatter puts out."

Chapter Twenty-Nine

THE MAN THROWS his hands in the air. "How was I supposed to know?"

"Sand in a washing machine? *Sand?*" His wife shoots him an incredulous look. They're a young couple, late twenties by my guess, married six months ago.

"These new machines, they are fickle. Get enough of those little grains in the system, and there's no fixing them. Don't make 'em like they used to." Ned pats the floor model they've just selected. "Come on over to my counter, and we'll get you sorted. Might want to think about an extended warranty."

The man looks to his wife. "Hun, do we want an extended warranty—"

"*Yes.*" She shakes her head at her husband as he trails Ned to the counter. "This is what happens when you marry a man who lives at home with his mother until your wedding day. I don't think he did a load of laundry his entire life."

"Believe me, I get it. I had to housebreak my ex when he moved in with me." I note the absence of that sharp sting at the mention of Bill. "It's April. What's with the sand?" It's not like he was washing grimy beach towels.

"Indoor beach volleyball. But don't ask me how he brought so much home with him. Anyway, thanks so much for your help. *Way* better customer service than those guys across town."

"That *is* our official slogan."

She reunites with her husband just as Joe's assigned ringtone trills in my pocket. With no customers to focus on, I answer. "Two and a half weeks till the big day!" And three days until the bachelorette party—an event I'm still dreading, despite the opportunity to see Garrett again.

"Yeah, trust me, I'm counting down until the day *after*, when we're on a plane out of here." Joe's breath is uneven. Horns honk in the background. He must be on his way to a client meeting.

"What's wrong? Rushed wedding planning not fun?"

"No. Not when I'm drowning at work. And not when your guests leave you hanging. Sara needs to know if you're bringing a plus-one."

"Oh shit. She messaged me about that. I don't know." The plan was to bring Dean but now, with this thing with Garrett … What even is this thing?

He groans. "We're running out of time, and we need to finalize seating charts. We're doing a round head table instead of a long one for the bridal party. Sara and I'll sit alone together."

"Great. So I get to sit across from *them* for the entire night?"

"Fine. You want to sit with Mom and Dad? I can do that."

I hesitate. "What did Garrett put in?"

"Who, Sara's cousin? The fuck if I know." A horn blasts. "Wait, why? Are you telling me that wasn't just a drunken one-night thing? Is there something going on between you two?"

"No! I don't know. Just … find out what he put down for me, okay? But don't tell Sara you're asking."

"Why?"

"Just because! Then she'll tell him I'm asking, and what if it's just a casual hookup for him—"

"You know what, I don't want the details. But can you please make sure you don't want to kill two of my groomsmen by the time my wedding day comes around?"

"No promises. Hey, I could kill Bastard Bill and use the sperm from one of Garrett's condoms to frame him."

A weird, strangled sound answers me.

I grin. "Was there anything else?"

"Yeah. Have you talked to Mom yet today?"

"No. Should I?"

Joe's sigh fills my ear. "Okay. I figured you'd want to hear it sooner rather than later."

"Hear what?" Unease slides down my spine. I think I already know what he's about to say.

"Bill and Isabelle are engaged."

———

I hiss as a pin pricks my skin.

Dottie winces. "Sorry, love. I'm better at doing this on myself, if you can believe that." She carefully slides the pin through the seam line at the bust. "There, that should do it." Taking a few steps back, she cocks her head. "What do you think?"

I study myself in the mirror. "I can't tell." The dress looks more like Frankenstein's monster, the material hacked apart and handstitched back together. But she has brought the hem up to a suitable short-person length. I'm not even telling Sara. In the grand scheme of ways I can ruin their big day for them, my altered hemline should be the least of her worries.

"Trust me. With my sewing machine, these seams will look fabulous."

"It's a definite improvement already." Scarlet scoops a spoonful of yogurt out of the cup and sucks on the utensil.

"Wait. Maybe we should tighten it a bit there?" Dottie adjusts her glasses and shifts her focus to the collar.

My phone chirps with a text from Joe. "Am I allowed to move?" I've been standing in the middle of the living room for almost an hour.

"Of course." She waves me off.

I dive for my phone.

Joe: *He's down as a plus-one. Someone named Mindy.*

My insides clench. "Who the fuck is Mindy?" I furiously type.

Scarlet frowns. "What's wrong? What happened?"

"The plus-one Garrett's bringing is some woman named Mindy." I watch the three bouncing dots on my screen.

Joe: *No idea. Ask Sara.*

I toss my phone onto the coffee table and wander back to my spot, my mood sinking. "Whatever. Like I said, this isn't serious." Except my chest feels tight, and it's not because of this stupid dress.

Dottie refocuses her attention on my collar. "Garrett ... that's this developer fellow, right?"

I huff. "Yeah."

"I'm sure there's a good explanation," Scarlet offers. "I mean ... he spent the entire weekend here with you. And he texts you every day."

"But we've kept it light. Surface stuff. Flirting and banter. He could have something going with someone else." He's away enough. "And I was *living* with Bill while he was fucking someone else." Will I ever be able to trust another man after that experience?

Her forehead wrinkles. "Maybe it's time to have a frank conversation."

"You know, I've never been good at playin' hard to get." Dottie inserts another pin. "But there is something called 'impossible to get.' You sure you haven't been playin' that?"

"We had a fifty-hour sex-a-thon here. He got me," I add with an eyebrow waggle, "in *every* position imaginable." Except missionary. It's like he intentionally avoided it.

Dottie's face ignites with joy. "*Do* tell." She loves a good sex story.

"But you haven't had a conversation about feelings," Scarlet pushes, steering the conversation away from the sordid details.

"Because I don't have feelings for him." If I don't allow myself that, then he can't hurt me.

Scarlet shakes her head, seeing through my mulishness.

I'm not fooling myself either though. The truth is, it's too late.

I have plenty of feelings for Garrett John Harrington *III*

Chapter Thirty

DIETER'S MEAT Shop and Delicatessen is the busiest I've ever seen it, the line of customers waiting to take advantage of the clearance sale on its last day at this location extending almost to the door. Yesterday when I stopped in for lunch, Todd was frantic, stressed. Today he's all smiles. I think he's looking forward to the coming change.

By the time I reach the counter, I'm stealing frequent glances at the clock. It's a two-and- a-half-hour drive to Manhattan, plus there's Saturday traffic and parking to contend with, plus I need to find out who Mindy is and then either murder Garrett and dispose of his body *or* divest him of his clothes and play with my favorite parts.

I'm running out of time.

"Hey, Justine, you look fancy."

"I clean up once in a while." I spent the morning perfecting my hair and makeup. The little black cocktail dress and heels for the night are waiting in the back seat of my car.

"How was last night at Bonny Acres?"

"Interesting. Three different residents asked if I'd be running bingo from now on, right in front of Nancy. She did not appreciate that." The side of my face still feels the searing heat from where her glare burned holes.

"And Shirley?"

I grimace. "Wasn't there." Saul and Gertie sat at her table. When I asked Harper if anyone'd checked on her, she confirmed with a pitying smile that Shirley announced she had no interest in seeing anyone who might be visiting. I know she didn't mean Garrett.

There's not much I can do except give her space and time, and hope she comes around.

"I'm heading to New York for the most uncomfortable bachelorette party ever."

"That's right. A whole night being civil to *Isabelle*." That name curdles on his tongue, and it makes me smile. He's never met her and likely never will, but the solidarity is appreciated.

"I'd say that I'd fill you in on the gossip next week, but ..." *You won't be here.* After almost a hundred years, tomorrow, this place will be empty of life.

"I'm not dying, Justine." He chuckles. "The new shop is only a seven-minute drive away."

But it's not right next door. It's not the same. I don't need to point that out, though. "I just wanted to stop by for your last day, but I have to hit the road—"

"Wait!" He collects a bowl and starts ladling soup. "Here's lunch for the drive. On the house."

"Have you tried eating soup while driving?" I inhaled Scarlet's half-eaten tray of sushi before I left, so there's no need to attempt it.

"Fine. Dinner. Or a late-night snack." He tucks it into a paper bag and passes it over the counter. "You know, I don't think I've ever told you this, but Ned's lucky to have you watching out for him."

"He is, isn't he? Make sure you tell him that." But hearing Todd acknowledge that spreads warmth through my body.

Todd smiles. "You keep an eye on him for me. And drive safe."

———

A flush crawls over my skin as I step out of the elevator on the fourteenth floor. I'm equal parts excited to see Garrett and dreading the confrontation—a rarity for me. I thrive on confrontation, especially when it involves challenging him. But this whole plus-one situation has rattled me far more than it should.

Garrett opens the door, and my tongue catches in my mouth for a few beats as I appreciate how utterly beautiful this man is. He must have just stepped out of the shower because his hair is damp and the smell of soap clings to his skin.

Meanwhile, I look like a Sherpa with my garment bag slung over one shoulder and my duffel bag over the other, and a paper bag of Todd's soup gripped in my fist.

Why am I sweating?

I need to unload all this weight—my belongings and my worries.

"Who's Mindy?" I blurt by way of greeting.

Garrett blinks, caught off guard. But that's the best way to get the truth out of a guy who always seems to have handy the answer you want to hear. "A friend?"

"You don't sound sure."

"I'm one hundred percent sure."

I cross the threshold into his condo, struggling beneath bags that aren't that heavy. "A plus-one-to-a-wedding kind of friend?"

Realization washes over his face. "Did they put Mindy down as a plus-one for me?"

"Apparently."

He shakes his head. "Aunt Audra figured she should, because I hate weddings, and I usually bring Mindy to make them less painful. They never even asked."

"She's just a friend?"

"Yeah."

"Like, *I'm* just a friend?"

The corner of his mouth twitches. "Like that guy you brought to the engagement party is just a friend."

That I could have had sex with a hundred times by now. "Smooth, but you didn't answer my question."

He bites his bottom lip in thought, struggling to hide his amusement. "We had a thing in the past, but now we're platonic."

The thought of another woman's hands on Garrett makes blurry spots appear in my vision. "So you're *not* bringing her to the wedding?"

"Why would I do that?" He gingerly slips my bags off my shoulders and carries them to a plush leather couch. "I'd ignore her all night because I couldn't keep my eyes off you."

My pulse throbs in my throat, hearing his candid admission. "Good answer."

He cocks his head. "Are you jealous?"

Insanely jealous, also a rarity for me.

"Nice place." I not-so-smoothly divert the conversation, refocusing my attention on his condo, a stunning loft with black metal, glass, and wood features, and charcoal grays and camel-brown décor. Vaulted tin-clad ceilings loom above, and a floating staircase reaches to the second floor. It's nowhere near the size of the Waltons' penthouse, but it's a mansion by Manhattan standards. Drew could fit his condo in here three times over. "How many bedrooms?"

"Two bedrooms, three baths. You want the tour?"

"Depends." I check the time on my phone. "I have to be at the Laurier at six for *high tea*." Some posh hotel a few blocks away from here. "Do we have time for a tour and a fuck?"

A sly smile stretches across his face. "Have I told you how much I like that mouth of yours?"

"Refreshing, right? Why dance around what we both want." I rake my eyes over his T-shirt and track pants. His feet are bare. And pretty. "How did I never notice your pretty feet before?"

"You were too busy obsessing about other parts on me. Are

you okay? Your face is all red." He comes closer, pressing the back of his hand to my forehead. And frowns. "You're hot."

"I know I am, but please tell me as often as possible. My ego never tires of hearing it." I'm *not* feeling okay. The Mindy situation is resolved, and my baggage has been unloaded, and yet with each moment that passes, I'm feeling weaker, my insides churning more.

My phone trills from my back pocket. It's Scarlet's ringtone, which is unexpected. She always texts. She *never* calls. "Give me a sec?" I pull it out and answer, my hackles raised. "What's up?"

"Please tell me you didn't eat the sushi that was in the fridge," she croaks, her voice feeble.

Oh no. "*Why?*"

She groans.

I slither up against the wall, the cool gray tile refreshing against my cheek.

"Justine?" Garrett's voice calls out from the other side of the door. "How are you doing in there?"

"Peachy." Even that one-word answer takes effort.

The first wave of intense nausea hit me minutes after I hung up with Scarlet, who informed me that both she and Shane were ill, and they suspected the sushi. I demanded that Garrett lead me to a private corner to hole up and die in for the night, and he led me to the spare bedroom. I darted in here just in time.

"I've got a glass of water for you."

"I drank from the tap." Then splashed water all over my face, dousing the countertop and the floor around the sink in the process. But at least I found a fragrant candle and matches, and now the scent of leather and brandy permeates the posh little en suite bathroom, helping to mask odors.

"What about ice?" The door handle twitches.

I had the good sense to lock it. "Nope. All good."

"Come on, Justine. I can handle vomit. Let me help you." His voice is soft, pleading.

"The vomiting portion of this show is now over." I hold my breath and grit my teeth against the cramp twisting my insides. We've moved on to the less pleasant symptoms of food poisoning.

This is what I get for reveling in Nancy's stomach bug to my own gain.

"Okay, then let me in." He jangles the handle again.

"Garrett, if you step foot inside this bathroom, we are *never* having sex again. I'm not even remotely kidding." Just having him hover so close to the door—where he could hear certain bodily sounds—is enough to stir my anxiety.

Silence hangs.

The cramp finally passes. "What time is it?"

"Almost eight."

I groan. I was supposed to be at the hotel two hours ago.

"I messaged Sara. It's all good. She understands."

All that stress over tonight, and six pieces of sushi solved my problems. Sort of. "When do you have to leave for the bachelor party?"

He snorts. "I'm not leaving you here alone like this."

"I'm fine. I just"—What's a sexy term for explosive diarrhea?—"have to deal with this for a few more hours, and then I'll fall into a coma." I think. I've never had food poisoning before. "You can go off with the guys for your pretend tequila-tasting pub crawl. Honestly, I'd rather you be gone."

There's another long pause. "I'm going to run out to the drugstore and grab you some electrolytes. I'll be back in twenty."

My lower intestines snarl at me. "Good idea. Run along now. Take your time." I crawl to the toilet.

———

"These sheets smell nice." My words are garbled as I face-plant into the pillow. "Like lavender."

Garrett sets a tall glass on the bedside table. "You need to drink this. It's Pedialyte."

"M'kay," I mumble, making no effort to lift my head. I took my time in the shower, letting the water sluice over my body to remove the stale sweat and sickness from my skin. The rest of my energy was depleted from digging my pajamas out of my bag, scrubbing off the Marilyn Manson-esque smudged eye makeup, and brushing the puke taste from my mouth.

I have nothing left in me.

I am a limp piece of lettuce.

But at least I feel clean again.

"Aren't you supposed to be gone?" I crack an eyelid to check for a clock, but there isn't one in this spare room, and I left my phone in the bathroom. I have no clue what time it is.

"I told you I wasn't going." The mattress sinks under his weight.

"If you think for one second—"

"I don't."

"*No* hokeypokey tonight."

"Don't you mean hanky-panky?"

"That too."

"I think you're delirious." The mattress shifts more, and then a palm smooths over my back, rubbing in circles.

A feeble moan slips from me. "That feels good. Keep doing that."

"See? You do need me here."

But a bridesmaid and groomsman both skipping out on tonight? "Joe's gonna think I faked this just to get out of the bachelorette."

"Would you if you weren't sick?"

"*No.* I'd go and be utterly miserable."

"Then I'm sure he'll understand."

"I should have taken a picture and sent it to him."

"Of what?"

"Don't ask."

"Sara did say you two are close."

I grimace. "I'm sorry you're missing the bachelor party."

"I don't care. Besides, I don't think I can spend an entire night around your ex without punching him in the face."

"That's *so* sweet. But, when you think about it, Bastard Bill did you a favor. If he wasn't such a supreme douchebag, you wouldn't be having the best sex of your life."

"Is that so?" Laughter laces his voice.

"I may be projecting a little bit." But I'm not lying. Maybe it's because this all feels so new and different, not weighted down by the kind of bedroom boredom that comes with a long-term relationship. The thing is, Bill and I were never bored in the bedroom. If he ever claimed anything else, I'd call him on that blatant lie, and I'd see the truth of it in his eyes.

No ... something electric happens every time Garrett and I connect.

"I'm glad to see you're feeling better." His fingers pick up where his palm left off, the circles more defined, digging into sore spots earned from all that retching. "And you're right. I should be shaking his hand."

I smile into my pillow. "I still think you should punch him. But I want to be there to see it."

Hands curl around my shoulders. Garrett gently rolls me over to fit into the crook of his arm. He brushes strands of damp hair off my forehead. "You're still pale."

"I'll be fine." I mold myself to his torso with a sigh, my ear pressed against his chest, listening to his steady heartbeat.

And that's how I drift off.

———

"... kill with a stranglehold to its neck."

My eyelids crack open in time to see a cheetah murder an antelope on the wall-mounted TV. "I've done that before," I croak. I'm draped across Garrett's body, my leg thrown over and wedged between his thighs. It's the most satisfying way I've woken up in eons.

Garrett aims the remote at the TV to mute it. "Morning."

I respond with a groggy moan.

He strokes a few loose hairs off my face. "How are you feeling today?"

"Empty." I woke up in the middle of the night with my tongue stuck to the roof of my mouth, so I inhaled the tall glass of Pedialyte before burrowing back into Garrett's warm body. "I'm never eating sushi again." Not grocery store sushi, anyway.

"That's fair."

The TV screen flips to a tiger closing in on a wild boar. "Do you normally spend your mornings viewing animal slaughter?"

"No, I spend them at the gym. You looked so comfortable, though, I didn't want to wake you by moving. But, yeah, I do like nature shows."

Something to file about this man I know so intimately but also not at all. I'll have to buy that fornicating mammal calendar as a Christmas gift.

If we're still talking by then.

His phone vibrates on the far nightstand, but he doesn't so much as twitch in response, his free hand smoothing over my hip instead.

"Any news from last night's debauchery? Pictures?" I hope Joe had fun, despite my hatred for the night's organizer.

"I doubt there'll be any evidence of whatever went on." He clears his throat. "You know, at that tequila tasting."

"Probably for the best. At least I didn't miss too much on my side."

Garrett's chest shakes with his laugh. "You really don't know Sara at all, do you?"

"Why?" I ask, a prickle of wariness stirring. "Is high tea code? Like tequila tasting with a sommelier is code?"

"I'm no expert, but I don't think high tea is served that late." He pauses. "And not by men in bow ties and G-strings."

I gasp. "Are you telling me I missed dirty teatime? Where's my phone? I need to text Sara. There had *better* be pictures."

"You like that sort of thing?"

"Hot bodies and large penises? Yes, I'm partial. How have you *not* figured that out yet?" Scarlet may have been mortified at the Polson Falls charity auction but I was in my element. "What else did I miss?"

"I think they were also heading out to Sara's favorite drag show."

"Nooo!" I pout into the crook of Garrett's neck.

He pulls me tighter against him to press a kiss against my forehead. "I'm sorry you missed hot bodies and large penises last night and had to spend the night with me instead."

"I didn't even get to do that. I spent it with your toilet. Which is the nicest one I've ever puked in, by the way." And this body of his is the nicest I've ever had the pleasure of touching. My hand slips under his T-shirt to admire the ridges of his abdomen. "Oh look, we're back to the cheetahs."

"They've been back and forth all morning."

"How long has this been on?"

"At least an hour."

"You watched me sleep for an hour?"

"No, I watched the cheetahs sleep. They were under a tree, looking peaceful and harmless. Like you do when you're sleeping."

"Funny." I poke his ribs, earning his flinch. "Hey, you know what *I* like first thing in the morning?" I slip my hand under his shorts before he has a chance to answer, wrapping my fist around his hard length. I give it a little squeeze before I slowly stroke it all the way to the tip.

A heavy sigh sails from his lips. He leans in to press a gentle kiss against my lips. "Are you sure you're up for that?"

"I need to make this trip worthwhile." I tighten my grip, earning his sharp inhale.

His gaze searches mine. "Give me a minute." He slips from my grasp, out from under my weight, and leaves through the bedroom door, heading downstairs.

I take that opportunity to stumble to the washroom and give my teeth a quick brush. A wave of dizziness hits me, and I have to brace my balance with a fist against the sink. When I come out, he's setting a tall glass on my nightstand. "Drink this." And then he vanishes again.

I shed my pajamas for ease, climb back into bed, and chug the entire glass of electrolytes, hoping that'll clear this fog and renew my energy. I finish just as he strolls in, a square foil wrapper between his fingers, his T-shirt and sweatpants gone.

My mouth hangs as I admire his naked body. When I look up, he's watching me, the usual arrogant smirk when I'm drooling over him absent, a soft, knowing smile in its place.

He knows.

My infatuation with him must be splayed across my face.

I swallow against the vulnerability. "Gosh, those feet of yours really are pretty."

He slips beneath the covers again. "You drink all of that?"

"Yeah."

"And how are you feeling?"

I hesitate, before admitting, "I'm not a hundred percent."

He pauses, his eyes searching my face. "We don't have to do this, Justine."

"Yes, we do. I missed strippers and drag last night. Don't take *everything* away from me."

He blinks. "You are the horniest woman I have ever met."

"Thank you. Now, are you going to put out?"

With a chuckle, he seizes me by my waist and drags me over to the center of the bed. Cradling one side of my face, he steers it into his, brushing his lips across my jaw before teasing my lips open.

I lift my head to catch his mouth, but he evades, bracketing my head with his elbows resting on my pillow. "I know what you like, but we're taking it easy this time, got it?"

I make a frustrated sound that might pass for agreement.

He leans down. Our lips meet in a painstakingly slow and sensual kiss that is a hundred times more intense than the animalistic teeth- and tongue-clashing ones we usually find ourselves in during foreplay.

I realize something then.

There are clear, strong feelings woven into this kiss. Mine, I'm aware of. I've been trying my damnedest to ignore them, to keep them behind the wall that will protect my heart from more pain while I'm still healing.

But my feelings aren't the only ones at play here. The way Garrett is kissing me …

It's making my heart ache with need for him, and that's not a place I want to visit yet.

My restlessness grows as an overwhelming swirl of conflicting emotions surges in me. My hands find their way to his hair, collecting fistfuls.

"Uh-huh." He deftly pins my wrists above my head and, fitting his hips between my thighs, presses me down with his weight. Entwining his fingers within mine, he returns to kissing me with a slow desperation palpable with each stroke of his tongue. Between us, his hard length presses against my core, a promise that I'm growing eager to collect.

I need to anchor us back into the "this is just sex" column before it's too late.

I roll my hips, sliding my warm center across his velvety soft skin.

He groans, but he doesn't make a move for the condom waiting on the nightstand. "I know what you're trying to do," he whispers, his lips never leaving mine.

"I have no idea what you're talking about." Another hip roll brings him closer to an accidental slip.

His hands tighten around mine. He shifts his focus to my jaw, dragging his tongue along the edge, down toward my neck. "It won't work. You can wait. Besides, I thought this position didn't do it for you."

I hiss as his teeth nip at my throat, feeling the aftershock of it skitter across my nipples. But he soothes it immediately, lapping against my skin with the same tantalizing skill he uses on other parts of my body.

And then his lips are back on mine, worshipping them again.

I use my feet and pinned hands as leverage, and shifting the angle of my hips to catch the tip of him, I push down.

Garrett inhales sharply as he slides into me. "I wasn't expecting you to do that."

"You should know better than to tease me." I leave him seated halfway inside me before shifting my hips to slide him out.

But he bears down on me, pushing himself in. All the way. "Fuck." His body tenses. "I can't remember the last time I felt this." With another curse, he bows his head. "You feel incredible." His flexed arms tremble.

This one moment feels more intimate than any other we've had yet. And at this moment, I want it.

I nuzzle my nose against his ear. "I have an IUD. And I got tested after Bill."

"I'm clean too." He lifts his head and our gazes touch, and an unspoken agreement passes between us.

I wrap my legs around his hips, opening myself up more, the idea of him coming inside me stirring a new, deeper ache of anticipation.

With a shaky sigh, Garrett presses his forehead against mine, our eyes mere inches away from each other, too close to focus, and yet I can't look away from the intensity.

I feel like a live wire, waiting to spark.

He begins moving, my body stretching around him. But unlike other times, where he's met my demands with wild, pummeling thrusts that leave his lungs heaving and his breathing ragged from exertion by the end, this time he keeps a steady, easy pace, his hips rolling with ease.

It's raw.

Emotional.

Somehow, this feels harsher.

He won't leave my lips alone, but I don't fight him anymore, clinging to them as intense pleasure builds inside me, my legs splayed to either side, my hands clenching within his as we move in tandem, our breathing as tangled as our tongues. He shifts his position, forcing my hips up a fraction, and then he's hitting that delicious spot inside me.

Heat floods my core.

He groans with the sensation, a guttural sound that tells me he won't be able to hold off for long.

"How thin are these walls?" I ask.

"It's brick." He pants. "Do you care?"

"No." Let everyone in this swanky building know how completely Garrett can unravel me.

My orgasm crashes like a tidal wave, my body clamping down on him as I cry out his name and buck against his hips. He follows seconds later, his arms tensing with guttural moans. He swells and then pulses inside me as he empties. With the last shudder, he collapses on top of me, his weight nearly unbearable.

For several long seconds, we say nothing. I lie limp, reveling in the combined feel of his heartbeat pounding and where he's still buried inside me. "That was ..." I can't find the rest of the words to describe it.

Incredible.

Intense.

Terrifying.

"See? You just haven't been with the right person."

If missionary feels like *that* did, I'll gladly burn my *Kama Sutra*. But something tells me it has nothing to do with the position and everything to do with the man lying on top of me.

"I love making you scream like that," he whispers, pressing a kiss against my neck.

I close my eyes, warmth blooming in my chest. "What a coincidence. *I* love it when you make me scream like that." But what's more, I love hearing him use the word *love*.

And I think I'm falling in love with Garrett.

The words itch my tongue, waiting to be spoken.

Oh God. How did this thing between us get so out of hand? I don't even know him. At least not the laundry list of favorites and bad habits I'm supposed to be able to recite before I can declare *I know him*.

But I know how I feel every time he walks into the room. I know how he consumes my thoughts, infuriates me, and sparks my laughter, how my adrenaline spikes with the anticipation of every interaction, no matter how big or small.

I'm addicted to Garrett. I can't get enough of him.

But this can't happen. I'm still stewing over my last heart-break. I'm not ready to set myself up for my next one.

"Your heart's beating so fast," he murmurs.

"I know." Because panic is exploding inside me. I think I'm having an anxiety attack.

His fingers have loosened their grip. He rolls off me, slipping out in the process, his hand smoothing over my hip. "You must be starving. One of my favorite places is a few blocks away. It's an easy walk, if you're up for it? We can give Joe and Sara a call, see if they can handle brunch. If they're not too hungover." His chuckle is soft. Oblivious.

I'm feeling light-headed.

Brunch at Garrett's favorite place … with the family.

Sounds perfect.

Sounds like a relationship.

But that's *not* what we are. We're just great sex. How long before Garrett sees that? How long before he finds someone more appropriate to settle down with like Bill did?

"You know what? I should get going home." I need to put space between us, to give myself time to think before I let this go any further.

"Now?" He pulls himself onto his elbow to stare at me. A flash of something skitters across his face that I can't read but leaves me feeling cold.

I swallow against the urge to recant, to tell him I want to stay forever. "Now."

———

Garrett's bare feet pad over the hardwood as he carries my things to the door for me. "You sure you don't want to stay?"

"I have a ton to do at home." Like get my mental state examined because I'm scurrying away like a feral cat caught in an alleyway, running from this man I'm falling head over heels for.

And my gut tells me he knows it.

"I've got work to do too." He smooths a hand over the back of his head, but I don't miss the way his throat bobs with a swallow. He may have work, but he was going to put it all off to make time for me.

Justine, you're such an idiot.

A confused, scared idiot.

"Hey, I never asked you about Friday night. What happened with Shirley—she still angry?"

"She wasn't there, so I assume so."

His forehead wrinkles. "Is that normal? For her to not be there?"

"Nope. She's never missed a Friday. Anyway, if you're still looking for my help with the meeting—"

"Justine." He sighs heavily. "If you still think this is some elaborate ruse to get my project approved, you are giving me way too much credit."

That's the problem. I *don't* believe that anymore, which makes this whole thing too risky. Because now it involves my heart. "Listen, thanks for everything. I'm sorry about last night." I don't even sound like myself.

An awkward pause hangs over us. Normally, this is the time when I ask him when he's going to be back in Polson Falls, and he kisses me and tells me he'll message. Except now we stand frozen, staring at each other.

"What's going on?" he finally asks. "One second, you're screaming my name, and then you're shutting down. Did I do something to upset you?"

"No, nothing. It's just … Things between us are good the way they've been, right? Casual."

His lips twist as he studies me. "You mean straight-up fucking."

"Exactly. Let's not complicate things."

"Wow, this is a first. Normally, I worry about women being after my money." He smooths a hand over his jaw. "Whatever you want, Justine." Strolling to the door, he opens it. "Drive safe."

I swallow and march out the door, my insides in knots.

Chapter Thirty-One

"I CAN'T BELIEVE what you did with this, Dottie." I angle my body from one side to the other in the mirror. "I mean, I still look like a corpse in this color, but at least I'm a well-dressed corpse." Sara let us choose our own shoes, and the soft gold stilettos I've paired dial the dress's appeal up by a hundred notches. "Thank you."

"My pleasure, darling. You know you're my favorite."

Scarlet coughs from her perch on the couch.

"Well, of course, my favorite after *you*, daughter. But you know what? You feel like my daughter too." Dottie pinches my cheek. "Now, I've gotta rush out. I promised Griffin my famous chicken Parmesan."

"What famous chicken Parmesan?" Scarlet frowns. "Have you ever made that before in your life?"

"No, but he doesn't know that, and it won't matter. He's always *extra* grateful after a home-cooked meal." She winks at me as she collects her purse. "Good luck at the wedding." Dottie opens the door and startles. "Oh! Hello, boys. Perfect timing. You almost missed me."

A chorus of "Hey, Dottie," fills our hallway as Shane and Dean wait for her to step out before they enter.

"Hey, babe." Shane sets his toolbox down before crossing the living room to plant a kiss on Scarlet's forehead.

"How's the ring of fire today?" I ask, checking my reflection in the mirror again.

Shane groans. "It's gonna be a long time before I ever touch sushi again." Of the three of us, he got it the worst, hovering close to the bathroom for almost thirty hours. At one point, Scarlet wanted to drive him to the hospital.

"It's on the cocktail menu for next weekend."

"I'd rather starve, thanks. You guys want to hear some good news?" He peers back at Dean. "Tell 'em what you just bought."

Dean grins. "A farm."

"What?" Scarlet and I both explode in unison.

"Yeah. Thirty-five acres about five minutes outside of town. A house, a small barn. There's even a pond and a forest."

"Farmer Dean!" I hoot with laughter. "Oh my God, this is going to be *so much fun*. Are you getting any sheep? What about cows? A bull?" I waggle my eyebrows.

Dean shakes his head, chuckling. "No animals. Just thought it'd be a good idea to invest in some land."

"When do you get it?" Scarlet asks.

"The deal closes in thirty days."

"Wild, right?" Shane collects the toolbox again. "Okay, we better get started on putting this grill together. It'll take us a few hours."

"I left it out on the patio stones in the back." Dean lingers, appraising my bridesmaid dress. "That looks a lot better. Still not like the red one."

"Nothing will ever be like the red one, but these shoes ..." I stretch my foot out, angling the toe down. "Imagine me in these and *nothing* else."

My phone chirps. I dive for it, holding my breath against all hope that it's Garrett, who I haven't heard from in three days.

It's just my mother, asking what time my flight to Boston is ahead of the wedding.

"Call him!" Scarlet prods.

I toss it back on the table, deflated. "No." Garrett texted to make sure I made it home, and then responded with "Great," and I haven't heard from him since. He hasn't responded to any of my playful messages. "It's over."

Her lips pinch with frustration. Climbing off the couch, she smooths a hand over Shane's shoulder. "I'll keep you company."

"Be there in a minute." Dean refocuses on me. "What's going on with the guy? Last I heard, you were shaking this entire house with him. What happened?"

"Nothing. I don't know. I just … I had to leave his place. I had this overwhelming need to get away from him and his penis voodoo powers."

Dean folds his arms over his broad chest, smirking. "You realized you like this guy, and you got cold feet."

"If you need to define things, *sure*," I mutter. "So?"

His brow furrows with thought. "If the tables were turned, what would you say to me?"

"I would tell you that age is just a number, and if you want to ask Abuela out, you should do it."

He barks out a laugh. "Can you, for once, just give me a straight, serious answer? No fucking around."

"None?"

"None."

"Fine! I would tell you … I would tell you …" My eyes rake over Dean as I try to fit him into my size six women's shoe. "That your ex is the biggest idiot for cheating on you because you are amazing. But something ten times better has come along, and if you let this guy go—I mean, woman—if you let her go, you will regret it for the rest of your life."

"See? Was that so hard?" He shakes his head. "Now take your own advice."

"I can't." I shrug. "What can I say? Bill did a number on me. I'm not ready to go through that again. But I'll be fine. It's no big deal. Garrett was my rebound. A really good one."

Dean scratches his chin. "What are you going to do about the wedding?"

"I don't know. Eat some more bad sushi." Though that didn't help me last time either. I traded one problem for another.

"Meera asked me to go with her, but I can bail if you need me to be your plus-one."

"That's sweet of you to offer, but don't do that." Who else is there to take, though?

A thought strikes me. "Oh my god, what if he brings Mindy?" Not only will I have to deal with Bill and Isabelle, but Garrett and "we had a thing in the past, but now we're just friends" Mindy, all at a table together?

My bottom lip begins to wobble.

Dean's seen the signs of my impending meltdowns before. "Just a rebound, huh?" He pulls me into his arms.

———

I poke my head into the office. "Hey, I'm going to run down the street to grab a sandwich from Vinnie's." I desperately miss having Todd's next door. All that's left are bare metal shelves and empty refrigerators. The new place won't be open until next week. "You want something?"

Ned looks up from his crossword to wave me away. "I brought my peanut butter sandwich. Go on. I'll hold down the fort."

I'm veering toward the hall that leads to the back when I hear a man call out, "Hello?"

I frown, searching out the owner of that voice. "Hi, I'm sorry, we didn't hear the door chime." I'm startled to discover Richard Harrington inspecting the inside of the retro refrigerator at the front of the store. He's dressed in his typical business attire. A quick peek outside shows the Town Car waiting to whisk him back to his offices.

His mustache lifts with his smile as he taps the fridge door. "What's old is new again?"

"Don't tell the mayor." I mock wink as if we have a secret. "What are you doing at Murphy's? Shopping for your new place?"

"It'll be awhile before that's ready for appliances. No, I was in town doing some site visits and I thought I'd stop in." He studies the store's interior as Garrett did that first day. "Good bones here. Lots of potential. I can see why my nephew wanted to invest in it."

"Don't tell me *you're* coming to make an offer now." This is déjà vu.

"No, my focus is on larger projects, like the ones across town. Besides, next door is already causing enough headaches for HG."

I raise my hands. "I have hung up my anarchist's badge. I am no longer the poster child for the movement. You will have no resistance from me at next week's town meeting."

His laugh is soft but jovial. Genuine. "That's welcome news. You're quite the adversary."

"That's not me. That's Shirley." Who likely isn't backing down.

"I don't know about that. It's not Shirley my nephew has been talking nonstop about for months now."

"Only good things, I'm sure." I smile slyly, even as my heart races. Have I been on his mind that much? "You should know, he has been working *really* hard to win people over and get the project moving." It's the least I can do, put in a good word with the man who Garrett clearly idolizes.

"Hmm, yes, that was evident when he came to tell me that we've added a costly town park remodel to our budget."

"He went all out. He even brought in pastries for the residents at Bonny Acres."

Richard's eyebrow arches. "My future home?"

"That's the one."

"Did it work?"

"I don't know. Shirley thinks I've crossed enemy lines. I'm *excommunicado*."

"But you haven't?" There's something in his tone that hints he knows more than he's letting on.

How do I answer that without going into sordid details that I'm sure a man like Richard doesn't care to hear about? "Let's say I straddled it for a while." A lewd memory of what I've been straddling pops in my mind, and I usher it away.

Richard smothers a smile. "The variance approval is just one more step in a complicated process. It'll go through, one way or another, and then some other problem will rear its head to challenge us. That's the nature of the business. Garrett is getting a good feel for it, and he is nothing if not invested in his career."

"Are you considering him to take over HG?" Was that true?

"Am I retiring, do you mean?" His palm smooths over the fridge's door handle. "Yes, that has been on my mind. But that takes years of planning for a company like this. And Garrett still has a lot to learn." He checks his watch. "I suppose I should be on my way. But it sounds like our paths will cross again next weekend."

"Small world, huh?"

"Indeed." He makes to move.

"Hey. It's a good thing, what you did, having Garrett revise the plans to save the old building. I know it all comes down to money, but ... still. I'm sure people around town will remember that."

He pauses, scratches his chin. "Is that what Garrett told you? That *I* made him do it?"

"You didn't?"

He falters, as if choosing his words. "If it were up to me, those tenants would have been out as soon as I could legally vacate them, and that building would be slated for demolition. Garrett is the one who insisted on reexamining the plans. He created himself an enormous amount of extra work and added cost. He didn't need to."

"But he told me ..." My words drift. Why would he lie?

"I don't think it's the senior citizens who Garrett's been trying to win over." He smiles. "See you soon. I hear the linen closets at Cliffside are nice." With a wink, he strolls out.

Leaving my cheeks flushing while I try to figure out why Garrett would lie to me. Again.

Chapter Thirty-Two

A SUDDEN URGE to pee hits my bladder as I step into Bonny Acres' common room.

Shirley is at her usual table tonight, her copper-red hair freshly colored.

"You need your wingman for this?" Ned asks.

"Only one of us has to die tonight. Say nice things at my eulogy, okay?"

He shakes his head, shuffling to where Vicki waits for him, a bouquet of tulips in his grip.

Nancy is busy wiping down each numbered bingo ball with a cloth and ignoring me. She's wearing another Easter sweater—her third one this month. The bunny stretches from her neckline to the hem and looks like a creature that gnaws on children in a horror cartoon.

With a deep breath, I march toward doom, my chin held high.

"You must be getting bored with solitaire by now." I settle into the seat across from Shirley without asking.

"Nope." She doesn't make eye contact, her hands moving over the cards, flipping and lining them up. This week's nail color is a vibrant purple.

I place the tin of cookies in front of her, and then bite my tongue and watch her play, waiting for her to crack.

It takes three minutes. "Is your developer coming tonight?"

"I have no idea where he is. Off developing things." Hopefully, not other relationships. "We haven't talked in a while." Five days feels like an eternity.

Her eyes flip to mine before refocusing on her game, but she says nothing.

"Bastard Bill proposed to Isabelle."

Her hand falters. I knew that would get her attention. "I'll bet that felt like a kick to the teeth."

"More like the shin. I hopped around a bit, but then I walked it off."

The creased corners of her lips twitch with a small smile before she smooths it over. "You were always too good for him."

"You haven't met him."

"Don't need to."

I smile at her steadfast loyalty.

"What are those?" She pokes at the tin. "From the bakery?"

"No, I made them." They're Ned's secret shortbread recipe, but with pistachios. I'm sure he won't mind. It's for a good cause.

She harrumphs but doesn't make a move toward them.

"The wedding's next weekend. I've managed to avoid Bill and Isabelle up until now, but I won't be able to avoid them there."

"You need a date. Why don't you bring the developer? He'd look good on your arm."

Is this a test? I never know with Shirley. "Funny thing, he's already going. He's Sara's cousin, and also in the wedding. I found out at the engagement party in February."

Her hands drop as she glares at me. Another secret I've kept from her.

I offer a sheepish look. "I was trying to keep Polson Falls separate from New York."

"You did a piss-poor job of that." She rips off the tin's lid and digs out a cookie. Her first bite is tentative, but then she takes another. "When'd this thing between you two start?"

I hesitate.

"Oh, give me a break. The way you two were mooning over each other. Even Phyllis could see it from across the room without her glasses, and she's legally blind."

When *did* it start between Garrett and me? Was it at the engagement party, when he came to my rescue? Or was it the first moment I laid eyes on him? "I don't know, but it's over now."

Fury twists her features. "Why? What did he do?" she snarls.

Despite everything, I smile. "He didn't do anything. It was all me." It feels strange to be divulging secrets about Garrett after we've spent so many hours plotting to dismantle him. Then again, HG was Shirley's true target. HG and the mayor. Garrett was just collateral damage. "We had this amazing night and morning, minus the food poisoning—long story—and I felt myself falling, like *truly falling* for him. But after Bill … I figure it's only a matter of time before Garrett gets bored or realizes I'm not marriage material and ends it. So I left. And now he won't call me."

"You panicked and ran scared, huh? That doesn't sound like the Justine I know." Her lips twist with thought as she pulls out another shortbread. "Did I tell you I had a Bastard Bill once?"

"No. You've never mentioned that." Though Shirley doesn't talk much about herself. She guards her life stories as if they could be wielded against her.

I wait quietly as she chews and decides how much she'll divulge.

"His name was Arnold."

"Asshole Arnold?"

She smirks. "I like that. Asshole Arnold. Arnie, for short. Gosh, we fought a lot. He was so stubborn."

I purse my lips together.

"Not buying what I'm selling, huh?" She cackles. "Fair enough. It was usually me that was the problem. He called me his firebrand. But when we made up, *did we make up*. We went on together for almost two years. I sat back and waited for the big question, figured it was a matter of time. Turns out he never had any intention of asking it. I caught him one night, having dinner with Daisy Mulligan. We had it out in a big way, and he told me I was too hotheaded, too opinionated, too strong. Daisy was more marriage material. Polite and agreeable, never raised her voice. The right kind of woman to raise his children and all that." She shakes her head. "He didn't want a firebrand. He wanted a wet noodle. But boy, did he ever shred my heart. After that, I didn't trust any man at their word. Convinced myself they'd all leave me for a Daisy eventually."

She flips a card over, but I can tell she's no longer paying attention. "Then along came Daniel. He was a nice man. We were both working at the newspaper in Philly—"

"*You* worked for the newspaper?" How has she never mentioned this?

"I was there for ten years before I moved back to Polson Falls."

"A reporter?"

She scoffs. "Secretary. God forbid they allow a woman to write a story." She rolls her eyes. "He kept courting me. Sending me flowers, asking me out to dinner. We had a lot of fun, kept things casual. *I* kept things casual until they started feeling like they weren't. And I wasn't going down that road again. Anyway, I can't remember what that last fight was about. Some problem I created in my head and then got all worked up about. Told him I didn't love him, we were done, and I walked out." She shakes her head. "I've never regretted anything in my life, but I regretted that move."

This sounds eerily familiar. "Did you ever see him again?"

A smile touches her lips. "I did. I ran into him back in the '90s, at a funeral for a colleague. He'd never married either, and he'd never stopped thinking about me. We picked right back up where we left off. He proposed within months, and I said yes."

"You *were* married?" She's never mentioned a husband once; there's no ring on her finger.

"I was. For six wonderful months, and then Daniel died of an aortic aneurysm just before Christmas."

"Oh." My shoulders sink, sadness for Shirley dragging my spirits down. "I can't decide if this is a good story or a terrible one."

"It's a cautionary one. I lost decades because I was scared of rejection for being who I am. But Daniel saw who I was from the start and loved me for it. He never wanted a wet noodle. There are men out there like that. And if this developer ends up wanting a wet noodle, then you dust yourself off and move on, to bigger and better things. You don't run and hide in an assisted living home every Friday night, playing cards with crotchety old ladies."

"That's not why I'm here! I happen to like crotchety old ladies. And you should be proud of yourself. When you stir up shit, people listen." I dig out a cookie and shove it into my mouth. "I think half the town is afraid of you." Cookie crumbs scatter onto the table.

She chuckles. "You're gonna choke on that."

"I know. Bad habit." I force down the mealy mixture with a few swallows. "I don't know what to do about him. Garrett and I haven't had a normal start."

"No, it's been an exciting start." Her eyes flash with wicked amusement. "You've put that man through the ringer, and yet he's still coming back for more."

That's true. I was his tiny menace, after all. "It just feels like there's been too many lies and half-truths." This latest revelation, courtesy of Uncle Richard, has me perplexed. "Did you know HG is reworking the plans to keep the main building?"

"I heard something about that."

"Garrett's the one who pushed for it, but he told me his uncle was forcing him to. I don't understand why he lied. If he was trying to win me over, the truth would've gotten him there faster."

"Would you have believed him?" She raises a doubtful eyebrow.

"Maybe not." I've been second-guessing his motives from the start, scoffing at his goodwill gestures.

"Sounds like you two need to have an honest-to-goodness reckoning. Put everything on the table and see what you've got to work with."

"I'm good at making jokes and antagonizing people. Having serious, mature conversations about feelings is not my strength." In the rare case that it happens, it's because I'm falling apart in a fit of tears. "Besides, he's not even answering my messages."

"You'll figure out a way to get him to listen. You're awful clever." The shortbread crumbles on the way into her mouth, sprinkling specks. She brushes them off the table, stealing a surreptitious gaze around to see if Harper is watching. "You know he'll be in town on Monday for the council meeting."

"Yeah." I'm counting down the days. Do I show up there and pin him down? "You still going to fight that variance?"

Her mouth works over her words. "I saw the plans for that condominium. It's not the *worst*-looking building," she admits.

"It's not," I agree. "And that park looks nice."

"I'll believe that's happening when I see it." She jabs the air with her finger, as if warning me not to believe it either, but then her hand falls, as if the fight in her deflates. "I'll be at the meeting, but I'm not going there to raise a stink."

An unexpected wave of relief washes over me. For Garrett's sake, I want him to succeed.

Shirley watches me closely as if sensing it. "But do me a favor —if you talk to him before then, don't tell him I'm easing off. I'd rather he sweat until the last possible moment." A wicked cackle sails from her lips.

"That secret, I will gladly keep." I grin, but my mind is working on overdrive, her words of a reckoning triggering an idea.

Chapter Thirty-Three

"YOU'RE GOING to this town meeting dressed like *that*?" Scarlet stares at my all-black ensemble—leather trench coat, wide-brimmed hat, and stilettos to cap off the menacing look—as I stalk through the house.

"I'm not going to the meeting." I need the time to prepare. "Garrett's meeting me after." The relief I felt when he answered my text and agreed to this little rendezvous was overwhelming.

I collect the cardboard box of supplies I started gathering as soon as I hatched this plan.

Scarlet peruses its contents—rubber gloves, Clorox wipes, bleach, black trash bag, handcuffs. "Will I be bringing a shovel to an undisclosed location later?"

"I don't know. I guess we'll see how this goes." I double-check that the old spare key is tucked in my pocket, and with a wink at my ride-or-die best friend, I flip my collar up and stroll out into the evening.

"Justine?" Garrett's voice echoes through the long, dark corridor, wariness lacing his tone.

"Back here. Close the door behind you." Wouldn't want any surprise visitors this time.

The heavy wooden entrance shuts with a bang, sealing us into the basement of Todd's old building. Garrett's footfalls sound along the dirt floor. "How'd you get in here?"

"You think a mere lock can keep me out?" It just so happened that Todd found a spare key when he was clearing out the last of his old office. He hadn't had a chance to turn it over to HG, and after an hour of me badgering and promising that my intentions were not felonious, he handed it over.

"What's going on?"

"We need to talk."

"Right. Look, I know we left things off ..." He appears around the wall of crates and falters, his gaze dragging down the length of my all-black outfit. He looks positively delicious tonight, dressed in tailored navy-blue pants and a crisp white shirt. He's even wearing a tie.

"Take a seat." I point at the sole chair, the sturdiest of the four.

He surveys the crime scene. "I thought you wanted to preserve this?"

"I saved what made sense." I snapped a dozen pictures and then tucked the playing cards and ashtray into the cardboard box. The rest, I wiped down. "Apparently, a century-old murder of criminals isn't high on the museum's priority list." The lady I spoke to suggested I drop the furniture off at Goodwill.

His attention shifts above to the measly twenty-watt bulb I swapped in, casting a dim and ominous glow over my interrogation area.

The corners of his mouth twitch. "Am I in trouble?" He's piecing this entire charade together quickly.

"I guess we'll find out." I gesture toward the chair again.

With another head-to-toe scour of my outfit, he strolls over to the chair. He eases in slowly, as if afraid it'll collapse under his weight.

His focus latches on my shoes as I take measured steps around him. "Here's what's going to happen." I reach down to collect one wrist, guiding his arm behind the chair. "I'm going to ask you a few questions." I collect his other wrist and join it with the first. Moving with skill, I slide the handcuffs from my pocket and lock him in. "And you are going to answer truthfully, got it?"

"Did you just cuff me?" He tugs against the binding, testing the strength.

"I wouldn't bother. These are regulation-grade police cuffs." I circle around to stand in front of him. "Ready?"

His nostrils flare with the challenge. "Fire away."

I lean back against the table—also tested for my weight—and adjust my stance, allowing my trench coat to part past my knee and show off my bare leg. It does the trick. Heat ignites in his gaze as I watch him ask the unspoken question—what's underneath this coat? "The first day we met, did you purposely mislead me?"

"In what way exactly?"

"All your flirting, acting like you were attracted to me."

He stares up at me through his heavy fringe of eyelashes. "No. I've already told you that." His answer is firm, unyielding. He almost sounds angry that I'm questioning him again.

"What about wanting to buy Murphy's so you could run it? Was that false?"

He exhales. "Yes, but—"

"Next question."

He grits his teeth but stays quiet.

"Were you trying to hide the sale of Dieter's building so you could get the project through approvals before anyone could cause problems?"

He opens his mouth, and I can sense the elaborate "it's complicated" explanation coming, so I adjust my stance farther, letting my coat part more, until he gets a peek at the black lace beneath.

"Yes or no?"

He falters until his gaze shifts up to meet mine, as if deciding something. "Yes."

I tsk. "Finally, some honesty." I stand and circle him again, lingering at his side as I drag the tip of my fingernail along his jawline, down his neck, tracing his collarbone. "The night of the engagement party, were you trying to win me over as an ally because you knew you'd have that variance meeting?"

"No."

I press against his flesh with my nail. "The truth, remember."

"That *is* the truth. The absolute last thing I was thinking about that night was a stupid variance meeting. All I wanted was another chance." His attention is locked on my face, his expression sober.

"But you knew about the meeting."

"Yes."

I shift behind him, lingering there a moment, leaving him in suspense over my next question, our next contact. Gooseflesh crawls over his neck as he waits. I smile. "It's not that cold in here, is it?"

"You tell me."

"Hmm … Good question." I yank on my belt, letting the leather ends drop and the sides of my coat fall open. Stepping around to the other side, I stall just within his line of vision. "What do you think?"

A sharp hiss sails through his lips, his eyes burning as they take in the bra and panties set. "Can't tell. Come closer?"

I want to. A handcuffed Garrett is impossible to resist. My thighs itch to feel his hips between them, but I hold back. "Who decided to rework the building plans and keep the original structure?"

His lips part, but then he stalls, looking up to see my smug smile. Seeing the answer there. "When did Richard tell you?"

"He came into the store last week."

A long exhale sails from Garrett's lips.

"Why'd you lie about that?"

"Because I knew you wouldn't believe me if I told you it was my choice, that you'd see it as some other ploy, like the park project. I figured I'd give it time. Give *you* time to realize I'm not the slimy developer you think I am."

Exactly what Shirley suspected. "Richard said he would have torn it all down. That you didn't need to do any of this."

"No, I didn't *need* to. Though, I could argue that it has its own set of benefits."

I have no interest in delving into those. All I want to understand are his motivations. "Why are you doing it?"

A small smile touches Garrett's lips. "Contrary to what Shirley thinks, not every developer gets an erection for a bulldozer. I like old buildings."

I knew that. I saw it in the way he studied the skyline in New York with genuine admiration, the way he spoke. That was the first time I felt like I might be seeing the real Garrett.

I settle in front of him, taking up the space between his parted thighs. "Any other reason?"

He swallows hard, peers up at me. "Because it mattered to you, and you matter to me."

I could joke about all the power I must wield, making the baby developer buckle to my whims, but for once, I don't even feel the urge to hide my feelings behind humor. "You matter to me too."

His eyes soften. "I wondered if you'd ever admit to that."

"It's not easy for me. Not after Bill."

"I know." He sighs heavily. "So, is that it? Is the interrogation over?"

"Not quite." I hesitate. "What is this, between us?" Vulnerability hangs in my voice.

"You tell me. You're the one calling the shots. I'm following your lead." He searches my features in earnest. "Am I just your rebound? Is this purely physical?"

"No." Despite whatever foot we started off on with each other. "But I'm scared."

"I know you are. But of what? I am not your ex."

I bite my bottom lip. How do I explain this? "That you'll

decide you don't want your tiny, beautiful menace anymore. That you'd rather have a wet noodle."

A blank look takes over his face. "I can't even pretend that I understand that. What ... why would I want a *wet noodle*?"

I shake my head. "Nothing, it's just something Shirley said about firebrands and wet noodles, and it resonated with me in a weird way. I am who I am, and for some people, I can be too much. Admit it, I was too much for you and your posh life and upbringing."

"I can't admit that because it's not true. You were *never* too much for me." His lips twitch with a smile. "That first day we met, when you told me I've never met a woman like you? Were you ever right. Because no other woman has invaded my thoughts so utterly and completely like you have. And it's not even the sex, which believe me, is fucking mind-blowing. But I catch myself wondering what you'd say or do in any given situation, what snappy comeback you'd have." He shakes his head. "No woman has made my blood boil, or challenged me, surprised me, or made me laugh, or made me care as much as you have. I wouldn't ever want you to mute yourself for anyone, especially not me."

My heart swells at the ring of honesty in his words. "I'm sorry I bolted last weekend."

He nods. "I figured out why you did. I didn't like it, but I knew it wasn't me."

"It *was* you. You're too perfect. And I ... am the woman your mother found on her knees in a closet with her son."

"Man, did I hear about that one." He chuckles. "But she's a lot more open-minded than you might imagine. I think you two will get along."

The air is chilly, but I barely feel it, my skin burning in anticipation.

Garrett tugs at his restraints. "I've never been handcuffed before. You did that awfully fast. Like you have experience."

"A girl never tells." I reach up to remove my hat and toss it to the table. My long hair tumbles down over my shoulders as I move in to straddle his lap. "There're all kinds of things we can do with those."

He leans forward as far as he can, his lips just inches from mine. "Such as?"

"Hard to describe. Better if I show you." I keep my lips out of reach as I shimmy my hips closer until I can feel his hard length against the apex of my thighs. I grind against it, earning his groan. The ache to feel him inside me is building quickly.

"I have a question for you," he asks, swallowing hard. "Sara told me about Bill and Izzy. How hard was it to hear that he's getting married?"

"It was hard," I admit. "But not nearly as hard as I thought it would be." Because as often as Garrett claims he thinks about me, my thoughts have been consumed by him for months. I smooth my hands over his cheeks, admiring the sharp angles. "If he could do that to me, he's not the man I convinced myself he was. That person doesn't exist." I give Garrett's tie a gentle tug. "Besides, he's got nothing on you. He can have his wet noodle."

Garrett grins. "It's starting to make sense now. Yeah, you're definitely a firebrand."

Mention of that brings me to Shirley. "How'd your big town meeting go?"

"Anticlimactic. I thought you'd be there."

"I couldn't. I was busy staging all this."

His gaze drops over my lacy outfit and bare skin. "And I appreciate it."

"So ... no issues with your variance?"

"My request passed, and no one lobbied against it, if that's what you're asking." His eyes narrow. "But I think you already knew that."

"I may have heard something through the grapevine."

"Thanks for the warning," he mutters, his smile crooked.

"Sorry, couldn't. I made a promise to a friend to let you sweat. Besides, Ralph was off the clock."

"Yes. Busy getting dressed for a felony. And *your friend* cornered me after."

"Oh no." I wince. "How bad?"

"I don't know. She told me that if I hurt you in any way, she'll come back and haunt my ass every night until I'm dead. And then we'll both be in hell together, and she'll *really* fuck with me."

Laughter rolls out of me, filling the dingy old stone basement. "If there's anyone who can do it, it's Shirley."

"I believe that. But I told her she has nothing to worry about. It's you who's going to break my heart." His brown gaze drifts over my lips, raw adoration shining in it. "But I don't even care. I'm here for it."

I lean in until our lips find each other in a kiss that soothes the gnawing ache that's been lingering in my chest since the day I left him.

"Any chance you can uncuff me now?" he whispers.

"Why on earth would I do that?"

Chapter Thirty-Four

"I COULD GET USED TO THIS." I accept the flute and lean back in the last vacant Adirondack chair overlooking the channel, my sunglasses shielding my eyes as the sun hints at descent.

"To what, exactly? Me, serving you? Or watching yachts coast by while sipping on pricey champagne?"

"Both. All of it." Especially this magical little slice of American Richie Rich heaven, tucked on an island that isn't an island. Garrett and I arrived in Newport Thursday night and spent all of Friday touring around in his Porsche—a sly surprise—before the rehearsal dinner.

I met his father, Garrett the Second, and I managed not to reference Stuart the Second even once. I again met Blair and bit my tongue against the urge to highlight how her son's pants were on this time.

All in all, I'd say that was a success.

But my biggest triumph was that I saw Bill and Isabelle in the hotel lobby, and I didn't want to crumble, I didn't want to hide. I wouldn't say I didn't care. It's going to take time for me to detach years of memories—so many good ones—from the man he is. Maybe we'll be friends again one day.

Maybe not.

But I didn't feel that hollow ache in my heart, that punch to my gut. And there's one dashingly handsome explanation for that. Garrett's been my anchor, attached to me the entire weekend, save for the few hours earlier today when the two sides of the bridal party were separated. I've dreaded for months looking across the aisle and seeing Bill standing there, but Garrett's face was the *only* one I cared to look at the entire wedding ceremony, when I wasn't mouthing "you big baby" to Joe for crying as Sara came down the aisle.

Even now, Garrett hovers next to my chair in his three-piece pale gray suit, like a sentry to protect me from dark moments. But there aren't any looming. "I can't wait to get you out of those clothes." The sage tie matches my lace dress. "Except for the tie. You can keep wearing that."

He steals a glance around, crossing gazes with several guests who clearly heard my blatant come-on because they're chuckling, before hiding his smirk behind a sip of his drink.

"You love it." I wink. I may be a tad tipsy.

"Hey, guys." Scarlet sounds out of breath. Trailing behind her are Shane, Dean, and Meera, who clings to Dean's arm as she maneuvers the grass in her heels. "Picture time. They're looking for you."

"You're kidding. I thought we were done!" We spent two hours grinning for the camera.

She holds her hands in the air, a champagne flute still gripped in one. "I'm just the messenger."

"Well, it's too late. I can't get out of this chair."

"Come on." Garrett reaches down, collects my hand, and pulls me up.

Scarlet swoops in to take my place. "Thank you!"

Dean looks dashing, as usual, but especially with the good doctor on his arm, her straight, raven-black hair shimmering in the sunlight. He swears it's just casual. For her sake, I hope she's reading from the same page.

"Aren't you two cute." I grin slyly at Dean. "Has she had a chance to check—"

"No. Stop." His cheeks turn red.

I pinch his side on my way past, but I don't miss Meera asking, "Check what?"

My wicked laughter carries over the grassy knoll.

Garrett ropes his arm around my shoulders. "You truly are a menace."

"Thank you. Can we please skip these pictures? This is excessive. My cheeks still hurt."

"You know what? I agree. This *is* bullshit." He scans our surroundings. "But we can't stay here."

I gasp with delight. "You know this place. Where should we hide? Besides our room, because if we go in there, we're never coming out, and I'm hungry."

His focus lands on the hotel, aptly named for the deathly drop leading down to the water. A devilish gleam sparks in his eyes. "Follow me."

Epilogue

ONE YEAR LATER ...

"Low-income apartments were part of his campaign promise." Shirley jabs at the park bench with her hot pink–painted index fingernail. "I didn't vote to reelect him, but I'll make damn sure Gump keeps his promises, if it's the last thing I do."

Some things don't change around Polson Falls. Shirley's grim determination to make Ferris Gump's life hell is one of them. I smile at her energy. "You know, *you* should run for mayor."

She scoffs at my suggestion. "I tried that once. Didn't work out."

"What?" I gawk at her. "You never told me that."

"It was back in the '80s. You think getting elected mayor as a woman *now* is tough?" She snorts. "People said I was too confrontational for politics."

I bite my tongue. Sometimes I can get away with poking at Shirley if her mood is right. Today is not that day. But after three missed bingo nights, it's still good to see her.

"Besides, do you have any idea how old I am now?"

"No, actually. I don't." But I feel like she's lived ten lifetimes.

"Good. Let's keep it that way." She waves me off with a cackle.

A little girl of maybe five squeals as she sails down the slide, pulling Shirley's attention behind us. The park redesign started and finished within six weeks last year, ending in a ribbon-cutting ceremony that Garrett insisted Shirley be a part of, given it was her relentless voice that inspired the project. Though she wouldn't admit to it, I know she loved it. Harper said the front-page article with her picture that Colin took is pinned to the wall in her suite.

"That's Gertie's granddaughter."

"She's cute. You know, for a kid." A man who I assume is her father points out a nearby butterfly, and the girl chases after it, her hands in the air, heading toward a row of tall grasses and a lilac bush. "Does she know Grandma's banging the Bonny Acres' dog?"

"Not anymore." Shirley's grin is wicked. It always is when she's downloading juicy gossip. "You've missed a few doozies. Let me fill you in."

———

I cross the street toward the Revive Project. The safety fencing came down a few weeks ago when they completed the last of the outside work, and the finished product looks even better than the designs. Anyone who knew the building that stood there before can still see it hidden within—the color of the brick face, the shape of the second-floor windows.

The process to get here, though, wasn't as pretty. Working next to construction for the last year has been noisy, dusty, and altogether not enjoyable, and I made sure Garrett heard about it daily.

But it's almost over. Every condo unit was spoken for within a week of sales opening up. They'll be move-in ready next month.

"Since when do you hang around past three o'clock?" I holler at the figure standing on the sidewalk where the laneway cuts between Murphy's and the new building.

John the contractor looks up from his clipboard and grins. "When the boss is a tight-ass."

"He *does* have a tight ass." I wink.

Garrett appears around the corner from the back then. His flat look says he heard me.

My pulse kicks up a notch as it always does when I see him. If there is a honeymoon stage for us, we haven't reached its end yet. The past year has flown by, and each day I learn more and fall more in love with him, more thankful for Bill's selfish life choices that led me to Polson Falls, to Murphy's, and inevitably, into this man's arms.

"Any other delays I need to know about?" That question is directed at John, but Garrett pauses long enough to lean down and kiss me hello. I haven't seen him since Wednesday.

"Do I get one too?" John puckers his lips.

Garrett shakes his head at me. "What have you done to my people?"

"*Me*? How is this my fault?"

"It's not. It's mine, for exposing them to you."

"Hey"—I hold up my hands in mock surrender—"you're the one who came to me on your knees, groveling for help to save your little project from total ruin." Garrett was drowning in work, and John is too nice when it comes to getting answers, so I offered to make a few calls and track down some missing building materials and replace lazy city tradespeople with locals I trusted. I guess I was too proficient because somehow that turned into dealing with day-to-day construction site challenges, administrative paperwork, and an official job offer from HG that I've been sitting on for a month.

Garrett says it's a baby-developer-in-training role, with potential to move up.

"From total ruin, huh?" His dimples pop with his amusement. "Is that how that all went down?"

"More or less."

"So? Delays?" he pushes.

"Nothing major." John looks to me to elaborate.

I roll my eyes. "The bathroom faucets are on back order, so I'm going to swap them out for comparable ones. They'll be here next Thursday." There are *so many* moving pieces and decisions in this development game. I'm enjoying it, but I won't admit it to Garrett.

He smirks. "See? Was that so hard?"

"No. But do you know what is *so hard?*"

"Have a great weekend, John." Garrett waves, effectively cutting me off from delivering the rest of my lewd and inappropriate comment.

The general contractor saunters toward the back where the vehicles are parked, chuckling.

Garrett throws an arm over my shoulders, pulling me into his side. "You're such a pain in my ass."

"I know."

We stand in silence on the sidewalk for a long moment, regarding the For Lease sign in Murphy's window. Beyond the glass is nothing but an empty space and seven decades of memories.

With Lowes opening across town last fall, Ned's little business took an even bigger hit, and he decided it was time to shutter the doors for good. He didn't seem too distraught about the decision, though. I think he'd been mulling it for some time. It could have been because he was already making other plans, ones that involved Vicki.

He sold his building to Garrett in March. We had the grand closing celebration a month ago. Now Ned spends most of his time visiting with Vicki at Bonny Acres. I wouldn't be surprised if his house is on the market soon and he finds himself a suite there as well.

Maybe they'll get one together.

I lean my head against Garrett's chest. "Your place or mine?"

"I'm in the mood for the city this weekend."

"You know what? Same." We're spending more time in New York as Garrett gears up for another, much bigger project. We see

Joe and Sara often, which has been a treat, watching her pregnant belly grow with my niece. It's beginning to feel as much like home to me as Scarlet's, and given I overheard her and Shane talking about selling both places and buying something bigger, I think my days in my claimed room behind the kitchen are coming to an end soon.

But that's okay. I'm ready to move on.

Garrett tightens his arm around me. "Besides, you don't even have a place, squatter."

"Don't you start with that too. And, hey, you were squatting up *there* for a few months." I point to the window above where Dieter's used to be.

"Barely." He scoffs, leading me down the laneway toward the back parking lot—a much smaller one now, and riddled with potholes from months of construction, waiting to be regraded and paved. "I stopped at Todd's on the way here to grab steaks for tonight."

"Bacon-wrapped?"

"Naturally."

"Gosh, you're *so* well trained."

"He says hi."

I haven't been by the shop in weeks, but I heard through Dottie that Todd hired on more staff to handle the busy grilling season. It looks like the move across town was a smart one.

Garrett waves at Morgan and a couple standing near one of the back doors.

"Who're they?"

"New tenants in one of the commercial spaces. Here to check it out."

"Already? Nice!" Morgan has taken over much of the rental management for the area—a busy full-time role that has her considering a move to Polson Falls to reduce her daily commute from Philly. "What's the business?"

Garrett frowns in thought. "Bubble tea shop."

The Player Next Door

Want a sneak peek from Scarlet and Shane's story, The Player Next Door? Here you go!...

———

Chapter One
2007

I survived Day One without puking or crying.

Do they make T-shirts with that slogan? They must. I can't be the only person to head back to school after summer vacation with a broken heart. Though, I'd be lying if I wore that T-shirt. I *did* cry today; I just didn't do it in public. I ducked into a restroom stall as the first fat tear rolled down my cheek and then spent my entire lunch period with my butt planted on a toilet seat, struggling to muffle my sobs as giggling girls streamed in and out, oblivious.

And all it took was one look from Shane Beckett to cause that reaction. Or rather, the lack of a look. A passing glance as we crossed paths in the hallway between third and fourth period, when his beautiful whiskey-colored eyes touched mine before flickering away, as if the momentary connection was accidental.

As if the seventeen-year-old, six-foot star quarterback for the Polson Falls Panthers and I hadn't spent the summer in a semipermanent lip-lock.

As if last night, sitting in his father's car outside my apartment building, he didn't tell me that we were getting too serious, too fast, and he couldn't handle a relationship right now, that he needed to focus on football, and I was too much of a distraction.

That one vacant, meaningless look from Shane Beckett in the hall today was worse than anything else he could have done, and it sent me stumbling away, dragging my obliterated spirit behind me.

The rest of the day has been a painful blur, with me cowering in the same restroom stall after the last bell rang to avoid the crowd. I foresee myself spending a lot of time in there. Maybe I should hang an occupied sign and declare it mine for the school year.

"Hey, Scarlet." Becca Thompson, her stride buoyant, flashes a sympathetic smile as she passes me on the steps outside the front doors of Polson Falls High.

"Hey," I manage, but the bubbly blond is already gone, trotting down the sidewalk, no glance backward, almost as if she hadn't greeted me at all. She's nice enough, but I shouldn't be surprised by the lukewarm friendliness. We've never traveled in the same circles, her being the popular cheerleader and me being the reticent mathlete who slogs away at the local drive-in movie theater every weekend in summer. We'd exchanged nothing more than polite greetings before Shane and I started dating, despite our mothers working together at the hair salon for years.

Couple that with the fact that Becca is best friends with Penelope Rhodes—a.k.a. the Red Devil, otherwise known as the worst human to walk these dank halls—who was away in Italy all summer, and I'm not surprised that I'm persona non grata once again.

Becca obviously knows Shane and I broke up. They *all* must know. But at least she acknowledged me, so I guess there's that.

She's heading toward the parking lot now. That's where the jocks and cheerleaders and otherwise popular crowd hang out, congregated around the cars their parents bought for them, talking and laughing and ignoring the peasants.

I check my watch. It's been twenty minutes since the last bell. Most of them *should* have left by now. With a heavy sigh, I tuck a wayward strand of my mouse-brown bob behind my ear, hike my backpack over my shoulder, and amble down the path, ready to avoid eye contact and walk the eight blocks home where I can hide in my bedroom for the rest of my life—or at least for the night.

Rounding the bend, I spot Steve Dip heading this way with two other guys from the football team. My stomach clenches. There's a reason the wide receiver and Shane's best friend is nick-named Dipshit. He's an obnoxious ass with a cruel sense of humor.

I hold my breath, hoping he'll ignore me, like everyone else seems to be.

Our eyes meet and he winks. *No such luck.* "Hey, BB. You cost me fifty bucks!"

I frown. *What?* I have no idea why he's calling me that, but it can't mean anything flattering, especially not with the raucous laughter that follows.

He brushes a hand through his cropped hair. "Tell Dottie I'm gonna come in for a *quickie* later, will ya?"

"Bite me," I throw back, my cheeks burning as we pass. How long has he been sitting on that stupid joke? It's far from the first time I've heard something along those lines. When your mother's the town bicycle, everyone feels the need to share their punch line with you. He never dared say a word about her when Shane and I were together, but I guess it's no holds barred now.

"Is that an offer?" Steve grins. "'Cause it sounds like that'd be more action than Bex got this summer."

I lift my middle finger in the air and speed up, wanting to put as much distance as possible before this knot in my throat explodes into tears. I told Shane I wanted to take it slow and he said that was fine. He never pushed me.

Did he tell his friends? Was he laughing about it with them? Mocking me?

The parking lot has emptied out with only a few students lingering. Aside from Dean Fanshaw, no one left is associated with Shane and that crowd. Thank God.

Dean is Shane's very best friend and, unlike Steve, isn't known for being a jerk. What he *is* known for—and for good reason, based on what I witnessed—is boning every girl who's willing. Currently, he's too busy mauling Virginia Grafton's neck against the hood of his truck to notice me.

I keep my eyes forward as I rush past them and his red pickup, trying my best not to think about warm summer nights stretched out in the back of it, cradled between Shane's long, muscular thighs, my back resting against his chest, struggling to focus on the movie playing on the drive-in screen ahead.

I'm so focused on *not* catching Dean's attention that I almost miss the two sets of legs dangling over the open tailgate, tangled in each other.

Almost.

One set, long and male, I recognize instantly. It's the shoes I recognize, actually—white Vans. Shane's favorite.

The other legs are shapely and lead into a short, powder-pink skirt that I distinctly remember from second period English.

I'm frozen in place as I watch Shane and Penelope Rhodes lost in a kiss, Shane's fingers woven through her fiery-red hair, while his other hand slips beneath that tiny skirt.

I was *so* wrong.

Ignoring me earlier was *not* the worst thing Shane Beckett could have done today.

———

Chapter Two
  August 2020

I inhale the stale air in the living room, rife with the smell of old wood steeped in summer's humidity. The widow Iris Rutshack left the house spotless, at least. Or rather, her children must have, because I can't imagine the ninety-year-old woman on her hands and knees, scrubbing grime off the thick pine baseboards.

I smile with giddiness.

This place is *mine*.

I used to walk past this charming clapboard house every day on my way home from school. I'd admire the pale blue exterior and the covered porch running along the front, adorned by a matching set of rocking chairs that Mr. and Mrs. Rutshack—old even back then—filled every afternoon, watching the kids go by. On the odd day that their watchful gazes were distracted by a singing bird at their feeder, I'd stick my hand between the fence pickets and steal a bloom from the wild English-style garden that bordered the sidewalk.

Then I'd keep going all the way home to our low-rent apartment complex, my feet growing heavier with each step closer. When I closed my eyes at night, I'd imagine I was drifting off to the rhythmic sound of creaking chairs and cricket chirps, and not to the barfly screwing my mom on the other side of a too-thin wall.

"Thanks, Gramps. Whoever you are." My voice echoes through the hollow space as I wander. Technically, my father's father bought the house for me. He was never a part of my life, but he knew who I was—the product of a fling between his twenty-eight-year-old, truck-driver son with a criminal record and my then-fifteen-year-old mother—and was kind enough to name me in his will.

The house needs some TLC, more evident now that the furniture is gone. Nothing fresh paint, new lights, and a belt sander to the worn golden oak floors can't fix. I knew that when I put an offer in, and ever since I signed the sale papers, my butt's been glued to the shabby couch of my Newark apartment while I've binge-watched home-reno shows for inspiration. Of course, most of it I can't afford. Slowly but surely, though, I'll turn this place into the charming seaside retreat—minus the sea—that I've always envisioned.

Checking the time, I fire off a quick "Where are you?" text to my best friend, Justine, and then head to the porch to wait for the U-Haul. They were supposed to be here an hour ago. I'm annoyed, but I can't be too annoyed, seeing as Joe and Bill—Justine's brother and boyfriend—are driving two hours each way to move me in exchange for beer and burgers and a night on air mattresses.

Well, I'm sure Justine will repay Bill in some sordid way that I'd rather not think about.

Leaning against the post, I smile at the hum of a lawn mower churning through grass in the neighborhood. I'll have to pay a neighborhood boy to cut my front yard until I can afford my own mower. The gardens, I'll tend on my own. Iris and her husband doted on this property for sixty years, and I promised her I'd keep them thriving. Maybe that's a tall order, seeing as I have yet to keep even a cactus alive. First stop tomorrow is to replace my long-lost library card so I can borrow some gardening books.

The low picket fence—more decorative than purposeful—that lines the front yard has seen better days, the layers of white paint peeling away, many of the boards needing new nails to secure them upright. The wooden rocking chairs will need attention too. They rest where they always have. Iris left them, saying they belong on this porch. I can't bring myself to sit in one just yet, so I settle on the slanted porch steps instead.

Two children coast along the quiet, oak-lined street on their bicycles, throwing a curious glance my way. I'm sure they saw the For Sale sign out on the curb weeks ago. In a town this small, everyone is interested to know more about the woman moving into the neighborhood.

They don't have to worry about me, though. I'm a native of Polson Falls, Pennsylvania, merely displaced for twelve years when I dashed away to college in New York, allured by the idea of starting over in a big city where people hadn't heard the names Scarlet or Dottie Reed. It was fun for a time, but I've since learned big cities aren't all they're cracked up to be, and the luxury of anonymity has its own set of challenges. Like, how hard it is to catch a break in a school board where you have no connections. Seven years of substitute teaching while waitressing in the evenings to make ends meet dulled the luster for that life.

It seemed like providence then, when I made the obligatory trip home to visit Mom for her birthday and ran into my elementary school principal at the 7-Eleven. Wendy Redwood always loved me as a student. We got to talking about my teaching career. Thirty minutes of chatter and what felt like an impromptu interview later, she asked me if I'd ever consider working for her. Lo and behold, she's *still* the principal at Polson Falls Elementary and was looking for a sixth grade teacher for the fall. Sure, there were hiring considerations and board rules and all that, but she could navigate around them. Wink, wink. Nudge, nudge.

I smiled and thanked her and told her I'd think about it. At the time, I couldn't imagine entertaining the thought, but then I drove down Hickory Street for shits and giggles, only to see the open-house sign in front of my childhood dream home.

Within fifteen minutes of stepping inside, I was dialing Wendy Redwood for the job and considering what I should offer on the property. It all seemed like kismet. I mean, the house was at a price almost too good to be true, and the school was two blocks away!

I sigh as I sip the last of my cold, burnt gas station coffee. This is a fresh start, even in an old world full of familiar faces. Besides, it's been more than a decade since I last roamed the halls of any school here. Those painful years and cruel people are far behind me.

The peaceful midday calm is disrupted by the chug of a garage door crawling open, followed by the deep rumble of a car engine starting. A long, red vintage muscle car backs out of the garage next door and eases into the open space beside a blue Ford pickup. I can't tell what kind of car it is, but it's old and in pristine shape, the bright coat of paint glistening in the August sun.

I never asked Iris about the neighbors. The two times I've been here—once during the open house and once after I'd signed the paperwork for the offer—nobody was home on either side. Both properties look well maintained, though. The bungalow with the muscle car has new windows and a freshly built porch off the front. There isn't much in the way of gardens—some shrubs and trees—but the lawn is manicured.

I watch curiously as the driver's side door pops open and a tall man with wavy, chestnut-brown hair steps out, his back to me as he fusses with his windshield wiper. Coffee pools in my mouth as I stall on my swallow, too busy appreciating the way his black T-shirt clings to his body, showing off broad, sculpted shoulders, muscular arms, and a tapered waist. He's wearing his dark-wash jeans perfectly—not so baggy that they hang unflatteringly off his ass, but not so tight that cowboy boots and a wide-brimmed hat come to mind.

Damn.

I hold my breath in anticipation, hoping my neighbor will show me a beautiful face to match that fitness-model body. What a stroke of luck that would be, to live next to a gorgeous man. A *single*, gorgeous man, I pray.

Finally, my silent pleading is answered as he turns and his gaze drifts my way.

I struggle not to spew coffee from my mouth as my keen interest turns to horror.

Oh my God.

Someone, please tell me this is a mistake.

Please tell me I'm not living next door to Shane Fucking Beckett.

———

Chapter Three

What is Shane even *doing* back in Polson Falls?

The last I heard, he was flying high on a full-ride football scholarship, somewhere in California. Mind you, I heard that way back in senior year, when people were strolling through the halls, bragging about the college offers they'd opened after school the day before. Back when all I could think about was getting out of this town and all the assholes in it—him being the king of them.

Shane Beckett can*not* be back in Polson Falls and living next to me.

He just can't.

But, oh my God, he *is* heading this way, stalking smoothly across his lawn to mine, his long legs easily maneuvering over my picket fence. He strolls along my driveway toward me, eyeing my dented Honda Civic on his way past.

He must not realize who I am. There's no way he'd be so casual in approaching if he did. I look a lot different from the girl he slummed it with for a summer, back before our senior year. The boring, mousy-brown bob I used to sport in high school is gone, replaced by sleek, tawny hair that stretches halfway down my back. My once-average figure has been honed by years of running and yoga. And while I still sometimes shop at thrift stores for my clothing, I've acquired a discernible palate for higher-end consignment purchases. Even now, on "moving day," my worn Guns N' Roses T-shirt looks trendy paired with black leggings and jeweled sandals.

Shane has changed too, but not by much. Being the star quarterback, he was always lean, but fit. He's much bigger now, his neck thicker, his shoulders broader, his top clinging to a solid, curvy chest, his jaw more sculpted and angular. And the hair he always kept cropped is longer, gelled in a tousled, messy style.

He's *still* gorgeous. In fact, he's *more* gorgeous than he ever was. I'd recognize him from a mile away, even all these years later.

I'd recognize him as the guy with the deceptively sweet dimples who smashed my seventeen-year-old heart into a thousand pieces.

I sit up straighter and pull my shoulders back to meet him head-on, readying myself mentally as my gut churns with nerves and my pulse races. Thank God I slipped on my sunglasses when I sat down. At least I can hide the panic from my eyes as he comes to a stop three feet from me.

Those full, soft lips that I remember kissing for hours—so long that my own were left chapped and sore some nights—stretch with a wide smile. "Scarlet Reed."

His voice is deeper and sexier than I remember, and my stupid, traitorous heart jumps at the sound of my name on his quicksilver tongue. The first time he said my name, the night he asked me out, it took me forever to pick my jaw up off the drive-in concession counter. I was so shocked he knew who I was.

Obviously, he knows who has moved in here.

I clear my throat, trying to maintain calm. "Shane Beckett."
Shane Fucking Beckett.

Sliding his hands into his pockets, he climbs the first step and leans against the railing. It creaks under his weight. "Your dream came true." His warm eyes drift over the face of the house. They're as stunning as I remember them, speckled with gold flakes and rimmed with dark brown. "You bought the old Rutshack house."

"You … you remembered?" I sputter, unable to mask my

surprise. I mentioned my secret wish to own this place on our first official date—a balmy night in early July, the humidity making my hair frizz and my skin slick. I was so nervous, I babbled the entire time. I was sure he regretted asking me out.

Shane's gaze drops from its inspection of the porch ceiling to settle on me. His eyelashes are still impossibly thick and long, his nose still slender and perfect. "I remember a lot about that summer."

My chest tightens, and pain I'd long since thought faded flares with renewed vigor. "So do I." The sweet words, the longing looks, the gentlest touches. He told me I was one of the coolest girls he'd ever met, and it didn't matter that my few misfit friends would never gel with his many popular friends, or that I wasn't a cheerleader or an athlete.

He said he didn't care that my mom and I lived in an apartment on the shady side of town, or that she was caught in a compromising position with our *married* town mayor the night of our school's Christmas pageant when I was twelve.

He swore he wasn't the player everyone said he was, and he was okay with taking things slow, that he wouldn't push me to give him my virginity.

He told me that he thought he might be falling in love with me.

I remember it all because it was in stark contrast with the personality one-eighty he pulled in the last week before school, when he started avoiding my calls and breaking plans. He dumped me the night before classes began, claiming he wasn't looking for a serious relationship through senior year.

What he meant was, he wasn't looking for a serious relationship with *me.*

Worse, he wanted it with Penelope Rhodes, the daughter of the scandalized mayor having the affair with my mother. She'd made my life hell since seventh grade, and he knew it.

Shane flinches ever so slightly, the only sign that he's aware of what a thoroughbred douchebag he was in high school. "You look different."

"I'm surprised you recognize me."

"Iris told me who she sold to." He chews his bottom lip, hesitating. "I probably wouldn't have known it was you at first. Not with those giant sunglasses covering half your face."

"They're Prada." Five seasons ago, but still. And I feel stupid for announcing that.

His eyes bore into the lenses as if trying to see beyond them. "Take them off."

I hate Shane Beckett with every fiber of my body, I remind myself. Even the fibers between my legs that are stirring right now, as I imagine him asking me in that deep, sexy voice to take something else off. *Everything* else off.

A medley of short horn blasts sounds and a moment later, the U-Haul pulls in.

I release a shaky sigh of relief, saved from the risk of bending to his will. I need to regain my composure before I come across as the love-struck teenager I used to be. I'll *never* allow myself to be that around him ever again.

"My friends are here."

"Do you need any help with—"

"Nope," I cut him off curtly, hauling my body up to charge down the steps, inhaling the intoxicating hint of bergamot and mint on my way past. My annoyance flares. He even *smells* sexy.

I march across the lawn, needing to get away from Shane and fast. "Finally!" I holler as Bill slides out of the passenger seat, followed by Justine.

Her sharp, hazel eyes immediately land on Shane. "Who is *that*?" she asks in her thick Bostonian accent.

"Can you wait until I'm out of earshot before you drool over another guy?" Bill shakes his head as he wanders to the back of the truck.

"Nobody. Can you stack the orange- and blue-stickered boxes in the dining room? That way we can get to the bedroom furniture as fast as possible. Pink-stickered boxes go upstairs. The ones with the green stickers are for the kitchen." I spent three days researching how best to organize my belongings for efficient unpacking.

Justine studies me warily. We've lived together since freshman year of college, and she can tell when I'm pretending to be indifferent while there's a four-alarm panic fire burning inside me. But because she's my very best friend, she also knows when not to push.

"Come on, guys, you heard the boss!" She claps her hands. She's barely five feet tall and diminutive in every regard except the range of her voice and her larger-than-life personality.

Her brother, Joe, jumps out from the driver's side. "Gotta take a piss first," he announces, heading for the porch.

"Put the seat down when you're done!" I holler after him. I don't know how many times I've fallen into the toilet in the middle of the night because Joe was crashing on our couch and had forgotten the common courtesy.

Shoes crunch against the gravel driveway behind me, setting off a fresh wave of tension.

Just keep on walking back to your side.

Justine thrusts out her hand. "I'm Scarlet's best friend, Justine. And you are …"

Despite my greatest effort not to, I steal a glance in time to see the deep dimples form with Shane's sexy smirk. Those dimples fed a lot of girls' fantasies, including mine. Back before we dated, I used to spend all of chem class waiting to catch a glimpse of them.

"Shane. I live next door." He accepts her hand.

"*Shane*. From *next door*." God, I'm going to get an earful of lewd suggestions later. "Well, it's nice to meet you, Shane. Have you lived in this thriving metropolis long?"

"All my life, except for a few years while I was away at college." He nods toward me. "Scarlet and I go way back. We were friends in high school."

A loud, unattractive snort escapes me, earning raised brows from them both.

"Where'd you say you want these?" Bill rounds the corner, his arms laden with a cumbersome box, the top marked with a blue sticker.

"Dining room. Far wall."

He juts his chin at Shane on his way past.

Shane looks from him to the truck, and back again. "Are you sure you don't want my—"

"I don't want anything from you," I blurt, and my cheeks immediately burn. But I'm not going to let myself feel bad for being rude. Shane deserves it and far worse.

He holds up his hands in a sign of surrender and backs away slowly. "All right, Scar …"

Ugh. I always hated that nickname.

"But, just so you know, I'm around if you ever need help." He juts his thumb in the direction of his house.

"Thanks. I'm good." I spot Joe storming down the steps and add on impulse, "Because I have him!"

"Huh? You have me for what?" Joe's face fills with confusion.

"For *everything*." I rush over to loop my arm around his waist and sidle close to his tall, lanky body, giving off the impression that we're a couple. *Just play along*, I silently will him, staring up into his baby-blue eyes.

If there's one thing I know about Joe, it's that he's had a not-so-secret crush on me ever since I went with Justine to Boston for Thanksgiving, back in sophomore year of college. He knows I'm not interested, but that hasn't stopped his shameless flirting. Pretending we're together isn't an issue for him.

He throws an arm around my shoulder and pulls me close until my face is mashed up against his chest and my sunglasses are sitting crooked. "That's right, babe. You don't need nobody else."

Shane's gaze flips between the two of us before shifting to my house, an unreadable look touching his face. "I hope you're a handy guy." With that, he heads back over the white picket fence.

"Does this mean I get to sleep in your room tonight?" Joe whispers.

I give him a hard shove in the ribs, earning his grunt.

———

Read The Player Next Door

Acknowledgments

I began this story in January 2021 but then shelved it until I was in the right mood. I'm so happy I did because it would not have been the same story you just finished reading (which I had so much fun writing.) For those waiting, thank you for being patient. I hope you feel the delay was worth it.

I will be the first to admit that town ordinances and building codes are not key ingredients in a sexy romance. They can be tedious and convoluted, and they vary between towns, cities, and countries. What is real in one township can be opposite in another. For the sake of this story (and my sanity), I found elements from various sources and spun them to suit my needs. If you work in town planning and are shaking your fist because "this is not how it works in my town!" … this is (fictional) Polson Falls.

A few special thank yous I'd like to say:

Dina Silver, for answering my real estate questions (I can't remember what they were because I asked them two years ago but I know you were at least moderately helpful.)

Melissa Campion, for feeding me invaluable information about town development and all that (unsexy) stuff that comes along with it.

Christy M Baldwin, for letting me pick your brain about life in an assisted living center.

Jenn Sommersby, for your editing prowess.

Chanpreet Singh, thank you for finding all the last little messy things lurking within these pages.

Hang Le, for designing not one but two fantastic covers for this book.

Nina Grinstead and the VPR team, who work so hard to help get my books into readers' hands and are so wonderful to work with.

Stacey Donaghy of Donaghy Literary Group, for a decade of championing my work.

My family, for giving me a reason to work hard.

About the Author

K.A. Tucker writes captivating stories with an edge.

She is the internationally bestselling author of the Ten Tiny Breaths, Burying Water and The Simple Wild series, He Will Be My Ruin, Until It Fades, Keep Her Safe, Be the Girl, and Say You Still Love Me. Her books have been featured in national publications including USA Today, Globe & Mail, Suspense Magazine, Publisher's Weekly, Oprah Mag, and First for Women.

K.A. Tucker currently resides in a quaint town outside of Toronto.
    Learn more about K.A. Tucker and her books at katuckerbooks.com

Made in the USA
Monee, IL
12 January 2023

25188220R00184